THE WOLVES COME AT NIGHT

NEW YORK TIMES BESTSELLING AUTHOR

J.T. ELLISON

"The Wolves Come at Night"

Digital ISBN: 978-1-948967-51-8
Trade ISBN: 978-1-948967-53-2

For more, visit Two Tales Press.

ALSO BY J.T. ELLISON

Standalone Suspense Novels

It's One of Us

Her Dark Lies

Good Girls Lie

Tear Me Apart

Lie to Me

No One Knows

Lt. Taylor Jackson Series

The Wolves Come at Night

Whiteout

Field of Graves

Where All the Dead Lie

So Close the Hand of Death

The Immortals

The Cold Room

Judas Kiss

14

All the Pretty Girls

Dr. Samantha Owens Series

What Lies Behind

When Shadows Fall

Edge of Black

A Deeper Darkness

A Brit in the FBI Series,

Cowritten with Catherine Coulter

The Sixth Day

The Devil's Triangle

The End Game

The Lost Key

The Final Cut

Amazon Originals Short Fiction

These Cold Strangers

For my mom, who has always loved Taylor Jackson the best.

And as always, for Randy.

THE TALE OF TWO WOLVES

One evening, an elderly Cherokee brave told his grandson about a battle that goes on inside people.

"My dear one, the battle between two 'wolves' is inside us all. One is evil. It is anger, envy, jealousy, sorrow, regret, greed, arrogance, self-pity, guilt, resentment, inferiority, lies, false pride, superiority, and ego. The other is good. It is joy, peace, love, hope, serenity, humility, kindness, benevolence, empathy, generosity, truth, compassion, and faith."

The grandson thought about it for a moment and then asked his grandfather: "Which wolf wins?"

The old Cherokee replied, "The one you feed."

—Cherokee Legend

PART ONE

"She slept with wolves without fear,
for the wolves knew a lion was among them."

— R.M. Drake

ONE

RADNOR LAKE, NASHVILLE, TENNESSEE

"CARSON? CARSON! HOLD UP."

Carson Conway halted on the trail, using the moment as an excuse to catch her breath. They'd been hiking straight uphill for thirty minutes now, and she was feeling every ounce of the dreaded freshman fifteen she'd put on since arriving at school. At home it was so much easier to stay balanced, to get the prescribed amount of exercise, especially with her doctor mother's gimlet eye on her at all times. At school, with the massive course load she was taking and the stress of being away from home and the infinite choices in the dining hall and the sudden influx of excess calories in the form of alcoholic and cannabidiol treats, she was struggling.

She'd joined the Lat & Long Club precisely to start getting this under control. She set herself a number of rules. More fresh air, more exercise, salads during the week, beer/gummy enhancement on weekends only. She was already feeling better, though at this particular moment, she felt like crawling the rest of the way to the location the club's random latitude-and-longitude generator had assigned them.

Randomness. Arbitrary, unplanned, unpredictable outcomes. That's what the Lat & Long Club promised. Set an intention, plug in your location, and boom, a random sequence of latitudinal and longitudinal numbers would appear. The idea was to head immediately to those coordinates, and if all worked according to plan, you'd find something directly related to your intention.

It was all the rage on campus right now. The club had blown up after a sophomore Tri-Delt filmed herself saying she needed to find the meaning of life and had been led to a box of books in the free bins in front of McKay's Used Books. On top of the stack was a book titled *The Meaning of Life* with a green frog on the cover.

After that, everyone wanted a piece of Lat & Long.

It didn't hurt that the guy who'd started the club and built the app, a senior applied physics major from Cambridge, England, called Simeon Chase, was a blond god hottie of epic proportion. With a British accent, to boot.

If she didn't want to spend the rest of her life in Spanx, Carson needed to get back to fighting weight. Maybe then, Simeon Chase would look at her twice. And her mom wouldn't look down her nose with that disapproving glare when they FaceTimed, as if she somehow knew Carson was now living in high-waisted yoga pants...

"Carson, my God, you're marching up this damn hill."

Carson's roommate, Isabel Heathcote—Izz to everyone—caught up and bent over, hands on her knees, puffing air in and out so heavily Carson could smell the remnants of the brown-sugared oatmeal Izz had enjoyed for breakfast.

"What is the rush? We're supposed to be finding enlightenment, not giving ourselves a heart attack."

"Just trying to burn some calories. Are you okay? You look green."

Izz stood up, adjusted the bun on top of her head, the tendrils floating around her face. "I'm fine. I shouldn't have had so much to drink last night. How close are we?"

Carson checked the app. "Actually, we're nearly there. We're supposed to go another hundred feet, then turn right."

"I still think we should have said we wanted to see a bear."

"Oh yeah, I want to get caught up here on the side of a mountain with a bear."

"You know this isn't a mountain, right? Only a tall hill. It's basically a geographic speed bump. We could roll down the side into the lake if we take the wrong step and not get hurt."

Carson laughed. She couldn't help herself. Izz was still red-faced and panting and looked so cross even while she made her amusing comments. She'd gotten lucky to be assigned a fun roommate. Izz was fearless and adventurous, and cute enough to draw the attention of all the right people, as shallow as that was. Carson brought the brains and a desire to fit in. They were a solid match.

"Come on. It'll be worth it. I know it will."

They set off again, albeit slower this time. The brush started to obscure the trail. The birds stopped singing. There was a distinct rustling to Carson's right.

"Careful. I think I just saw a snake."

Izz screamed and practically hopped on Carson's back.

"Get off, you goof. We're in the woods. What did you expect?"

Izz's voice was shaky. "I don't want to die out here, Carson. Maybe we should go back."

"Because of a snake? This from the girl who wanted to see a bear. Where's your sense of adventure gone?"

"Apparently into a slithery, nasty hole." Izz reached down gingerly and plucked a branch from the path. She started off again, this time swishing the stick in front of her. "Go away, snakey snakes. Go away."

Carson followed, still laughing to herself. She'd caught her breath now, and the app was showing that they were very close to their target.

What were they going to find? Enlightenment was a rather broad concept, yes. But the Lat & Long Club hadn't failed anyone yet. Members had been coming back from their adventures starry-eyed for weeks now. Carson could do with some mystical starry-eyed shit, that was for sure. College was hard. Harder than she'd anticipated. It felt too close to the real world, to being an adult. Her mom hadn't coddled her, not at all, but since her dad died, she and her brothers had been more sheltered than their friends, for sure. She missed New Haven. Nashville was cool, but it was different. She missed her bed. She missed muffins from the bakery. She missed—

"Oof."

Carson went down, painfully scraping her shin on a rock. She landed hard, her breath leaving in a *whoosh*. Her glasses flew off, and she scrabbled in the leafy undergrowth to find them.

Jamming them back on her face, she took stock of her injuries. Her shin was scraped but not bleeding, though it would have a bruise. Her rump hurt. So did her wrist. Topical problems; her pride was more injured than anything. She looked up, expecting to see Izz doubled over with laughter at her accidental pratfall, but her roommate was standing stock-still five yards up the path as if she hadn't seen a thing.

"What the hell, Izz?"

Izz hurried back to Carson. "Shh!"

"Why? What—"

Izz knelt and slapped a hand over Carson's mouth.

"I hear someone," Izz said quietly.

"Where? Up here? It's probably just someone from the club.

There's probably some sort of celebration when you find your intention."

"I don't think it's a party for us, Carson."

Carson heard it now, too. Voices. A man and a woman. Raised in an argument. And getting louder.

"How could you do this to me? How could you ask this of me?" The woman's voice was met by one rougher, deeper.

"Please, Georgia. Everything depends on you."

"Don't give me that. I don't have a choice here. I don't care if it ends things between us. I'm tired of all of it."

A snarled reply, no more pleading, no more cajoling. "You will regret you ever said that to me."

"We should go," Carson whispered to Izz, who nodded and helped Carson to her feet.

The gunshot was loud, echoing through the trees, bracketed by the panicked flight of birds, rising into the air like a dark cloud. Carson thought it was a firework at first, an M-80 like her brothers used to set off in their neighbors' trashcans. Her ears rang with sparkling echoes of the resonant boom. Her mind caught up, and her heart rate spiked. It wasn't a firework.

A second shot, and a choked male scream followed. They heard shuffling, and branches breaking. Was he covering the body? No, it sounded like he was running away.

They had to get out of here, too.

"Go," Carson whispered.

Izz, frozen again, shook her head, but Carson yanked at her arm. "Now. Go, now!"

She pushed her roommate, who stumbled before righting herself and running away down the path, bushes and branches crashing apart in her panicked wake. So noisy. *Damn it, Izz, he can hear you.*

Carson glanced back once before following, shocked to see a stranger pushing aside the branches of the oak tree at the apex of the hill. He was big, burly, and looking for something. Or someone. Them.

Heart stuttering, she burst into motion, following Izz down the mountain.

She'd seen his eyes, wild, searching. The glint of metal in his hand—a gun?

God, he'd just shot someone with that thing.

The question was, had *he* seen her?

They plummeted down the path, tripping and falling in their hurry, Carson looking over her shoulder, knowing, just knowing he was behind them, about to grab her ponytail and throw her to the ground... But he wasn't there when she looked.

At the end of the trail, they hauled ass to the car and back to campus, not stopping until they were inside their room in Crawford House, inside the perceived safety of the school's persistently watchful eyes. Still panting, eyes wild, Carson had bolted the door and heaved out a breath. Safe. For now.

Izz paced their room, hands on her slim hips, still catching her breath. A trickle of blood ran down her cheek; she'd caught a branch to the face toward the base of the hill.

"Should we call the police?" she asked.

"We just witnessed a murder. Maybe a murder. A shooting, for sure. Of course we call the police," Carson said. She was trying to be calm, to be an adult, when in actuality, she wanted to scream and cry and call her mother to come get her, right now, no questions asked, like the contract she'd signed in high school about drinking and driving proclaimed. Her mother swore it up and down: "You will never get into trouble calling me for a ride if you've been drinking, though there will be repercussions."

Her mother, the doctor. *Repercussions* were often day trips to the morgue or a shadow shift at the emergency room. Her mother wanted her to be a doctor—*you're so studious, darling, you're so smart.* Carson knew in her soul she would never, ever commit to that life. It wasn't her. She had no idea what *was* her, what her life held, but she knew what she didn't want. She didn't want to be tied down. She didn't want to have to report for duty. She didn't want a uniform. She didn't want to witness the pain and the loss on a daily basis. She wanted life on her terms.

Still. Mom's arms and clucking sounded pretty damn good about now.

"My mom's going to kill me," Izz said.

"I hardly think that's the case. Do you want to talk to her first? Before we call?"

"I think we should stay out of it." There. Now having spoken the verboten words aloud, Izz halted, arms down at her sides, her stance pugilistic. The idea floated in the air between them.

So easy. Such an easy path. Ignore. Pretend. Stay out of it. Don't take a chance.

It's how so many lived these days anyway, afraid to put a head above the crowd for fear of it being shot off. They all lived in the trenches of an unseen, highly consequential psychological war, children and adults alike.

But having an opinion that wasn't compatible with the on-campus *au courant* was entirely different than witnessing someone lose their life.

At least, Carson thought the woman was dead.

"Izz. No. We can't pretend it didn't happen. We should have gone back to check, and instead, we ran. That woman was probably killed. We have to say something. I'm calling now."

Izz put her hand over Carson's. "Wait. We need to plan. We need to talk this out. I think it would be dangerous for us to get involved."

"We have to call. We have to tell someone." A pause. "I think he saw me."

"He saw you?" The edge of hysteria in her roommate's voice made Carson grit her teeth.

There was a knock on their door, and Izz screamed. Carson rolled her eyes.

"Come on, he couldn't have followed us to our room. He doesn't have a keycard to the front door."

She sounded much braver than she felt.

She flung open the door to see Simeon Chase, app developer extraordinaire, in the flesh, looking down at her with concern in his whisky-brown eyes. Up close he was even more impressive than witnessed across the dining hall or wandering the quad. Six feet two inches of swimmer's physique, broad shoulders tapering to a narrow waist, a straight nose, plush, kissable lips... Carson flushed, speechless.

Izz draped herself over her roomie's shoulder, though, suddenly all good with the scenario. Carson dropped her right shoulder so Izz couldn't use her as a coatrack.

"Hey, Simeon," Izz drawled, as if she knew this glorious creature intimately.

"Um, hullo. I wanted to check on you two. I saw on the app that you set off on an adventure earlier, but you never checked in after you hit your coordinates. I was worried. But since I see you're okay..." He turned slightly as if to walk away, and Izz stamped on Carson's toe, gesturing at the god's departing back.

"Tell him," she stage-whispered.

Simeon whipped around. "Tell me what?"

Carson stared at Izz for a moment, then shrugged. "Not out here. Come in."

Simeon smelled like pine needles and blue sky, and Carson had a moment's disequilibrium, standing so near him. Her practical mind said aloud, "Can I get you a soda or something?" while her animal mind darted longingly toward the bed. She'd once seen a meme online that made her giggle, of a totally hot guy standing shirtless in a kitchen with a frying pan, smiling charmingly, overlaid with the headline "How do you like your eggs?" and the woman in the frame below with a shit-eating grin on her face—"Fertilized!"

That's how she felt in the presence of Simeon Chase.

Simeon, not realizing the effect he was having on her hormones, plopped down on their little couch and tossed a leg onto the arm.

Oh, to be so in command of yourself that you don't think about the space you take up in the world.

"Uh, no. I'm fine. What did you see out there? You two seem a little...spooked."

Carson sat gingerly on her desk chair, Izz on the opposite sofa arm. She'd gone all colt when Simeon showed up, legs and arms akimbo, giggling and flipping her hair. If Carson didn't take charge, Izz was going to topple over into his lap.

"We were almost to the coordinates when we heard a couple arguing. There was a gunshot. No, two. We think the man may have shot the woman. Her name was Georgia. He called her Georgia, at least. I suppose it could have been a nickname."

"He shot her? With a gun? At my coordinates?"

Horror crossing his face, Simeon pulled out his phone and tapped a few times on the screen.

"Are you calling the police?"

"I'm locking the coordinates first. I don't want anyone else going there. Why didn't you call the police immediately?"

"We're going to. We just got back here. We were scared. The man seemed really pissed off. I think he saw me," Carson finished, annoyed at how small her voice sounded. "We were about to call the police when you knocked."

Simeon gnawed a thumbnail for a moment. This gesture

made Carson's heart swell. It was the response of a child, not a man. So vulnerable, was Simeon Chase. Who knew?

"We should go back up there," Carson said finally. "Just to make sure. If there's not a body, and we waste everyone's time... we could get into trouble."

"No, no way. Bad idea," Izz said. "What if he's still there?"

"You say her name was Georgia?" Simeon was tapping away again.

"Now what?"

"I'm looking to see if there are any missing people named Georgia in the area."

"That's a waste of time."

"What if he shot her but she isn't dead?"

"Why would he have started to bury her, then?"

"He buried her?" Simeon asked.

Did he? It seemed like he was moving brush around, but maybe he was just walking across the top of the hill. Or running through the trees. "Maybe? It sounded like he was covering things up."

"All right. No one by that name in the news."

Carson tried once more. "Not to be argumentative, but this happened less than an hour ago. I don't think someone would be identified as missing that quickly. Look, let's just call the police, tell them what we saw, and let them deal with it."

Simeon looked briefly pained but nodded. He had the campus police on speed dial. Vanderbilt had its own force that handled most of what happened on campus. He watched Carson as the call connected.

"Hello? I need to report a possible crime."

TWO

CARSON FOUND herself on the trail up the mountain again an hour later, leading a group to the crime scene. Simeon was behind her, and the cops, too. Campus police had called Nashville Metro immediately, and there were four of them, two patrol officers, a crime scene tech, and a smoking hot homicide detective who'd tagged along at the last minute. The officers in uniform and the crime scene tech were huffing and puffing, their equipment clanking away. It was only a matter of time until one of them went into cardiac arrest and she was forced to perform CPR until the Life Flight helicopter could meet them at the top of the mountain.

"We there yet?" the older of the two cops called. "Hotter than Georgia asphalt up here."

"Nearly," Carson said, cringing inside. Georgia was the woman's name, at least that's what she'd been called by the furious man. Though Carson hadn't heard the euphemism before, she'd bumped into a few strange southern sayings since she'd moved to Nashville, and brushed it off. It *was* hot for a fall afternoon, and tiny gnats were buzzing around their head, delighting in the salty treat that came from landing on necks and arms.

Simeon backed her up. "We're getting close to the coordinates, sir."

Carson's legs were screaming. She hadn't planned to climb this hill twice in a single day. The hill seemed more like a mountain the second time. Geographic speed bump my ass. She was puffing as hard as the cops.

"It's here," Simeon said finally, his face lit by the phone in his hand. They all stopped, and Carson looked around, catching her breath, getting her bearings.

Yes, there was the mossy rock formation she'd tripped over. She pointed ahead of them. "He was on the other side of these trees."

"You kids stay here," the detective said, setting off with the two patrol officers. Carson thought his name was Marcus something; she'd been in the bathroom freaking the hell out when he'd shown up to join their outing. He had a hand on the holster at his waist, and so did the two uniformed cops. She glanced at Simeon to see if he'd noticed, suddenly feeling very, very unsafe. She was alone in the woods with four men, three of whom were armed, and a possible dead body. She heard her mother's horrified voice say, "What the hell were you thinking, Carson?"

An excellent question.

Simeon was quiet and watchful beside her. If this weren't such a horrid situation, she'd be in heaven being near him. As it was, she simply took one step closer and was surprised when he put an arm around her shoulders.

"It's going to be okay," he said, and she thought he was reassuring himself as much as her.

"Got something here," one of the patrol officers called, and without thinking, Carson moved toward his voice. She wanted to see, and that was horrible. But Simeon walked with her, clearly just as curious.

The detective stood over a mound of branches and leaves tucked haphazardly around the body of a woman. Carson could see her face through the screen of branches. The impressions flew through her mind. *Open eyes, slitted and swollen. A huge hole in the side of her head, lopsided in the leaves. Brain and blood and matted hair. She looked surprised to be dead.*

Granted, no one thinks they're going to die on the top of a mountain after an argument.

"Hey, hey, hey, you two, back it up. This is a crime scene." Hot Marcus what's-his-name shooed them away. Simeon took Carson's hand and pulled her back ten yards. He was pale, the light in his beautiful eyes dimmed by distress.

The police started talking on their respective phones, calling for backup.

She realized Simeon was shaking, ran her hand up his arm. "Hey, you're okay. It's okay."

"You could have been killed," he said, eyes closed. "If something had happened to you, while you were using my app? It would be the end of everything."

"Good to know you're more worried about the integrity of the app than my safety," she snapped.

"That's not what I meant, and you know it," he fired back.

"You two want to put the lovers' spat on hold?" The detective stood with his arms crossed. "I need all of you to come down to the station. Make your statements—and Carson, I'd like you to sit down with a sketch artist. Will you do that for me?"

"Yes, sir," she said. What was she going to say? *No, thanks, I've got to study for my midterms?* And a lovers' spat? With Simeon Chase? Izz would laugh her out of the dorm.

Still, her heart sparked for a moment, and she groaned

inside. *Stow your crush, Carson.* What a damn wreck of a day this was.

They marched away dutifully, and Carson took a moment to look around. *So much for the path to enlightenment.*

"Hey, look at this," Simeon called quietly, and she looked over to see a mossy green circle of stacked gray rocks, what she now knew was Tennessee limestone because it built every fence in every park all around the city. Inside were several fallen slabs of what looked like ancient concrete.

"Are those...gravestones?" she asked, a little breathless.

"Yeah," Simeon said, jumping into the circle and moving the heavy, collapsed stones around.

"You're standing on their graves," she scolded, and he looked up with a raised brow.

"Hate to break it to you, but there was a lot of Civil War fighting in this area. Plus, this land originally belonged to the Indians. You've heard the history of Fort Nashborough, surely. It's all graveyards around here, whether you can see them or not."

Carson looked at her feet, imagining bodies stacked like cordwood underneath her, and scrambled closer to the stone circle.

Simeon was running his hand across the carved lettering of the headstone. "Wow, look at this. Born 17... Damn, I can't make that out. Is that a three?"

"I don't know. But look at his death date. December 5, 1776. Not Civil War era. Revolutionary."

"Tennessee didn't have any official regiments in the Revolution." She raised a brow. "My minor is in history," he said.

"Gotcha. Well, you're assuming he died in battle. This is a family graveyard. Look, there are three other stones. Smaller ones."

"Wife and kids, maybe?"

"Maybe." The names and dates on the three smaller headstones were unreadable, but Carson took photos anyway. It was a lovely, eerie spot.

"I'm curious," Simeon said a few moments later. "What did you ask to find when you set out on your adventure today, Carson?"

She smiled ruefully. "Enlightenment. Not quite sure this was what I had in mind."

They were on the mountain until dark, retrieving the body. The crime scene tech found the bullet casings, so now they'd have a way to match the gun, which the detective was thrilled about. "Every gun has a signature, just like your fingerprint. Find the gun, we can match it ballistically, and that goes a long way toward making a court case."

He was ridiculously chatty on the trip down the mountain. He asked her repeatedly about what she'd seen and heard, then Simeon engaged him with a thousand questions, and Carson wished they would both stop talking. By the end of the afternoon, she'd added one more thing to her *don't want to be when I grow up* list—law enforcement. God, what a bore, all the details, all the time they took with every little thing, crawling around in the dusty leaves searching for blood spatter, taking hundreds of photos. She didn't have the kind of patience it would take; the attention to detail she observed was off the charts. Her mother would appreciate the thoroughness. And, Carson supposed, if she were being morbid, she'd be glad they spent so much time making sure things were right if she'd been the one lying under the branches instead of a girl who went by the moniker Georgia.

When they got to the station to make their statements, the police split up the two of them, Simeon walking off like a man condemned, stealing glances back at her. In a generic, chilly room, Carson provided as much detail as she could to the artist who came in to do the sketch of the suspect. The cops must have been satisfied with both of them, because as soon as she finished, a patrol officer was assigned to drive them back to campus.

The one good thing was Simeon. He was an inquisitive man by nature, and on the ride back, he asked her a hundred questions and offered to swing by tomorrow so they could have lunch together. She'd agreed.

"I'm sorry you had to go through this, Carson. I'll see you tomorrow."

For a brief second, he looked at her, really looked at her, and she thought he might kiss her, but he just nodded and loped off.

Don't be a dope, Carson. Simeon Chase is not interested in you. He's just making sure there's no blowback on him because of this.

Izz was all over her the second the door closed. "Oh my God, what took so long? The cops were so weird, they wouldn't tell me anything, just made me repeat what I saw like a hundred times then dropped me off back here. What happened?"

"They found her," Carson said, feeling her stomach turn at the memory. "Her body was under some branches. Whoever the guy was, he didn't do a good job of hiding her. It took a while to secure the scene."

"You sound like a true crime podcaster. We must have scared him off. Car, I'm so freaked out. What if he saw us, for real? What if—"

"Stop. You're getting worked up. We're safe here on campus. I promise."

"The news was talking about it. They've identified her. Georgia Wray. She's a singer here in town. She's, like, semi-famous or something. She's working on an album. The reporter said there were no suspects."

"Except for the creeper we saw. They're going to be looking pretty hard for him. I gave them as good a description as I could."

"What was he like?"

"Dark hair, stocky, light eyes. Brownish shirt?"

"Silly. I meant Simeon."

Carson smiled. Naturally, Izz was already onto the possibilities of being friends—or more—with Simeon Chase.

"He's nice. More thoughtful than I expected. He said he'd come check on me tomorrow. I think we're having lunch. But we'll see if that happens."

"Wow," Izzy said, totally dazzled. "Carson and Simeon. Who would have thought?"

"Izz, come on. We're not going on a date. We bonded over something tragic. I'm sure he'll forget about me by next week. I have to go to bed. Let's talk in the morning, okay?" Carson was already shutting down. She was exhausted, the combination of adrenaline and two massive hikes taking her down. Her legs were sore, her feet were tired, and her soul was crushed. She'd witnessed a murder. A *murder.*

"Fine. But you have to promise to give me every single detail in the morning."

Carson thought she'd have trouble getting to sleep, but was out ten minutes later, the man's face haunting her dreams.

THREE

METROPOLITAN JUSTICE CENTER, NASHVILLE

TAYLOR JACKSON HATED her new office.

She hated not having a view of her beloved Nashville downtown. She hated not having a view into her Murder Squad bullpen. And she sure as hell hated the always-open-to-anyone door in her current line of sight, labeled with the word that now preceded her name.

Captain.

Better pay, better hours, better benefits.

Desk. Desk. Desk.

She had fought this promotion, begged and pleaded and threatened to quit, and yet here she was, sitting in the shiny new headquarters building, surrounded by stacks of paperwork and trying not to grit her teeth every time her new admin knocked gently on the door frame to remind her of her next meeting. She spent her life in meetings now. Half of them virtual, half of them in person, at an appropriate distance. Such a perfect metaphor for her feelings toward her new gig—she was distanced from everything she used to love about her job.

"Captain?" Knock, knock.

Speak of the devil.

"Commander Huston wants to talk to you. I told her you'd be right up."

"Thanks, Delila. If you want to leave at lunch, go for it. They're saying there might be severe weather this afternoon, and schools are closing early. You might as well get home ahead of the kids."

Delila's look of gratitude made Taylor feel bad for her earlier uncharitable thoughts toward her admin. "I appreciate it, Captain. I hate this weird tornado weather. You be safe, you hear? Don't hang out in the sky in your condo watching this one come at you, all right?"

"I'll be fine," Taylor said, grabbing her notebook and stretching, little pops breaking out along her spine. "And tomorrow, do me a favor and find me another chair? This one hurts my back."

"Will do. Thanks, Captain. See you tomorrow."

Taylor opened her phone to the Nashville Severe Weather Twitter feed to see what was in store for the afternoon. With luck, she could have her chat with Huston and then head out herself. She supposed that was one perk of the new job: she could work from home on the ridiculous mounds of paperwork and do many of her meetings on the computer just as easily as here. And she'd have a view of the incoming weather, as Delila warned against. The condo she and her fiancé, John Baldwin, had bought during the first summer of the pandemic was on the forty-fourth floor. She dug that she could watch the storms blow in, but tornados weren't her favorite. Their building had been only blocks away from the monster that tore through Nashville just a few days before the earliest lockdowns began.

According to the local meteorology gurus, the line of severe weather would be passing through between 2:00 and 3:00 p.m. It was 11:00 now. She had time.

Taylor rose with a small groan from the wildly uncomfortable fancy modern chair and headed down the hall to Huston's office.

Commander Joan Huston was busy *umm-hmm*ing someone on the phone and gestured for Taylor to hold on a moment. Happy to wait, she rested a shoulder against the jamb and crossed her feet at the ankles. Huston had the better view: the city at a distance. Nashville's copious new skyscrapers rose like beanstalks into the sky, and the edges of the Batman Building were blue in the gray haze.

"Hey hey, if it ain't the Cap." Taylor looked down the hall to see Detective Marcus Wade and newly minted Lieutenant Lincoln Ross hurrying down the hall toward her. Her mood lightened immediately.

"Y'all are a sight for sore eyes. What's up?"

Marcus gave her a high five; Lincoln, a fist bump.

"Murder and chaos, as always. What's up with you? You look like you've been tearing out your hair."

Taylor whipped her hair out of its ponytail and smoothed it before piling the whole mess on her head and anchoring it with a rubber band, noticing ruefully that it was an actual rubber band, snatched from her desk drawer in an earlier moment of duress. "You spend the morning digging through requisitions and see how slick you look. Though you're getting a taste of that now, aren't you, Linc?"

"Yeah, but I always look slick." Lincoln gave her a gap-toothed grin. She'd long thought he was a dead ringer for the singer Lenny Kravitz. All he needed was a nose ring and some cool tattoos. He was dressed casually today in a black half-zip sweater over a white button-down, sleeves pushed up, and a pair of black jeans. Marcus, too, looked well-put-together though casual—dark jeans, blue button-down, cowboy boots, his thick brown hair flopping over his forehead.

Taylor, in her uniform, expected of all the brass, felt a pang of jealousy. "How's Flynn?"

Lincoln's smile got even bigger. Lincoln had adopted Flynn last year after the boy's mother, the wife of a fallen officer, was killed. "Getting bigger every day. That kid's eating me out of house and home. He's getting good grades, too. He's smart, like his momma was. Marcus saw him last weekend. You and Baldwin should come over soon, we can grill and you can see for yourself."

The sense of isolation widened around her. They used to be a tight-knit unit, in each other's business and lives constantly. Now, she had to catch up with them in hallways.

"He's a cute kid," Marcus agreed. "Oh, speaking of, have you talked to Renn this week?"

Renn McKenzie was the fourth of their former team. She'd been reluctantly paired with him and ended up welcoming him into their circle. He was a fine detective and a good man.

"I haven't," she said. "What's up?"

Marcus blushed immediately. "Oh, you gotta call. I'll let him tell you."

A light sparked in Taylor. "Tell me the baby is happening."

"I am sworn to secrecy. Call him." Though while he spoke, he grinned and nodded.

"That's a bright bit of news. I love babies."

"So long as they aren't your own," both men said in unison.

"So long as they aren't my own."

Lincoln cocked his head. "You know, you really should rethink that. You and Baldwin would make really pretty babies."

"A—sexist. B—why does everyone keep telling me that? C—we aren't even married yet, and you've already got me knocked up. One step at a time, boys. One step at a time. And when we do get married, it's going to be quiet, and we aren't going to tell anyone. Elope Central. And then maybe—and I say maaaybe—" She let it drag on a moment for effect, enjoying how their eyes lit up. "A hamster."

While they guffawed, she shuddered at the memory of her own interrupted nuptials. Taylor had come inches from marrying John Baldwin in a traditional, elaborate, tons-of-guests church affair, but was kidnapped by a psycho on the way to the altar.

But that was years in the past, and now, she was actually ready again, if one can ever be ready to make such a life-altering change, especially when you've been alone for so long. They'd do it on a beach somewhere. Someplace no one knew about but her best friend, Samantha Owens, and Sam's fiancé, Xander Whitfield, the two people she would not marry without. Vows in private, a huge party back home once the deed was done.

Her friend from New Scotland Yard, Memphis Highsmith, had offered his castle estate in Scotland, with him and his wife, Evan, as witnesses, but Taylor had demurred. As glorious as the home seat of the Viscount Dulsie was, she still had too many bad memories of her time there.

"Y'all quit jawing and get in here," Huston yelled.

They shuffled in, the guys letting Taylor go first.

Huston looked entirely harassed, a view Taylor saw more and more these days. Being in the leadership of Metro was for the birds. Law enforcement in general was having a rough go of it, with the cultural shifts happening throughout the world. A lot of their own cops had quit, or been forced out after the mandates, but many had doubled down on their commitment to keeping people safe, focusing tremendous amounts of energy on finding a new path forward that worked for all involved. Huston was in the latter camp and had made serious strides in making sure body cameras were on at all times, instituting new sensitivity training at the academy, doing high-level outreach to the community at large, and shutting down even the tiniest whisper of complaint from the troops. As a result, though

Nashville still had problems, community relations were improving, and Taylor was grateful for the steady hand at the helm.

Still. A hard job had been made harder, and Taylor felt utterly neutered. As much as she enjoyed outreach to the community and sit-downs with younger cops, teaching them how to do it right, how to show respect to people who rarely experienced it, how to get to the root of the issue with a young repeat offender instead of just tossing someone into the back of a car, she longed for the streets. A teacher she was not.

"Georgia Wray," Huston said, pulling Taylor from her reverie.

"The country singer?" Lincoln said. "What about her?"

"That's the ID on the body Detective Wade pulled off the mountain last night."

"Oh, what a shame. She's been hitting it pretty big lately." Taylor said. She was more inclined to listen to the New Wave romantics and punk rockers of her youth, but even *she* knew about Georgia Wray. Nashville born and bred, a gorgeous blonde, wrote her own songs, and had a voice that didn't need a whopping dose of auto-tune. A real star in the making. They were saying she was the next Taylor Swift.

"Her family and label are up my six, as you can imagine," Huston said, gesturing toward the phone. "We need a quick close on this. There's a witness, I understand?"

Marcus nodded, and for Taylor's sake, said, "Two Vandy students were on a GPS hunt yesterday and heard arguing and a gunshot. They hightailed it down the trail and called us. I hiked up there with one of the witnesses, the app's founder, a tech, and a couple of patrols to find the body. Poorly buried, recently deceased. I've already started on it," he said to Huston, who shook her head.

"It's a high-profile murder, the record label wants a high-profile cop. No offense, Marcus. But Taylor, this one's yours."

Taylor's heart lit up in macabre reaction to the news of a dead girl. Finally, something to do.

"No problem. I'm happy to help." She hoped she sounded serious and not gleeful. She hated like hell that the girl was dead but was already seized with the frisson of a new case, even without knowing much about it.

"I assume you're both okay working with the captain, Lieutenant Ross, Detective Wade?"

Lincoln nodded. "Always."

"Yes, ma'am," Marcus chimed in.

"Good. Get to it. There's a presser scheduled for this afternoon, and Dan is expecting you to brief him on where you stand."

"Thank you, ma'am," Taylor said. "We'll figure this out."

Huston already had a hand on her phone. "You better. That label has clout. It's all of our asses on the line."

FOUR

TAYLOR STOPPED in her office long enough to grab her keys before following Lincoln and Marcus to the Violent Crimes offices. Clean, sterile almost, brisk. Their new building was modern, all glass and wood, steel beams—a beautiful, functional, aesthetically pleasing box, surrounded by a black metal fence. It didn't have the sordid, sloppy personality of their old office downtown—the rabbit warren of desks crushed in cheek to jowl, the dirty windows and ashtrays outside the door, sliding stacks of printer paper atop coffee-soaked carpeting, random tourists wandering into the courtyard. Of course, the old Criminal Justice Center had been demolished; that squalid room in the CJC lived on in her memories only. Change. She was becoming a dinosaur, resisting the benefits of the new space. Metro now had their own lab, a successful decentralization to the precincts, better coverage across the city. All positives for them.

Maybe it was her.

Taylor fingered the tiny, puckered scar on her temple, a souvenir from a madman. He'd taken her voice, her autonomy, nearly her life. A year removed, so much had changed. She was back...but was she? When she returned from her medical leave in Scotland and was cleared by Dr. Willig, the department shrink, for active duty, she'd been summarily promoted, ostensibly taken out of harm's way. But was the city trying to keep her safe, or keep themselves safe from her? Sometimes she wondered.

Lincoln's office was on the far side of the room. He hesitated a moment, sending a glance her way, before sliding behind the desk. Taylor didn't mind. This was his domain. He'd worked hard to get the promotion to sergeant, and with her recommendation, the step up to lieutenant. Her old position.

If Marcus felt any qualms about Lincoln's new leadership role changing their dynamic, he didn't show it. He flopped in the chair to the left. Taylor more sedately took the one to the right. Even the chairs were nicer. They were all going to get soft, riding a wave of high-end interior design glory.

"Linc, for the presser, what do you want to say? Do I need to write you up some talking points?"

Lincoln shook his head. "Marcus, tell us what you know, and we'll go from there."

Marcus opened the folder he'd been carrying. "Well, my gut is, we should wait. We have a solid description of the suspect. Our witness said she thought it was a personal thing between them, so before we blast this all over the airwaves, I'd like to see if someone in her immediate family or her label knows who this is. If we could get a couple of hours..."

"I'll take care of that," Taylor said. "There's no reason to have a presser if we need to be chasing down a lead." She already had her phone in her hand, sending a text to Franklin. "There. He'll get it rescheduled."

Lincoln grinned at her. "Huston won't like it."

"Let me handle Huston. What else? Tell me about this witness."

Marcus consulted his notes. "Witnesses, plural. Carson

Conway, and her roommate, Isabel Heathcote. Vandy freshmen. Carson is the one who physically saw the shooter. She's scared, as you can imagine. The campus police are keeping an eye on her dorm, just in case the shooter identifies her and decides to look her up. The sooner we can get with Georgia Wray's people and find a suspect, the easier the kid will rest."

"I'll want to talk to her. Do you have any contact info for Wray's people?"

"Two steps ahead of you. I've already talked to her manager, he flew in from LA. Caught the red-eye last night. That's who tuned up the chief, I think. Her folks are on vacation, in New Zealand, of all places. Arrangements are being made to get them back here, but it's going to be another day at least before we can sit down with them. But her manager is expecting me—us? If you want to join me—as soon as we can get to Music Row."

Taylor nodded. "Yeah, I'll tag along. Your show, though. I'm just observing."

"No need, Cap. You step in whenever you want. I'm not picky about who gets the solve."

"God, stop calling me that. I hate it."

Both men laughed, knowing full well her opinions of her new job. They liked to poke at her, though. It was part of how they'd all operated for years.

"Taylor," Marcus said. "Better?"

"Yes. What do we know about Georgia Wray outside of the public persona?"

"Not a lot yet, actually. We've pored over her socials and searched her house—her purse and cell were on the counter, her car in the drive. She was wearing workout clothes and an Apple watch, had a house key tied on her shoelace, so I'm assuming she went for a walk or a run and was taken. I'm still waiting on data from the cameras around her neighborhood to see if there's any credence to that theory."

"How far is her place from Radnor? Could she get there easily on foot?"

"No, not easily. She's in East Nashville. Nice place. She could have met up with a friend who drove her to the lake, for sure, but I can't imagine planning to be gone for a couple of hours and not having your cell with you."

"No, me either. Not someone her age. She was pretty active online, too," Lincoln added, handing Taylor his tablet with Georgia Wray's feed pulled up. "Couple of posts a day, at least. Nothing since Tuesday morning."

Georgia was pretty, delicate, with a pouty mouth and rosebud cheeks against a spill of wheat hair. If her dark eyebrows were any indication, the hair was chemically lightened, and the smile looked like she'd had a run at some decent orthodontia. She was lithe and strong, built like an athlete. There were photos from earlier in the year of her finishing a 5K with some friends in the East Nasty Running Club, so Marcus's assessment made total sense. These personal shots were interspersed with show pictures and professional photo shoots, shots from her tour bus, reels of her singing. It was an altogether adorable feed, and Taylor felt bad for all involved. A budding, talented life cut short.

"Does she post herself, or does her team do it for her? You know how it is with celebrities—it's not always them behind the curtain."

"We can ask the label, they'll know." Marcus flipped a page in his notebook. "The witness heard Georgia arguing with the killer before the shot was fired. She thought it was a lovers' spat, though the kid's in shock, so no idea how accurate that observation is. She can't remember it word for word, but she did say it was heated. That's all we've got so far."

"That's a good start. All right, puppy, you're with me. Lincoln, you keep running interference with Franklin while we go track down who might be responsible for the girl's death."

"You got it. Be in touch, though. If Huston comes down here and yells at me, I want to be able to give her updates."

Taylor had a moment of sheer pride at his command. She'd trained him well. A lieutenant, a father, a leader. He fit his new roles perfectly.

She saluted. "Yes, Lieutenant. I will make sure your ass is not in a sling for the rest of the day. Permission to take your detective on a joyride?"

Lincoln's eyes sparkled with merriment. "Take him off my hands. He's worthless."

Marcus flipped Lincoln the bird. "Hey! I resemble that remark."

Giggling, Taylor bumped knuckles with Linc, then jingled her keys. "Come on, Marcus. Let's get out of the big man's hair."

"That's *Lieutenant* Big Man to you. *Captain.*"

FIVE

OUTSIDE, the western sky was purpling, and a breeze had kicked up. Taylor checked the radar on her phone again. "Yuck. Nasty storms. Looks like we're gonna get wet." She dangled the keys. "You want to drive?"

"Naw. Riding shotgun will be like old times."

They piled into her new service vehicle, a black Tahoe with Metro Nashville Police stenciled on the side, headed toward downtown and the impending storm.

Marcus caught her up on the rest of the case, all the steps he'd taken to this point, the evidence procured, all the finer details, finishing with "Whoever did this shot Georgia in the face. Knocked off half her head. That smacks of someone who's pretty pissed off, if you ask me."

"I agree. That's never good. Does it feel weird to you that he'd march her up a hill to shoot her? I mean, she could have made a break for it, or he could have stumbled and sprained an ankle. If you want to murder someone, this is an odd setting for it. Plenty of other deep woods spots that don't take a fitness buff to pull off easily."

"Maybe he was just trying to get her someplace that he

could buy some time before her body was found? This spot is isolated. It's off the main path and straight up a hill. Honestly, it feels like a total fluke that there were witnesses. Bad luck for the killer, but good luck for us. It could have been weeks before we found her."

"Which is what's bugging me. What are the odds? After we do this possible ID, I want to speak to the kid who designed the GPS program. I'd like to know how he picked this particular spot."

Rain began splattering on the windshield, and she turned on the wipers.

"Linc seems happy," she ventured.

"Bossing us all around? Hell yeah. But he's good at this, you know? Not just the investigative side, you know how great his instincts are. But with all his computer geek background, he's going to streamline the entire system for how we manage our paperwork. He just put in for all of us to have tablets on scene so we can upload the photos and make our notes on-site into a program he's written that automatically feeds into CODIS and iAFIS, all the other databases. We can take fingerprints on it, too. It's an all-in-one solution, and it works fast. Pretty slick."

"I know. I approved the requisition," she said, smiling. "Anything to cut down on our paperwork is a bonus for me. You're right, he's a genius. Violent Crimes will run much smoother with him at the helm."

"Maybe. We miss you, though. Miss having your brain on a case. Hell, we even miss Baldwin sticking his nose in all the time."

She smiled, ridiculously pleased to hear this. Her team had welcomed the FBI's brilliant profiler into their lives with open arms, and into their cases, with deep respect. It made her proud, of both the team and her man.

They got to the record label's offices just as the rain started to come down heavily. The front was pushing through early and fast, which was good. She hoped there wouldn't be enough storm fuel to make tornadoes. Nashville didn't need any more natural disasters.

Georgia's record label was housed in a renovated Craftsman with navy blue siding and black-framed windows, the tapered columns a fresh cheery white. The foyer was bright and airy, opening into a sitting area with a white-painted brick fireplace. There was a black metal staircase to the second floor, and Taylor could smell freshly-baked cookies. Her stomach growled in response.

There was a rustling from the hallway, and a woman with unnaturally red hair and a sleeve of intricate multicolored tattoos stepped into view. Her face was blotchy, and she held a tissue in her right hand. She beckoned to them from the foyer into a conference room, calling into the room in a thick voice, "Cops are here."

Georgia Wray's manager sat at a smoky glass rectangular table, a wall of signed guitars over his shoulder. He was wearing gold sunglasses, and there was a single red file folder and an iPhone in front of him. A plate of cookies sat on the sideboard.

He stood at their approach. "Travis Bloom," he said, gesturing to the chairs. "Have a seat. We're all just devastated about Georgia." He didn't remove the glasses, and the tattooed assistant backed out of the room, closing the glass French doors behind her. Lightning flashed, and Taylor caught herself counting off *one Mississippi, two Mississippi*, and thought briefly of Samantha Owens, her best friend—and the former mid-state medical examiner—who had bad OCD and tended to count while washing her hands, before dragging herself back to the present just as the thunder crashed. They all jumped.

"Whoa. That was close," Bloom said. "Of course, I'm a bit jumpy today anyway. What can I do for you? How can I help? What do you know, and what do you need to know?"

"First, thank you for helping us, sir," Marcus said. "We're very sorry for your loss."

A small sniff. Not being able to see his eyes, Taylor was going off his body language. He seemed upset but contained.

"There's quite a bit we don't know. Georgia was killed in an isolated location, and there was a witness who heard her arguing with the killer before she was shot." Marcus slid his tablet with the sketch pulled up across the table. "Any idea who this is?"

Bloom was tense, Taylor could see that despite his eyes being hidden. When he looked at the screen, he sighed heavily, and the head bobbed.

"Aw, shoot. Yeah. That's Justin Osborne. Her boyfriend. Ex-boyfriend. Man, I knew that wasn't gonna end well." He took off the sunglasses and rubbed his forehead. His eyes were red; he'd been crying. So: genuinely upset. She filed that away.

"How so?" Taylor asked.

"They just had a pretty bad breakup. You know the drill, I'm sure. They came to Nashville together. He played guitar, she sang. They booked a bunch of gigs around town, started to get a following. She got better than him, fast. One of our scouts saw them open at Mercy Lounge, pitched a record deal at her. We wanted her as a solo act, so Georgia wrote Justin out of the picture pretty quick. He went away without too much fuss, but clearly, he's back. He's always been upset that she wasn't dependent on him, that she bailed when the label asked her to. I mean, what's a kid gonna do, right? He made some threats, then disappeared, only to show back up like the leech he was."

"What kind of threats?"

"You know. Toothless. At least, I thought they were. 'You'll never make it without me, watch your back,' that sort of stuff. We thought it was bluster."

Bingo. Taylor excused herself and stepped out of the room, dialing her phone as she went.

“Linc? Got a name to run. Justin Osborne.”

“On it,” he said. She could hear typing in the background and the murmur of voices from the conference room, Marcus getting as much information as he could.

“Justin killed her?” a soft voice queried. The redhead was lingering by the stairs, dabbing her cheeks with a tissue.

“You know him?” Taylor replied.

The redhead laughed mirthlessly. “We *all* know Justin. Total hothead. He sneaks around every once in a while, looking for scraps. Georgia didn’t have the heart not to throw him some every once in a while.”

“Meaning?”

“Gigs, mostly. A few co-writing credits. She knew he was holding her back, but she felt so beholden to him. And now he killed her. God. That just sucks.”

“We don’t know that, and I must caution you not to say anything to anyone until we get a chance to speak with him. Do you have an address for Mr. Osborne?”

“Over in East Nashville. She bought him a house, if you can believe that.”

“That’s some scrap.”

“She was too generous with us all.” Tears spilled down the girl’s face. “Let me get you that address. I’ll be right back.”

Lincoln spoke in Taylor’s ear. “I’ve got it—it’s out on North Sixteenth. I’ll get a warrant started so we can toss it to a judge as quick as possible if you think it’s a go.”

“I’ll grab Marcus and head there. Might you be persuaded to call for a couple of patrols from East as backup, just in case?”

“Will do. Be careful out there, ya hear?”

“Yes, Mom.”

She left him laughing and went back to the conference room. Marcus was clearly itching to go; he was already half out of his seat, his notebook closed.

“Get everything you need?”

"For now. Thanks so much for your time, Mr. Bloom. We'll be in touch. And if Justin reaches out to you, call us, please. Do not try to talk to him yourself."

"When can we have her body? Her parents...they're a close-knit family. They've been a dream to work with, actually supportive without trying to hog anything for themselves. They're wrecked about this already. When they find out it was Justin..."

Marcus shook his head. "We don't know it was Justin, sir, so please keep that to yourself."

"They're coming from New Zealand. They were out in some secluded resort, they're having to hike back in. They might be out of touch for the moment, but they will absolutely want to talk to you as soon as they're back. They're going to want their girl's body."

"I understand. I'm afraid you'll have to talk to the folks at Forensic Medical about the release. I know they are doing her autopsy today, but I haven't gotten the call as to when yet. I'll stay in touch with you, okay?"

Wind lashed the tree outside the conference room window, making it wave and spin crazily, and the rain came down in sheets.

The sunglasses went back on, and Travis Bloom retreated into the chair with a grimace.

"Sure thing. I'm heading back to LA as soon as this storm breaks, but you have my contact info. Keep me looped in. And thank you. She is—was—ah, damn..."

His shoulders began to shake, and they left him in the conference room with his grief and his guitars.

SIX

"ANYTHING I SHOULD KNOW ABOUT?" Taylor asked Marcus as they drove to East Nashville.

He flipped through his notebook. "You didn't miss much. According to Bloom, Georgia was an angel. Everyone loved her. No stalkers, no hate mail. No issues with employees. Band loves her, agent loves her, manager loves her. She got into it with a few folks on her social feed every once in a while, but it was more complaints about her tours not coming to their towns than anything else. Girl's a paragon of young singers."

"Well, that's all easily checked. You know how I feel about the faultless. She has to have some flaw stashed away in her drawers."

"No doubt. Bloom was overdoing it a bit, I think. I get not wanting to speak poorly of the dead, but no one's perfect, especially a kid her age."

Taylor caught the light at Demonbreun Street, a lucky move. The bridge traffic was thinning. Marcus had pulled up Georgia Wray's website, hit Play on the latest single. The girl's voice filled the truck—deep and smoky, a hint of southern, pure and clear on the high notes. Taylor got goose bumps when she hit a high C then took it up a notch without a hitch.

"She's got some pipes," Taylor said. "Auto-tuned?"

"Doesn't sound manufactured. She was a looker, too. The whole package."

The final notes of Georgia's song bled away, and they drove a few blocks in appreciative but subdued silence. "Damn shame. Bloom seemed rather certain Justin was involved, especially after he saw the sketch."

"Adamant is more like it." Marcus turned off the song and slapped his notebook against his knee. "He really dislikes the kid."

"Well, if he's a murderer, I'm gonna dislike him too. That's the place over there?"

"Yeah, that's it."

She whipped the truck to the curb. The house Georgia Wray had gifted her ex in East Nashville was clearly being renovated: the company that was doing the work, OHB Designs, had a sign riding high above a sea of muddy sod, and a full construction dumpster stood by the garage. The workers themselves had been chased off by the rain; the lights were off inside, and the place looked deserted.

They ran to the front door, hands above their heads. Taylor was drenched in the few seconds it took to make it up the sidewalk. She shook off like a wet dog, then rapped on the door. Not fully latched, it swung open, helped along by a perfectly timed gust of wind. A dank scent wafted out of the darkness.

"Uh-oh," Marcus said, hand on his weapon. Taylor unsnapped her holster and drew her Glock, held it down by her thigh. With her left hand, she called it in.

"Linc? We're at the address, there's a problem. Send those patrols *stat*. We're making entry. I'll leave you on speaker."

She could hear him barking instructions, slid her phone into her breast pocket. She nodded at Marcus, who had a flashlight in his left hand, his nostrils pinched and white at the smell.

"Ready?"

He nodded, and they went in hard and fast—her high, him low, perfectly timed, like they'd done too many times to count.

A flash of lightning showed them the worst of it. Marcus hit the scene with his Maglite and they saw the rest. The body was faceup, but the face was gone. Blowflies bumbled drunkenly in the sudden light, disturbed from their feast.

"Shit," Marcus said.

"Linc, we've got a body here, gunshot to the face. Better send everyone." And to Marcus, "Let's clear the house," though it felt very clear and very empty. They moved through the space room by room. The fetid stink of the body coupled with the smell of fresh paint followed them. It was nauseating even to Taylor, who had an iron stomach.

Nobody was inside.

House cleared, they moved carefully back to the living room. The rain was lessening, and two patrols were standing in the doorway.

"House is clear," she called to them. "Someone want to hit the lights?"

"Power's out." The patrol saw it was Taylor and straightened up. "Ma'am."

"Gotcha. Can you give us a hand with your Mags, then?"

Three Maglites beamed down on the body. It was male, brown hair, but otherwise unrecognizable. The gunshot had been to the face, pulping the flesh and taking off part of the jaw; the bugs were happily doing the rest. Circle of life.

"Someone get me his wallet," Taylor commanded.

She crossed her arms and ignored the pained looks, though almost laughed at the patrols' quick game of Rock Paper Scissors. That's how they'd always decided who was in charge of the unsavory things when she was coming up, too.

A small squelch and gag later, the younger of the two called out, "Got it. Name on the ID is Justin Osborne. Male Caucasian, DOB nine-fifteen-ninety-eight, five-nine, brown on blue. Address matches this residence."

"Looks like our suspect managed to get himself dead, Marcus. Is there a weapon?"

He circled the body carefully. "Don't see a weapon. There is something trapped below his shoulder...it's a little mucky."

He teased out a piece of paper with ragged edges, as if torn from a spiral notebook, the blotch of dark blood nearly obscuring the two words written on it.

I'M SORRY

"Think the gun is under him?"

"I don't know," Marcus said, face white. "But if we don't take this outside and get some air, I might boot all over him."

"Puss," one of the patrols said, and Marcus tossed him a grin. "Your mother."

"Boys, play nice," Taylor said, tamping down her own inappropriate giggle. Crime scenes always made people uncomfortable, and they all reacted differently, but gallows humor and smart-ass comments were the primary forms of coping. She pulled her phone from her pocket. "Linc, you still with me? What's the ETA of the 'gators?"

"Forensic Medical is an hour out, at least. Another scene across town. You okay cooling your heels, or do you want me to send someone to get you?"

"I'm fine, I've got my car. We'll be on the porch for the time being, but send a tent. I don't want to set up the command close to the house. This scene's been marinating, and without lights, I don't want to risk messing anything up."

"Suicide?"

Taylor looked down at the mess of a man lying at her feet.

"Maybe. I don't know. If this is the guy who killed Georgia Wray, murder-suicide could be a logical call. The head of the label said their relationship was strained, that he'd been making threats. There's no visible weapon, though, so until we get this processed, I don't want to make any judgments."

"Roger that." Lincoln sighed.

"What?"

"I'm just thinking about how Huston's going to come down on you. Back in the field five minutes and you've already got yourself another body."

"I'm a magnet," she said, smiling at his teasing. "Don't worry about how Huston reacts. Let her know and tell Dan we won't be able to do that presser until tonight. And Linc?"

"Yeah?"

"Thanks for having my back. I appreciate it."

"Always," he said, and the phone went dead.

Taylor turned and took in the scene, and the three men watching her. "All right. Y'all know the drill. Crowd control, tight lips, no video from the neighborhood lookie-loos. Start a canvass, see who knows what about Osborne's movements over the past week. Get me the contractor, too, name's on the sign out front. If we can get a schedule of when their people were in and out of the house, maybe we can narrow down when this occurred. And someone find me a Diet Coke, yeah? It's going to be a long afternoon."

SEVEN

BY THE TIME they cleared the scene and the 'gators had removed the body, the skies had followed suit and moved from gray to black. The cold front responsible for the storms had swept through, dropping a couple of nasties from the sky but leaving the evening air in its wake crisp and clean. Taylor dug a North Face puffer vest from her back seat and donned it to ward off the chill. She stood under the tent, her third Diet Coke of the afternoon discarded on the table in favor of a hot Earl Grey tea wrestled up by a thoughtful patrol officer. The little tab of the tea bag swung in the breeze until she tucked it into the paper holder.

Justin Osborne was, so far, a relatively open book. They'd found a series of journals in the second-bedroom closet, one that was staged as an office/music room. His hurt and resentment of Georgia Wray was so visceral Taylor couldn't help but assume that he'd been the one who shot the girl.

THAT WAS MY SONG...MINE! I WROTE THE WHOLE THING.

HOW DARE SHE GIVE IN TO THEM?

WHY DOES SHE HATE ME? SHE WON'T ANSWER MY TEXTS OR CALLS ANYMORE...

FUCK HER. THE WORLD WOULD BE A BETTER PLACE WITHOUT HER..

I MISS HER SO MUCH...

There were a few oddities, though. Justin did have two weapons registered to him—a Winchester .22 rifle and a Taurus 9mm handgun, and both were located in his gun safe in the garage. The gun that was found under him was a Glock 40—hence the gaping face and head wounds—with the number filed off. A street gun. The shell casing retrieved from the scene was an initial match to the casing found on the mountain. The bullets would have to go through forensics to see if the rifling matched the gun, but there was a strong chance the weapon found under Justin's body was the same one used to murder Georgia Wray. If Justin Osborne planned to kill himself, why go to the trouble of procuring a street gun instead of using his own Taurus?

The other thing was more of a hunch than anything concrete. Based on her extensive experience with entry and exit wounds, it seemed the gun had been fired at least an arm's length away from his face. Something about that felt...wrong. Taylor had handled her share of suicides, and usually, the gun was held close to the body. It was entirely possible the gun had kicked his arm back—the 40 packed one hell of a punch—but to start that way? Like Justin was taking a selfie, but with a pistol?

But...if he had, it would have taken two hands to hold the gun steady and pull the trigger. He'd have to use his thumb, and the recoil would make the nose of the weapon tip up, possibly missing his face. Perhaps he was trying to shoot himself in the chest and that's exactly what happened, the gun jerked up and the bullet caught him square in the nose instead of the heart.

Possible. But still, weird.

Don't borrow trouble, girl. Cut and dried. They were having serious troubles. He killed her, came back home, killed himself. Everything points to murder-suicide, even the witness who saw him after the gunshot. A shame, but logic matters. You just want things to be complicated so you don't have to go back to that damn desk.

It was Samantha's voice interrupting her thought process, so ingrained into Taylor's psyche that she appeared without Taylor summoning her. She argued back as if Sam were standing five feet away.

Why come back home? Why not just shoot himself there?

He freaked out and ran. He knew there were people up there with him.

Logical. Still. Something feels all wrong here.

You're bored and looking for fun. Wrap it up, sister. Presser's waiting on you. Family, too.

Marcus joined her under the tent. "Talking to yourself again?"

"What?"

"You stare off into space and your lips move. Like you're talking with a ghost. You've done it for years."

She laughed. "I was arguing with Sam."

"Ah. Gotcha. I miss her. You talked to her recently?"

He reached down and snagged a rolling ball of something being pushed into the scene by the breeze, neatly deposited it into a trash bag helpfully provided to ensure they didn't contaminate the scene with their crap.

"I have. She's doing well. She and Xander are up in the forest at their cabin, hanging out with Thor. Can you imagine our Sam, camping? Well, glamping—his cabin has a baby grand."

"Nope. She must really love that guy. And the dog. I never thought she was a dog person."

"She wasn't. And she does love Xander, and Thor. They worship her, not surprisingly. They're a good match. Anyway, I was having a mental fight with her because of two things: the unregistered gun, and the selfie gunshot."

"Yeah, that's weird. I mean, we've seen that kind of distance when they use their toes to pull the trigger on a shotgun, but yeah, with a handgun? Weird, but I doubt it's enough to sway a jury one way or another."

"And what about the fact that he came all the way back home?"

"Guilt got to him."

"I'm overthinking this?"

"Totally. But I get it. It's a quick and easy, albeit sad as hell, wrap. You were hoping for more."

"Not hoping for more. Just...expecting things to spiral out of control, as they are wont to do."

"You wanna take one more pass through the house before we shut it all down?"

She shook her head. "No. There's not much else to see, and the journals really do spell it out. Do we have a lead on Osborne's family? Want to get them notified, and talk about things. Their lives just got complicated."

"I'll handle it."

She nodded, squaring her shoulders. "Okay. Let's have a quick run at a few of the neighbors, see if we can find the kid's family, then go give our summary to the cameras."

It was only later, when she was driving home, that the third discrepancy jumped out at her.

None of the journals in the house were spiral bound. They were all Moleskines, with lay-flat bindings.

So where had the notepaper come from?

EIGHT

HOME AGAIN, home again.

Taylor pulled into the underground garage of their condo and parked, happy to see Baldwin's BMW in the second slot. She grabbed her gear and headed upstairs. She didn't look over her shoulder at all.

Nashville was different now than when she'd been running these streets after dark with a rather unsavory crew of miscreants from the local high schools, eluding the very police force she was now in charge of. This particular area used to be very rough, nearing dangerous, but now it was slick. Sophisticated. Packed with upscale hotels and condo buildings, elegant restaurants, art galleries, and a few blocks away from the happy chaos of the music venues handling the innumerable bachelorette parties and concert traffic that mobbed downtown. Even with the tourists, or especially because of them, Nashville was safe again, thanks to Taylor and all of Metro's hard work.

The move downtown was a good one for her and Baldwin. Never one to enjoy a crowd, she was getting used to the constant, throbbing hubbub. The building had tight security, too, which was the main reason they'd made the move. Taylor had gotten crosswise with an assassin at a conference up in Maryland—the same conference where she'd met Thierry Florian of the Macallan Group. They'd faced off, and Taylor had shot the woman, but in the shoulder. The assassin had disappeared off a cliff before she could be apprehended. That moment haunted Taylor's nightmares still. Why she hadn't taken the kill shot, she didn't know. Or maybe she did. Maybe she'd recognized a professional doing their job, or maybe she'd just lost her edge. Either way, she and Baldwin had decided it was important to have some barriers to entry just in case said assassin decided she wanted to get back in touch. Not that Baldwin hadn't made his share of enemies along the way, too. Their home in the suburbs, while patrician and lovely, was simply impossible to secure, and their neighbors didn't take kindly to lurking security teams camping in the bucolic tree-lined street. The condo was...easier.

The elevator purred to a stop at the forty-fourth floor, and the doors whispered open to reveal a small, tastefully decorated antechamber. Baldwin had made several upgrades to the condo's security, including a biometric reader that allowed them into the hallway off the anteroom. If someone managed to get into the building, into the elevator, to this floor, and into this room—an unlikely set of circumstances—they'd then have to get through three more layers of completely personalized security to get the doors open to the hallway. Key. Keypad. Iris scanner.

If someone got through that, they still needed to bypass a handprint biometric at the door itself. They were secure. Overkill, but secure.

Taylor didn't want to tell Baldwin she hated being locked away like a princess in a castle. That she'd prefer to take on Angelie Delacroix headfirst, *womano e womano*, instead of hiding. That if the assassin who wreaked havoc in Maryland wanted Taylor, she could get her anytime, outside of the building. She could end her in a heartbeat.

But this setup made him feel better, so she could hardly argue.

Baldwin hailed her as she entered. The sharp scents of peppers and onions wafted from the kitchen. So normal, so real, she felt all the tension leave her. She could worry about poor Georgia Wray tomorrow. For tonight, there was her home, and her man, and her life. She dropped her bag and slid her arms around his body, hugging him from behind.

"That smells delicious, hon. What's for dinner?"

"Carnitas."

"Oh, yum!"

He turned in her arms, spatula held high. "I kind of like the whole role reversal here. Me making dinner, you out on the beat."

"Ahem. If I recall, I was the one who made the carnitas, and you're simply heating them up."

He looked wounded and gestured to the counter, where a colorful stack of peppers awaited their turn in the pan. "I will have you know I cut all these peppers into little bitty thin matchsticks, just like you do."

"Oh, forgive me, Sir Pepper Cutter." She gave him a little bow and accepted a glass of Tempranillo. "Now that's the way to get to my heart." She took a deep sip, relishing the peppery taste of the red wine. "I fear my case is solved."

Baldwin set down the spoon and took up his own glass, clinking it into the side of hers. "*Ching ching.* That was quick. Confession?"

"Suicide. Her ex-boyfriend. Looks like he killed her, went home, killed himself."

"Odd."

She thumped the glass onto the counter. "Exactly what I said. Why wouldn't he kill himself near her body? Why would he take her up a mountain, shoot her—granted, interrupted by a couple of co-eds who stumbled upon him—then go home? I'm overthinking it. It's a righteous close, I'm sure."

He nuzzled her neck, then turned the burner down and sat at the counter. "I'm sure it is. Speaking of overthinking, you won't believe what I have to do."

She raised a brow and licked her lips. "Your talents are wide and varied, good sir. I can believe most anything."

Baldwin laughed. "Later, if you're good. No, yours truly is off in the morning to speak at a writers' conference. On a damn cruise ship."

"Wait. *You're* going on a cruise with a bunch of writers?" A laugh bubbled up inside her at the pained expression on his handsome face.

"Yeah. Garrett roped me in. Charlaine Shultz was the speaker scheduled to go, but she's caught some sort of bug, and Garrett doesn't want to disappoint the organizers. I told him it was a disaster in the making, that me stuck on a boat for a week with a crowd peppering me for information on cases that I can't possibly provide information about wasn't in anyone's best interest, but Garrett gave me a speech. 'You're a rare commodity, and you owe me. Go speak, thrill their pants off that they're in the room with a famous profiler, and relax a bit. You need a break.'"

She smoothed a hand over his jaw. "You do need a break. We both do."

"You can come with me. Or better yet, for me."

She picked up the spoon and gave the carnitas a stir. "Last time I went to a conference in your stead..."

He groaned and ran a hand through his hair, making it stand on end.

"And here I thought you loved me."

She gave him a grin. "I'll love you more if you finish off those peppers and plate dinner. I'm famished."

The lead story on the ten o'clock news was the suspected murder-suicide of the country singer Georgia Wray, supplanting the storm-damage story that imparted the unwelcome news: an EF-2 tornado had whipped through both Dickson and Mount Juliet; the damage was substantial.

Taylor cringed at that news, then again when the story switched to the murder-suicide. The cameras panned to her giving the statement, truncated into an appropriate sound bite.

"This afternoon, we followed a lead in the Georgia Wray homicide investigation to a home in East Nashville that had ties to Ms. Wray. We found a body in the house, whom we have tentatively identified as Justin Osborne, Miss Wray's ex-boyfriend. We're waiting on DNA results to confirm this identity. We can't release the cause of death for either party at this time, but I can share that we are not looking for additional suspects. Autopsy results will be released at a later date pending toxicology. We are pursuing the theory of murder-suicide at this time, and the families request your indulgence to leave them in peace while they process this information."

She wasn't vain by any means, but wow, she was looking pretty rough. Tired. Circles under her eyes, drab skin. Just worn down by the world. She needed a vacation.

Baldwin slid into the bed beside her. He, too, was looking ragged. Soon, though, they could go away together. She made a mental note to start looking for a place. She'd surprise him. Make it a romantic getaway. The thought made her smile. It had been too long since they went somewhere just the two of them, without work—or death—looming.

"How's it feel?" he asked, snuggling in, his long arms sliding around her.

"How's what feel?" she replied archly, pushing her hips

back against his. She was rewarded with a low rumble of laughter and a nip on the neck.

"I meant being back in the field, but if you have other things in mind..."

"I always have other things in mind." She flipped off the television and rolled onto her back. Her hand threaded through his hair, and the inky night of Nashville bled into the room, the lights of the other buildings near them shining. It was never completely dark in the condo, despite the automated louvers installed between the glass panes of the windows. He kissed her neck gently, and she sighed.

"What's wrong?"

"Huston read me the riot act this evening."

"About what?"

"Not following orders. I was supposed to do a presser midday, put it off. Didn't call her immediately when we found the body. You know, power-play crap. Said my being in the field on this case was conditional and she'd slam me back to my desk without a second's hesitation."

"I assume you told her to go jump?"

"I told her 'yes, ma'am, sorry, ma'am, I'll never do it again, ma'am,' like a good little captain."

Baldwin was silent. They could hear the faint strains of music drifting up from Lower Broadway, the honky-tonks in full swing. The city was vibrant until late in the night now; the tourists didn't come here to sleep.

"She never used to be like this. I mean, she's always been tough, but since I moved into management, she's been quite the bitch. Toward me, mostly. Working for her is...complicated."

"She knows your next step is her job. That makes people anxious."

Taylor scoffed. "Captain is bad enough. Commander? No way, no how."

"You don't have to do this, you know. You can come work with me. Sam, too. You'd be a huge asset to the team."

"I appreciate the vote of confidence, but Baldwin, honey, we've been over this a hundred times. Metro brass is bad enough. The FBI would be even more stifling. No offense"—she stroked his arm—"but you're much better at following rules than I am."

She didn't need to see his face to know he was smiling. "None taken. Someone has to, or we lose all credibility. So what are you going to do? Open a restaurant? Italian food, homestyle. You know how much I love your meatballs."

"Oh, the jokes, they write themselves... That's tempting. Actually, though, I was thinking about the offer I got from Thierry Florian last year. You know, at the conference in Maryland."

"To go to work for the Macallan Group? Really?"

He shifted onto his right arm, and she looked over. God, he was handsome, even in the dark. Especially in the dark. Black hair with strands of silver, moss-green eyes, sharp nose, full lips. He could have been a model but instead was the FBI's most celebrated profiler. Beauty and brains. A small thump of desire lit her lower stomach. She could never get enough of him.

"He wants you too, you know."

He spit out a wry laugh. "Like you, I have enough taskmasters."

She knew that in addition to Garrett Woods, his boss at the FBI, he was talking of the shadowy man known as Atlantic, the head of Operation Angelmaker, an offshoot of the CIA that claimed Baldwin as their own personal assassin whisperer. What a side gig. When one of the governments of any nation's wet work specialists went off the grid or started unsanctioned killings, Baldwin was called in to do an "assessment." Get the creeps back on track, killing for the right people, not themselves.

A nasty job, but Baldwin was up to the task. He had a deep, unassailable conscience, and the psychopaths, for the most part, listened to him. Yes, he did have too many people to answer to.

Taylor didn't. She was responsible now to Baldwin, and the city, but her team was no longer hers. Sam had moved to DC and was consumed with consulting for the FBI and teaching at Georgetown, and her burgeoning relationship with Xander Whitfield. Taylor, should she choose, was a free agent.

"I don't know," she said, as she'd been saying since Florian offered her a job. "It would mean time away from Nashville, and from you. Plus wads of training, and riding a desk until I could get up to speed. That's not something I'm interested in right now. I'm already stuck in the office as is."

"But you aren't happy. And I hate seeing you like this."

"I'm happy with you. That's enough."

He kissed her softly. "It won't be. Not forever."

"Why do you say that?"

He sighed deeply. "Honey, you are like a feral cat, and I mean that in the best possible way. You will come inside eventually, and accept the warm cushion and bowl of milk, maybe even consent to have your back scratched, but you will never be happy as a house cat. You will only be happy roaming the woods."

"Are you profiling me, Dr. Baldwin?"

"Do you want me to?"

"No. I can't imagine what you might dig up."

She touched the healing scar on her temple, a habit she really needed to break. At least it kept her hands off the well-faded scar on her neck. She'd spent enough time being psychoanalyzed when she'd had the aphonia after the gunshot that nearly took her life. Not being able to speak had freaked her out. She'd done a cool technique for her PTSD called EMDR—Eye Movement Desensitization and Reprocessing—and the legit portion of it worked. The non-legit—offered at the hands of a madwoman—nearly killed her. Regardless, she had her voice back and wasn't flinching and getting overwhelmed with adrenaline every time someone snuck up on her or a car backfired. She'd even been spending time at the gun range again, something that had always relaxed her. She was healed from her recent run-in with the serial killer the press called the Pretender. Mostly. At least on the outside.

"Wanna talk some more about Georgia Wray?" Baldwin said, interrupting her thoughts, and now it was her turn to sigh deeply. He knew her too well.

"Honestly? I'm probably reading into things, but I get the sense there's something else happening, though I have no idea what. The more I think about it, I really don't think my guy today was a suicide. It was set up too perfectly. There was a note, a piece of paper ripped from a notebook. And though there were a ton of notebooks in the house, none were spiral bound. We found the gun under him, just where it would have been if he shot himself and collapsed onto it—but who shoots themselves in the face? Under the chin, in the mouth, the temple, the chest, yeah. But who holds a handgun a couple of feet from their nose and pulls the trigger? That, and the whole placement of her body on the mountain and the shooting... He was up on that mountain with her, no doubt, because that's who our witness identified. But what if someone else was there, and Justin somehow escaped and was followed back to his house? What if *he* was the target and Georgia Wray was a casualty? And...I mean, the odds of these two college kids wandering into a murder hiking near Radnor Lake, following a specific set of GPS coordinates? It's wildly coincidental. And don't even get me started on this whole GPS thing. It's too weird."

"That's a lot of what-ifs. So do you think the developer of the GPS game is in on it?"

"I don't know. Also feels like quite a stretch. He's a kid. Then again, so are Georgia Wray and Justin Osborne." She rolled to face him. "See what you've done to me? I'm being handed a cut-and-dried case to make me shut up about not being in the field anymore, and I'm turning it into zebra hooves instead of horses."

"I love it when you Occam's razor me, honey."

"Shut up and kiss me, goof."

He did.

NINE

WEDNESDAY: NEW HAVEN, CONNECTICUT

DR. AVERY CONWAY arrived home from a long overnight shift in the emergency room and followed all her usual habits: dropped her bag and shoes and everyday mask in the mudroom, plugged in her phone, washed her hands thoroughly with plain soap, not antibacterial, divested herself of her clothes, which went straight into the wash. She had a stack of clean yoga pants and T-shirts folded neatly in the laundry room cabinet. She pulled on the fresh clothes, put her hair into a stubby ponytail, and wandered into the kitchen. She poured a glass of wine and took a deep sip. She was one of the few people she knew who drank wine in the morning, but that's the weird way her day was structured. Took another deep drink, then topped off the wine and sat at the bar counter where the mail waited for her. Her housekeeper always brought it in for her before she left for the day, separating the stack of the weekly circulars and other junk from the good magazines, letters, and bills.

Avery riffled through it with half an eye, trying to reorient herself from the noise and chaos of the hospital to her quiet, serene sanctuary, stopping only when she saw the envelope from Vanderbilt. The crest said *From the Office of the President*, and the linen was thick and creamy, as befitted her alumnus. Oddly, the envelope wasn't sealed.

Sloppy of them, she thought. *Must have had the prospectives there for the weekend and made them stuff envelopes.*

Avery had suffered just such an indignity the summer before her senior year in high school when she'd gone to Nashville for a prospective visit. She had no idea they'd be put to work for two hours stuffing envelopes for an alumni mailing. It was drudgery, and she was annoyed, but she'd gotten her own early acceptance letter the following week and all petty grievances were put aside. She was a Vanderbilt graduate now. Her darling daughter was following in her footsteps. Anchor down!

Not that it mattered.

Avery glanced around her spacious kitchen, the leathered marble and white cabinets, the champagne brass fixtures, the monstrous Italian stove and refrigerator large enough to park a battleship inside. Vanderbilt had put her on the path to these... things. A degree. A career. Even a husband, a boy she'd met in her freshman English comp class whom she'd loved with all her heart and married the first chance she'd gotten. When she'd graduated from Vandy med school and started her residency in New Haven, she'd discovered she was pregnant, and she'd never been happier. A full life. The life she always wanted.

The babies came quickly, three in four years—two rambunctious boys, Riordan and Julian, and a sweet little girl she named Carson after her own mother—while she was finishing her residency and getting her practice up and running. The people around her marveled, called her superwoman. She was. She was invincible. Driven. Dedicated. Brilliant. So incredibly happy.

Then Richard died. An aneurysm exploded during a bike

ride down the Farmington Canal Heritage Trail. Avery thought she might curl up and die along with him. Her scripted, perfectly planned life was suddenly off the rails. She had three teenage children and was a widow at thirty-nine, bereft of her soul mate, the man who made her laugh, who shared her ambitions, though his were cozier in nature—Richard had started an organic bakery in New Haven that catered to the students with fresh, delicious, allergen-safe pastries. He'd dedicated his life to helping others, and he was gone in an instant.

Unable to juggle everything, she'd sold the business to Richard's friend Alan Rooney, who, alongside his husband, Santiago, had turned it into a hugely successful, now nationwide business. Richard would have been so proud—both of the bakery and its new business model, and how his people had rallied around his precious wife once he was gone.

Alan and Santiago never did an interview without mentioning Richard and Avery. There was a dedication page on the website, and a small logo of a bicycle on all of the packaging, an homage to Richard's favorite pastime. (Avery thought it morbid, considering he'd died while on the bike, but didn't say anything.) The profit-sharing scheme they'd cooked up meant Avery didn't have to work if she didn't want to, and gave her plenty of cash to take care of the children, in addition to her own healthy paycheck from the hospital.

And there was a fresh cooler of everything bagels and lemon blueberry muffins on the front porch every Sunday. She didn't have the heart to tell them once the children were gone, she gave them away. Sometimes she'd run them to the shelter on Fourth Avenue, or she'd drop them at the retirement home down the street.

They were trying to take care of her still, but the constant reminders—that logo, the stylized R coiling around the bagel she saw everywhere (even the hospital cafeteria stocked the brand); the periodic requests for interviews when the bakery opened a new branch; the way the children's faces fell when they were forced to drive by the original building housing the bakery; the dividends—all of it was too much for one woman to bear.

She'd thought of moving from New Haven, maybe finding a cottage by the sea, but this was her home. Eventually, her heart would heal. She wouldn't be picking off the scab daily.

She told herself that, year in and year out, as the children grew older, one by one, went off to college, started their own lives, and she rattled around the big old house alone, exhausted from her shifts, too sad to sleep. Alone.

She took the letter and her wine to the table, berating herself for the thoughts of Richard, as she inevitably did when she saw anything related to how they'd met.

It had taken such strength to send Carson off to Vanderbilt. It was different with the boys—Rory and Jules were always independent, raucous, happy, full of life, throwing footballs in the kitchen and borrowing the car keys for nights out with their friends. Carson was so much quieter. A sweet, bookish girl who was more content to read, even as a little one. A dreamer, her baby girl. Avery prayed nightly her lovely, fragile daughter wouldn't meet a handsome, studious young man or woman and fall in love. Love did nothing but cause pain.

She turned the envelope over and pulled out the sheet of paper, half-smiling thinking about Carson wandering lonely as a cloud around campus, her nose in a book. Instead, there was a thick, heavy notecard with a small sprig of ivy at the top. On it were three lines of block print that made Avery's heart stop.

WE HAVE YOUR DAUGHTER
TWO MILLION
NO COPS

TEN

AVERY DROPPED the paper with a cry of revulsion. What the hell? Surely this was some sort of terrible joke. She yanked her phone from her bag and speed-dialed Carson's number.

"You've reached Carson Conway. I'm sorry to miss your call. Please leave a message."

So polite. Even her voicemail message was well mannered, unlike the boys'. Rory's was "You know what to do." And Jules' was simply "What up?"

"Carson? It's Mom. Call me back as soon as you get this."

She sent a text, too, waiting, waiting, waiting for the three dots that said her darling daughter was writing back.

When they showed up, she nearly sang for joy.

Then the text came.

Two million. Clock's ticking.

The cry from her lips startled the cardinal from the feeder outside the kitchen window.

"Dr. Conway?"

Avery screamed and jumped, her hand clutching the phone to her chest. Teddy, Alan and Santiago's teenage son, stood at the entrance to the kitchen, holding an envelope.

"You scared me, Teddy."

"Oh, Dr. Conway, I'm so sorry. The door was open, and I rang the bell. Someone dropped a letter for you at the bakery, I told my dads I'd drop it by on my way home."

He took a step toward her, and Avery took a step back, slamming into the Sub-Zero, the handle digging hard into her back. "You can leave it there, Teddy. Tell your dads I said thanks."

Teddy frowned, but listened, setting the envelope on the table. "You sure you're okay, Dr. Conway? You look upset. Do you need me to call anyone?"

"I'm fine, Teddy."

She went through all the motions of what fine might look like — smiling, ushering him to the door, closing it behind him with a little wave— then went back to the kitchen and stared at the envelope on the table as if it might bite.

Finally, hands shaking, she opened it.

NOW ARE YOU TAKING THIS SERIOUSLY?

She sprinted to the door and threw it open. Teddy was just pulling out of the drive. Lord, time flies. When had he gotten his license? She waved wildly, and he stopped at the mailbox, rolled down his window.

"Where's your daddy? Santiago?"

"At the bakery."

"I need to talk to him, right now. But I need to do it in person, and I have to stay here. Would you please go get him and bring him to me?"

Teddy didn't hesitate. "I'll be right back, Dr. Conway."

He sped away, and Avery went back inside the house,

dialing Carson again. The phone rang and rang, no voicemail coming on.

Why would someone take Carson?

Where would she get two million dollars?

She should call the police, right this moment. She wasn't an idiot, she didn't have cash money like this on hand, and they would know what to do.

But Santiago might have another idea. She hoped and prayed that the rumblings and rumors she'd heard over the years were right.

That he used to work for the government before he retired and moved to New Haven.

That he used to be a spy.

That he used to be in a gang.

That he'd killed ten men with a fork.

That he was incapable of being hurt.

That he'd spent three years in prison.

That he was a ghost.

She called her boys, one after the other. Got their voicemails. Shit. This wasn't something she wanted to say in a message, she needed to talk in person. "Call me," she said to each.

She heard the squeal of the truck's tires and dropped the letter on the table. Santiago Diaz-Rooney strode into the room, still wearing his apron, a dusting of flour on his cheek and in the fringe of his dark hair.

"Avery? What's wrong?"

"Teddy, please excuse us, all right?"

With a glance toward his father, who nodded, eyebrows drawn tight together, Teddy melted away into the hall. When she heard the front door slam, Avery thrust the notes into Santiago's hands. He read them, paling a bit.

"What the hell?"

"Exactly my thought." Avery struggled to keep her voice

even. "I've been calling and she's not answering. Why would someone take Carson?"

"For the money, apparently. But do you have this kind of cash to access?"

"No, of course not. It's all tied up, in the house, the bakery, investments. But Santi—what do I do?"

She moved suddenly, knocking the wineglass to the floor. The ruby liquid purled on the hardwood and reminded her of lifeblood. She burst into tears, ragged sobs that racked her body. *Damn it, g-g-get yourself together,* but even her inner voice was weeping.

Santiago held her while she shook, murmuring soothing nothings until she got a grip on herself and could take a big, shuddery breath.

"Okay," he said. "Better?"

"I'm sorry. I didn't mean to fall apart like that. I just...after Richard...I can't lose her, too."

"You won't." His jaw was tight, dark eyes flashing with anger.

"What do I do?" she repeated. "Call the police?"

"No," he snapped. "You let me handle this, okay?"

"You're a baker, Santiago," she said, praying he would disagree with her.

She felt a little thrill inside at how dark and dangerous he looked when he said, "I wasn't always."

ELEVEN

NASHVILLE

TAYLOR DROPPED Baldwin at the airport for the flight that would get him to Fort Lauderdale and the port where the thriller writers' cruise departed, then grabbed a biscuit and Diet Coke and headed to Forensic Medical for Georgia Wray's postmortem.

The city was buzzing about Wray's death, and Huston wanted a quick close to settle everyone down. Taylor wanted a quick close, too, naturally, but wouldn't have minded a couple more days in the field. She had her weekly staff meeting later, two slogging hours of PowerPoint decks on crime statistics, and already felt the internal yawns starting.

She greeted the new receptionist—*Cookie? Callie? Connie!*—and headed through the security doors into the heart of the building. Downstairs, Taylor put scrubs and protective gear on over her clothes, wondering just how many times she'd been in this position over the fifteen years she'd been on the force. Hundreds. Thousands, maybe. She'd never kept track of how many murders, accidents, unattended deaths she'd worked, before and after she'd been moved to plainclothes. That would have been much too grim. Forensic Medical was someplace she had spent too much time over the years. Just a part of the job, but one she never relished.

She entered the autopsy suite, glancing over to where Sam was usually setting up shop for the day's guests. Taylor was never going to acclimate to not seeing Sam's head bent over the long desk on the far side of the room, the skylights causing warm red highlights to show in her hair. Without Samantha Owens there, everything felt lopsided. Out of place.

Sam had moved on. Why couldn't Taylor?

All eight stainless tables were occupied. The bodies of Georgia Wray and Justin Osborne were at stations side by side, separated by scales and sluice drains. Their left and right hands trailed off the table and toward one another, a grotesque Romeo and Juliet tableau.

Dr. Fox had proceeded without her and was currently cutting the upper and lower lobes of Justin Osborne's left lung into squares and triangles.

"Hey, Cap. If you've got someplace else to be, I'll call it now. I'm ruling it a murder-suicide."

Taylor blew out a breath.

"You're sure?"

Dr. Fox nodded. "Without any evidence to the contrary? And a witness, and a note? Georgia's pretty straightforward — the bullet caught her in the face and opened up the back of her head. She had her arm up in a defensive posture, the bullet went through her wrist before it hit her jaw. There's bruising and lividity, consistent with her falling backward, and she's covered in dirt and leaves, I assume from the attempted burial. Cause of death was the gunshot wound to the head, manner of death is homicide.

"This guy"—he gestured with his elbow toward Osborne's pale body—"is consistent with suicide. The bullet lodged in the wall at the perfect angle to show the weapon being held approximately thirty-four inches from the body, angled up, just like I'd expect from a man standing, arm extended, with the weapon pointed toward himself. Could have been aiming at his heart and the gun kicked up, caught him in the face. The gun is the same as the one that shot Georgia Wray, rifling was positive. GSR tests were also positive, and the dirt under his nails is soil preliminarily consistent with the soil we pulled off and around her body, so that puts him at the murder scene. His arm's reach is about perfect for that shot. Not to mention your witness was pretty clear they were arguing before she was killed, and saw him moments later, gun in hand."

"Oh, I'm not doubting he shot her, just that he shot himself afterward."

"Yeah, I mean, it was a weird angle, but it's not unthinkable. There was a little bit of fabric in the wound, wedged near his jaw, that I have to send out for analysis, but visual inspection suggests it came off his shirt. The collar is missing a small corner." He popped his own collar, held out his hands, and angled his head slightly to the right. "Bullet could have easily caught it as it went in. Not to do your job for you, but his girl just hit it big-time and left him behind. That causes problems in a relationship. He shoots her, goes home, shoots himself. Murder-suicide feels like a slam dunk to me. I've collected a bunch of fibers and a dizzying array of dirt, rocks, leaves, and branches, which I'll send off, but nothing is standing out. Definitely nothing that would indicate otherwise."

"Thanks, Fox. I know you're right. That is what the notebooks seem to indicate, too. He was really upset with her, made threats in person and on paper. I haven't had a chance to cruise their phones yet, but I'm sure there will be more of the same. Anything on the suicide note? It didn't come from paper that matched anything we found inside the house."

"Nope. Run-of-the-mill notebook paper. Find it in any

drugstore. You're sure there was nothing that matched it in the house?"

Taylor nodded. "Positive. He used Moleskines exclusively. We found about a hundred of them."

"Maybe it was from one of hers?"

Hmm. "Good thought. I'll check. Nothing else?"

Fox shook his head. "Sorry, Taylor. This one's pretty straightforward."

"All right. Thanks. Send me your reports when they're ready, and barring any unforeseen new evidence, I'll close it."

"It's such a shame," Fox said, staring thoughtfully at the ravaged body of the young singer as his assistant stowed the plastic bag of organs inside her open body cavity and sewed the incision shut with three large looping stitches—two top, one bottom. "She's a doll. I really loved the single she released."

"What's it called?"

Fox stared at Taylor in mock horror. "Seriously?"

"I'm more inclined to listen to The Police or Duran Duran. You know that."

"Sacrilege," he said, popping a stick of gum in his mouth. "You live in the country music capital of the world, and you know nothing about it. The single's called 'Breathing Your Air.' It's all over Spotify. Very pretty ballad, though I might have started in B flat. Her tone could have been better and the chorus would have ended up like this." He sang a few bars in a surprisingly good alto, playing an impressive air guitar, finishing with the line *"That's what it's all about, I just wanna breathe your air, baby."*

Taylor clapped. "All these years, and I had no idea. You never told me you were a singer."

"Taylor," he intoned with mock severity. "I live in Nashville. It's a requirement to have a side gig in the industry. Like every waiter in LA is writing a script, everyone here is, or was, trying to get discovered."

"Don't tell me you're going to leave me for auditions..."

"Hey, I did my time with the stage crowd while I was at Meharry. Though I admit, med school was a bit too all-consuming to let me get any real breaks."

Three tables down, there was a high-pitched whine, the skull saw doing its grisly business, and one of the lab attendants called out, "Head's ready."

"Duty calls," Fox said. "I'll send you that report."

Outside, the air was shockingly clear of humidity, but not cold, the desired effect of the previous day's front and storms. Taylor breathed deeply, ridding her lungs of the clinical, antiseptic scent of the morgue, and looked toward downtown. One full day in the field, a case closed, and now she had to go back to her stuffy, overdecorated office and do paperwork before the staff meeting. Ugh.

On impulse, she pulled out her phone and thumbed open her contacts. She pressed the name on the screen, calculating the time difference. Cocktail hour in France.

A male voice, heavily accented and slightly suspicious, answered with a simple "*Oui?*"

"Mr. Florian? This is Taylor Jackson."

"Captain Jackson. A pleasure."

"How did you know I was promoted?"

She could envision the dapper man shrugging a single shoulder. "If I did not pay attention to the people I value, I would not be much of a leader, no? Have you considered my offer?"

"I have. I..."

Shit. What was she doing? Florian saved her, though. This was one hell of an escape hatch.

"I happen to be in New York this week. Why don't we get together, *chérie*? We can discuss things. You needn't make any commitments to me over the phone. I sense you are still conflicted. I am very happy to give you as much space and information as you need."

"I don't know that I can come to New York. I have responsibilities here."

"It is no matter. I will come to you. Shall we say lunch, tomorrow at noon? I do love the Oak Bar at the Hermitage Hotel. Their *frites* are remarkably good."

"I didn't know you knew Nashville."

"One always studies one's adversaries, and one's potential recruits."

Why was she not surprised to hear he'd been checking up on her?"

"Well, I hate to break it to you, but they've closed the Oak Bar."

He made a very French sound of indignation. "That is a shame. I will find us someplace else suitable. If you agree?"

"All right. Yes. That would be lovely. Thank you, Mr. Florian."

"Thierry, please, *chérie*. If you come to work for me, you will be my equal, not my subordinate."

"Thierry. Tomorrow, then."

"*Au revoir, chérie*."

She hung up feeling lighter than she had in weeks. Despite what she was telling herself—and Baldwin—aloud, she *had* been contemplating Florian's offer since he made it. At some point, she needed to make a decision and settle herself, once and for all. For a decisive woman, the events of the past few years had shaken her to the core. That's what the Pretender's reign of terror hath wrought—she didn't trust herself anymore. And that was a dangerous place to be.

She called Sam on her way back to the office but got her best friend's voicemail.

"Give me a call. I want to talk to you about something."

The phone rang before she hit Ellington Parkway.

"Hey, cookie! Sorry, I was in the backyard with Thor. That silly dog misses his daddy, who is off on yet another protection detail. We just got back to the city, and Xander's gone for at least a week or two. How are you?"

"Good."

"Uh-oh. Do I detect a tone?"

Taylor laughed. "You know me too well. No. No tone. Just heading back to the office after a whirlwind twenty-four hours on a case. Murder-suicide. Case closed."

"Oh, the Georgia Wray murder? That girl was going places. I was sick when I heard."

"Everyone is. Her boyfriend killed her, we have a witness, but then the boyfriend ended up dead at his place. GSW to the face."

"Ugh."

"Yeah. So now I traverse the lonely road from your former office back to my new one, and the boring world that has become my life. Fox says hi, by the way."

"I'm worried about you. You sound more than bored."

"Don't be. I'm taking steps."

"Do tell."

"First, I'm going to have lunch with that guy from Macallan. And then I'm going to take Baldwin to a beach somewhere and bang his brains out for a few days."

Sam's throaty laugh spilled into her ear, maybe her smile. "You're incorrigible. But yes, a little getaway is just what the doctor ordered. So you're really thinking of quitting?"

"*Retiring* has a much nicer ring to it. Take the twenty and run."

"But that would mean staying for a few more years."

"I can manage."

"No, you can't. You're sad. And that is awful for everyone around you. Who cares about the pension and benefits? You've got enough if you need it."

"I'll never take my parents' money, Sam. You know that."

"And there's also that tall drink of water you're bedding down with. He's got some income, too."

"If I'm not taking it from my parents, you think I'd take it from my partner? Hells to the no."

Sam laughed. "I'm just saying, it's not like you're going to starve. And this new gig would pay. Get out while the getting's good. That's what the rest of the world is doing. The Great Resignation, they're calling it."

"I will definitely not be making any decisions because of the downstream fallout of the pandemic. This is about me. What I want, and what I don't. And I do *not* want to be a captain. I've never wanted this job. I am not suited for it."

There, she'd said it aloud, for the first time, too. She was being snappish, but Sam could take it. They'd been best friends since they were little girls; their bond was deeper than any sister, because they'd chosen each other as blood.

Sam, recognizing the moment, whooped. "There's my girl. Why don't you just go straight to Huston's office and lay down your badge and gun while you're all tuned up?"

"Maybe I will."

Her call waiting beeped, and a quick glance at her watch showed it was Huston. "Crap. Speak of the devil. Call you later?"

"You better. Love you."

"You too," but she was already flipping over to her boss. Just knowing she had to talk to Huston, the tension was back in her shoulders in a heartbeat. And at her boss's frantic tone, it stayed there.

"Where are you?" Huston demanded.

"On my way there from Forensic Medical. I—"

"Turn around and get yourself to Vanderbilt. Carson Conway has gone missing."

TWELVE

NEW HAVEN

AVERY PACED while Santiago lifted the phone to his ear, waited a moment, then spoke such rapid-fire Spanish that her generic emergency room doctor's version of *¿Donde duelo?* couldn't begin to follow. He spoke, then listened, then spoke again, nodding and gesturing as if the person on the other end could see him. Finally, he hung up and gave her a reassuring smile.

"This is both good news and bad news. The Nashville police are already involved. Carson's roommate called them this morning. She worried when Carson didn't come home last night."

"Why in the world didn't she call me?"

"I don't know. Maybe she tried and you didn't see the call?"

She grabbed her phone and sure enough, damn it, there was a call from an unknown number that had gone directly to voicemail and wasn't showing on her main screen. A wonderful way to combat telemarketers, but she cursed the software trick now. She pressed the speaker button and played the voicemail.

The voice was watery, apologetic. "Um, Dr. Conway? This is Izz, Carson's roommate. Any chance you've heard from her? Give me a call if you have."

Not frantic or scared, just concerned, and it allowed Avery a moment to take a deep breath, gathering herself. She dialed the number back and waited for a heartbeat before the same voice answered.

"Um, hello?"

"This is Avery Conway. Have you found her?"

"Oh hi, Dr. Conway. Um, no, she didn't come home last night, and with all the weirdness going on, I kind of reached out to the police, since I had the card—"

"Whose card? What weirdness?"

"Oh, Carson didn't tell you?"

Avery's last nerve was shredding. "Tell me what?"

"We, well, we kind of witnessed a murder? On Tuesday? Of this real pretty singer? And we called the police and they took her and Simeon up to the spot and told us it was a murder-suicide and not to be worried, and then Carson didn't come home last night and I sort of freaked out this morning and called them. I think they are going to look for her, too."

Santi was running his finger in the air, telling her to wrap it up or keep her talking, she didn't know which. Her heart, God, her heart was pounding so hard she thought she might faint.

"When did you see her last, Izz?"

"Yesterday evening. We had a hot yoga class, then she booked it to the library while I went to dinner. She wasn't here when I got back, and she didn't come back all night. So I called the detective."

"Good. That's very good. You did the right thing." Even as her brain was screaming *Why didn't you track me down? I am her mother.* But she could hardly blame the girl, it sounded like they'd been in enough trouble this week. But Carson hadn't told her a thing.

"Can I have the name of the detective?"

"Um. Marcus Wade. Here's his number." She rattled it off and Avery wrote it down.

"What did he say? Exactly?"

"That he was sure she'd turn up, but because of the situation—he said that, *situation*, like there were quotes around the word—he would start checking into things right away."

"All right. You hang in there and call me if you hear anything."

"Sure. You think she's okay, don't you, Dr. Conway?"

The girl sounded ten, not eighteen, and Avery understood exactly how she felt.

She half laughed, half sobbed, "I'm sure she's fine, but she's going to get grounded when I get my hands on her."

She hung up and looked at Santi. "Do you think the police know there's a ransom demand?" Her voice sounded hollow and weak, and she cleared her throat. She would not falter, not now.

"No. I— No. There's no way, unless you tell them. That's just between us. And her kidnapper."

"I have to call Nashville." She already had her hand on the phone.

"Wait. Let's talk this through."

"There's nothing to talk about. I have to see what they know. I have to see...it's Carson, Santi. My daughter. I can't just sit here. I need to call...I need to go down there. Right now. I need—can you book me a ticket? There's a direct flight. You do that while I talk to the police there." She realized she was turning in circles, stopped, put a hand on the counter, and took a breath. She was trained to handle crises; she knew the first thing she needed to do was breathe.

Santiago's espresso eyes were troubled. "You can't run off, Avery. There's a ransom demand. And whoever is making it is here, in New Haven. The letters..."

"You can handle this end while I go to Nashville."

"No. I can't let you run off without protection."

"Santi, I am a grown woman. I'm not in danger. Carson is. And we're wasting time."

He ran a hand over his face, coming to a decision. She stopped moving again, curious.

"I understand. I'll get us a flight, but I'm going with you. Alan can stay here in case Carson comes back or calls. Sit down."

He pulled out a stool for her, and she sat, worried. He sat too, and took her hand in his.

"I will say this in all seriousness, Avery, and you must listen to me closely. I know how hard this is, but I also know how this works. Kidnapping for money, I mean. Please, don't ask me how, just trust me. I agree, going to Nashville is exactly what you should do. It would look strange if you didn't. But you cannot, under any circumstances, tell them about the ransom note. We will start raising the cash to get her back and handle that on our end. If we involve the police there in our negotiations, we endanger Carson."

"Putting aside the fact that you're scaring the crap out of me right now, Santiago, why, exactly, should I lie to the police?"

"Not lie. Omit. You can't be blamed that the roommate called the police. But if the Nashville police know there's a ransom demand, they will shift into high gear in a whole different way. They will be forced to pull in the FBI and other agencies that you do not want to be involved. You must trust me, Avery. I wouldn't tell you this unless I knew it was the right thing to do."

"How do you know? How?"

"I...I was in the military, a long time ago. I've seen these things. I want to call another friend, someone who might be able to help. Will you excuse me? Just for a moment."

She nodded, and he disappeared out the back door. Images

of Carson in various stages of duress were flying through her mind, and she fired off another text.

Where are you, honey?

Nothing.

She could hear bits of Santiago's conversation, but again, the words were too fast for her to follow. She heard him say *muerto* once and cringed. Her daughter was not dead. At least not yet. The notes proved it.

Didn't they?

Please let the notes prove it, she prayed. *And please help me understand why Santiago is so sure this is the right path.*

Santi came back inside and this time, the smile was strained but real. He rubbed her shoulder. "She is going to help us."

"Who?"

"An old friend of mine. Others will be searching, too. But this woman, she has a vested interest."

"What's her name?"

She was shocked when Santiago's handsome face turned cruel, and Avery realized that yes, all the rumors she'd heard about him were very, very true.

"Vengeance."

THIRTEEN

CHÂTEAU RODAUNE, BURGUNDY, FRANCE

ANGELIE DELACROIX STARED in abject horror at the man in front of her, standing with his hand outstretched, the small package dangling precariously from his thick fingers. He was tall, heavy through the shoulders and brow, covered in dirt, and to this point, had done everything she asked perfectly. But now, he had deviated from the plan, and she had to get him back in line. Her heart raged in her chest, and her first instinct was to simply kill him immediately and dump the remains in the river, despite the fact she had no gun to hand. No matter. Angelie had myriad ways to kill.

Breathe. Focus. Fury gets you in trouble. You need him.

In a clipped, tight voice, she said, "Please put that down. Carefully. It's worth more than your home. Perhaps more than your life."

The workman dubiously eyed the small sculpture that could fit into the palms of his calloused hands, but complied, setting the box holding its precious cargo gingerly on the table, as if it carried a grenade instead of an original Rodin she had unearthed from a niche in a forgotten bedroom. He backed out of the room before she could lose it, closing the battered French doors behind him.

Smart move.

Angelie collapsed onto a Louis XIV chair that she suspected might be original but hadn't yet had time to track its provenance and sighed in relief.

Another disaster averted.

She'd had no idea when she tackled the restoration that she'd be just as tense as if she were on a job.

She'd been restoring the château for almost fourteen months now, and each room, each hallway, each cracked wall and fallen chimney and tarnished iron gate, brought new and interesting problems to her door. Rotting tapestries, gaping holes in the roof, flooring eaten alive by termites, cracked Napoleonic-era marble mantels tumbling into the fireplaces. The château had once been a grand and seductive summer palace for the kings of France, but now was a shadow of itself, not so gently collapsing into the forest that guarded its rear.

She'd visited this place once when she was a child. It was in ruins then as well, and her father had stood in the gravel drive with tears in his eyes. "It is a beautiful place, *ma chérie*, one worthy of its history. Look at the carved wolf head above the door! If I had the money, I would snap it up and restore it, top to bottom."

Her mother, Genevieve, laughed. "You know nothing of restoration. How would you do this?"

A grin, white teeth flashing. "I would quit my job and hire you and Angelie as decorators. I would buy a donkey to carry timber from the town, and a hundred men to swarm over the ruins like bees. We would buy art books and interview craftsmen to determine what it was supposed to be like originally. And we would dance in the ballroom at midnight and give offerings at the folly under the full moon. It would be glorious, my darlings. We could live here, be happy here."

Angelie had no idea at the moment that this would be the last time she heard her father laugh. The last time she'd spy the small kiss on the forehead her mother gave him when she was amused, as if a promise for later. An hour hence, they were dead, butchered, ambushed at a crossroads, and for all their assassins knew, so was Angelie.

She rubbed her left shoulder. A bullet had caught her deep in the muscle almost a year ago, and the wound still ached when she did too much with the arm.

She owed the woman who'd shot her a visit, a conversation, perhaps a bullet in return, but this, too, she'd been putting off. She'd lost her taste for blood. After she healed, after she'd finally put the traitors who murdered her family into the ground, she'd hung up her guns and had since been consumed with continuing the fulfillment of her father's last dream, restoring the decrepit château.

Was it punishment, spending all of her time in the last place the sun had ever shined for her, where the memories of that horrid day were tempered with sweetness and joy, even if only for a moment? Perhaps. Was it punishment that she had to drive the small interchange where they'd been ambushed all those years ago every time she went to the south, to the closest town, where the majority of bistros, shops, and artisans existed? Perhaps. Was it punishment that she had given up her job, the one thing she was good at, to secrete herself in the French countryside with only a crumbling monolith of a house and a bevy of terrified Corsicans in dirty jeans and work boots for company? Perhaps.

Was she happier here, doing this time-honored labor, than she had ever been before, when revenge was her only true companion? Definitely.

Angelie Delacroix, wolf, domesticated.

She pushed herself out of the uncomfortable chair with a grimace, favoring the permanently sore arm, and took in the room. This was once the ballroom, and when she finished, she would honor her father by dancing through the space at midnight, as he'd promised her mother. For the moment, though, there was a large hole in the middle of the floor, and she had to get the joists rebuilt. At least the stairs to this floor were intact, solid French oak, as yet unstained but no longer black with mildew after years of disuse. She trailed down them, admiring the satiny finish that had taken her a week of sanding until her hand cramped, running her mental checklist for the rest of the day. She had no more deliveries, no more artisans coming. It was still sunny, but a chill lingered; there would be fog curling around the gate in the morning, and she would need a fire to warm the kitchen.

She had a small apartment on the first floor, went there now. Yanking open the vacuumed-solid door of the Sub-Zero with her good arm, she unearthed a bottle of Sancerre and a block of Laruns from the cavernous interior. She took her treasures to a small wooden table. The kitchen was the first room she'd tackled, updating appliances, repairing the monstrous hearth, tiling the floor with the encaustic terra-cotta ubiquitous to the area. She'd put a bed in the scullery and outfitted a serviceable bathroom with a toilet, bidet, and shower—the barest necessities. There was no heat yet; the kitchen, though, was thoroughly warmed by the fire, and the thick stone walls held enough warmth to get her through the nights. Soon it would be freezing again, and she would be forced to move her bed nearer the fire, or get the wiring in place for the water heater, but for now, she was comfortable enough. She'd slept in worse places, with far less armor around her.

The cheese was hard and salty, the wine crisp and cold, and she felt the tension leave her shoulders. This project was going to take her years, and as sore as she was, as stressed by the little things, she was happy to bask in the journey. She could see where life was ready to spring into being, feel the walls shuddering with happiness at their careful repair.

As far as Angelie was concerned, she was going to spend the rest of her days making this place the masterpiece it once was, and to hell with her old work, and the people she did it for. She'd gotten out, for good this time.

She toasted the not-so-empty air around her and drank deeply.

A small beeping brought her back to earth. Her phone. She never knew what excitement a call held these days, which artisan or restorer or inspector or local antiquity board member was coming to help—or hinder—her progress.

The screen held a text, and all of her hard-earned tranquility fled.

Mr. Brown requests a meeting.

"*Merde.*"

She dialed the number by heart.

"*Hola.*" The voice was deep, and made too many memories flood her senses.

"What do you want?" she asked curtly, also in Spanish.

"No time for an old friend?"

"I swear to you on my father's grave, Señor Brown—"

"I have a small problem. The daughter of a friend has been kidnapped."

"Pfft. Get her back yourself," she replied lazily.

"There is a complication."

"There always is."

"She's been taken from Nashville."

Angelie's heart stuttered. "Jackson—"

"Will be working the case. Yes. I thought you might be interested. Kill two birds, as they say."

Angelie slowly placed her wineglass on the ancient French oak table, and stood, moving to the fire. She poked it with her good arm, sparks flying at her vehemence.

"Do you have any idea who's taken the girl?"

"No. But the sooner you're on a plane, the sooner we can wrap this."

"Who's the friend?"

Diaz was silent for a moment, then said, "Avery Conway."

"*Merde*," she said for the second time in less than a minute.

"Where should I meet you?" he asked.

She was already calculating the time difference and knew the easiest flight to take. She had a solid cache in Virginia she hadn't touched in years that would give her the tools she needed on the ground in America. It was strange, how fate works. She and Jackson were tied together, whether they wanted it or not. And now, Avery Conway and Santiago were tied to them as well.

"There is a hotel called The Willard, in Washington, DC. You know it?" she asked.

"I do. Awfully public."

"Good cover. I have a legend that uses the hotel when she visits. The cameras at the service entrance are permanently disabled to give the famous people who stay there a private entrance. Bring Avery in the back, to the service elevator. Sixth floor. The Thomas Jefferson Suite. There is a secondary ingress to the suite on the northwest side of the building. Meet me there."

"When?"

"As soon as possible. I'm leaving now."

"Thank you." The relief in his voice was palpable and set her teeth on edge.

"Do not thank me yet, Señor Brown. You may end up regretting your words."

FOURTEEN

NASHVILLE

THE VANDERBILT UNIVERSITY campus was as familiar to Taylor as if she'd attended the school herself. Though Taylor was a University of Tennessee grad (*Go, Vols!*), she'd been living with Vandy in her life since she was a child. Not to mention the number of crimes she'd investigated in this area over the years.

As she strode across the quad, her uniform drew attention, and a line of students was soon trailing her. Mentally pushing away Pied Piper jokes, she finally stopped and turned to face them.

"Do any of you know Carson Conway?"

Nothing.

"Then I ask that you let me do my job in peace. I have nothing to share at this time. If *you* do, please come forward now. The sooner we can find Carson, the sooner you can go back to your normal lives."

An extremely willowy blonde who looked about sixteen—

damn, the students seemed to be getting younger and younger—raised her hand as if Taylor were teaching an open-air class.

"Ma'am?"

"Captain," someone hissed behind the girl.

"Captain," the girl amended. "I'm in Carson's American Lit class. They're saying she was killed out by Radnor Lake. Is that true?"

"Who is *they*?"

"Just some kids online." The girl looked down. "I didn't know whether to believe them. They also said she had a gun in her room, and there was a note that she was planning to take out the campus. Like she's going to be some sort of active shooter. That you found all that stuff but didn't want to tell us because you didn't want us to be scared."

Lord, save me from the rumormongers. "Let me put your mind at ease. None of that is true. We've found nothing like that. And we don't have any indication that Carson has been murdered. Right now, all we know is she didn't come home last night, and we're going to be searching for her. You can help by signing up to be a part of the search—if we get to that point—and if you have any credible information to share, please do. Don't listen to rumors. And don't spread them," she finished, glowering at the tall girl, who blushed and nodded.

"Anything else?" Taylor asked.

"Are we safe?"

Oh, child. You do not want me answering that. She understood the place the question came from and answered with the simplest platitude she could.

"Listen to me. You are not in danger. We don't know that Carson is either, we're just starting to look at why she might not be answering her phone. Please don't worry, okay?"

There was a chorus of assent. The world-wise little cynics clearly didn't believe her, but obediently melted away. Taylor set off again toward the dorm where she was going to meet

Carson's roommate. A Vandy cop had been stationed by the Crawford House entrance and straightened at her approach. God, she missed the days when she wore jeans and boots, and sometimes even needed to whip out her badge to prove who she was—the uniform itched and the bars on her collar scratched her chin and caught in her hair when she turned her head too quickly, not to mention she was about as subtle as a heart attack in it. A six-foot wall of blonde, blue, and gold.

"Captain Jackson."

"Hi there. I'm supposed to have a chat with Carson Conway's roommate."

"Yes, ma'am. Detective Wade is already upstairs. Need me to show you the way?"

"I can find it, thanks. Have you heard anything?"

His eyes darted around, making sure no students were around. "No. Everyone here is pretty freaked out, though. My leadership is talking about a curfew."

"I don't know that we're quite to that point yet. We don't even know for sure that she's really missing, not just holed up somewhere."

The officer nodded sagely. "Right. Chances are she's just off somewhere with a friend."

"That's the hope. Hold the fort."

She took the stairs two at a time and found the room easily. The door was open to the quad—two bedrooms that shared a bathroom—and the room Carson shared with her roommate was nice enough, for a dorm. One side was covered in colorful posters and hangings, the bed piled high with layers of knitted afghans, the other more subdued, only a single framed piece of art—an oil of a boat sailing away from a rocky shore—over a blue-and-white interlocking key-patterned comforter. Both beds were lofted with desks underneath, leaving enough room for a small sofa under the window. The roommate was perched on it, eyes swollen from crying, hair tucked into a batik-printed kerchief.

Taylor knocked on the door. "May I come in?"

The girl nodded and waved Taylor in. "I'm Izz Heathcote," she said, holding out her hand.

Taylor shook it. "Captain Jackson. You can call me Taylor."

"Got it. Your partner is getting me some water. Nice guy."

"Detective Wade is one of the good ones."

Izz gave her a wan smile. "Cute, too." The girl's voice rose at the end, making it a hopeful observation.

No way, no how, kid. "Taken, I'm afraid." Like she was going to encourage an eighteen-year-old first-year to go after a seasoned homicide detective. Marcus *was* cute, without a doubt, always a hit with the ladies. They used it to their advantage—people opened up easier when you were as charming as Marcus Wade.

The object of their conversation appeared at that moment, two glasses of water balanced in his hands. "Hey, Captain. Here you go, Izz."

She batted her lashes at him, but he'd already turned to Taylor, his notebook in hand.

"Izz says Carson went to the library after their yoga class last night and didn't come home. That's all she knows."

"That's all you know?"

Izz nodded. Taylor waited. The girl was building to something. Finally, she said, "She got a phone call that upset her."

"From who?"

"I don't know. Seriously, I don't. She took the call, got all pale, said she had to go to the library, and that was the last I saw of her."

"We need paper for the phone records," Taylor said.

"On it already," Marcus replied. "Also for the cameras in the area, including the road behind us."

"Good. So, Izz, tell us what else has happened since you two stumbled across Georgia Wray."

"Simeon Chase hung out with us for a while. That was almost worth it."

"The GPS game developer," Marcus reminded, sotto voce.

"And Simeon is a friend?"

"No. He's, like, unattainable. But he and Carson had lunch yesterday, and she came back looking sort of upset. I mean, it's not like there's anything romantic going on, not between her and Simeon, but she was, I don't know, edgy, all afternoon." Izz pointed to the desk. "She'd been studying before coming to yoga, her books and laptop were just like that, sitting open, when I got back."

"Is her laptop password protected?" Taylor asked Marcus, who nodded. "Izz, do you have her password?"

"Mm-hm. But don't you need, like, a warrant or something for that?" Izz's eyes were huge and scared. She was just trying to do the right thing. Taylor knew this, but decided to shake her up a bit, just in case.

"Do you genuinely believe your roommate is missing and in trouble?"

"Yes. She's not the type to just walk off without her stuff."

"Then we need to get into her laptop and see what she was up to. If you'd be so kind?" Taylor gestured to the laptop, and Izz scrambled to Carson's desk.

Moments later, the computer was open and Marcus was surfing through Carson's email and texts. "Here it is. She and Simeon have an exchange going. Just setting up their lunch date, talking about the app, 'sorry for getting you involved in this.' And one last message from him, at midnight last night. 'This is the program I mentioned. Don't forget to download a VPN, too.' Here, I'm opening the attachment."

The screen flashed with a website called MalwareFree.

"Huh. That's weird. Izz, was Carson having problems with her phone or laptop?"

"Actually, yeah. We had to use my phone for the game because hers wouldn't work right when she opened Simeon's app. She thought maybe she'd picked up a virus or something."

"Interesting," Marcus said.

Taylor cocked a brow. "Interesting why?"

"Well, her phone isn't pinging. The new phones will ping even if they're turned off, safety features have been upgraded. But if hers is old, it's possible that it doesn't have that feature. And if she has a VPN on, it would confuse it even more."

"VPN?"

"Virtual private network. Gives her an IP address from another area. Not insurmountable, but it might throw off the pings."

"Yeah, she'd said something about wanting to see a show from the UK that wasn't available here. You put on your VPN, say you're in England, it hooks into that network, and you can stream the program." Izz said apologetically, "It's a shortcut. We all do it."

"Okay. This is good information. What about the malware program? Any idea why she'd need that?"

"Nope. But I bet Simeon knows."

Simeon Chase was as lanky and handsome as his posh name foretold. Add in obvious brains and a British accent, and Taylor understood why Izz swooned every time the boy's name came up. They met him at the Student Center, and he was clearly agitated by Carson's absence.

"Tell me she's okay, and that I didn't get her killed. I can't sleep, I can't eat. Just the idea that I might have led a murderer to her..."

"Why do you think you got her killed?" Taylor asked in surprise. "I thought you two were on a lunch date."

"I don't mean that, exactly. I didn't do anything directly to hurt her. But she played with my app, and they walked into a murder, and now she's missing."

"That doesn't exactly make you culpable, Mr. Chase. Unless there's more that you know?"

"No!"

"Okay, okay. Calm down. I had to ask."

He ran a hand through the springing curls of his blond hair. "Yeah. I know. I can't help but think that if she just hadn't played, she'd be okay." He paused, took a breath. "Do you think she's okay?"

"We're doing all we can to find her."

He moaned softly.

"Listen to me." Taylor touched his shoulder briefly. "The girls went on a hike and walked into a bad situation. It was a fluke."

"But what if it wasn't? Her phone was screwed up."

"What do you mean?"

"Carson's phone was acting up. She told me, at lunch. It wouldn't stay on the network while we ate, and she complained that it had been happening for a few weeks. She knew she needed a new one but didn't want to call her mom and ask. She even had apps opening that she hadn't touched in months, which felt like she'd probably downloaded something hinky. I thought she should scan it. I don't know that she did, I just recommended it so that she could use the GPS properly if she ever wanted to do something with the Lat and Long Club again. I tried to fix it, but I couldn't without downloading a bunch of software to see what was amiss, and she didn't have time, had a class. I told her I'd send her a program to download that could sweep the phone and her laptop and see if she'd been infected or not."

"Is there any way to tell if she downloaded and ran the programs?"

"You'd have to get the phone itself to see."

"Marcus, do you have anything else?"

Marcus had been quiet during the whole interview. He shook his head shortly.

Taylor stood, brushing her hands down the front of her uniform. "Thank you, Simeon. If you think of anything else, please don't hesitate to reach out, all right?"

"Yes, ma'am." The kid looked both terrified and relieved, and she felt for him. She'd keep him on the suspect list for now, but only because the list was short, not because she thought he was really involved. Her gut had been wrong before, though. Not often, but it had.

They crossed campus toward Taylor's car, but neither of them was ready to leave. They took a seat on a bench in the quad and talked it out.

"I don't know," Marcus said. "Something doesn't feel right, does it?"

"Nope. I'll be damned if I think that kid is responsible for anything but creating a cool app and maybe starting a crush on Carson. But I've been tricked before."

A small knot of girls in white tennis shoes and slouchy cable knits streamed by, looking over shoulders with apprehension. Taylor forgot, sometimes, about the uniform. Not that she blended in on the local campus before, but in jeans and boots and a messy bun, at least she could be mistaken for a guest lecturer. Not in the blues. Especially not with a girl missing.

"I was texting with Lincoln while you talked to Simeon Chase. He wants Carson's phone. If we can find it, he can run diagnostics and see why it was being weird. Something there, though. If there was an app or download sophisticated enough to disrupt her network, we at least have a place to look. But why Carson Conway? Why would she of all people end up with malware on her phone, stumble into a murder, then go missing? It doesn't add up."

"Agreed," Taylor said. "Think someone was tracking her?"

"I think that's a leap, too. But all right. Let's play that out. Why would someone be tracking a Vandy first-year?"

"Either she got into something, or her family is in trouble. Have you talked to her family?"

"Oh, yeah. Her mom called right before you got here. She's on a plane down today. She's an ER doc in Connecticut. The dad's dead. Drugs, maybe? Though no one's breathed even a hint of this girl being anything but a weekend warrior."

"Drugs are an angle. Either her own relationships went south, or she stumbled into a situation and didn't realize what it was, but just in case, someone wanted to cover themselves?"

Marcus rubbed his chin, the stubble rasping under his fingers. "I don't know. According to the roommate, they've done nothing more exciting than yoga classes and crashing a few frat parties. Doesn't sound terribly suspicious. And if they had, don't you think the roommate would have been targeted, too?"

"Good point. She probably just clicked a bad link then. And we could be overreacting. She could have run, you know. Gotten scared with all the press and took off."

"Could have. Though I don't get the sense Carson's terribly independent. The roommate said they do almost everything together. No, I think we gotta assume she's been taken."

A few minutes passed. Taylor was surprised to realize the sun was starting to set. They'd been at it all afternoon and gotten exactly nowhere. The campus was quiet, holding its breath; squirrels and birds emerging to fill the air with chirps and song while they feasted before their overnight naps. The students were giving Taylor and Marcus a wide berth now, concerned, obviously, but still so wrapped up in their own lives that the alarm wasn't too high. Not yet.

That would change. She knew it.

Marcus's phone chirped. He glanced at the screen. "The mom's in town. She's going straight to her hotel and wants to meet us there."

"That's fine."

"Guess we should go see her, huh?" Marcus said finally, not moving.

"Yep," she replied, also staying put. After a few beats, Taylor sighed. "Let's press hard on that warrant to track all the activity on Carson's phone. See if anything pops."

"Will do."

The birds chirped. The squirrels foraged. The students wandered. Somewhere, there was a girl. Hiding. Scared. Alone. Dead.

"We're missing something, aren't we?"

Taylor pulled out her keys and ambled toward the truck. "Yes. We are."

FIFTEEN

WITH THE MISSING girl's mother from out of state, Taylor felt a bit at sea—she was used to being hands-on with the families, being in their homes, searching through the detritus of the victims' lives. She'd solved more than one case by physical searches through a victim's personal items. She'd had a chance to see Carson's room at Vanderbilt, yes, but it simply wasn't the same. Now, she had to make do with the anonymity of the mother's hotel. Taylor had happily granted the request to speak to Avery Conway there instead of dragging her into headquarters or trying to interview her in her missing daughter's dorm room. The media were crawling all over town, and she had a feeling they'd need the privacy.

The opulent lobby of the Hermitage Hotel wasn't terribly crowded, but Taylor still drew attention striding across the marble floors to the elevators, Marcus at her shoulder. She'd last been here with Baldwin before a Predators hockey game, eating at one of their favorite downtown venues. She wished that was her mission today. Speaking of...Florian had wanted to meet at the now-closed Oak Bar, downstairs in this very hotel. Odd.

She'd sent Florian a brief text earlier, cancelling their lunch date. When she checked her phone, he'd gotten back to her.

Dinner, then? I'll find someplace discreet. I do want to see you. Very much.

She sighed. Florian was persistent. *He might be your new boss, Taylor. Play nice.*

Assuming things calm down, I can make that happen. Let me know when and where.

Merci. You won't regret it.

They were quiet on the elevator, each lost in their own thoughts. At the door, Marcus said, "I'm going to let you take the lead."

"Jump in anytime," she said, and knocked.

The door was opened by an older version of Carson. The resemblance between mother and daughter was incredible.

"Mrs. Conway? I'm Captain Jackson, Metro Nashville Police, and you've already talked with Detective Wade. I'm assisting the detective with your daughter's case. Thank you for agreeing to meet us."

"Thank you for arranging this meeting so quickly." Conway ushered them in, and graciously offered to order up some coffee or tea, or dinner, considering the hour.

"We're fine, ma'am, thank you," Marcus said, gesturing toward the sofa.

Avery Conway had booked a two-room corner suite with a beautiful view of downtown. The sun had set, and the lights twinkled in the foreground, so similar to Taylor's view only a few blocks away. Taylor thought all that space was a hopeful gesture—that her daughter would be found and they could bunk down together, try to forget a bit of the terror Carson had suffered. *Let her be safe,* she thought. *Let her come home.*

They got settled, Taylor surreptitiously assessing the woman. Conway was probably only a few years older than herself but ravaged. Her hair was mussed, her eyes were red, her skin was gray with worry. But she sat tall, back ramrod straight, and her voice didn't waver.

"Have you gotten any leads?"

Taylor shook her head. "Nothing that has our attention at the moment. I know this is difficult, and you must be scared, but we need information. We need to find out as much as we can about Carson. About her state of mind, the way she acts when she's scared or threatened. Is it possible she's run away?"

"No. There is no chance she's run away."

"Considering the situation, I think there is a small chance. The death of Georgia Wray has created a media blitz—"

"Trust me. She didn't. I am 100 percent certain of that."

There was a finality in Conway's tone that made Taylor sit up.

"Can you tell me why you're so sure?"

Conway sucked in a breath. "I know my girl. She's just not the type to run away from a situation, especially without looping me in. She's brave and smart and cautious. She's also still very dependent on me, and on her family. Losing her father the way we did brought us closer together than you might expect for a teenager. She would reach out to me before she ran away from a situation."

"She didn't tell you about the murder she witnessed."

The look Conway shot her dropped the temperature in the room ten degrees.

"Someone's taken her. You're wasting time following any other theory."

"Fair enough. I hate to say I tend to agree with you, because of the situation she found herself in, though I don't know what the connection is yet."

"I just don't understand how someone disappears from the

middle of a city, from a campus as populated as Vanderbilt. The university has ever-present security, and I know the cameras are on most corners. Have the videos been searched? Have all of her friends been contacted?"

"They do have cameras, and we did think of that. There's been nothing unusual thus far. It's possible she was taken from somewhere off-campus. Nashville is a big place."

"We were worried about that."

"We?"

"My friend." Conway glanced toward the bedroom door, and on cue, a stocky, dark-haired man appeared in the doorway. Taylor and Marcus both shifted in surprise, but he called, "Friendly," and put his hands up. "I'm Santiago Diaz-Rooney, we bought the bakery from Mrs. Conway when her husband passed. I didn't want her traveling alone."

He came to stand behind Conway's chair, putting his hands palm down on the back. "Sorry, didn't mean to startle you. Avery called me when she got word about Carson disappearing, and I offered to help in any way I can."

Diaz-Rooney gave off the air of a professional. Taylor could practically smell it on him. Interesting. "You say you run a bakery?"

He nodded. "Yes. Now."

Now. Sure, pal. You're just the friendly neighborhood baker.

Conway dragged a hand through her hair and shook her head. "My God, what a mess. I just want to find my girl."

Taylor brought her focus back. "Dr. Conway, I hear you. That's all we want too, to find Carson safe and unharmed. This is a terribly difficult moment for you, I know. But if there is anything, *anything*, you know that could help me find your daughter, now is the time to tell me. I sense we're not getting the whole story. Maybe there's something we've missed that we can use to find Carson. Anything you can share, even the most inconsequential thing, could make all the difference."

Conway twisted her hands in her lap. Her knuckles were turning white. Taylor couldn't help the thought. *You know more than you're saying. And it's eating you up inside.*

"I don't know what I can give you that will help. I don't know what she's gotten into. Yes, she didn't tell me about the murder she witnessed. I've been very careful to keep out of her hair since she left for school. I was trying to help her build some autonomy. If I called four times a day, she'd never have a chance to grow up properly. So we established we'd talk once a week. Sundays." Her voice grew softer. "She loves school. She loves the freedom. She might not say it aloud, but I can hear it in her voice. This is an adventure, and after her father's death, she needed an adventure. She needed something to pull her away from the bad memories." A single tear slipped down Avery Conway's lovely, ravaged face. "And now, she is going through something unspeakable. She will be forever damaged. And it's my fault. I should have insisted she stay in New Haven, go to Yale, where I could keep an eye on her."

"This isn't your fault, Dr. Conway, nor Carson's. We haven't established that the murder is related to her going missing—"

"Being kidnapped. You can say the word. She isn't missing. She didn't run away. She was taken against her will. And she is probably dead. It's been twenty-four hours. I know the statistics."

"Statistics are irrelevant," Taylor snapped, then caught herself when Conway's mouth dropped open. She tried again, slower and calmer. "With all due respect, ma'am, that's a fact. Every case is different. I am certain we can find your girl. We just need to know where to look. There are things we need from you. Phone records, bank statements, and access to all of her accounts so we can see what she's been up to recently. Have you taken a look at her social media feeds to see if anything leaps out at you?"

Avery Conway shut her eyes, just for a moment, and rubbed

her temple as if a migraine was taking hold. Taylor waited her out.

"She's not a huge social media kid, never has been. Some of the girls her age are rebelling against it because they feel it undermines them as people, reduces them to objects. They aren't fans of the system. But there was a post on her page the night she went missing that did feel...odd to me. We use it mostly to communicate between the extended family, and it's usually dormant—I rarely have time, and my boys couldn't care less. But Carson did post a photo, a selfie she'd taken somewhere in Nashville, with some sort of white lace painted on the bricks in the background. I don't recognize the place. I know it's a reach, but it almost felt like whoever took her posted it because they think a girl her age would post selfies. I'm probably grasping at straws, but it didn't feel like the kind of post she'd do. She wasn't much one for showing herself off, if you know what I mean. She's a delight, and very engaging in person, but she can be shy, especially with strangers. If you look at her feed, it stands out. She's much more likely to post photos of other people, and photographs she thinks are beautiful, when she does post at all."

Marcus was tapping on his tablet, held it up for Taylor to see.

"That's the 'Wings' mural in the Gulch," he said.

Taylor nodded. And to Conway: "A very popular spot for tourists to take pictures. There's usually a line around the corner. The artist, Kelsey Montague, does street art with the hashtag What Lifts You. Anyway, we'll see if we can geotag the photo and get the information about when it was taken, and when it was uploaded."

Taylor scrolled through the rest of Carson's social media feed. It was mostly lovely nature and cityscape photographs. Her mother was right, the selfie stood out.

"He'll kill her," Conway said quietly. "That's what the angel wings are saying. He probably already has."

"Don't think that way," Taylor replied. "That's why I need all the help I can get. I want to bring in more agencies, get help from our TBI, maybe even the FBI."

Conway looked up at her friend pointedly, a look Taylor read as *Your turn to step in here.* He did.

"You need to keep it local."

Taylor crossed her long legs. "Frankly, sir, I don't need to do anything you tell me. Why in the world would you not want me to bring in every available resource to find Carson?"

"Of course we want you to do all you can," Diaz-Rooney said, not at all flustered, as she expected. What in hell was going on here?

"Then you'll understand that I may need to bring in additional team members."

"If you can't keep this local, you have to do it quietly. You can't spook him."

Taylor glanced out the window, assessing her next words carefully.

"You speak like you have an idea what's going on. Do you know who's behind this, sir?"

Diaz-Rooney crossed his arms, which turned him into a wall of man. "I just have a vested interest in seeing Carson home safe. I've known her since she was a baby. It's killing me, the idea that she's hurting somewhere. I don't want to set off whoever's taken her."

"Hmm. I understand." She did, now. Avery Conway's protector was an operator, without a doubt. Former law enforcement or military. He had that hawkish look about him. He'd know the odds, and he'd know the machinations that happened when the Feds got involved. "You weren't always a baker, were you, sir?"

"I'd rather not make this about me, if you don't mind," he

said, eyes shuttered and jaw set. Military, she'd bet her life on it. Special Forces, probably. Those guys were uber-contained like this, coiled up inside like snakes readying a strike.

Dr. Conway pulled Taylor back to the details. "Izz, Carson's roommate, said she and Carson were hiking using some sort of app? Have you talked to them?"

"Marcus?" Taylor said, and he nodded, stepping in.

"We have. The app developer is a student at Vanderbilt, and he's torn up about all of this—from the girls stumbling onto a murder to Carson now going missing. We're looking into his background, but as of now, he is not a prime suspect. We are, though, looking into the possibility that Carson downloaded some sort of malware. According to both her roommate and the app developer, Carson's phone was acting up. If that's true, there could be remote access to her phone. This means anyone could be using it to post, text, all of that. Just FYI."

Conway shot a glance at her friend. "That seems...sophisticated. Why would anyone target my daughter? She has nothing to do with this singer's murder."

"That's what we're trying to find out," Marcus said. "Do you have any enemies, Dr. Conway?"

The ghost of a laugh. "I'm a doctor. I'm sure somewhere along the way I've upset someone, but I don't have any lawsuits against me or nasty letters from former patients. I am a relatively benign presence in the world, except for what I do for strangers and my children."

"Okay. Could this be something to do with your husband's business?"

"The bakery? No. Richard was beloved by everyone. He was the heart of the bakery, of this town, and of our family. Since he's been gone...it's been rather gray."

"I am sorry," Taylor said, automatically, though she genuinely meant it. "I want to get moving on all of this right away. Are you planning to stay here in town, or go back to New Haven?"

"I—I've taken a leave of absence until my daughter is found. I'm reachable."

Taylor and Marcus stood, and Marcus handed over his card. "We're going to get to the bottom of the photo that was posted, set up traps on your phone, dig deep into Carson's last few weeks. Here's my personal mobile number. Call or text me anytime, all right? If you hear from Carson, or see anything unusual on her socials, or hear from anyone—a ransom call, specifically—please loop us in immediately."

Conway tensed but accepted the card. "I will."

Taylor resisted the urge to touch the woman on the shoulder to comfort her, knowing nothing would make it better. She settled for a vow. "We're going to find her, Dr. Conway. We're going to do everything we can. Hang in there, all right?"

With a bleak nod, Avery Conway saw them out.

"What do you think?" Avery asked Santiago when the cops were down the hall and on the elevator.

"I think Captain Jackson's a bulldog, and I think this is going to go public, fast. My friend is on her way. I want her looped in and on the case as quickly as we can. I need to go to DC and meet with her. You will be fine here. Safe, here."

"I don't feel very safe. I think I should go with you." Santiago shook his head, but Avery squared her shoulders. "Take me. I want to meet this friend."

He shook his head again. "No. You really don't."

"If she's going to help find my daughter? Yes. I do."

SIXTEEN

IN THE CAR, Taylor waited before turning over the engine. "Thoughts?"

Marcus was already tapping on his tablet, starting a background check on Santiago Diaz-Rooney. "The guy with her seemed like some sort of bodyguard. Yep, here he is, all over the bakery website. He really is a baker."

"You heard him. He wasn't always. See if you can do a little digging. I got the sense they know something they aren't sharing."

"You know how it is with parents, Taylor. They don't always like to admit when their kids have done something that might have led to their problems."

"Yeah. Well, there's nothing more we can do tonight. Let's call it a day, and I'll see you in the morning. We'll hopefully have the warrants by then and be able to look at Carson's phone records. It might be time to start a physical search, as well."

"Agreed."

Taylor dropped Marcus at the downtown precinct to do some digging with the camera techs who ran the city CCTV systems, then headed back to HQ. She was happy to find Huston still in her office and ran her through the conversations she'd had, the steps they'd taken, the warrants they needed to draft and get signed, and the people tasked to the various leads they were following.

She was surprised when Huston said, "Good job. This feels odd. And the mayor is all over me. Students going missing, country music stars being murdered. None of this is good for business. We even had a tourist rolled, down by Municipal. Stepped out for a cigarette and got knocked on the head and his wallet stolen. Everyone's on edge."

"I agree. We're doing all we can. We may need to form a task force. We need a cohesive effort. She's been missing for long enough. I want to start a physical search, and I need more people digging into Carson's world."

Huston was not stupid, nor did she play games when the stakes were high enough. She may have been riding Taylor lately, but in this, they were in agreement.

"Do what you think is best."

Back in her office, Taylor made some calls, setting things up, then sat back in the chair, noting with pleasure that it was a different make with actual lumbar support. Much more comfortable. She still hated the building and the office, but at least her back wouldn't scream every time she stood up.

There was nothing more she could do at the moment outside of walking along the river with a switch hoping Carson hadn't fallen into the Cumberland. The biggest problem with being a cop...sometimes, the world was spinning without you. The case was happening, the energy was there, but a brick wall that climbed to the sky was right in your path. You couldn't do anything until the pieces began to fall into place, and that felt worse than anyone could ever know. Her team was working every angle. She had to trust that one of the facets would reveal the truth they were looking for before the worst happened.

With a last glance at her email and texts, she shut off her

light and headed to the parking lot. Carson Conway was out there. Taylor just hoped she got to her in time.

Taylor fought the last of the street back downtown, took the split to Second Avenue, caught all but one light, and was at the condo twenty minutes after she left. Without the turtle train of vehicles, the drive took no more than five minutes. Another strike against the new HQ—inching along in the terrible downtown traffic with the rest of the Nashville hoi polloi was such a huge waste of her time.

She hurried into the condo to change out of the blues, then sent Baldwin a text about what was happening, unsure where he was and what sort of access the writers' cruise was going to have. When he didn't reply immediately, she sent a kiss emoji and pocketed the phone. She missed him when he was gone. Would he miss her when she was off gallivanting through Europe in search of baddies to neutralize? Of course he would.

Taylor glanced at her watch. She needed to leave to make her date with Florian. Feeling much more herself in her normal uniform—dark wash jeans, a cashmere T-shirt under a black leather jacket, and her battered Lamas—she loped down the street through the pulsing crowds on Lower Broad to the Omni Hotel and the restaurant inside, Bob's Steak & Chop House. Full of nooks and crannies, locals and tourists alike, it was not only a bastion of fabulous food but was also a perfect place to either be seen or hidden away in privacy.

The head of the Macallan Group, Thierry Florian, waited in the back room of the restaurant, looking dapper and extremely French. For a pseudo spy, he stood out, and Taylor wondered if it was on purpose. Any time she'd been undercover, she'd found trying to be nondescript sometimes drew more notice than being dressed to kill. Some people stood out no matter what. Taylor was one of them. Thierry another.

He'd ordered a bottle of wine already, a good one, judging by the dark ruby liquid in the decanter on the ledge behind him. And managed a table in the corner that put both their backs to walls and had them angled away from the main dining spaces. An exit was nearby. They were alone in the room and had line of sight to all ingress and egress. *Now that's more spy-like,* she thought.

She accepted the black napkin from the server, spread it in her lap, and watched him pour a glass of wine for them both. She waited for the server to depart before pointing toward the decanter. "Are we celebrating?"

"We are," Florian said, rolling the wine in his glass. "A lovely little Pichon Lalande. I was surprised to see it on the menu. A token of my gratitude. I am hopeful that you will soon be a member of my team, and these meals will occur more regularly. You're excellent company, Captain Jackson."

"I'll be even better company if you call me Taylor. Why do you want me to be a spy so badly?"

Florian laughed, showing small, even teeth. "I don't particularly identify with that word. Spying sounds so vulgar, as if we're some sort of voyeurs. I—and Macallan—are merely facilitators. Investigators who work in that gray space between law enforcement and criminals. We do what must be done to save the masses from total destruction. As I told you in Maryland, your unique style and searing insights would be a godsend. And I know that you're bored. I can offer a more exciting life. A more fulfilling life."

"People die around you an awful lot, Thierry. And I have plenty of excitement here."

Those even teeth flashed in the dim light, and Taylor was reminded of a small wolf she'd seen bounding across her backyard several years earlier. Noticing her on the back deck, it had stopped and stared at her with an almost comical grin on its face. It looked harmless, even beautiful, but she knew if she'd gotten closer it would have happily ripped out her throat.

"My dear Taylor, please don't. Games do not suit us. We both know you're leaving Metro and coming to work for Macallan."

Hell, she *was* going to do this. She thought she was, at least. The excitement of solving Georgia Wray's murder and searching for Carson Conway was going to fade away into the ether, leaving her stuck down the hall from Huston pushing paper for the next few years until Huston decided to run for mayor and Taylor got shoved up the ladder again.

She took a sip of the wine in acknowledgment of this truth. The deep, dry red exploded in her mouth, berries and truffles and cedar. "You serve me wine like this at every meal, and I'm in. So *if* I join you, what's my first assignment?"

"That is to be determined. There are steps we must take to secure you. Legends to build. You've been in the news enough that we'll have to reduce your footprint for a while. You need training, most of all."

"I know how to handle myself."

"You are excellent with a weapon, yes. But you'll need more tools in your arsenal than a gun. And you must learn the theater of operations. My preference would be for you to establish residency in Paris. It is a central location, easy to reach me, our headquarters, and all the areas we would travel while you're training."

Better than the Virginia countryside or Quantico. "Paris. For how long?"

"To be determined."

Oh yeah, Baldwin was going to love this. *I have to move to Paris for a while, honey. Be back before you know it.*

"And Baldwin?"

"Is more than welcome to arrange visits. Not in Paris, of course, we'd have to find safe houses out of the country for you to meet in. It will take a bit of coordination, but we're hardly asking—"

"Thierry. Let me stop you right there. No offense, but that just isn't going to happen. I'm not going to move halfway around the world away from my fiancé for an indeterminate amount of time in order to—how did you put it? Reduce my footprint?"

"Then convince him to join you." Florian leaned forward, the charm offensive forgotten in favor of intensity and earnestness. "You work well together. Couples in general work well in this arena. We can send a pair like you and Baldwin anywhere in the world to operate. You're both smart, you're both capable. With the right training and fewer fetters on your talents, you could save so many from harm."

Taylor shook her head, but internally. This was nuts. And Baldwin didn't want it. She'd never convince him otherwise.

"What else?"

"Compensation, obviously, will be quite generous. You will want for nothing. You will have the best training in the world, from the finest instructors. Weapons, hand-to-hand combat, languages, covert actions. You will be operational within a year, and then, my dear, you will change the world."

"A year?"

"Ten months at the outside. You are a quick study, and you've already had some training. We have some less orthodox ways to train that will leapfrog you ahead. If you were to join your own intelligence services, it would be much longer. With much less freedom on the back end, I might add. At your age—not that I am commenting on it, my dear—they are less likely to take on more seasoned operatives for fieldwork. I am the opposite. I much prefer experience to enthusiasm."

"And Angelie Delacroix? What of her?"

She could have sworn Florian flinched.

"Retired."

"Retired. Your best assassin retired. Is that supposed to make me feel safer?"

"Oui," he said with a small French shrug, flexing his hand in memory. She saw the tip of his finger, the one Angelie had removed, had been expertly reattached—in no small part thanks to Taylor's quick actions when the injury was inflicted. "She is of no consequence to you. Angelie exorcised her demons. While she is one to hold a grudge if the matter is, shall we say, personal, I know for a fact she does not harbor ill will toward you. You were doing your job. She was doing hers."

"I shot the woman, Thierry. That's pretty damn personal."

"Angelie is not an issue," he said with an air of finality. If he was lying, he was very good at it.

The server took that moment to approach the table, breaking the spell. They ordered and talked of things more general while their meal was served. It was only when the plates were empty and Florian glanced at his watch that Taylor circled back to their earlier conversation.

"You aren't thinking I'm going to be a hired gun, are you, Thierry? Because I won't go any further if you think you can put a weapon in my hand and send me out to take a life. That's not who I am, and we both know it. I have no interest in ridding the world of these losers myself. I'm only in this if you can guarantee you will never ask it of me. I have spent my entire career trying to save lives. It's not negotiable." When he didn't reply, she said, "Tell me this is bigger than that."

He took one last sip of wine. "It *is* bigger. The world is at risk. All the time, constantly, threats emerge. Some are state-sponsored. Some are individual. When you see what's happening out there, Taylor, when you see what we face on a daily basis, the tragedies we manage to avert..." His sigh was deep and melancholic. "I need you. I need you both, yes, but I need *you*. I want to reshape the narrative, and I want to do it well. Diplomacy doesn't work. People talk and talk and nothing happens, and meanwhile, dark forces gain strength from all quarters. Losing Angelie has been a blow, it's true, but you won't be filling her shoes. Anyone can be trained to kill. And you won't be asked to take a life unless you are in grave danger and there is no other option."

"That's a relief."

He waved his hand. "And this is exactly why we need you. Not everyone can chart a new path, find solutions to the hard problems. You can. I've seen you do it. You aren't afraid to take risks, you're smart, and people gravitate to you. You are the finest investigator I've ever met."

"Flattery isn't necessary, Thierry. If you knew me at all, you'd know I don't respond to manipulation."

"All right. Let's talk reality. What I'm offering you is complete autonomy. Once you're up to speed, it's all on you. Your decisions, your team members, your cases. I will, of course, want to work with you from time to time, perhaps give you some guidance, but you will call the shots. I'm offering you a life of proactive law enforcement, Taylor. Stop the crimes before they happen, on an epic scale. You'll be brilliant at this. I promise."

She took another mouthful of wine. Before she could chicken out, she swallowed and nodded. "When would you need me?"

"Yesterday."

"I have to solve a missing person case first."

"There are many people who can step into your shoes. There will be this case, then another, then another. They will never end. You will never be truly finished. And you are needed, Taylor. We need you now."

"Carson Conway's need for me comes first. There's no way I'm walking out on this case, so don't ask again. And I still want to run all of this past Baldwin. We've talked about this, but not with all the details. I need to be sure he's totally on board. The moment I'm sure, and my case is closed, I'll tender my resignation and be on a plane. Deal?"

Florian toasted her, grinning like a pirate. "Deal."

SEVENTEEN

THURSDAY: WASHINGTON, DC

ANGELIE DELACROIX DISEMBARKED from the charted private jet with a single bag in her hand. She went through the motions of handing over her legend's passport and getting it stamped, then entered the car waiting on the tarmac. As it moved toward downtown DC, she reapplied her lipstick and got her things in order. The city was so busy—always had been, but it seemed even more so now. Externally unchanged by time or enemy, Washington seemed vaguely romantic to her, though she despised each and every one of the leaders the people of this country had recently voted into office.

None of the new ones had been as good for business as the ones a decade earlier. With the threats moving online and pushback from the ever-more-politically correct electorates, her job had gotten harder, not easier. Moving around was more difficult than ever; electronic surveillance had multiplied exponentially over the past few years, which meant she had to disguise herself well to travel unseen through the cities and countries she visited. Even then, beating the AI was becoming harder. People in her line of work didn't usually last long enough to be affected by these sorts of changes. They certainly rarely, if ever, secured a genuine retirement. Angelie thought of herself as a very hardy cat, though she suspected her multiple lives were running out.

The old Angelie enjoyed this dressing up, camouflaging herself. Enjoyed the challenge of evading capture, of inhabiting the skin of another for a time. She didn't want to admit to herself the small thrill she'd had when choosing her identity for this emergency trip to the States. This persona was always fun.

Today, she was dressed in rich fabrics with a tailored jacket, tall boots, and pearls, capped off with a wildly curly auburn wig. A bright red lip, large black sunglasses. She stood out, but for all the right reasons. It was sometimes easier to disappear behind a more flamboyant persona—and the uber-rich, uber-beautiful Sònia Masot-Mallofré was one of her favorite masks. She hadn't become Sònia for many years—fitting, as Angelie herself had aged as well. Sònia had taken a small mental health vacation in the South Aegean four years earlier and hadn't returned to the scene. After a small emotional breakdown exacerbated by a raging addiction to Adderall and clear tequilas, she'd chosen to stay on the island to continue her recovery in sun-soaked solitude. Sònia was brash, and not a little unbalanced, a perfect combination. People remembered Sònia. Angelie could disappear into the fabric of the city while this alter ego held court in the hotel.

Forty minutes later, the Town Car crossed the Key Bridge into Georgetown, snaking down M Street through Foggy Bottom and into the city proper. White marble buildings whispered secrets as she passed by. The core of DC had not changed since she last saw it, outside of the fences everywhere holding back knots of tourists and malcontents both. There was a small group of protestors gathered in front of the White House, colorful signs and raised fists bobbing in time. She had no idea what they were demonstrating about—it seemed all of the world was engaged in some form of protest, from her own France to America to Australia to Hong Kong, an entire generation unsettled by cultural change, sweeping technological advances, terrifying biological attacks, and their own self-worship. Perpetual misery, must take it out on all around. Sometimes she was glad of retirement.

Stepping from the car without a word, she barely glanced at the full set of Louis Vuitton hardback suitcases being unloaded from the trunk. She shifted her bag onto her shoulder, and, as befitted the woman she'd become, swept into the hotel like a tidal wave, gathered her key, dropped a few hundreds into the hands of the desk clerk and concierge who'd arrayed themselves to meet her, ordered bottles of Perrier-Jouët to be brought up to the room, and disappeared into the elevator, almost without breaking stride. The Willard knew what to expect when Sònia Masot-Mallofré arrived and made things as seamless as possible. Her entrance was that of undercover royalty, a rock star, a movie mogul. Everyone now knew she was here.

The game had begun.

Full of a single glass of the delicious rosé Champagne, half a sleeve of water crackers, and a bag of almonds, Angelie showered, changed—this time into slim jeans and a sweater, her hair in a chic black bob—and pulled the key to the room below out of her handbag. It had been inside the smallest of the Vuitton cases, nestled against a suppressor and a Ruger Mark IV .22. Having divested herself of Sònia, she tested the weapon, screwing on the suppressor, making sure the sights were in order, slapping in a magazine and doing a press check, then removed the suppressor, tucked it into the zippered makeup panel of the purse she was carrying, and slipped the pistol into a sleek, worn, molded-to-her-ribs harness. She tucked a knife into her boot in the slot built for it, looked in the mirror to make sure nothing was amiss. She was a ghost again. Perfect.

She set all of her traps to ensure no one entered the suite while she was taking care of business, and left through the back entrance. She was down the flight of stairs and into the spare room moments later.

Santiago was waiting. They didn't touch, though she was surprised to feel the urge for contact. It had been a long time, and Santi had been a good friend. Once.

"I thought I told you to take her in my back door?"

"You know I don't like rules. And in case someone was listening... It's good to see you, Ange."

"You, too. Is she here?"

He nodded, inclining his head toward the closed door to her right. "Asleep. I gave her a slight sedative when we got here so she could get some rest. She hadn't slept for two days. She should be waking up shortly."

"All right. Want to tell me what the hell's going on? Who took her daughter?"

"We don't know. They demanded cash, which, of course, was a signal they wanted to talk."

"Or they actually want money, and are willing to hurt a child to get it."

Silence crawled around them. Angelie went to the window, standing by the wall, looking from the side of the heavy drapes out into the city. The wig itched. She hadn't had to wear a disguise in so long, she'd grown soft. Her hair was too long, grown out unchecked for the past year. She'd have to cut it if they went operational.

Who are you kidding? You already are.

"You know who took her," Santiago finally said. "He wants to talk."

She whirled on him. "You said you didn't know who took her."

"Ange, come on. Can we stop? The odds of Carson Conway being kidnapped by a stranger are as likely as a giraffe growing a second head. You and I both know who. The question is: Why now? And why from Nashville, instead of New Haven? What sort of game is he playing?"

"The question is: Why the hell didn't you tell me you know who took my daughter!"

Angelie had to hand it to her, Avery Conway was still a looker, and stealthy as hell. She stormed toward Santiago, hands on her hips, clearly restraining herself from exploding into furious punches and slaps.

Faced with the surge of anger from his old partner's widow, Santiago took two steps back, raising his hands in defense, just in case. Angelie put a shoulder against the wall, folded her arms across her chest, hooked one ankle over the other, and leaned back to enjoy the show.

"Avery, it's not what you think," he started, but she advanced, rage and panicked fear making her as unpredictable as a rattlesnake.

"Santi..." Avery growled.

"Stop, okay? I'll tell you what I know. Sit down, and stop... doing that."

Avery breathed once hard, through her nose, then retreated to the elegant couch, took a seat, and crossed her legs demurely. "There. I'm not doing anything. Now, talk."

With a glance for help to Angelie, denied with a single shake of her head, Santi took a chair opposite Avery and steeled himself. "It's about Richard."

"What?"

"The people who've taken Carson. They're the same people who killed Richard."

EIGHTEEN

ANGELIE WATCHED with cool curiosity as Avery Conway fell completely to pieces.

The woman clearly didn't know her husband had worked for Macallan. There was no way anyone was this good an actress. Angelie almost felt sorry for her, if she was able to feel such things, but pity was not going to solve this situation.

Santi was still trying to explain the situation calmly, gently, and Angelie was getting bored. She pushed off the wall and strode to Avery.

"Get yourself together. Richard would not want you to be like this."

"Who the hell are you?" Avery spat, tear-filled eyes blazing in her chalk-white face.

Angelie smiled grimly. Good. Richard's widow still had some steel in her. She was going to need it.

"That's not necessary—" Santi started, but Angelie shook her head sharply.

"*Non*. She must know. We must act before they come for us all." To Avery: "My name is not important. What matters is this.

Richard worked for us. We are an international consortium trying to rid the world of the vermin who seek to destroy it."

Avery blinked once, twice. "My husband was a baker."

"Your husband was a spy. He ran his operations out of the bakery. He did not tell you?"

"No. Of course not. You're insane." Avery cast her eyes about the room. "This is all insane. I'm leaving."

Santiago put a hand on Avery's shoulder, keeping her planted on the sofa. "What she says is true. It's why Alan and I 'bought' the bakery from you after Richard died." He used little air quotes, and Avery shook her head. "We'd been using it as a cover for years anyway. Of course, it gave us the added benefit of watching over you and the kids. We owed him that much."

"Richard had an aneurysm." Avery pronounced each word slowly, with great effect. "I saw the autopsy report."

"You saw what we paid for you to see. His bike was forced off the road and his head bashed in with a rock."

"By who?"

Angelie and Santiago met eyes, and she nodded.

"He's called Game. Joseph Game. He's a sadistic son of a bitch who works for a group of very bad people. You don't need to know any more than that."

"Like hell, I don't." The tears were gone now, the calm, collected ER doctor reasserting herself. "This is my family you're talking about. My daughter is missing and you're saying my husband was murdered by some sort of, what, assassin? You have to tell me everything."

"Avery. Trust me. The more you know, the more dangerous this is for you, for the boys, and for Carson." Santiago's voice was soothing but had exactly zero effect.

"Carson's already in serious danger. Does this Game person have my daughter?"

Angelie shrugged. "Possibly him, possibly someone he

knows. He won't hurt her. Not badly, anyway. He just wants me."

"You? Why?"

Angelie smiled. "Professional jealousy."

"Sònia," Santiago warned.

"It's true. I killed someone he wanted for his own. A contract. He's mad."

"So go apologize to the bastard and bring my daughter home." Avery was on her feet now, still pissed off, and starting to think clearly again. "I'll go with you. Where is he? Where are they? We have to go, right now. He must—"

"Stop," Angelie said. "You will not come with us. We have to find him, and he's very good at hiding. But yes, you will go back to Nashville, or New Haven, whichever you prefer, and wait. The police are involved, and you must continue on as if you are simply a grieving, frightened mother, nothing more. Trust me, Game is nowhere near your home. He is most probably already out of the country. He—they—could be anywhere by now. It will be up to us to hunt him down."

"You say this like you know something more. What aren't you telling me?"

"Nothing," Angelie said.

"You're lying."

"Yes, I am. It does not concern you, nor your situation. I will bring Carson home. I promise. You must follow all the instructions the police give you. Play your role. Do a public plea for your daughter's return. You will not mention me, you will not mention Richard's death, and you will *not* mention this meeting. They will go in circles, and while they do, we will track down Game and kill him."

"The note said no police."

"Your daughter's very clever roommate resolved that for you. He can't complain. You followed instructions. *You* did not involve them."

"And the money?"

"This is not about money. That was a message for Santi. So he would reach out to me. We're complying with Game's wishes at this point. We will do so until we have Carson back, and then?" Angelie ran a long finger across her throat. "And then I will kill him. Slowly. For you. And for Richard."

"What am I supposed to do? I can't just sit around in hotel rooms waiting for news."

"I would prefer Santiago take you back to New Haven."

"The Nashville police will think that's strange."

"I will deal with Taylor Jackson."

"No. I am going back to Nashville. I want to search for my daughter."

"If there was a sighting of your daughter in New Haven, you would of course go home immediately. I will arrange it. And you will be safer there with Santiago and Alan."

"You're going to manipulate a police investigation? Is that wise?"

Angelie forced a smile. "Go home, Dr. Conway. We will get her back for you."

Avery stood tall and still. Her eyes were hooded, strong emotion coursing through them. Finally, she nodded once, tersely. "Just find my daughter. Please. For Richard's sake."

The woman's eyes were hooded. "I will. I promise."

Santiago and Angelie spoke briefly again before he hustled Avery back to New Haven.

"Game is taunting you."

"*Oui.* It does not matter. I have a chance to right a wrong."

"You can't go after the cop."

"I can. And I will. She is the key to all of this. She is why Game has come for me now. Why he took Carson from school instead of from home. He knows I will come running to Nashville and try to address things. I will use that to my advantage. Two birds, one rock."

"One stone. Two birds, one stone."

She laughed and kissed him swiftly, on both cheeks. "Take care of her. And trust me. I will make this right."

"Do you want Alan to meet you? Or me?"

"I have a few things that need my attention first. I'll call if I need you. But Captain Jackson is good at killing, too. She will help."

Santiago spit out a small laugh. "Like you're going to turn the savior of Nashville into an assassin for us? Give me a break, Ange. She's as pure as the driven snow."

"She is not pure. Trust me. I will give her a nudge in the right direction. She might even find she likes it."

This was a surprise; she could see the flicker of disbelief in his eyes.

"Just be careful, all right? Don't burn down the city to make a point, okay?"

"*Moi? Non, mon chéri.* I would not dream of it."

NINETEEN

NEW HAVEN, CONNECTICUT

AVERY WAS TORN between anger and terror during the trip back to New Haven, sitting in confused silence next to Santiago on the private jet his "friend" offered.

Santi, though, had talked most of the time, nonsense, really, telling stories about the "unit"—himself, Alan, Richard, Angelie, and Joseph Game. He spoke of the early days when things were hopping worldwide and they were in an almost constant rotation, until she finally snapped.

"You can't possibly expect me to believe Richard was a part of this. He was never gone from home. He raised the children while I worked. You're trying to tell me he was a part of these exploits? Give me a break, Santi."

"He was. He was our SIGINT—signal intelligence—as well as the lead SysOps—systems operator. He gathered all the data and planned all of our operations. He didn't have to be on the ground, he was with us virtually. And he did all the paper—passports, IDs, backstopping legends, the works. He was an incredibly talented forger."

"My husband. *My* Richard. Was a *forger*? These fairy tales you tell, Santi. How in the world am I supposed to believe you?"

Santi shrugged. "Believe me or don't. I'm telling you the truth. Alan will tell you the same."

She thought about it. According to Santiago, Richard had been lying to her practically their whole life together.

But when could Richard have possibly done all of these things? He was always around. Always there for her, for the children. He worked at the bakery, yes, but the bakery was only a few blocks from their house, so he was always popping in to handle their lives.

And they had a marriage. They vacationed together. They went on bike rides together. The only time he was ever truly unreachable was when he had his poker game, and those impromptu events were only held when the guys could get away. Richard had a few buddies from school who had also moved to the area, and they got together in various places on occasion to play cards. It was his sanity break from the kids. She never begrudged him a minute of alone time. It wasn't a regular thing.

Her husband's smiling face animated in her mind, the soft hazel of his eyes teasing, the fullness of his mouth right before he kissed her goodbye as she left for her shifts at the ER. "Don't wait up," he'd say. "I feel a streak coming on."

"The rolling poker game?" she asked finally. "That's when he worked? That's why there was never a set night?"

"For one. Listen, Avery, you were at the hospital a lot. He worked when you weren't around, and sometimes when you were, if he had to. He was just very good at compartmentalizing, making sure you didn't ever suspect he was anything but a loving husband, a father, a baker, a friend, so he could keep you safe."

The plane landed and she followed Santiago to a car waiting for them on the tarmac. He took a moment to glance at his phone, then stowed it and buckled himself in carefully. She couldn't imagine this cautious, careful, gentle man as some sort of lunatic spy running all over the world. Nor could she see her husband in that role. There had to be a darkness in someone to be such a good liar. She'd seen that darkness in the woman Santiago called Angelie, as deep and unfathomable as the midnight sky. But never in Richard.

When Santiago pulled onto the highway, she spoke again. "So you say he lied to me to keep me safe?" There was a sharp edge of hysteria starting now, and Santi's hands gripped the wheel tighter.

"Let's wait to discuss the rest until we get home. Right now we need—"

"No. Do you have any idea how hard it is to find out your husband, who you cherished, who died and left you to raise your children, to make a home, and keep the family you made together from spinning into oblivion, was nothing more than a liar?" The last word ended on a shriek.

"He was doing it for you, Avery. For the kids. To help make the world a better place. Alan can tell you more—he was the one who recruited Richard in the first place. They met right after you graduated."

She slapped a hand against the window, her ring making a deep *thunk*. "This is obscene. What am I supposed to tell the boys? 'Your sister's been kidnapped by your father's old spy buddy'? They'll have me committed."

Santiago went still. She stared at him.

"What? What is it? Tell me right this instant or I am going to call the State Department and ask them to confirm all of this, and then I'm calling the media. Joseph Game and your problems with him be damned, I want my daughter home."

The Santiago who answered made her blood run cold. She'd never heard that voice before. Sharp. Staccato. Emotionless.

"I would recommend against that, Avery. You'll get nowhere

—we didn't work for the US government. We worked for a group called Macallan, and Macallan works for themselves. And if Game thinks you're not playing ball, he won't hesitate to kill Carson just for fun."

Her hand convulsed on the door handle. "Fuck you, Santiago. Don't you dare threaten me."

"Avery, come on. I understand. Really, I do. I've always hated that you didn't know the truth, but you couldn't. It wasn't safe for you, it wasn't safe for the kids. It especially wasn't safe for Rory and Jules."

His voice caught again, her friend returning from the depths of the stranger beside her, and she started to piece it together. "Tell me Richard didn't recruit one of his sons to work for this shadow organization."

Santiago was silent.

"Both of them?"

He nodded. "Rory is training to be our SIGINT now. Jules is showing remarkable aptitude for operations. We'll have him on the ground soon."

Her heart. She could swear it stopped for a moment.

"This is unbelievable. No. I won't allow it. You are going to cut them both loose immediately. I will not have them dying because their father thought he could play spy. No."

Her head fell back against the rest, and she shut her eyes. *This is not happening. This is not happening.*

"They are grown men, Avery. They make their own choices. They understand the risks, and they understand the rewards. They're honorable boys, and we're damn lucky to have them. We have a lot of family lineage in the service. It's not uncommon for children to get curious, see something they shouldn't, and be read in and trained."

He took their exit. She was running out of time. She recognized that once they were back at the home, out of this strange bubble of confession that existed in the jet and the car, Santiago would stop talking and start acting, and she needed as much information as she could get.

"And you and Alan? Are you retired now?"

"For the most part, yes. We're detailed to you. That was something we decided as a team when the five of us started working together. Should something happen to one of us, the others would take responsibility for their families. We don't mind. We never have. Alan and I love you and the kids. And it's given us a chance to settle down. Macallan didn't have an issue with us as a couple, but we would never have had a life together, not like this, if we were still operational. We wouldn't have Teddy." She felt his gaze, and kept her eyes shut. She couldn't take this, she couldn't. "Richard was our friend, Avery, and so are you, though I'm sure you don't feel that way right now."

"And the woman? 'Sònia.' I know her name is Angelie. I heard you call her that at the hotel when you thought I was asleep. How does she fit into this little scheme?"

"Hmm." If he was upset that she'd figured out the woman's real name, he didn't show it. He stayed silent for a few moments, maneuvering the car through the New Haven traffic. Everything looked strange to her, unfamiliar, as if she'd never seen these streets, never walked beside her husband here, played with her children in the park there. The world she knew, the world she relied upon, was no longer her own.

"She is special," Santiago said quietly. "She'll die before she actually gets out. She lies fallow and then emerges from her chrysalis a completely different person. She's brilliant and loyal, and sometimes unstable. She had a terrible tragedy when she was a young girl—she and her parents were ambushed in their car, shot to pieces. She was left for dead with their bodies. That shapes a girl, you know? She grew up too young. Too fast. Too bloody. She had no chance. We are made, people like us."

"And you? You were 'made'? What's your story, Santi? How did you get involved with this group?"

"I'll tell you another time, all right? I want you to hear all of it, but it's a long story, and we're nearly home. I think we've had enough revelations for one day."

She turned her face to the window, to the yawning, unfamiliar darkness, and pretended not to be hurt.

Alan was at the house when they arrived, concern etched on his face, and the table set for dinner. Something in the back of her mind noted the smells coming from the kitchen, roast chicken and rosemary potatoes, one of her favorite meals, and while her stomach gnawed with emptiness, the idea of eating when Carson was missing, possibly dead—no, she wasn't dead yet, Avery would feel that loss keenly, in her very bones—didn't seem right.

Alan practically threw himself at Santiago. "Where have you two been? I've been worried sick since I got your text that you were taking a meeting."

"DC," Santi answered, giving him a brief kiss. "She's here."

"Oh." Alan's gaze grew thoughtful. "And she met with you both?"

"She did," Avery said, "and I know. Not everything, but I know. You've all been lying to me, and I will hate you forever. When we find Carson, I never want to see either of you again."

She stormed from the kitchen, leaving Alan and Santiago staring open-mouthed at the empty doorway.

Avery called Rory, relieved when he answered on the first ring.

"Mom. Have they found her?"

"No. Rory. Tell me they're lying. Tell me you're not—"

"Not on this line, Mom. Seriously. I'll come home, we can talk when I get there. We'll find her. I know we will."

"Son of a bitch," she screamed and hung up on him. She didn't even bother Jules. She knew they were telling the truth, and it was going to break her in two.

Richard, working for some nefarious organization trying to save the world. Killed by a former teammate. Her sons co-opted into the same nonsense. And her daughter, her darling, sweet, shy daughter, kidnapped, in the hands of a mass murderer with no conscience and a twisted sense of humor.

This was all too unbelievable.

Avery had no idea what to do.

So she texted the detective from Nashville, who seemed like the only person in her life who hadn't lost their goddamn mind.

We need to talk.

The cop got back to her immediately.

Give me five.

Avery sent back a note.

I've found out some things, but it's not safe to talk on the phone. How can we have a conversation that's secure?

...

Three dots. It reminded her too much of the night Carson went missing. She swallowed back the rising hysteria that threatened to engulf her. Finally, the screen filled with words.

Are you okay? I can come by the hotel and we can chat.

I'd prefer to speak like this.

Okay. My lieutenant will call you in a few, and he's going to have you download an app that we can use for a private conversation. Hold tight.

"What are you doing?"

Santiago stood at the kitchen door, a look of genuine concern etched on his face.

"I'm going to talk to someone sane about all this," she snarled.

She sensed the mood changing in the room almost immediately.

"We can't let you do that, Avery. You know that. You've been entrusted with a secret, and you have to keep it."

"Or what? You'll have me killed like you did my husband?"

"I didn't kill Richard. I loved him like a brother. And of course I'm not going to kill you." He'd stalked across the room while he spoke, and she had nowhere to go. He held out a hand. "But I can't risk you drawing unwanted attention to this situation. We are handling it from within. I swear to you we are. Give me your phone."

"No."

Santiago sighed and snatched the phone from her hand so quickly he might as well have been a snake striking from hidden grass. She gasped and yanked back her hand, but she was unwounded. Untouched.

But now, also unable to communicate with the one person she thought might shed some light on what was happening around her.

The phone began to ring, but just as quickly, the battery was twisted out, the SIM card yanked from its tiny slot, and the phone crushed beneath Santiago's heel.

"Don't do that again," he said, then marched from the room.

TWENTY

NASHVILLE

TAYLOR CALLED Avery Conway's number three times before she set the phone on the table and rang Lincoln.

"I don't know what happened. She said she needed to talk, securely, and now she's not answering."

"Weird. You don't think something happened to her?"

"I don't know. I'll keep trying, and if I can't get through I'll head over to her hotel. What's your status? Everything okay?"

"As okay as it can be. We're crawling through Carson's email and social media, trying to pinpoint when that photograph was taken, but nothing's popping. Someone else took it and posted it. Besides, it's early days. Marcus will shout if we get anything. You know how this is. Legwork. It will take time. Without a sighting or any other physical clues... You might as well shut down for the evening."

"All right. But don't hesitate if you find anything. I doubt I'll be asleep."

"Roger that. See ya."

She called Avery Conway's cell again, to no avail. Prowled the kitchen, opening the fridge, the pantry, the fridge again, settling at last on a beer. She paced—into the living room, the bedroom, back out—worrying. She wasn't used to letting others do the work. Leadership was for the birds.

Why had Avery Conway ghosted her?

She couldn't just sit here. She'd never get to sleep worrying if the woman was okay.

Taylor grabbed her keys and drove the few blocks over to the Hermitage Hotel.

She badged the valet, who paled and backpedaled, waving her into a spot. He probably had an outstanding warrant, but she wasn't worried about him now. She parked the Tahoe directly in front of the hotel's portico in between a fiery red Ferrari and a gleaming black Audi Quattro, ran up the stairs into the lobby, then headed up to Conway's suite.

She heard muffled cursing after she pounded her balled fist against the door. Moments later, the door opened to reveal an unshaven man with red-rimmed eyes wearing a white bathrobe. Surprising, to say the least.

"What?"

"I'm here to see Dr. Conway."

"Wrong room."

"I'm certain it's not." She lifted her jacket, her badge gleaming on her belt. The man yawned widely, not impressed.

"I checked in a couple of hours ago. No idea who that is. Maybe they switched rooms."

"I'll need to look inside your room, sir. And I'll need ID."

"Be my guest. Then leave, would you? I just flew in from Belgium and I'm freaking exhausted."

Taylor cleared the suite, noticing there were no signs of Conway's luggage. Her internal concern meter started thrumming. She took down the man's name, Brian Hodson, looked at his plane reservations, which showed he had flown British

Airways from Antwerp to Heathrow to Nashville, and concluded he was most likely telling her the truth. She left him her card and hightailed it to the front desk.

"I need to know where you've moved a guest. Avery Conway. She was up on the eighth floor yesterday, but someone else is in the room." The desk clerk started to protest, but she slapped her badge on the counter. "Now."

He typed for a second then shook his head. "She checked out."

"When?"

"Yesterday. Checked in yesterday, too. Guess she decided she didn't like the place."

"Get me security. I need to see their videos."

The clerk looked alarmed but nodded and made a quick call.

The security chief was amenable to helping without waiting for a warrant, and she followed the man to their offices. Something was wrong. Very wrong.

"I was here with her at approximately six p.m. yesterday, so it would be after that."

The videos were well organized; timestamped and searchable. Sure enough, Avery Conway and her friend, Santiago Diaz-Rooney, checked out around 8:00 p.m.

What the hell?

"Thank you," she said, heading to the Tahoe. As she walked, she tried Avery Conway's phone again, and again got the voicemail.

Great. Now she had a missing mom on top of a missing kid.

Don't jump to conclusions. Maybe she heard something about Carson and went home.

Before Taylor got to the truck, she realized she was starving. She decided to grab some truffle fries and a burger to take home with her. She knew it would take fifteen minutes or more, decided to get a beer while she waited. The staff knew her and politely stayed out of her way while she sat in the back corner of the room, sipping.

Taylor texted Lincoln while she waited.

Conway checked out of the hotel yesterday. Looked at the footage to make sure all was well. She didn't seem under duress. Want to call the New Haven cops, see if she went back home?

His reply came immediately.

Weird. Will do.

Her food came, and she paid the check, took the stairs up to the lobby two at a time, and hopped in the Tahoe. Their building was only a few blocks away, so the food was still hot and fragrant when she laid it on the counter five minutes later.

She opened a beer. Ate. Thought. Tried Conway a few more times. Wandered, pacing through the rooms. Her team was out working and here she was, sitting alone at home, doling out orders. The isolation Taylor was feeling was exactly why she didn't like her new position. Too many decisions to make, too little action to take.

The beer was nearly empty and she'd logged a mile wandering the condo when the phone rang again.

"Linc? Is Conway okay?"

"No word from New Haven to the contrary, which is good. But I've got something else for you. Georgia Wray's parents were just in touch. They're finally back in town. They'd like to have a conversation with us. Tonight, if possible. I can send Marcus, but you sounded bored, so I thought you might want to talk to them."

"Ha ha." She glanced at her watch. Nearly nine. "I'm up for it if they are."

"Are you sure? I'd do it, but I'm covered up here."

"No problem. I'll go to them, where are they?"

"Georgia's place. East Nashville. Not far from the house she bought for the boyfriend." He reeled off the address.

"Got it. I'll report back. Don't bother Marcus, I can handle it."

"I kind of like this—me giving you a detail."

"Me too. Wanna trade?" He laughed and hung up. Taylor rinsed out the remnants of the beer and tossed the bottle in the recycling, brushed her teeth, then pulled on her boots and leather jacket again. Talking with the parents of a dead girl was not her favorite thing to do by any means, but at least they already knew the contours of the situation. There was nothing worse than having to do a notification. Breaking apart a life wasn't something she ever got used to.

Then again, she had nothing to give them. A dead daughter, a dead boyfriend, and a couple of hunches that she was definitely going to keep to herself.

Lincoln texted her the address as a backup, though she remembered it easily. She set the alarm and took the elevator to the garage again. This late, the drive to East Nashville was quick. She had no trouble figuring out which house it was; the renovated bungalow was glowing with light from every window.

Loss makes people afraid of the dark.

She knocked, and the door was opened by a young man dressed all in black: skinny jeans, Bluestones concert T-shirt, Converse. Even his hair was dyed black, falling into his reddened eyes. The fingernails on his right hand were longer than the left and painted black. She pegged him as a member of the band, a little edgy for country, but not unusually so, even before he said, "Hi. I'm Meddows. Georgia's guitarist. Was. Damn. Come in."

"I'm sorry for your loss," she said, stepping into the foyer.

"Thanks. They're all in the kitchen," Meddows said. "I was just heading out. Nice to meetcha."

He shouldered a broken-in leather jacket and closed the front door quietly. Just as softly, he opened it again. "Ma'am? Make sure you ask about the issues we were having with Travis." And he was gone before she had a chance to speak.

TWENTY-ONE

THE KITCHEN WAS full of people. The group was far from jovial, but they weren't weeping, either. The chatter decreased as she stepped into the room. She spied a few faces she recognized from the music scene around town, and a couple of acoustic guitars leaning against the walls, though no one was playing anything at the moment. The music community in Nashville was close-knit, a loving communal family who spoke not only in words but in sounds, as well. Soon enough, they'd all be circling the fire pit, singing Georgia's favorites into the wee hours.

"You must be Captain Jackson," a stocky man said, standing and putting out a hand. "I'm Georgia's dad, Kurt Wray. Thank you for coming this late. Can I get you anything?"

"No, sir. I am very sorry for your loss."

He nodded, mouth a grim line. "Georgia was an incredible young woman. I wish you could have known her. Come on, her mom's out back."

The patio was screened in, and a fire roared and sparked in the pit, warming the area and sending tiny flaming fireflies out into the night. Couches and chairs were set up in a conversational square, and a petite woman with shiny blond hair was curled in one, rocking slowly.

"Heather? Captain Jackson is here."

Heather Wray's eyes were red, but she seemed pretty well contained, considering. Granted, she'd had some time to get used to the idea that she'd never see her daughter alive again, but Taylor still sent up a private thanks as she sat in the chair opposite. Kurt took the corner of the sofa closest to his wife. The remaining people bled away without a word. When they were alone, Kurt Wray took the lead.

"We wanted to talk to you privately, and we appreciate you being here. We're concerned that because of our daughter's lifestyle, things may get overlooked. We understand you've already talked with Travis about Justin and his issues with how their careers were going?"

"Mr. Bloom told me Justin was causing serious disruptions, if that's what you mean. So did some of the staff at the label. Is there more?"

Bloom hadn't mentioned any problems with Georgia other than Justin Osborne's animus, but he'd also seemed completely shocked by the news, and jet-lagged from his red-eye from LA. Of course, there were always two sides to every story.

The Wrays met eyes, and Heather Wray took over. "We want you to have the whole picture. Justin and Georgia were a lovely couple, and they made great music together. When it was clear Georgia was going to be the star, the label did everything they could to drive a wedge between them. Everything. Georgia was put in a terrible position. A career in the spotlight over the boy she loved. She felt pressured into breaking up with him, and it was eating her alive. Justin was heartbroken, absolutely. But homicidal? No way. We've known the boy nearly his whole life. He was upset, but he wasn't mad at Georgia. He got it. We all knew Georgia was the more talented of the two. He was proud of that, proud that he helped get her into the position to have a career. But Travis didn't want Justin hanging around. A boyfriend made Georgia less appealing to the masses, you know? Travis created as much animosity as he could between them."

"I have to interrupt you here, ma'am. There is some pretty incendiary stuff in Justin's notebooks. He was most certainly mad at Georgia. Furious, in fact. Furious enough that it seemed quite clear he was upset enough with the situation to kill her."

Heather shook her head. "Blowing off steam, maybe. Trust me. He would never hurt her. Hear me out, there's more. Here's what else Travis Bloom doesn't want you to know. Georgia was fed up with his manipulation and was threatening to pull out of the contract. Everything was going too fast for her. She was being isolated from all of us, not just Justin. Bloom and his flunkies were putting up a wall between Georgia and everyone who genuinely cared about her. They were dominating her every moment, her every thought. They were even offering her drugs, and she told us Bloom was always around when she was pulling late nights in the studio, hitting on her. Anything they could use to get her under their thrall. She was scared enough to buy herself a cell phone they didn't know about to communicate with us. The texts between us will corroborate everything we're telling you."

Kurt handed over a sheaf of papers. "I took the liberty of printing them out for you."

"That's very helpful, thank you."

Taylor glanced through the stack. It certainly looked like a regular exchange between the parents and their daughter. She was going to have a long night digging through all of them.

"Does Mr. Bloom know about these communications?"

Kurt shook his head. "No. No way. He would have taken the phone away from her. I'm sure if you took her phone, or Justin's, into evidence, you'll see a different story entirely. She was doing everything she could to maintain the facade while our lawyers looked for loopholes in the contract." A small sob escaped his lips. "We were too late. We told people we were on vacation, but we were holed up with an entertainment attorney. Georgia called us and said Travis had threatened her, and we should have just come here immediately and taken her home with us. I will regret that for the rest of my life. I had a chance to save my baby, and I failed her."

Heather reached out and touched her husband on the knee. "Kurt. It's not all on you. We were all trying to get her out."

"Could she not have left of her own accord?" Taylor asked. "Was there a physical component to this? Was she being held somewhere, detained?" At the look Heather Wray gave her, Taylor followed up. "I need to ascertain if she was being held against her will, because that changes the complexity of what we're dealing with here. Travis Bloom being a Svengali isn't illegal. Holding her against her will, that I can maybe work with. Drugs, of course, complicate things, depending on what they were, but if you didn't see him give them to her..."

Kurt sighed. "She could have left. She was trying to handle things herself. She was trying to save her career. She loved singing so much. And she was so headstrong. She thought she could handle him."

"Have you spoken with Mr. Bloom?"

"We left word, but he didn't return the call. He's already back in LA, looking for his next mark."

His next mark. Damn. That got Taylor's back up. Young women being taken advantage of pissed her off.

"This is very compelling. I will look into Travis Bloom, I promise. But I have to tell you, there is no indication anyone but Justin was involved in her death. He was on the trail with her where she died, and we have a witness who saw him moments after the gunshot. All the forensics prove he shot the same weapon that killed Georgia."

"Justin didn't kill her," Heather said. "You'll see." She rose from the chair. "If you'll excuse me, I need to go to bed now."

When it was just the two of them, Kurt said, "She's holding up remarkably well, considering. That's where Georgia got her strength, from her mom. I know this is a lot. I know you think we're just grieving parents, unable to believe the truth. I'm telling you, when you read the texts, you'll understand."

"Do you have any idea where Georgia might have stashed her phone? The one she was using to send texts? I don't recall anything like that on the evidence sheets."

"She said she hid it in the bathroom, under the lid of the toilet. It wasn't there when we got here. We searched the whole house. She must have had it with her."

"Okay. One more thing. Are you going to go public with these accusations, Mr. Wray?"

"Will I need to?"

Taylor smiled, but there was no warmth in it. "I can assure you we will look at every bit of evidence. The girl who witnessed the murder has gone missing, and that has my attention. Finding her is my primary goal right now. I don't want another dead girl on my hands."

Wray flinched.

"Sorry."

"Yeah. Are you asking me to be patient?"

"I'm asking you to talk to me before you go to the press. I understand your frustration, I truly do. Georgia's case has been declared a murder-suicide by the preponderance of evidence found by both our team and the medical examiner. I'm going to have to get the case reopened, which has some technical back end, and is going to cause some chatter. And in the meantime, I've got a missing girl. The pressure to find her is intense, and now, even more so." He started to speak, and Taylor held up a hand. "I promise you, I am going to look into reopening the case. I just want to do it very quietly, and only with my people.

If Georgia's murder and the witness's disappearance are tied together, I don't necessarily want to broadcast that to the world. Do you understand where I'm coming from?"

Kurt looked her over for a moment, then stood. "I do."

Taylor stood as well, handing over her card. "Then let me do this my way. You've given me a lot to work with here, Mr. Wray. I will get justice for Georgia, I swear it. If there's anything else, don't hesitate to call me."

He nodded. "I'll be in touch. And I'll echo my wife's sentiments. It wasn't Justin. He's as much a casualty of Bloom as Georgia was."

In the car, Taylor turned on the interior light and flipped through the printed pages. Text after text of Georgia detailing all the things Bloom was doing and saying to her. If this was for real, it was incendiary.

She called Lincoln. "Oh man, do I have some stuff for you to play with. The parents think Bloom was somehow responsible for this mess. And I'm starting to wonder if they aren't on to something."

"The head of the record label? Travis Bloom?"

"Yeah. Georgia was trying everything she could to nix her contract. Allegedly he was isolating her, pushing her into decisions she wasn't comfortable with, offering drugs, et cetera. She had a burner phone she was using to connect with her folks, and I've got a stack of texts her dad printed out for us. I haven't gone through them all yet, but the gist is certainly there. It's your basic nightmare scenario for a young female artist. She wanted out, and her parents were trying to help her. They are 100 percent convinced Justin didn't murder her."

"All right. Where's this burner phone?"

"Your guess is as good as mine. We need to find it, though.

Corroboration of these claims would be helpful. Her parents aren't as rocked as I might expect. Granted, they're in shock, and they've had a couple of days to process, but it's almost as if they thought this might happen. There could be something to their testimony."

"Damn. Just when I thought things were going smoothly."

"No kidding. We're going to have to reopen this case. Can you do it under the radar? If the press gets wind of any of this, or worse, Travis Bloom thinks we're looking at him, this could spin right on out of our control."

"I hear you. I think we can do some digging into Bloom without raising the red flags. Especially since he's in and out of town. We can be discreet."

"Good. Do it. I don't want to turn him into a suspect, publicly or privately, unless we have a damn good reason. I think her parents believe what they're saying, but they weren't here in town, and without the actual phone to get records that corroborate this text string, this won't hold up in court. We'll need the phone itself."

He sighed. "Get some sleep. We'll start looking tomorrow."

She heard a noise in the background that sounded like giggling. It made her smile immediately. "Is that Flynn?"

"Yes. I put him to bed an hour ago, but the silly rascal thinks he can fool me into reading him another story. I better go deal with him."

The joy and light in Lincoln's voice made her heart sing. "You do that. Tell him Auntie T loves him. And Lincoln?"

"Yeah?"

"Something is going on here. We need to figure out if Carson Conway and Georgia Wray are connected in any other ways, and we need to do it fast."

Shit. So much happening, so many balls spinning. Her mind jumped from case to case, issue to issue. Two girls—one dead, one missing, somehow tied together. The mom acting sketchy and dropping off the radar. A possible criminally liable label head. Justin Osborne and the phantom notebook paper. Malware on Carson Conway's phone. Carson stumbling onto Georgia's murder. Coincidence?

Coincidence that Taylor had gotten assigned a case that was going supernova?

Yes, Huston had given her the assignment to get back on the street, but what about when all this was over? This was temporary, something to appease her. There wouldn't be more. Which brought her full circle, back to her dinner with Thierry Florian.

She had almost managed to push away the worries about Thierry's offer to join Macallan. She wasn't going to do anything until she and Baldwin had a nice, long, sit-down in-person chat, so there wasn't pressure building to deal with it, but she couldn't help but think of the assassin Angelie Delacroix.

Could she work for the same organization that employed the sort of people she was blood sworn to hunt down?

The indecision was killing her slowly. She had to get a handle on this, and fast.

She was two steps into her foyer when her phone rang. Her stomach dropped.

"Linc?" she answered.

"Hey. Good news, for once. New Haven cops swung by Conway's house. She's there, unharmed, with the guys who own her husband's bakery. One of their detectives is going to have a chat with them shortly."

"Well, that's a relief. Wish I knew why she bolted."

"I'm sure we'll find out. For now, you should get some rest."

"Talk to you tomorrow, Linc."

Maybe she would sleep tonight after all, knowing at least Avery Conway was safe.

TWENTY-TWO

NEW HAVEN

AFTER THE PHONE INCIDENT, Avery stormed out of the room after Santiago, screaming at him. What if Carson called, and couldn't get through?

Santi explained, quietly, in no uncertain terms, that Carson would not be calling. That she was being held hostage, and Game would never, ever let her go until his terms were met. He told Avery to be patient, then he huddled with Alan, who soon after drove off, leaving Santiago on the porch and Avery inside, roaming like a caged lion.

She wasn't afraid of Santiago, though she knew she should be. She was afraid of the woman who called herself Sònia. Angelie. *"Ohn-jhee,"* Santiago had called her, which sounded like a nickname. She had no idea if that was the woman's real name, nor did she care. All she wanted was her daughter back. She'd promised she was going to make that happen. Avery had no choice but to believe her. Santiago had gone to Angelie immediately and seemed to think the woman had the power to make Game comply.

How had Avery been so blind? Was she so dislocated from her family that she'd allowed this treachery to happen? Were they lying to her now?

Exhausted, Avery collapsed onto her bed. She still slept on the left side, all these years later, never encroaching on Richard's space. She was too tired to sleep; worry gnawed at her stomach to the point she rolled onto her side and drew up her legs, hoping to ease the cramps.

This wouldn't do.

She rolled onto her back. The tray ceiling, with its beautiful crown molding and chandelier, made her feel like she was sleeping in a high-end hotel suite. She'd always loved it. Now, it seemed almost sinister. Mocking. Her home, her life, was a lie.

Could she stay here, knowing what she knew now? Could she live in this house by herself, with her tainted memories? What if they were wrong? What if Carson never came home? Could she go on without her daughter? Her lifeline?

Don't think that way. You're being morbid. Be positive. Santi and Alan and that woman, they will get Carson back, or die trying. That has to be good enough for now.

A soft knock broke her from her reverie. Alan. Bearing a croissant and a cup of tea like she was simply home sick in bed, not having her world explode.

She sat up and gestured for him to enter. He set the tray on the bed. "Santi told me what happened. I'm sorry. I disagree with how he acted. I apologize on his behalf. He is quite distraught, you must understand that. He feels this is his fault."

"Why?"

"He had a chance to kill Game, soon after Richard's death. We were called off."

"By whom?"

"The head of our organization. He felt it was counterproductive. He was wrong. We see that now. We will fix this. Our friend, the woman you met with in DC—"

"*Ohn-jhee?*"

He started at her use of the name.

"I know her name is Angelie. I heard Santi call her that."

He sighed. "Yes. Angelie." He pronounced it with such a painfully perfect French accent—OHN-jzha-LEE—that she again wondered how in the hell her life had spun 180 degrees in such a short time.

"She frightened me, Alan. She is cruel."

"She must be cruel, Avery. To do what she does, to be who she is, she must act without conscience or hesitation. She is unique. She is very capable. And she keeps her word. She will find Carson. She will kill Game. All of this will end well. You'll see." He smiled, weak but genuine. "Richard was so proud of you. Do you know that? He thought you were the most spectacular person in the world. Everything he did, he did to make your world a better safer place to live in."

"He lied to me." She heard the flatness in her tone, the petulance right behind it.

"Yes. He did. Because he had to. He couldn't take the chance of our enemies coming to hurt you."

She lunged at him, upsetting the tray and spilling tea all over the duvet. "And where did that get him, Alan? Dead, that's where. My daughter could be dead as well. Don't make excuses for him. I will not forgive and forget. The second I get my hands on those sons of mine, I'm going to shake some sense into them, too. I refuse to let your company take everything I hold dear."

She stalked to her closet, ripped down a sweater, a pair of jeans, and grabbed some hiking boots.

"What are you doing?"

"Something. Anything. I can't just sit here waiting."

"You have to stay here—"

"No. I can't."

"You must." He took the boots from her hand and set them gently on the bench at the end of the bed.

"If we don't play this right, Game will kill Carson for fun, just to watch us squirm. He is trying to draw Angelie into the open. She is taking his bait. Let her do what she does best."

"And in the meantime? We wait?"

"In the meantime, you need to continue being the same person you were yesterday. A loving mother, a grieving widow, a brilliant doctor. You must talk with the police the same way you were. You must not let on what you know. Your call to the police captain in Nashville could have jeopardized all our lives, but Carson's most of all. You must trust us. We only want what you want—Carson home, safe, and Game out of our lives for good."

"Why are you both here, Alan? Surely one of you is sufficient to guard me. Why aren't you out there with your friend, helping her?"

"Because I am following orders, just as Santi is, just as Jules and Rory are. This is a delicate balance, and we must do as our leader tells us, or it all falls apart. We are doing what we need to from here. We will activate the second Angelie calls for us. If it gets that far."

She searched his eyes for some sort of truth, some sort of understanding.

"If she activates you, that means she's failed to retrieve Carson. Is that what you're saying?"

"Yes."

She grabbed the jeans. "Then I'm going to the hospital. I can't sit here anymore. I'm doing no one any good weeping in my bedroom."

He looked at her long and hard. "The police might misinterpret—"

"Fuck the police. And fuck you. I'm going."

"Before you do anything, I need you to unring the bell with

the Nashville police. From what Santiago said, the captain down there isn't the type to let your conversation sit."

"What am I supposed to say?"

"That there was a sighting, and you were worried about trying to get word to her. You're a grieving mom who's never been in trouble before. She'll believe you if you're careful. Santi has gone to get another phone. Will you please, please, just lie down for a little while and let us fix things?

"I'm never going to forgive you, Alan."

"I know," he said, sadly.

Somehow, she slept. Her body was well tuned to sleep when needed, even in a crisis, and she fell back on her training to do just that. She had thought she was too keyed up, but her mind was spinning from all she'd learned over the past twenty-four hours, and her subconscious agreed she needed a break. When she came to, it was still dark, and there were voices in the living room. She recognized the cadences of Alan and Santiago, but there was another voice, speaking with urgency.

Carson!

The men all turned when she rushed into the living room. She was right, a third man was there. Detective Turley. The man who investigated her husband's death.

Before she could even open her mouth, Alan was by her side.

"Avery, are you okay? You look like you need to sit down." He had a hand on her bicep, squeezing it hard in warning. She shot him a questioning look. He shook his head and she nodded. He let her go.

"Detective, is there news? Have you found Carson?"

Jeremy Turley was a good guy, she recalled. Earnest, thoughtful, truly devastated for her. *If you only knew,* she thought. *If you had any idea you are sitting with the very men who caused Richard's death...*

"No, Dr. Conway, we haven't, not yet. I'll be heading to Nashville as soon as we finish talking. I just wanted to touch base before I took off, to let you know I insisted on working Carson's case. We have traps on your phones, so if a call comes in, we'll be able to trace it."

"Speaking of. Your new phone came while you were asleep, Avery," Santiago said, handing over a new iPhone. "I've already got it charged and set up for you. Dr. Conway dropped her phone in a sink of soapy water," he explained to Turley. "We couldn't get it to turn back on."

The ease with which he lied astounded her. But it was also an apology.

"Throw it in a bag of rice," Turley suggested. "Might work. Do you have any questions for me, Dr. Conway?"

"What happens now?" she managed.

"We continue searching for Carson. Physical search, digital search, the works. That's why I'm going to Nashville. They're already up and running. You're in good hands here."

"I'd like to go with you," she blurted.

All three men made negative noises. Turley patted her knee. "I know you do, and you're welcome to if you want. But there's not much you can do there that you can't do here. Continue the public pleas, that's the most effective tack. Stay plugged in. We'll bring her home. I swear."

He stood, brushing his hands down the front of his pants. "Hang in. It's going to be okay."

"I'll see you to the door," Alan said.

When Turley was gone, Santiago ducked his head. "Forgive me. I overreacted. Seriously, Avery, we're trying to keep you safe."

"Funny way of showing it."

"You're a smart woman, and you know in your heart we are

telling you the truth. I promised not to lie. I swear, that will not happen again. We were worried we might have to move you, in case Game comes for you, too, but we've decided we're going to stay here. While you were out—and trust me, you needed some sleep, you haven't rested in days—we set our defenses. This place is hardened. Your new phone is encrypted, there's not a chance of anyone listening in. We just needed some time."

She shook her head.

"You went too far, Santi. Now the police will be suspicious. You should have let me talk to her."

"You're going to. Right now."

"What?"

"You're right, I'm sure you piqued her interest. We need her to stand down. Like Alan suggested, tell her there was a sighting and you bolted for home. It's believable, and it will buy our friend a little more time to assess what's happening. Please, Avery. For me."

He already had the captain's number pulled up, and the speakerphone on. She took a deep breath through her nose. She was not good at lying, but at least the woman couldn't see her face.

A deep, scratchy voice said, "Hello?

"Captain Jackson? It's Avery Conway. I'm sorry to reach out so late."

"Are you all right, Dr. Conway?" Jackson demanded, sounding both pissed and relieved. "I came by the hotel and they said you checked out."

"I did. I apologize for the confusion earlier. I am fine, my phone died. I'm here in New Haven."

A pause. "Are you alone?"

"Santiago and his husband, Alan, are with me."

"All right. Do you still want to talk to me privately? I can arrange that quickly."

"No." At Santiago's nod, she tried to make her voice sound

bleak. “There was a sighting of Carson, so you can understand I had to come back here.”

A pause. “I haven’t heard about a sighting. I’d like to hear the details.”

“Oh, it was nothing. A mistake. It didn’t pan out. I just wanted you to know where I was, that I’m fine, and to apologize for being panicked earlier. I’m sure you understand. I’m still very hopeful you’ll be able to bring Carson home. I know you will.”

She hung up, and Santiago patted her on the shoulder.

“Well done,” Santiago said. “That was very believable.”

Avery glared at him.

“I’m sorry, Avery. About everything.”

“You are no longer a part of this family, Santiago.” She went to her bedroom, trying to ignore the hurt in his dark brown eyes.

TWENTY-THREE

FRIDAY: WASHINGTON, DC

THE ASSASSIN STALKED the night streets, blending into the chaos that was the most powerful city in the world. The lights and noises made her long for the quiet of the château. *Soon,* she soothed herself. *Soon, you will be back there, arguing with the Corsicans and drinking a freezing cold glass of Sancerre.*

She'd spent the day searching, making calls, reinserting herself into her operational space. There were people who owed her, and they were more than happy to cancel their debts by sharing what they knew about Joseph Game.

She would be ready to move on soon, set up shop in the playground of the woman with the mismatched gray eyes. The anticipation of this moment was one she'd been reliving for nearly a year. She hadn't yet decided whether she was going to kill Jackson once she was finished securing Carson Conway and ridding the world of Game. She went back and forth. There was value in removing the maker of such a terrible memory. But Jackson also intrigued her. She could have killed Angelie easily

—she had the shot, had the upper hand—yet she'd shot to wound, not to kill.

Why?

Angelie wanted to ask the big blond woman that, and a few other things. Then she'd make her decision. But first, she needed her help. Finding Carson had to be the priority, and Jackson had a head start.

She had an encrypted burner in her pocket, one she'd been using to suss out information, so wasn't terribly surprised when it rang. She ducked into an alleyway near the Treasury Department, put her back to the stacked marble, and answered. She didn't recognize the number but had a dreadful feeling she knew who was calling. Damn Santiago. He couldn't manage to keep his mouth shut about anything.

"Qoui?"

An annoyed French voice shouted at her. "What the hell do you think you're doing?"

"*Bonsoir*, Thierry."

"Get on a plane and get the hell out of there, right now."

"Is this a warning or an order?"

"She'll shoot you where you stand, and no one will blame her for it. Get out of the country, now."

"I can't. Game is here. He's taken Richard's daughter."

It wasn't often Thierry Florian was shocked into silence. Finally, he said, "Go on."

"Santi didn't tell you? Pity. The girl's gone missing. I thought I'd help retrieve her."

"You thought you'd help how, exactly? By going to Nashville and murdering the captain of their police force?"

"You are no better than Game, thinking me so rash. I'm not here for that. I'm here to avenge Richard's death. I thought perhaps to touch base with the woman, assess the situation, but I can see you do not feel this is a good idea."

"No, I do not. You've had your acts of revenge, Angelie. On

me. On your uncle. On all who wronged your family. You've agreed to abide by the rules set forth in our agreement. I must insist you do not make Captain Jackson one of your...diversions."

"You really are serious, aren't you?"

"I am serious. You can't hurt her, Angelie. She is one of us now."

A small fire lit in her belly. *"Excusez-moi?"* she snarled, not bothering to hide herself. A tourist stumbling up the street gave her a curious but drunken look. Angelie ducked her head and marched farther into the dark of the alley, fury boiling in her veins.

"Jackson is going to join Macallan. Which means she is now your ally."

How dare he. How *dare* he? Bringing Jackson into their organization? Actually making them compatriots? It was preposterous. It was unfair and ridiculously stupid. Of course he would not do such a thing. Not to Angelie.

"You're lying so I won't kill her right now."

"Why would I lie to you? You've known I wanted her. She's agreed. Now, tell me what's happening? Why was I not informed about Richard's daughter?"

"That is not my problem," she said, trying to regain control. "I am retired."

"You'll be retired when you're in the ground, and not a moment before. As is evidenced by your current location and the outreach you've been doing. Everyone is buzzing. Now tell me what's happened."

Damn him. She laid it out, simple and straightforward, leaving out nothing, finishing with "Game wants our attention. I intend to give it to him. If only for Richard's sake."

Thierry was muttering expletives in French in his elegant way. "Santi is with you?"

"No. I have him guarding the widow."

"You need backup."

"I am aware of how to do my job, Thierry. Besides, if what you say is true, I'll have it."

A pause. "Jackson."

"*Oui.* If you are serious, and she's actually going to join our ranks, then she'll have no choice. Once she knows why, and who, she'll work with me."

"Is that why you've gone to the US, Angelie? To recruit her yourself?"

"No. I came to get the child, and to vanquish an enemy." She didn't bother to elaborate which one.

"I am in the country as well. We should meet."

"No," she said simply, and hung up.

She could not play this game with Thierry looking over her shoulder. She had to locate Game, and she had to retrieve Richard's daughter. Nothing else mattered now.

She pulled up her scarf against the chill and stalked into the night. The city sheltered her; murderers winding through the darkness with cruel secrets were, if not commonplace, not entirely unusual.

It was time for Sònia Masot-Mallofré to check out of The Willard and go about her life, and a new woman to make an appearance. She would go track Game, find where he'd stashed the child, take him out. And then, then, she would face her nemesis, and they would settle things, once and for all.

PART TWO

"Betrayal is the only truth that sticks."

—Arthur Miller

TWENTY-FOUR

NASHVILLE

THEY SEARCHED.

They combed through the meager online offerings Carson left behind. They put in warrants for the data, tracked the IMEI identification number on her phone to the most recent cell tower ping—unfortunately, that tower provided service to the campus. They opened a tip line, which was flooded with nothing of use. They watched her social media feeds, talked to her professors, her dorm mates, her friends. Carson's terrified roommate was making noises about pulling out of school for the semester. Frantic groups of students turned out to hike around campus and the outlying parks. Media trucks lined the streets around campus, reporters interviewing anyone who would come near their cameras. Dr. Conway had done a magnificent plea for her daughter's safety, which was being aired on a loop on all the cable news networks, and the hashtags #FindCarson #missingcoed #nashvillestudent were trending across the socials. So was #JusticeforGeorgia, just to confuse things further.

Nothing.

Carson Conway had vanished into thin air.

The cut-and-dried murder-suicide of Georgia Wray was blowing up, too, and though the connections between the two cases were murky, Taylor was grateful for the confirmation of her gut feeling something else was up. They hadn't found Georgia's burner phone, and the warrant for the records on the number was taking longer than she'd like. Lincoln had done a deep dive into Travis Bloom and was preparing a briefing. Apparently, it was a doozy. They'd have some answers, at least.

Taylor kept hoping they'd recover the Conway girl in the meantime. They needed a win. Every sunset that passed, the morale dropped.

It took forty-eight precious hours to get the task force officially into place, not to mention the weekend hampering their plans, so the first official meeting was on Monday, five days after Carson had gone missing. Task forces were usually a major pain in Taylor's ass, but right now, she was happy for the help. She needed all the input she could get to find Carson Conway alive. Missing Vanderbilt co-eds made her nervous; witnesses to crimes going missing made her sick to her stomach. And it had been too long with no word. She was so afraid they were too late.

In the old CJC offices, the conference room down the hall from the murder squad's offices would be the hive of the task force, but this was a new world, a new Nashville, with new government-mandated rules about who could meet when, and where, and for how long, so they circumvented the whole thing and, with Huston's taciturn blessing, quickly set up shop downtown on the nineteenth floor of a co-working building right around the corner from Taylor's new condo. It had a great view north to the Cumberland River through floor-to-ceiling glass walls that gave almost everyone a little vertigo the first time they stepped off the elevator. Not Taylor—she and Baldwin were on the forty-fourth floor of their building, and she was used to living in the sky—but most everyone else had a moment of sheer *whoa* when they entered the reception area.

The space itself was luxe in comparison to everyone else's home offices: the high-end coffee makers were a major upgrade, there were refrigerators stocked with Greek yogurt and LaCroix, bowls with nuts and candy in small packages, and two previously bored office attendants who were thrilled to have so many new people in their co-working space and something to do for them.

Though after giving the tour and handing over the keycards, the two were summarily dismissed to the eighteenth floor. Task forces were private things.

It was too big, too unwieldy, she knew that from the get-go. Despite her best efforts to respect Avery Conway's wishes and keep it small, there were representatives from Metro Violent Crimes, the TBI, the Connecticut Criminal Investigations Division, the New Haven FBI, Vanderbilt Police, Tennessee Highway Patrol, and a curious woman with white-blond hair and inky black eyebrows who was "representing" a private investigator who'd managed to get involved. After a perfunctory fist bump, the woman stayed silent and out of the way, drinking a cup of coffee through a rocking red lip, staring out the window, and humming what sounded suspiciously like The Clash's "Rock the Casbah." She looked familiar, though Taylor couldn't place her.

In their first meeting, it took half an hour for the group to sort out who was going to be on top. Taylor let them squabble. She didn't care at all about who got credit, she just wanted to find the girl and return her to the normally safe enclave of her college.

When they'd all established their places and had gone around the room with brief introductions and decisions on who was handling what, Taylor put a name to the face of the woman by the window. Schuyler Abbott. Sky. She'd briefly been a cop with Metro before she switched sides and went to work for her aunt's private investigation firm. Taylor made a note to talk to her separately afterward. If she was going to bail on working for Metro, Sky Abbott might give her some insights on what it was like working in law enforcement from the outside.

Finally, it was Taylor's turn. "I want to run through everything we know so everyone is on the same page. Even if you feel it's repeated information." She had precious few images, but at least it was something to share. Lincoln had popped them onto her laptop. She hit the button and the first image came on their screens.

"Carson Conway didn't come home from the library Wednesday evening. Cameras in the quad caught her at 8:11 p.m., walking past the Student Center. This is not the path back to her dorm."

"Meeting someone?" one of the Connecticut cops said, and Taylor shrugged.

"Maybe. Or getting a late-night snack. Or picking up a newspaper. Or heading to St. Augustine's to have a sit-down with the Reverend Stevens. Who knows? The point is, there's no sign of her after this moment. She never entered the Student Center, and no cameras caught her anywhere else in the vicinity. Her phone pinged the Vandy tower at 8:14 p.m. and hasn't shown up since."

The screen flipped, and a blurred image of a car came up. "This Jeep was idling near the Student Center. No image of the plates, and no idea if this is related, but it's all we've got to go on." *Click.* "You can see the driver is a male Caucasian, but that's it."

One of the Vandy cops interjected, "We can get you a listing of every Jeep registered on campus."

"That would be great," Taylor said. "Assuming this is a student, he's the closest thing we have to a witness. Let's talk about the mom. I met her, she seems very believable. You've all seen her on the news, I'm sure. She came here immediately but got a tip her daughter was back home, bailed on us, and has been acting odd. Is there any chance she's involved somehow?"

The Connecticut cop—Jeremy Turley—shook his head. Taylor assessed him quickly: good suit, salty hair, and round-cheeked, leather portfolio in front of him, well worn and slick with age, a thick notebook resting inside. He seemed solid.

"Avery Conway is the most attentive mom I've ever met. She's a widow, a well-known, well-liked doctor, and has serious community ties. No way she hurt her kid."

"Sounds like you know her personally?" Taylor asked.

"Unfortunately. I mean, not on her, she's a nice lady, just a bad situation. I said she was a widow—when her husband died a few years back, I worked the case. The autopsy said aneurysm riding his bike, but I always thought it was a hit-and-run. Terrible. Owned a bakery in town, a really popular place. They're well known in the community. Everyone pitched in to help after Richard Conway passed."

"Did you have any proof it wasn't an accident?" Taylor asked, and Turley shook his head, his ruddy cheeks growing more pronounced.

"No," he said slowly. "Though he had on a helmet, he had deep lacerations across his face, and some external injuries, so I asked some questions about whether his brain really blew up. Everyone thought I was nuts."

"Gut instinct?" she asked sympathetically, and he nodded.

"That's all it was. I had nothing tangible to argue with. It never smelled right to me, but hey, accidents happen. It was a quiet stretch of road, no witnesses. The back bumper of the bike was dented, too, but that could have happened when he turned it over. Anyway. Avery, Carson's mom, she's a good woman."

"Any enemies?"

"I didn't think so. We're looking into it, in case there's a disgruntled patient in her past, but so far, nothing." Turley sat back, finished. For now. Taylor sensed he might talk to her again privately.

"Anyone else?" Crickets. "Okay then. Cast the nets wider. We're looking for any ties between Carson Conway and Georgia Wray. Anything—and I mean anything—gets fed into the secure database Lieutenant Ross built for us. It will tie into all the usual databases, and if the NGI facial recognition can pull anything off the man in the Jeep...?"

"On it," the TBI rep said. "We're also monitoring Carson's social media feeds and cell phone. She hasn't posted to any of her accounts. There's a bunch of TikTokers putting out theories, jamming up our tip line. We're watching them, too, just in case one's plausible. We're all over all the places folks like to talk about crimes. So far, no joy."

"We have been too, but having a second set of eyes is very helpful."

Marcus was sitting to her right. He flipped his hair off his forehead and spoke.

"As far as our physical hunt is concerned, we've already searched all around campus, and are moving outward, checking dumpsters, alleys, and construction sites around downtown. But I think we should go back up the mountain where Georgia Wray was murdered. Georgia's boyfriend killed her, we're pretty well convinced of that, but his subsequent suicide is fishy." He glanced at Taylor, who nodded, and continued. "Hypothetical: Someone killed him, and whoever that was, he was on the mountain, too. He saw Carson and thinks Carson saw him, so he's eliminated her. Unfortunately, it's rained since we recovered Georgia's body, so chances are we won't find anything new, but it's worth a look."

"I agree," Taylor said. She didn't want to mention that they were trying to blow up Travis Bloom's alibi, not just yet. This task force had been assembled to find Carson Conway alive.

Taylor and her team could work the Wray murder quietly for a little longer, without confusing the issue.

She pointed at the TBI rep. "O'Roarke, isn't it? Can we borrow your cadaver dogs? I wouldn't mind doing a full grid search up there. Something about that setting has felt weird to me from day one. Let's make sure there's no one else up there."

O'Roarke frowned at her. "You're thinking a burial ground? Come on, Captain Jackson. Not every case is a serial."

"Nope, it's not," she replied, tamping down her annoyance at the man's tone. "But humor us. I've been at this long enough to trust my gut, and my gut says Carson Conway saw something she wasn't supposed to, whether she knows it or not."

Marcus set down his pen. "Do you think she didn't tell us the truth about what happened up there?"

"I think it's possible she didn't know what the truth was. Or else she wouldn't have gone missing." She looked around the table. "Detective Wade and I have talked to the roommate multiple times, but I want someone else to have a go. Lieutenant Ross's team has been running all the data from the two crime scenes, testing against others in the region. Nothing has popped yet, but the more information he has, the easier it will be."

O'Roarke, handsome in a coarse, been-up-all-night forgot-to-shave way, shook his head. "You're 100 percent she's been taken? Kids now, they wander off. Pretty girl like that, maybe she met someone and is holed up, having a party."

Taylor shook her head. "Freshmen co-eds at Vanderbilt who witness murders don't wander off. Where did her phone last ping?"

"The quad," he answered, suddenly very interested in his notes. "Wednesday at 8:14 p.m."

"Exactly. Gotta play the odds, O'Roarke. The girl witnessed a murder and then went AWOL. Her phone is AWOL and not pinging. Do me a favor and run all the cells in that area at the time she went *poof*. Maybe one of them will belong to our mysterious Jeep driver."

"Got it," he said. "And I'll call Donna Christie, see when she and her dogs are free."

"Thank you," Taylor said, trying hard to keep the sarcastic tone from her voice. It was clear O'Roarke wasn't thrilled with the direction she was headed, but she couldn't care less. Find Carson first. They could sort out the hurt feelings after.

There was a small, tonal beep. The PI had been silent until now, but she looked up in surprise. "Captain?"

"Yes, Ms. Abbott?"

"Sky is fine." She smiled, and Taylor was again struck by that sense of knowing her from somewhere, and not only as a rookie on the police force. "I agree with you about Avery Conway. My aunt Joy knows her, that's why I'm here, as a courtesy. My aunt went to school with Avery's mother—Carson's grandmother. They're all Vanderbilt legacies. Anyway, we've run a few reports, and there is a discrepancy in the information you've been given."

"There is?"

Sky nodded. "Apologies to you, Mr. Turley, but I just received confirmation that Avery Conway stopped off in DC on her way home to Connecticut on Thursday night."

"Washington, DC? Why in the world would she go there?" Turley asked.

Sky shrugged. "Probably need to find out. Unfortunately, I have a case out west, so I'll have to recuse myself. I just wanted to give you that information." She stood, and that was enough to break up the meeting.

Now that was interesting. The timing coincided with the strange phone call Taylor had received from Dr. Conway.

"I'll look into it, Sky. Thanks. All right, team. Tomorrow, same time. Everyone stay in touch. I'll be out by the lake trail with O'Roarke and the dogs this afternoon if anyone needs me."

The task force members began shuffling papers and laptops, murmuring to their teammates. Taylor called out, “Sky? Do you have a moment?”

The younger woman was almost out the door. She glanced at her watch, a flash of gold on her wrist. Old school.

“Just.”

“Let me buy you a cup of coffee. My place.”

TWENTY-FIVE

THEY TOOK the elevator to the ground floor and walked the half block to Taylor's building. Taylor liked that Sky wasn't chattering at her as they took the elevator to the forty-fourth floor. A very self-contained woman. Who looked so damn familiar...

"Oh! It just hit me. You're the lead singer of that awesome band who plays around town."

A smile cracked Sky's face.

"The Deathwish Bunnies. That's me."

"I remember seeing you at a New Year's Eve show at Grimey's a few years back. Pretty kick-ass gig. You're one hell of a performer. You've got a great punk rock voice."

"That's kind of you. Though now we're all off to many other pursuits, and I don't get many chances to sing anymore. Just the odd tribute show, like Grimey's." She'd lit up talking about her music. "You don't strike me as the punk rock type, Captain."

"Taylor, please. And trust me, I am. It's been driving me nuts trying to place you—I know you were on the force. That's what I want to talk to you about, but—"

Sky froze. "I'm not coming back, if that's what this is about."

"No, no. Not at all. So did you know Georgia Wray? I know the music's not the same..."

"Yes, I did. I mean, to say hello, nothing more. I met her at a Grammy party last year. We talked about British punk versus American country. She expressed a desire to expand her horizons."

"Interesting. Between us, her parents were trying to get her out of her contract. The case looked cut and dried, but we're reopening in light of the conversation I had with them."

Sky frowned. "Well, Travis Bloom is a shrewd businessman. The contracts will be airtight. She'd probably have to surrender her IP, which is, of course, exactly what no artist wants."

The elevator stopped and Taylor unarmed the door with key, code, and palm. Sky watched all of this with interest, but Taylor didn't explain. She opened the door, looked at the condo with the eyes of someone new.

Despite the Fort Knox measures, their place really was beautiful, as warm and homey as glass and marble could be made. The view itself was arresting; they had the corner of the building and could see north, east, and south, overlooking the bulk of downtown. The natural white oak floors were scattered with thick wool rugs; the furniture was modern but comfortable. By all appearances, it was the home of two very successful people. Happy people. She was glad their contentment showed. It was hard-won.

Taylor gestured to a leather stool in front of the counter, which Sky took.

"Coffee? Tea?"

"Diet Coke?"

"A girl after my own heart." Taylor grabbed two cans, cracked them, and dumped them over ice. Their refrigerator made cocktail balls, perfect-sized frozen rounds that went into old-fashioned glasses. They also kept a Coke cold and didn't melt right away, a major bonus for her.

"I'm thinking of leaving Metro," Taylor said, handing Sky a glass.

Sky simply nodded. "Sick of it, are you?"

Taylor blew out a breath. "No, it's not that. Chafing at the bit, I'm afraid. They keep promoting me, and I'm not really interested in the politics of it all. I like getting my hands dirty. Not my soul."

"Profound." Sky tipped her glass in salute, and Taylor laughed.

"That's me. Overthinking things. Anyway, you left. I'd love to hear about your decision process. Do you like working as a PI?"

Sky's shoulders were a fine line of tension. "I left. I'd rather not discuss why. But yes, I much prefer being a PI. A lot more freedom, a lot less bullshit."

Taylor took note of the discomfort. Interesting. Something had happened to Schuyler Abbott. She needed to look into that. "Understood. I'm more interested in how you're approaching law enforcement from the outside. Without the badge. How hard is it to accomplish your goals, get your solves, that kind of thing."

"You're considering becoming a PI?"

"Not exactly. Well, sort of, but on a different scale."

One inky eyebrow arched, then Sky shrugged. "It's like any other job. I grind it out. It's freeing, actually. Not as many rules. I have friends who can run interference if I need them to. Laws aren't broken, but bent every once in a while. Things that would get you shit-canned immediately for even thinking about, that's where we do our best work. You know there's a lot of gray space out there when you're working on an investigation. I lean into that. Your mileage may vary."

"Still reactive, though, yes? You get pulled into cases after the crime has occurred?"

"Yes, of course. Nothing to investigate if no one's been naughty. People don't come to us to prevent crimes. They come because their spouse had lipstick on his collar or a business thinks their employee on paid medical leave is bowling every Tuesday. Every once in a while we'll stumble into something bigger, head it off at the pass. But usually, it's routine."

"Don't you do corporate work, too?"

"Forensic accounting, yes. Some close protection, too, in the right circumstances. Most of my job is hands-on, out on the field. My aunt—the whole firm, really—is very technology-driven. Which is great, and gives us a lot of shortcuts. But I prefer the old-fashioned way, just me and a camera and my Walther, waiting for the nastiness to occur."

They chatted for a bit longer about both music and law enforcement before Sky looked again at that gold watch, men's size, almost drowning her wrist, and made her apologies. "I gotta bounce. My flight leaves in two hours. This has been fun, Taylor. Good luck with the decision. If I can ever do anything, you let me know."

"Before you go, tell me how you knew about Dr. Conway's stopover in DC."

"I could tell you, but then I'd have to kill you."

"Quit joking around. I'm dead serious, Sky. Something is going on behind the scenes with Conway, and the little tidbit you dropped confirms it."

She watched the woman calculate her answer. Finally, she sighed. "Macallan is trying to recruit you. I think you should reconsider. You're too good for Nashville to lose, and they aren't as squeaky clean as they look."

"Excuse me? How the hell do you know that?"

"PI, remember? It's my job to know things. Ask Thierry

Florian what he knows about all this. And seriously, I'm gonna miss my flight if I don't leave, right now."

"Are you warning me, Sky? Is that why you showed up at the task force meeting?"

That quirky black brow raised again, and she smiled. "You're a smart lady, Taylor Jackson. Figure it out."

Taylor saw Sky to the elevator, then returned inside and stood at the window looking over the city. Thinking. Thinking. What the hell was that? Did Macallan, and Thierry, actually have something to do with all of this?

Well, obviously, or Sky wouldn't have mentioned it.

You're an idiot, Taylor. Florian shows up right when things get spicy with Carson's kidnapping? Tries to lure you away in the middle of a huge case?

Didn't exactly endear the man to her. She lasered back in on their conversation.

"I have to solve a missing person case first."

"There are many people who can step into your shoes. There will be this case, then another, then another. They will never end. You will never be truly finished."

He wasn't entirely wrong. *Could* she give this up? When the next girl went missing, the next body was found, the next tourist was shot, or a serial killer dropped in to wreak havoc, would she be okay not fixing things? Could she possibly live here, in this glorious skyscraper, while the people around her suffered?

Proactive autonomy, she reminded herself. That's what Macallan was offering. *You'd stop the crime before it ever happened.* There wouldn't be any dead body or investigation if she beat the criminals to the punch.

But now a private investigator knew more about what was

going on than her team, and that didn't sit well at all.

She dialed Thierry Florian, but received a polite voicemail. She said, "It's Jackson. Call me ASAP," and hung up. Seconds later, the phone rang. Not Florian. Marcus.

She put the phone to her ear. "Hey, puppy. What's up?"

"We're ready to head up the mountain."

"Oh, good," she said, almost surprised at the strength in her normally cracked voice. "Pick me up in five."

She was putting the glasses in the dishwasher when it hit her. What had been bothering her for three days.

She leaned against the counter and called Marcus back.

"Almost there. Come on down."

"You go on ahead, I'll drive myself and meet you and Donna in the parking lot. I need to talk to the kid who wrote the GPS game again."

"Simeon Chase? Why?"

"How many people are allowed the same coordinates at the same time?"

"They're not. It's meant to be a singular experience, completely random."

"But what if it wasn't random? What if Georgia Wray and her boyfriend were playing the game, too? What if both Carson Conway and Georgia Wray had the same coordinates? What if what Georgia's parents think is true—that the fight Carson heard Georgia having with Justin was just that, a fight. And someone else shot her?"

"What are you saying, Taylor?"

"I'm making a leap, and this is assuming Jason Osborne didn't kill Georgia, but... They look a lot alike, don't you think? Georgia and Carson?"

A pause. "They have similarities, yes."

"What if the killer wasn't after Georgia at all? What if he was after Carson all along? What if he got the wrong girl?"

TWENTY-SIX

SIMEON CHASE ANSWERED Taylor's call on the second ring, sounding out of breath.

"Captain? Hey. Did you find her?"

"I'm sorry, Mr. Chase. No. I'm calling for a different reason. I have another question about the app you run. You said that the coordinates Carson and Izz followed were randomly generated. Would it be possible to have more than one player sent to the same set of coordinates?"

"That's not supposed to happen, no. I suppose a glitch could occur. The probabilities are incredibly slim, though every program is limited by its data points. Mine has over 50 million possible combinations per geographic space, so the odds of that happening are astronomical."

"So if two players asked for the same thing on the same day —enlightenment, say—the app wouldn't send those people to the same coordinates?"

"No. Definitely not. The algorithm is programmed to sense anomalies like that and generate different coordinates. Technically, thirty people could be standing in a group and all ask the same thing at the same time and be sent to thirty different places. It's meant to be completely random."

"But even random patterns can exist. Is there any way to look and see if the app has ever generated duplicate coordinates?"

She heard him typing in the background, waited patiently. A low whistle came through the phone, then a heartfelt and clipped "Bloody hell." Her heart sped up.

"Find something?"

"Unfortunately, I have. It never occurred to me that I could be the source of the malware on Carson's phone, but apparently, I was. My app has been hacked, Captain. There's code in here that I didn't write. It's going to take me some time to sort it out."

"Now we're getting somewhere," Taylor said. "How could your app be hacked? What sort of tools would someone need?"

"Only a decent keyboard, apparently," he grumbled. "Can I ask what exactly you need me to look for? I can spout hypotheticals all day long, but if I have an idea of what I'm looking for, that would certainly help."

"First, can you shut it down so whoever hacked it can't see what you're doing? I assume they'll figure out that you know now?"

"I'm not sure. I don't know how deep this goes. Without some serious diagnostics, I can't tell if whoever hacked me is still in the system, or if they've left a back door they can enter any time they want. I suppose I can take the app off the App Store, stop other people from downloading it in the meantime. Bugger. That's a project. This is not how I wanted my first app launch to go. I have an angel on the hook, too."

"An angel?"

"Angel investor. I was approached by a fellow from Oxford who wants to invest. I'd been planning to pitch some VCs—that's venture capital, the companies that invest in startups—but he came with a sweeter opportunity. He offered twenty million and only wanted a point in return. I couldn't say no. He won't touch me now. No one in their right mind would." He sighed heavily, and she heard the edge of tears in his voice. "This app is finished."

Taylor stared out the windows, thinking. "Before you pull the plug on your nascent entrepreneurship, Simeon, tell me about this 'angel.' Who is he, what access does he have to the app, and when did you talk to him last?"

"You can't think...bollocks, the bloke has access to it all. I had to show him the code to explain the possibilities, how I wanted to scale up. It was on a secure call, but...surely not, Captain. I would feel a right git if someone had offered me a sweet deal and simply walked in my front door."

"Sometimes the best criminals are the ones who screw you to your face, Simeon. Send me his details. Let me do some checking. And do not, under any circumstances, shut down the app. If someone is using it for their own purposes, we don't want to scare him off. I still need to see the records for last Tuesday, when Carson and Izz hiked the hill. See if anyone else had the coordinates."

"Yes, ma'am. I'll get everything to you straight away. The angel's name is Gareth Maughan."

"Is he well known in the industry? Someone easily tracked down?"

"No. Which is the only reason I haven't agreed to the deal. I was still doing my due diligence on his background. I'm too cynical by half, I'm afraid."

"Send me all you've done to track him, too. And thank you, Simeon. For being honest with me."

"I want her found as much as you do, I reckon. Maybe more."

"Maybe," Taylor said and hung up the phone. She called Lincoln, who yawned a hello.

"Sleeping on the job?"

"Flynn caught a stomach flu. We were up all night. What's happening?"

"I have data coming. Will you be able to run it?"

"Depends on what it is, but sure. What is it?"

"Simeon Chase's app was hacked, he's the source of the malware on Carson's phone. And he was recently approached by an angel investor named Gareth Maughan, who claims to be from Oxford, England. He offered a twenty-million-dollar investment for one point in return. Simeon showed the man the base code for the app, so there's a chance Maughan or his company have something to do with the hack. Also, Simeon is running the coordinates from Radnor to see if any of his players got the same ones. If we can find Georgia Wray's burner phone, we can see if she got the same coordinates. It's a big stretch, but with what Georgia's parents told me, I have to look at every possibility."

"Marcus told me you were running with the idea that the killer got the wrong girl. Do you think that's the case? He was after Carson all along, and Georgia and Jason got in the way?"

"I don't know. I feel like I'm grasping at straws. But something is hinky with the app, it's definitely been compromised. And we know Carson was having issues with her phone, and we haven't found the burner phone Georgia's parents told me she was using to contact them, either. There's something here."

"I'll start the second you get me the info."

"Thanks, Linc. You're the best."

She could hear the grin in his voice. "Don't you forget it."

She paced until Simeon Chase sent her a text that he had the data ready. She sent him Lincoln's way, knowing between the two of them, they'd find something worth looking at. Her gut was screaming at her. She was more than happy to listen.

That sorted, she pulled on her hiking boots and headed to Radnor Lake.

Maybe there was more to be found on the mountain.

TWENTY-SEVEN

THE INTENSE RAINS had left behind perfectly crisp fall weather—deep blue skies, low humidity, a tiny chill in the midday breeze. Yellow leaves littered the path. It was Taylor's absolute favorite time of year, the moment summer's back was broken and autumn paraded in. Summer seemed to last longer here in Nashville than it used to, well into September. Soon enough there would be cozy nights under blankets—though this year, their home's coziness was going to be manufactured: the fire was gas, not roaring, chuckling wood, and the view didn't encompass woods and deer, but soaring falcons and twinkling lights.

Quit it, she said silently, while rebelliously reveling in the woods surrounding her, taking deep breaths of fresh air as she climbed. *You chose to move downtown.* But at heart she was a country mouse—always had been. She missed nature, missed getting lost in the trees. If this wasn't such a somber errand, she'd damn well enjoy it.

The dogs were all business, a soft-eyed brown Labrador and a Bernese mountain beauty that came up to her waist, and she was a tall woman, nearly six feet in socks. The Bernese was a sweetie; the Lab, too. They had hard work to do, depressing, difficult, though rewarding in its morbid way. Their handler, Donna Christie, was also gentle and kind. Taylor knew she was a big reader, and respected her love for both her books and her dogs.

Together they hiked beside Taylor and Marcus, gamely trudging up the mountain. The path was steep enough that everyone was breathing heavily when they emerged into the small clearing by the graveyard.

"Will the graves throw them off?" Taylor asked, and Donna shook her head.

"Chances are they'll alert, you know they can pick up scents of bodies that have long since crumbled into dust. Did you know there are archeologists using dogs to search for ancient Egyptian tombs? Pretty incredible, if you ask me. I'd like to see it in action. So would the girls. Wouldn't you, babies?"

The dogs woofed.

Marcus staked out a perimeter for them to follow, and Donna let the dogs nose around the graveyard for a few. Both dogs alerted, sitting, vibrating with repressed excitement, which wasn't unexpected. Donna marked the spots, and then led the dogs to the northern perimeter, rubbed them on the chest, called "Search!" and unleashed them to do their jobs. She started back toward Taylor but was almost upended when the dogs rushed past her, right back to the graveyard, alerting again.

"Not there." Donna led them back to the northern perimeter. They went straight back to the graves. The Bernese added a mournful whine to her alert bark.

Taylor shrugged. "Maybe we need to take them farther away?"

Donna had a small shovel and brush out. "I might as well take a quick peek. They're pretty adamant. Until I look and satisfy their curiosity, we'll be here all afternoon watching them run back. It's strange, though. They're usually so good about listening when I give them a boundary. Give me five, we'll clear this area and start again at the northern perimeter."

Taylor walked to the edge of the path and checked her cell phone—the signal was down to one bar. "Marcus, how's your phone? Do you have a signal?"

"Got a hot date, Cap?"

She smiled. "Have you *met* Baldwin? I always have a hot date. I just wanted to check if there was anything new on that crazy website you love so much."

"WebDetectives? They're not crazy. They're—"

"A bunch of amateurs who like to cause trouble," she replied. "But a thread started yesterday that was interesting, about Georgia Wray being ambushed by a really aggressive fan a few days ago outside a nail shop. I thought we might track down the poster and see what they actually know. With all the accusations her parents made, I don't want to let anything slip through the cracks."

"'The Rules According to Taylor. Follow every lead, no matter how obscure.' I'm on it." Marcus looked at his phone, smiling. "Though my signal's crappy, too. I'll track them down when I get back to the office. I'm looking forward to Linc's briefing on Bloom. Could be something there."

"Agreed. There's just enough weirdness going on that I'm quite relieved we're looking deeper. The notebook paper, for starters. It doesn't match any of the notebooks in the house. Granted, it could be Georgia's. We need to nail that down. You up for another look through both their places?"

"Definitely."

The dogs began to bark, and Taylor looked over her shoulder. Donna was kneeling but rocked back on her heels, a look of sheer consternation on her face.

"What is it?"

Donna looked up and sighed. “The dogs are right. These graves have been disturbed, recently.”

Taylor’s stomach dropped, an awful burning sensation that signaled a spike in adrenaline and despair. “Disturbed?”

She moved closer. It didn’t take her mind more than a second to process what she was seeing. The long, thin whiteness of a bone. A leg bone, split apart in a compound fracture. White bone. Not the burnished look of one that had been buried for centuries.

Carson. Damn.

“Ah, hell.”

“Did we just find Carson Conway?” Marcus asked, voice low. No one bothered answering.

The Bernese whined. Donna shifted out of the way and Taylor saw the rest. A shock of blond hair, a piece of fabric. The body was clearly female, facedown. And beside it, a deep hole with a jumble of bones, hidden beneath the silty earth. Definitely fresher than she would anticipate from a grave nearly 250 years old.

Donna stood up, dropped her trowel, and whipped off her gloves. She pulled the dogs ten feet away and gave them a reward in the form of a hot dog split between them that she had in a baggie in her jeans pocket.

“Sorry, Taylor. I think we’re going to need some more help.”

More help needed was an understatement. They couldn’t just start yanking remains from the ground. While Taylor and Marcus paced and planned, dread building, Donna made some calls, pulling together her team.

“They’ll be here in an hour,” Donna said. “I don’t want to unbury her until we’ve had a chance to do a forensic sweep.”

"Makes sense," Marcus said, brushing dirt off his jeans. "I'll go down and meet them, bring them back up here."

Taylor shook her head. "No, that's okay. I'll do it. I need to call Avery Conway anyway."

"Is that the mom?" Donna asked.

"Yeah."

"Poor dove. Be sure you ask for her dentals, just in case."

"We should be able to do a visual, don't you think?"

"Most likely, but for confirmation, radiographs are a lot faster than DNA. Better to have them on hand, just in case."

"Roger that. See y'all in a few."

She hiked back to the parking lot, grabbed a couple of mints to crunch on from the console of her truck, then, steeling herself, called New Haven. Avery Conway answered on the first ring, breathless.

"Captain? Did you find her?"

"Dr. Conway, let me fill you in on what's happening. I don't want you to hear this from anyone else. We've found a gravesite—"

The animal wail was almost too much for Taylor to handle. She grit her teeth and fought back her own tears. *You're getting soft, Jackson. Pull it together.*

She could hear voices in the background, and the cries of a heartbroken mother faded.

"Ma'am, I need—" A man's voice cut her off.

"Captain Jackson? This is Santiago Diaz-Rooney. What's happened?"

"Hi. Is she okay?"

"Would you be?"

"No. Okay, listen. We found a grave, and a body, female Caucasian, that fits the physical description of Carson. I don't know for sure that it *is* Carson, but I promised to let you know anything as I found it out. It will be a few hours before we can confirm any identity. I wanted to be sure you heard this from me, officially, instead of through any rumors that might fly around. In the meantime, I need Carson's dental records."

She heard a huge gulping breath.

"It's just a precaution."

"Right. Right. Okay."

"I want to give you reassurances, but I can't. I'm glad that you're with Dr. Conway. I'll call you as soon as we have an identification."

"Thank you, Captain."

Taylor clicked off, took a deep, minty breath, then called Baldwin. She was shocked and delighted when he answered the phone.

"Babe? Where are you?"

There was frustrated laughter in his voice, and it soothed her. "I was about to call. You will not believe this. One of the organizers had a family emergency, they managed to get word to the captain through the Coast Guard, so we're heading back to port and will do the rest of the con from there. This means much more reliable service, so I can talk to you whenever I want. How is everything? Your last text was a little grim. You okay?"

"I'm sorry for the organizer, but glad to hear you're more reachable. I've missed you."

"I've missed you, too. So what's up?"

"We just found a burial site, and I'm afraid Carson Conway might be in it. It's on top of an old grave from 1776, if you can believe that. Out by Radnor, an old private family plot."

She brought him up to speed, happily accepting his words of comfort. She'd missed him, damn it. Too much for her own good.

They talked until the TBI mobile lab RV pulled into the parking lot.

"I gotta run, lab's here. It's good to hear your voice, Baldwin. I miss you."

"I miss you too, love. I'll be home soon. Call me later. I hope...well, I hope it's not her, though no matter what, it's bad. Anything you need from my people, say the word, and it's yours."

"Thanks, babe. Love you."

Taylor stowed the phone in her vest pocket, hailed the TBI team, and, grabbing a couple of packs, led them back up the trail.

TWENTY-EIGHT

NEW HAVEN

AVERY WANTED TO SCREAM.

She wanted to hit.

She wanted to rend the two startled men in her living room limb from limb until their shattered bones and dripping skin littered the floor and painted the walls.

She wanted to go to Richard's grave and demand answers.

She had never felt so impotent in her entire life.

She was an ER doctor. She knew pain. She understood it better than most. She knew exactly, empirically, what was happening in her somatic system, how she was overloading, how she was shutting down. How the grief was overwhelming her ability to think, to breathe.

She'd lost her husband. Her life.

And now her daughter.

The fractures developed, deep inside. Shards of ice, slicing through skin and bone and tendon. Her hands were numb. Her vision spotty. Her breath coming in panicked little sips.

Dead. Dead. Dead.

Stay together. Hold it together, damn it. There's still a chance...

The shrewd, nasty, subconscious monster who lived inside her, the beast who gave her powers and strength few possessed, who held her upright nightly in the face of hideous disasters, blood and gore, cruelty, silent killers, plagues and pestilence, all the horrors unimaginable to regular people, that monster inside her laughed.

Oh, get a grip. There's no chance; there never was. Your baby has been dead for days, deep in the earth, and you've known that, you just haven't wanted to admit it. And these people, these horrible people who have invaded your life, who have stolen your husband and now your daughter, they are to blame.

The stark words rose unbidden.

We have your daughter.

Two million.

No cops.

Why in the name of God would a murderer bother to make a ransom demand if he'd planned to kill Carson anyway?

The note said no cops.

You failed her, Avery. You failed your only daughter. Over and over again, you failed her.

All of this in a moment, an instant of delineated pain, and she realized there was a guttural scream filling the room, and it was coming from her, and she was crumpled on the floor with the arms of two men she used to love folded around her, her neck was wet from their tears as they cried together, a ball of confusion and agony and despair. Their loss was a bitter chasm; she would never find her footing again.

Just when she'd agreed to never come out, to stay in this Stygian place forever, her daughter's gentle eyes and sweet smile shone from within that darkness, and the barest whisper of a breath caressed her cheek.

"Get up, Mommy. Get up."

No no no no no.

"You must."

Avery came back to herself slowly. Carefully, carefully, finding the edges of her psyche, raw and sharp and burning, and yanking them together as one does the opposite sides of a billowing jacket on a cold windy day, until she was sheltered, only a bit, but enough to be able to shake off the men crouching with her, the men who'd loved her daughter as their own, and stand.

The breath she managed was great and shuddering, and her lungs reluctantly obeyed. Her heart beat once again. Her eyes cleared.

The audacity of the dead, to make the living continue on.

The men let her go. They watched with dark eyes as she stumbled to her feet, wiped a hand under her nose, knuckled the tears from her cheeks. Watched her spine straighten. Watched the animal caught in the toothy, rusted trap gnaw off her own leg to escape.

And looked toward each other for comfort when she snarled, "It is time we had a conversation."

TWENTY-NINE

CHANTILLY, VIRGINIA

THERE WAS a light on in the small office in the back of the warehouse, a golden shadow in the gloom. Angelie needed only to cross the space from door to office, the length and width of a football pitch. Easy, but for one small issue. Stationed every fifteen meters was a man with a gun. Six men. One Angelie. She didn't love the odds, but they weren't impossible.

There was no other way to reach Marcello Staley face to face. He lived in this warehouse, he worked from this warehouse, and he never, ever left. A hermit crab with a monstrous shell on his back. His server farm was always attended, the rows upon rows of cell phones in racks and the poor women he shipped in from Vietnam and Thailand practically strapped to their chairs click-click-clicking on the stalker programs went twenty-four seven. Running bots was a full-time gig; there were governments to topple and societies to ruin, after all.

Her finger tapped the scope of her rifle as she thought. The easiest thing to do was blast her way in, catch them by surprise, take out every guard, and put a knife to Marcello's doughy throat to get what she needed. Maybe let the women go free. But that sort of attack would draw notice from people she'd prefer to keep ignorant of her presence in the country.

In another life, Angelie Delacroix would not be sitting on the side of a hill in the mud debating her best course of action. She would have already taken the warehouse and gotten the information she needed from Marcello. Subtlety wasn't always necessary, and she'd never been concerned with it before. Once, the more people knew—and feared—her actions, the better. Now, she wanted to stay as far off the radar as possible. She was getting soft, worrying about the footprint she would leave behind.

There was another way in, and she was going to try it first. Since all of Marcello's physical security was inside, he relied on cameras only for the exterior. She could drive up, walk up, or otherwise present herself on the main grounds, and no matter what angle, what path, she would be seen.

But the tunnel was another matter. She knew Marcello well enough to know that there was no way in hell he didn't have a bolthole. And an underground egress was exactly the thing a snake like him would build.

If she could thread the needle between the cameras that were surely placed in a position to see the entrance, she could slip inside his lair.

She simply needed to find the entrance and disable the cameras. The map she brought had four possible places of ingress, unnatural mounds that stood out against the terrain on the detailed satellite views.

She packed up and started moving. The weather was about to turn, the air redolent of moss and ozone, and she didn't feel like getting any muddier.

She traversed the perimeter carefully, stalking the entrance. The first anomaly was a large rock, and the second was also natural. But the third, approximately 800 meters from the warehouse, had loose stones and what looked to be fresh sod. She knew there must be cameras and searched the trees but found nothing.

Too easy. But she was out of time.

She pulled a jammer from her pocket, a small device that would create a thirty-second series of blips on the monitoring screen, enough time for her to break cover and open the door.

Which was easily found if you knew what you were looking for. She pressed the button on the jammer and yanked open the door, waiting a heartbeat for alarms and shouts. Nothing.

Marcello was either getting sloppy or was so confident no one would think to come in through his rabbit hole that he'd left it unguarded.

She slung her rifle across her back, palmed her pistol, and headed into the darkness.

It all went to smash.

Of course it did.

Her intel was bad. They *were* waiting for her. The guards had been trebled because clearly someone knew she was in town. Three were waiting deep in the tunnel, all of whom she dispatched with six cadenced shots from the suppressed pistol —*head and heart, head and heart, head and heart*—and the rest were crawling all over the interior of the warehouse, on alert.

She didn't want to kill them all, but she had no choice. She did her job, and she did it well. Those who didn't go down in the first barrage of bullets she got in the subsequent firefight, sniping individuals from the tops of the multitude of containers. The very few who evaded the secondary assault, she took on by hand. It was noisy, and it was carnage. Exactly what she wanted to avoid.

Thirty minutes later, bloodied to the elbows, everyone dead

except for Marcello, who was on his way out with a stab wound to the kidney, she kneeled on his wet, meaty chest and snarled in his face, "Tell me, now. Where is Game?"

Marcello had the audacity to grin, his teeth rimmed in blood.

"Tell me," she shouted, but he shook his head, blew out a frothy red breath, and died.

"Fuck!" She screamed the word in English, then French, then dismounted the fat man and went to his precious computer. It was in a state of alarm, files erasing—he'd hit a self-destruct when she'd started the firefight—but she took a steadying breath and sat down, typing as quickly as she could to stop the chaos and reset the machine.

She was no hacker, but she had a few tricks up her sleeve for just this situation.

Marcello Staley was an information broker. He was the one dirty people went to for information on their enemies. He could hold entire governments hostage should he choose, and this information—invaluable information, years of intel, some of it provided by Angelie herself—was quickly deleting itself. Surely he had some backups for leverage and protection, and maybe she'd find them, but she had more pressing matters at the moment.

She searched through his machine—what was left of the programming—until she found what she needed. The last thing he'd done before he set his systems to crash was send a single text.

She's here.

The one person Marcello had reached out to in warning was the one she needed to find. Figures Marcello was in on it—at least her instincts were still intact. There was very little that passed Marcello Staley's notice, and Game was a favorite of his.

Always had been. Stray dogs manage to find one another, nip and bark and snarl until they find their place in the pack. Marcello was content to be the beta to the nasty alphas like Game, because he was the one in control of the shadows.

It was a shame that Game now knew where she was, and she'd remedy that immediately by getting the hell out of Virginia, but she had something he didn't know. His phone number. She could track him now. Sloppy, sloppy, sloppy.

She copied down the number, wiped the keyboard, and stepped out into the carnage.

Burn it. Burn it to the ground.

It was the only way.

By the time the animals of the surrounding forest registered the fire and began to scatter, the true danger to them was long gone.

THIRTY

NASHVILLE

AFTER HOURS OF CAREFUL WORK, Donna finally waved Taylor over.

"I'm ready. We've prepped the grave, and have the grid built. It's contaminated with the bones of the previous residents, so we're going to have some disarticulated remains to put together. We're going to remove the soil and screen it as we go, in case there's something here we're missing visually. When she's free, we'll move these remains to the west tarp, so the death investigators can get started, while I keep unearthing the rest. I'm assuming—well, hoping—that the original graves are still intact, because my ground-penetrating LIDAR shows multiple biologicals in this area. We're going to run late. My team brought lights so we can keep working overnight, and we're going to need guards on the site."

"I've already taken care of it," Taylor said. "We have patrols on their way. I've also documented your steps. Let's do this. If I need to make another phone call to an already distraught mother, I want to get it over with."

The bravado was just that, and Donna squeezed Taylor's shoulder. "I understand. Let's start."

These moments were always anticlimactic. So much effort to find someone safe, only to discover their body. Now it was just about the positive identification, and the case would turn from search to murder investigation.

There was no sound but the wind in the trees and the steady metallic bite of the trowel through the earth, the whoosh of the dirt hitting the screens. The group stood watch while the body of the girl was unearthed, letting the soul free itself from its resting place.

Marcus came to stand beside Taylor, arms crossed on his chest.

"You're quiet," she whispered.

"Yeah. I guess...I thought we had a chance. To find her alive." He shook his head, his hair flopping into his eyes. He brushed it back impatiently. "Have you ever thought about bailing on all this?"

She looked at him sharply. "Why do you ask?"

"So much death. It's everywhere."

"That's what happens when you work Violent Crimes, pal."

He knocked her in the shoulder. "You know what I mean. It's becoming oppressive. Nothing feels right anymore. You're not around. Price has that private security firm. Fitz is gone off on his damn boat and isn't ever coming back. Sam's moved to DC. Linc with a kid...even Renn and Hugh...I don't know. Our team was important to me. Maybe I'd be better off doing something else."

Now, this was interesting. She gestured, and they stepped farther away from the graves.

"If I tell you something, can you keep it to yourself?"

He nodded.

"I am seriously considering leaving Metro," she said. "If I do, would you be interested in going with me? It's a different kind of gig, but I sure would love to have someone I trust by my side."

"You're serious? You're really thinking about leaving?" There was hope in his voice, and she nodded.

"I have an offer I don't think I can refuse. And carte blanche to bring anyone I want. I would love to have you."

"And Linc, Renn? You're asking them, too?"

"No. They're not appropriate for this gig. There's a lot of travel, and a lot of risk. They have families. I wouldn't feel right offering to steal them away. And this is very much up your alley. International intrigue. Stopping crimes before they start. Proactive work."

"So I'm going to go all *Minority Report* on the bad guys? I'm in."

"You don't even know—"

Marcus huffed a small laugh. "Taylor. You've taught me everything I know about how to be a good cop. More than how to investigate, you've shown me how to work this gig with compassion and empathy, how to shut off my emotions and do what's right for the victims. You've taught me how to get justice for those who would never otherwise have a chance. I've tried to emulate you in all that I do in this job. If you think I wouldn't follow you down whatever path you lead, you're nuts. I'm in. You can give me the details later when we're not—" He waved a hand, and she nodded, pleased no end by his words and his decision.

"All right."

He tossed her a grin. "Just tell me we're not going to go be Fibbies. I don't want to cut my hair that often."

After what felt like a year, Donna finally said, "Let's turn her."

Taylor stood to the side while a Tyvek-suited TBI technician knelt into the soft earth, taking the body's shoulders. Insects that were still hiding under her body skittered away. Donna eased the head out of the dirt, gently twisting the upper half of the body free, and Taylor's breath caught. The face was missing, the insect damage and natural decomposition extreme. Too extreme.

"Oh, wow. That's not her. No way that's Carson Conway," Marcus said, kneeling down for a better look.

Donna nodded. "No, it is not. This one's been here a while. Six weeks at least." She used the small brush in her hand to gently sweep away dirt from the girl's hairline. "Who are you, sweetheart?"

"Shit," Taylor said. "I mean, thank God. Carson's still out there." Even in the face of the death in front of her, Taylor's heart lifted. A chance. They still had a chance to make this right.

It took another ten minutes to ease the body all the way out. The victim seemed to have been buried in an inverted pike position, bottom first into the grave, which was more like a pit, the remains awkwardly wedged in half, which had caused the long femur bone to crack apart and poke through the skin as if waving for attention. As the torso came free with a great spill of dirt, Donna stopped.

"Hold, hold, hold."

Taylor stepped forward. "What? What's wrong?"

"Come over here. Shine your Mag under her right arm."

Taylor listened, shining her Maglite at the dark space under the body. It took her mind a moment to catch up with her eyes. "Oh, God. Is that...there's more than one?"

"Definitely more than one, and definitely not that old. Older than these remains, but not as old as what I'd expect from these gravestones."

"Not Carson. Again."

Donna looked up, the glow from the Maglite and the setting sun casting her face an eerie silver. Taylor was able to clearly see the head and shoulders of another body, also awkwardly bent, also face down. But this body was far less recent, more than a year old, easily, the bones clearly showing inside the rotting fabric of what was probably a pink shirt at one time.

"No. Definitely not Carson. But Taylor, there are more bones in here. A lot more."

By the dark of the moon, and the white-blue beams of the portable lights, the grave reluctantly yielded seven sets of remains in total, in varying stages of decomposition. Donna quickly determined four had been added in recent history versus the ones that were buried nearly 250 years earlier. It wasn't hard to tell the difference, even to the laypeople. The depth of the bones, to start, was a dead giveaway. The new remains had been wedged into the ground above the three who'd lived there for so very long.

The nest, as they started calling it, was deep. Someone had taken their time creating almost an oubliette, boring down into the existing graves, stacking the bodies on top of one another, simply pushing down the previous inhabitants as new ones arrived to create a latticework of skeletons. Bones were broken, disarticulated, skulls separated from spinal columns at hideous angles. The burials had been violent, and unseemly. They felt impersonal, though, almost utilitarian. The nest was a disposal site, nothing more. It would be quite some time before they had an idea of the cause of death for these people.

Another tech was running over the whole site with a metal detector and hit pay dirt. A mobile phone, about 100 feet from where Georgia's body had been found. There was a declination in a fallen root, and the phone was nestled deep inside. The battery was dead, but with any luck, they'd discovered the burner phone.

They launched the drone when the sun came up, and it buzzed overhead like a mechanical hummingbird, searching the areas they couldn't easily access by foot, trying to find anything else out of place.

Taylor stayed until the bitter end, mainlining caffeine, waiting, watching, hoping, because she had to be sure, until the LIDAR and the dogs and the extremely skilled technicians and their fearless leader assured them all the bodies that rested on this land had been found, and then, with a slap on Marcus's shoulder and a thank-you to the team, she marched down the hill to break the news to Avery Conway that her daughter was not yet among the newly discovered dead.

THIRTY-ONE

CARSON CONWAY AWOKE TO DARKNESS. The room she was in felt small, and was devoid of light, devoid of sound. The wall she leaned against was covered in what felt like cushy foam, and the whole place reeked of some sort of chemical she couldn't identify.

The quiet was overwhelmingly claustrophobic. She'd grown up in a house full of noisy boys and their athlete friends, then moved into a dorm full of chattering people who couldn't care less about quiet hours. She'd been surrounded by a buzzing hive her whole life, and the only time she could remember such silence was the day they buried her father. The graveyard was so still that morning that even the breeze had died, and the birds quieted their trills. It was as if the earth had held its breath while they gave her father over to its eternal embrace.

She'd felt the same sense of claustrophobia then, felt the urge to scream and cry and shatter the air with her wails, and yet nothing would break the pervasive stillness, and its return was overwhelming. She longed for the dorm, for her home, for the bakery, the scratch of a rat, anything, anything. But instead, all she got was darkness and silence.

Is this what it's like to be dead? She'd wondered that more than once. Alone in the dark, surrounded by a velvet silence so complete she might as well be underwater? She was going to die; she just knew it. Would she meet her father immediately? The thought comforted her. If he was waiting on the other side of the veil, she could manage to stay calm until it was time to go.

She was tied to the wall, could feel something like bandages around her head and eyes. She was hungry and thirsty. There had been food and water at least twice, but she'd lost all track of time. She was alive, and for the moment, unhurt, though the quiet clawed inside her and made her want to scream. She'd tried that once when the food came but had been struck so hard she blacked out. She had kept quiet since.

She thought she must have been drugged because today—tonight?—her thoughts came with more clarity. Her memory was fractured, like looking into shards of a mirror, the reflections distorted. She remembered a Jeep. Thinking about the worry line between Simeon's brows when he talked. The stranger's face on the mountain, eyes wild and scared. Scared. He'd been scared. Scared that they saw him. But why? He had a gun. Izz! Was Izz here, too? Her mom was going to kill her. *Don't think about death, stupid. Bad luck.*

But she was going to die. She knew that. She was oddly at peace with the idea. That must be the drugs, or else she would be fighting to get away.

A scrape, to her left. She turned her face, heart smashing through her chest. She was blind but sensed a draft. The door must have opened.

He was here.

She whimpered.

He laughed.

THIRTY-TWO

WEDNESDAY: NASHVILLE

THEY MET BACK in the task force office a week after Carson had gone missing for Donna to give the presentation currently on the screens in front of them. Donna was a forensic anthropologist by trade and a natural leader. She'd kept her team busy, made meticulous notes, written up all the details, and took pictures as the bodies came out. It took a full day for her to work her magic, taking soil samples at every level, bottling the bugs they came across, everything they could find that would give them answers on how long the recent bodies had been there before she was willing to give Taylor more details. She was ready now.

The photos showed four skeletons laid out on the tarps. One was disarticulated entirely, one still semi-identifiable as female because of the remnants of a pink dress wrapped around her legs and the ratio of her hips. One was the girl they'd found first, and there was another, bones broken but still attached.

Donna laid out her conjecture for them. She pointed at each body in turn.

"Jane Doe Four, within the last ten years. Jane Doe Three, with the pink skirt, within five. Possibly a year or two for Jane Doe Two, she's the broken one. Jane Doe One, the one we recovered first, she's within the last six weeks, I'll bet. We've had a hot summer, the body was fully decomposed, but there was plenty of adipocere wax for me to get samples of. I have her in the CODIS database, looking for a DNA match. The rest will take me a little more time. All Caucasian, all between the ages of twenty and thirty."

"And for the record, that also confirms none of them are Carson Conway," Taylor said.

"Right. Not enough time has passed for this level of decomposition."

O'Roarke shook his head ruefully. "Man, Captain, I'm sorry I popped off. You were right. There is a serial up there."

Taylor gave the man a full-watt smile and enjoyed watching him blush. "Well, let's not get ahead of ourselves. We don't know what's going on yet. I just had a weird feeling and played a hunch. I'm sorry I was right. I didn't imagine we were going to find a killing field." To Christie, she asked, "Do we have any sense that there might be more?"

Christie shook her head. "The dogs and I did a full search, and nothing else showed up. I think this is it."

"Still, four bodies. I hope we can identify them."

"We will," Donna said. "They're all adult women, so that narrows it down a little. They're all in good enough shape to do the usual identification methods, and even better, we have four intact skulls with decent dentition. We'll take radiographs and put those into the dental databases, look for matches, but we'll also be able to do reconstructions, get an idea of what these folks looked like. Between that, dental records, and DNA, with luck, we'll be able to ID them quickly."

"How were they murdered?" O'Roarke asked.

Donna closed the laptop, and the photos disappeared from

their screens. "We don't know that they were. Yes, it's very strange to be burying bodies in someone else's grave, but until we get a thorough examination of these remains, we can't assume anything."

"But if they were murdered, you will be able to tell how?"

"I think so. It might take some time. We'll be working on all the angles. Dr. Fox and I have a date in an hour to start the process. It's long and drawn out, so the sooner I get out of here, the sooner you'll have your answers."

"Do you at least know who owns that land?" O'Roarke asked, clearly frustrated.

Taylor got it. Not having answers was always annoying, and this simply added to their workloads.

"The city, I think," Donna replied.

Marcus flipped open his folder. "Actually, technically, it's no-man's-land. Radnor Lake on one side, a new neighborhood on the other. The homeowners association owns the land up to the top of the hill. Richland Country Club is across the street on the other side. See?" He flipped a page and the screens lit up with a topographical map. "The city owns this side of the mountain. The HOA for the golf course owns this side. The graveyard straddles the edge of the HOA's greenbelt, but Radnor is parkland, and there's a case to be made that it's within the easement band that belongs to Radnor. Which means it would belong to the state. Your jurisdiction, O'Roarke."

O'Roarke threw up his hands. "Hey, I'm not about to start playing hot potato with all this. I was just curious. That graveyard dates back to the 1700s. Do we know who sold the land to the HOA?"

"I'm still digging into that," Marcus said. "No one has the records, but I've got a call in to the city archives. My buddy Kathy Lauder has retired, she would probably know this off the top of her head, but they're looking. Whoever it is is long gone, I bet. The HOA took over the land back in the '70s."

"What a mess," Taylor said, pulling down her ponytail and running her hands through her thick blond hair. "In the meantime, we need to pull all the missing person files for this region and be prepared to match them to DNA from CODIS. Maybe we'll get a few closes. Wouldn't that be fantastic?"

"It will, and I'm on it," Marcus replied. "Linc sent me the database. Remember all the old case binders we gave to the Cold Case Unit when they moved into our offices? They packaged them up and cataloged everything, so it's all online. Gonna make the search that much easier—assuming these ladies have been reported missing from the mid-state, of course."

"God bless Linc."

"No kidding," Marcus muttered.

"So what are our next steps?" O'Roarke asked.

"I propose we turn these four deaths over to Marcus to run full time," Taylor said. "We don't know yet if these people were murdered or just disposed of, though naturally, I lean toward the former. They need their own investigation, and I'm not willing to let Carson Conway's disappearance lose steam. Unless you're not okay with that?"

O'Roarke shook his head, though he hardly had a say in the matter. She'd learned through many experiences with multijurisdictional task forces that everyone needs to be respected and feel like they're being heard. That solves 90 percent of the problems.

Marcus said, "I can grab Renn and get on it."

"Good. I'll let Renn know we need him. The task force stays focused on finding Carson. This could be a giant coincidence, nothing more."

She wished she believed that.

"What about the phone?" O'Roarke asked. "Do you know whose it is?"

"We're waiting on our tech support to get it up and running. It was wet when we found it, might be fried entirely, but they're magicians. I gave them the passcode from Georgia Wray's parents, so if they can get the phone working, we can give it a try. It's a standard burner, digital SIM card. No usable prints or DNA. Chances are it's hers. But, and this is a big but, it doesn't negate the murder-suicide theory at all. It only means we have to look at Justin Osborne as a possible serial killer. He brought his ex-girlfriend to a place he knew was safe in order to murder her. Bad luck that someone was there and saw him. He panicked, ran, then shot himself when he realized his secret was going to be revealed."

O'Roarke fiddled with his notebook. "Feels weird, don't you think?"

"For a kid his age? Yes. But logic dictates we have to at least entertain the idea."

"I don't disagree. Can I see the man's home?"

"Sure. Not a problem. Anything in particular you're looking for?"

"I'll know it when I see it," he said, grinning.

THIRTY-THREE

TAYLOR DROVE O'Roarke to Justin Osborne's place herself, just to get a better sense of the man. She hadn't worked with him before. He was quiet, serious, and seemed to know what he was doing. She'd been fooled before, but he seemed like a decent enough investigator. Still, he'd challenged her, she'd been right, and now things were strained.

"Hungry?" she asked, lobbing an olive branch.

"Famished."

"I know this great little place. Donuts that will make you weep. That work?"

"I am more than happy to perpetuate our most overdone stereotype. Let's do it."

She got in the drive-through line for the Donut Distillery, ordered a six-pack of whisky glazed and an almond milk chai. "Coffee?" she asked him.

"I'll take a chai, too. Oat milk, please."

She parked in the lot, passed over his chai and some napkins, and they dug in.

O'Roarke moaned in ecstasy at the first bite. "I'm gonna be down here every day from now on. These are killer."

"They are. When'd you join the TBI?" she asked, wiping icing from her lip.

"What?" He looked over at her, then the question computed. He swiped at his own mouth with a napkin. "Oh. A couple of years ago. Moved here from Colorado, I worked with the CBI out there. Our daughter is at Belmont, we thought it would be better to be closer, so we all moved."

"Your kid's the same age as Carson, then?"

"Junior. But yes, this is hitting too close to home, if that's what you're asking."

"I bet."

The silence was less strained now. "What do you think's happening with that graveyard?" he asked. "Doesn't it feel strange to you that both Carson and Georgia Wray were so close to a killer's burial ground?"

"It does, absolutely. But honestly, now that we know Simeon Chase's app was hacked? I think a case can be made that someone was luring them to that spot. It makes much more sense to me than it being some sort of coincidence."

"So we have a killer who's managed to murder four women, and kidnap a fifth."

"Well...now we're getting into the area I don't feel comfortable speculating about. Until we get identifications on the bodies we dug up, and get an idea of how they died, we have no solid victimology. Without that, it's nearly impossible to profile the killer. Nor figure out if these are his only kills. Was he kidnapping people all along? If so, and Georgia Wray was his target, why didn't he kidnap her instead of shooting her dead on the mountain? How does Justin fit into all of this? Why go after someone so identifiable, like Georgia, and also go after Carson, who is a virtual nobody? We just don't have enough data to assume anything right now."

"You sound like the profilers we work with," he said.

"Not a big leap why. I'm engaged to one, after all."

"That's right. I haven't had the pleasure of meeting Dr. Baldwin, but I've read a lot of his work. He should write a book. His experience is invaluable."

"I'll tell him you said so." She finished the last piece of donut, smiling to herself. Baldwin writing a book was a great idea. She could just envision him, stacks of papers around him, piles of books and case files on the desk, cursing and pulling at his hair as he tried to pull together some knotty philosophical thread. Maybe she could talk him into buying a cabin retreat, pull a Walden Pond. They could disappear into the wilderness, and emerge with the definitive text on hunting psychopaths, with a twist.

They could call it *We Were Hunted*.

Maybe that wasn't such a cool idea after all.

"I wanted to be a profiler," O'Roarke said quietly. "Applied and everything. Didn't make the cut."

She looked over at him. He was pleating the knee of his pants, staring out the window at the renovated Victorian and Craftsman houses that lined the street.

"It takes a certain kind of person, O'Roarke. You don't have that darkness, I think. And that's not a bad thing."

"Hmm. Maybe. We're all dark inside, though, aren't we?"

"We're all made up of dark and light. It's the wolf we feed. Your wolf is light."

"Yours isn't?"

She didn't know how to answer that. "We better get moving," she replied instead, downing the last of the chai.

Ten minutes later, she pulled to the curb in front of Osborne's house. The scene had been frozen, but she noticed both the construction dumpster and porta-potty were gone. They'd been thoroughly checked, but damn. She didn't like it when material things changed around her scenes.

She told O'Roarke this as they stepped onto the porch. He frowned but didn't say anything.

The inside of the house was much as she'd seen it before, but the lights were working again, which was helpful. The bloodstained flooring was still in place; the cleaners hadn't been here yet. That was lucky. She had her photos from the day they'd discovered Osborne's body, and she showed them to O'Roarke, swiping slowly, so he got the full effect. He'd seen all of this before, in the files he held in his right hand, but it helped to be on-site, she knew.

The renovation had been nearly complete before the home's owner was murdered. Art leaned against the walls, guitar cases were stacked neatly in the dining room, and a full suitcase was open in the master bedroom. As soon as she released the scene, she knew Osborne's family would empty out the place. He had only an aunt and uncle on his father's side, it turned out, who lived out of state. Kid had given up everything to follow his dreams and the love of his life, and look where it got him.

Soon enough, the cleaners would remove the man's life essence from the living room floor. New hardwood would be laid, the renovations would be finished, and the house would go on the market. The neighborhood was trendy; homes aggressively priced and recently renovated were scooped up quickly. The turnover was extreme; this area drew the dreamers, and so few succeeded. Five years from now, no one would remember that a young man was killed in this space, except those who knew him.

What a damn waste, she thought.

O'Roarke walked through the house slowly, looking in closets and drawers. He lingered in the kitchen, relatively empty save for a microwave, three plates, two cups and two glasses, and a set of silverware. The counters were a gorgeous leathered marble, but the sink hadn't been set yet; the hole where it would go gaped at them accusingly. O'Roarke stood quietly, playing with what looked like a phone cord plugged into the wall.

"None of this works. Nothing in this place works with what's happening."

"I have to admit, I agree. Something feels off, but I can't place it."

"Roll with me here," O'Roarke said, leaning against the counter, crossing his arms on his chest. "So Osborne is our serial killer—"

"Like we said, he'd have to have started pretty damn young."

"Roll, okay? Let me play profiler for a minute."

She smiled and nodded. "Okay."

"So Osborne is torn apart over his girlfriend giving him the boot. Maybe he was already unstable, but this pushes him over the edge. He stalks a college freshman, hacks the app he knows she uses, programs the coordinates, lures her and his girlfriend to the top of the mountain, stages a fight with his girlfriend then shoots her, tries and fails to chase down the second target. He leaves the girlfriend's body out in the open and doesn't come back to put it in the graveyard he's been using for several years. The following day, he kidnaps the witness, stashes her away, and hurries back to his house to commit suicide." He shrugged. "Seems far-fetched."

"My point exactly. Too complicated, too many holes, too many illogical points. His laptop didn't show anything suspicious, and the journals, while upsetting, felt like the yearnings of a jilted lover, not a homicidal maniac. Was he upset? Did he make threats? Yes. And we can't for a moment discount them. That's how schools get shot up, when we pretend not to see the madness staring us in the face.

"But the creeps I've dealt with in the past have such an edge to them. Someone who's been curating a burial ground for ten years? That's a special kind of pathology. No. Osborne isn't our serial killer. Did he kill his girlfriend? Probably, especially because we know he shot a weapon because of the GSR on his hand, but I'm not 100 percent on that either."

O'Roarke was nodding. "Agreed. Assuming, though, murder-suicide, let's set Wray and Osborne aside for the moment. A stranger stalker, someone who is trying to get his hands on Carson Conway, learns all her habits, sets her up with the app, brings her to his graveyard so he can kill her, and damn bad luck, another couple is there at that exact spot having a homicidal fight. Your target freaks and runs. Now you have to lay low for a day and then snatch her off the street instead of having the privacy to kill her and bury her as you'd planned. Chances are, you know we've found your burial ground and you're on the run, too."

"Also possible, more likely, though still wildly coincidental."

He played with the cord again, looking closely at the end of it.

"What's missing from this scene? You've seen the evidence logs, I assume."

"Yeah. Nothing terribly exciting. A laptop, that's already been cleared by my lieutenant's team. The notebooks, none of which, from what I've seen, say he's suicidal or planning to murder his girlfriend. He's pretty pissed off at her, but it feels passionate, not desperate. Though who knows, if he'd been planning it for a while, maybe he just didn't record all his thoughts. Also, don't forget the paper of the notebooks doesn't match the suicide note."

"Right. But there's nothing about this."

He yanked the cord from the wall and tossed it to her. She caught it midair.

"A phone cord?"

"Look closer."

She did, running it through her hands until she got to the very end. It was a branded cord, from a major retailer. She looked up to see O'Roarke with a huge grin on his face and the file listing the evidence removed from the house open on the counter, a big forefinger stabbing the center of it.

"There's no mention of any sort of voice-activated home assistant. But that cord that goes to a smart speaker. I'm sure of it."

"Which means..."

"Someone took it before you got here."

"Again with the assumptions. It could be to an eReader. Or a phone."

"It could. There are plenty of universal cords. But this is a charger for a specific smart speaker. I know because I have the same one, and it doesn't charge any other of my devices because it's a different voltage and connector. There isn't a smart speaker on our evidence list."

She thought about this for a minute.

"Okay. Assuming he owned one, and that cord isn't something the contractors left behind—remember, this place has been under renovation—you think that maybe, if Justin Osborne was killed instead of dying by suicide, the killer took it with him, knowing he could have been recorded?"

"Criminals aren't always that smart, but it's not outside the bounds of reason. And these devices have been known to record accidentally. It's a shot in the dark, yeah. But it's something."

"Okay," Taylor said, setting the cord on the counter. It was just nutty enough to be a possible lead. "This is going to take some legwork. And paper. This company isn't going to hand over audio recordings for us to comb through. The hoops we have to jump through because of the expectation of privacy are mitigated because the owner is dead—assuming we can find the records that prove he was the owner of this phantom device —but you're still going to have to convince a judge to give you a warrant for the records, and that's only if you can prove there was one registered to this address."

"I can do that. It might be a challenge, but I've got a feeling there's something here." He grinned again. "My light wolf is howling."

"It's yours, then. Run with it. I'm open to most anything right now."

She glanced at her watch. "I gotta go grab up one of my detectives to work the graveyard IDs. Can I drop you back at the task force HQ?"

"That would be great. Fingers crossed I can get this moving quickly."

"Fingers crossed it gives us something to go on," she replied. "Good work, O'Roarke. We might make a profiler out of you yet."

THIRTY-FOUR

TAYLOR DROPPED O'ROARKE, now significantly more impressed with him, and headed across town to see if she could talk Detective Renn McKenzie into interrupting his paternity leave to back up Marcus on the new graveyard case. She wove her way through the city, took Granny White Pike to 12 South, marveling, as she always seemed to do now driving in Nashville, at how much it had changed. She used to drive up this road when she was a teen, off to do naughty things after her curfew in the park by Lipscomb University. It was a quiet place then, but now, the streets were jam-packed with houses, many of the original cottages torn down in favor of monstrous modern multilevel homes.

Hugh and Renn had been married for a year now, after the chaos that created their first meeting—Hugh's familial home had been chosen as a crime scene for a freak of a killer named Gavin Adler, aka The Conductor. They'd been discreet, but the connection between them was obvious to everyone on the case. Hugh was a hugely successful Hollywood script doctor—interesting, charming, creative, handsome—and thankfully, not involved in the crime, but a target of the killer himself. Renn was a stellar detective, one who'd surprised Taylor with his nuance over the years. Taylor thought they were great together.

Hugh, understandably, couldn't continue living in a home that had been desecrated by a murder, even one that had been in his family for years, so they'd taken all the exquisite art and books and moved to a slightly less charming but more family-friendly and spacious home near the university.

Taylor pulled up to the new Tudor, unable to stop the grin that split her face. A pink sign in the extremely green front yard welcomed a baby girl to the family. Staked in the grass next to it was a blue sign welcoming a baby boy.

Twins.

Taylor clambered from her truck and knocked. Renn answered, a finger to his lips.

"Come on in," he whispered. "We just got them down."

"Renn?" Hugh called loudly from the recesses of the house. "Who is it?"

On cue, there was a squawk, then a lusty cry. Renn sighed happily, shaking his head in mock disgust. "Hugh insists that we run the vacuum and play music and make all kinds of noise so they will be less anxious, but guess what that accomplishes?"

"No one's had any sleep this week?"

He hit the side of his nose. "Got it in one."

He noticed the bottle of wine in her hands, and the gaily striped bag stuffed full of gifts, overflowing with tissue paper. "You didn't need to do that."

"Yes, I did. I don't have any babies to spoil anymore."

As she said it, a wellspring of sadness ran up the back of her throat, seizing the rest of her words. She hadn't indulged a child since Sam's twins. Renn, knowing what she was thinking, folded her into a hug. He didn't ask; he didn't need to. He simply held her until she nodded, once, twice.

"Wow. I'm getting weak in my dotage."

"You're human, Taylor. Sucks, but it's true."

"Yeah. Maybe. Before we go through, I have an ulterior motive. I hate to tell you this, but we need you. We've discovered a grave near Radnor Lake, and there are four women in it who need names."

"You're kidding? That's awful."

"I know you're on paternity leave. Marcus is running it, and normally I wouldn't ask—"

He held up a hand. "Of course I'll help. Don't tell Hugh, though. Let me handle him. He might panic at the idea of being here alone. Twins." He laughed softly. "Who would have thought. Ready to meet them?" he said.

"Yes." She saluted. "Lead me to the progeny."

She followed him through the exquisitely decorated living room to a bright and sunny den stuffed full—a single-piece curved couch, two cradles, two cribs, and countless piles of stuff took all the available floor space. It looked like a pink and blue confetti bomb had gone off.

Hugh had both babies in his lap, staring at them like they were perfect diamonds pulled directly from the earth. He looked up at Renn, smiled, then grinned at Taylor.

"People will think I'm their grandfather."

"They already think you're my dad," Renn said, laughing, and Taylor's mouth dropped open.

"No! Tell me."

She settled on the couch, yanked off her boots, and drew her legs up under her.

"Oh, yeah. Went to dinner a couple of weeks ago and the hostess—who was ten, I might add—asked if my *dad* and I wanted to sit at the bar or in the dining room. I thought Hugh might stroke out on the spot."

"I was having a bad hair day," he said, and they all burst into gales of laughter. Hugh's hair, while thick and full, was a vibrant, snowy white, and at first glance made him look older than he was. Second glance, however, confirmed that he wasn't ready for Social Security just yet. Though he was a full thirteen years older than his husband, he hardly looked like Renn could be his son.

"You're the perfect age for babies," Taylor assured him. "You have just the right seasoning not to get spooked when one of them does something dumb."

"Perfect age for *a* baby." Hugh chortled. "Twins? I'm telling you, we couldn't believe it when it happened. Janey, our birth mother, was just as shocked. The doctors missed it until she was almost seven months. This little one"—he patted the baby on the head—"was hiding behind her big brother. We paid Janey double for the rent, and she was cool with it. She had them a few weeks early, which is why all of this"—he spread his arm around the room—"is still here and not up in the nursery. We weren't entirely prepared."

"One never is, I'm told," she assured him.

"And we didn't want to tell anyone until we knew they were both okay," Renn added, ducking his head in apology.

"No need to explain."

Renn smiled. "Well, a little need. We figure one belongs to each of us." At her confused look, he smiled wider. "We mixed the sample. So we'd never know for sure who was the biological daddy unless we did a test, which we have no desire to do. But now—I'm telling you, she looks like Hugh, and he looks like me. We may have just tricked Mother Nature."

With that, he picked up the pink bundle and held her out to Taylor. He wasn't kidding. The little girl had the shape of Hugh's face and chin exactly.

"So this is where we make a speech about how much you mean to both of us, and how valued you are in our lives, but I know you don't like speeches, so..." Renn's smile grew soft. "We named her Bethany Athena. Will you be her godmother?"

Taylor was stunned into silence. Bethany was her middle

name. Tears pricked her eyes, and she swallowed convulsively. Damn it. A little girl named after her? Renn McKenzie and Hugh Bangor knew exactly what button to push. Finally marshaling her emotions, she managed, "I'd be honored," and, after cleaning her hands with an antiseptic wipe, took the small bundle from Renn's arms.

Taylor snuggled her in like the expert auntie she was and ran the tip of her finger down the baby's perfect little nose. "Hi, little girl. We're going to have so much fun together."

Her namesake looked deep into the eyes of this new and lovely face peering down at her, gave a perfect, sweet little yawn, and shit her adorably tiny pants.

It was a solid thirty before they had the chaos reined in, and Taylor, now wearing one of Renn's T-shirts, her own in their washing machine, was once again holding her goddaughter in her lap, this time not an atomic weapon but changed, fed, watered, and making faint sucking noises in her sleep. Her brother, Byron Apollo, was tucked into Renn's arms next to her, his face perfect and elfin, just, she had to admit, remarkably shaped like Renn's. Hugh cracked the champagne and poured out three mimosas, and they were opening presents and telling lies when Taylor's phone rang.

She wanted so badly to ignore it, but with multiple cases revolving, she knew she had to answer. Hugh took Bethany, and she lifted the phone to her ear.

It was Lincoln, voice nearly shaking with excitement.

"We got a lead. Thanks to some reverse hacking and Simeon Chase's devious little brain, we were able to get into Carson's phone. We have a possible location."

THIRTY-FIVE

TAYLOR HURRIEDLY BRIEFED Renn on what she needed from him and was assured he'd be happy to help, especially if he could work from home. She had no issue with that and promised extended leave once the case was at a good stopping point.

She kissed the babies' heads and Hugh's cheek, then hightailed it to the task force office. Lincoln and O'Roarke had assembled the team. They were waiting for her. Energy thrummed through the room when she walked in, excitement and fear, and impatience.

"Okay. Show me."

Lincoln had a map projected on the wall, with a red X over the roof of a house.

"Simeon Chase did a reverse-engineering of the hack. There was tracking software on Carson's phone. You can see the path the phone took as it pinged." He clicked his trackpad, and a path of red dots lit up. "Straight from Vanderbilt to this house in North Nashville. It hasn't moved since. I've already called SWAT. They're gearing up if we want to make entry."

"Are we sure she's in there?"

"Her phone is there, for sure," O'Roarke said.

Taylor enlarged her screen. "If we go in with SWAT and it's someone who's bought the phone or found it, and something goes south..."

"I agree," Lincoln said. "I'd feel better much better with a visual. But I want to get into the house ASAP."

"Who lives there?" she asked.

Another screen popped up, this time with records from the state.

"Property records have the house listed in the name Alice Shay. Most recent records say there are three more living there —Shawna Shay, Roberta Shay, and Theodore Burnkin. Looking at the ages, I'd say three generations, and maybe a partner? Doesn't mean that's right, could be more living there, or less."

"Do we know who they are?"

"There's an Alice Shay who was a nursing student at Meharry that matches, and a Roberta Shay with that address who's a math teacher over at White's Creek. Shawna—I'm assuming the mom—looks to be in and out of town. The last employment I could find for her was with Metro, in the admin department, but that was over ten years ago. There's a disability claim with that name. The socials don't match, but it could be her."

"Chances are it's her. Okay. So tell me about Theodore Burnkin."

He flipped the image. Burnkin's face came onto the screen, nondescript outside of a badly set broken nose and thick jaw. The nose made her think he'd probably played contact sports, once upon a time. Taylor tried to read his eyes but got nothing.

"There's not much," Lincoln said. "Got a record, but it's simple stuff—a DUI when he was in his early twenties, traffic violations, a failure to stop. He did traffic school. Nothing harder. Nothing that screams kidnapper to me. He doesn't own a Jeep, either."

“Damn it. None of them have ties to Vanderbilt? If Alice is a nurse, she could have worked there. Maybe they—”

“She’s eighty, Taylor. Retired long before Carson got to Nashville. If there even is a connection between the two, it’s tenuous at best.”

She took a loop around the table, came close to the screen. Traced the **X** over the cottage with a finger.

“I’m the first to admit I’m grasping at straws. So what do you suggest? Surveillance? Or break down the door?”

“Honestly? I vote we knock. Try polite, be ready for all hell to break loose.”

Assembling an entry team took only an hour. They kept it quiet, off the radios, staged a couple of blocks away so they wouldn’t alert whoever was in the house until they were ready, but time was short. The media listened to the scanners, as did a number of civilians who broadcast on Twitter every move Metro Police, Fire, and Rescue made. If the knock went south, it would be all over town in a heartbeat.

O’Roarke had opted to join them, bronze hair sticking up in the breeze. Lincoln was barking orders, and Simeon Chase was on the Telegram app from back in his apartment near campus, giving Lincoln tracking data as it came in. Taylor had refused to allow the boy access to the crime scene—she had no idea what was about to go down, and didn’t want to chance getting a civilian hurt, even if he was helping them with the tech. There were things the city leaders would forgive, and things they wouldn’t. Simeon Chase was not a cop.

She also reached out to her assistant, Delila, and told her to let Huston know they had a lead on Carson, and that Taylor would be in touch shortly with more info.

“That is the best news, Captain. I’ll let her know.”

She did not call Avery Conway. After their last exchange, Taylor thought it prudent to wait until she had all the facts instead of keeping her promise to keep Carson's mother up to speed with every step.

SWAT rolled up, and Taylor greeted the team, giving them as concise a briefing as she could. The last time she'd made entry with them, it had been across town in Green Hills, at Hillsboro High School. She shook off the memory, as well as the slithering chill that subsumed her. She'd been forced to kill the teenage suspect to save the student he was trying to murder, and despite extensive therapy, she'd never truly gotten over it. It was only by the grace of her friend Ariadne that she'd found some semblance of self-forgiveness. By killing one, she'd saved so many. Still, the boy's black eyes haunted her dreams, too often morphing into another, darker presence. The Pretender was dead, too. She was free from his evil.

Get your head in the game, girl.

Once the teams were assembled, they didn't waste time. They had to be careful, couldn't just bust down the door without cause. They had no proof Carson was inside this house other than her phone, and Taylor knew the rules. To compensate, she put two snipers on the roofs opposite the little house, thankful, for once, for a tall and skinny that gave them such an advantage over the cottage across the street. There were eight SWAT members geared up behind her. Joe Keller, the department's hostage negotiator, stood with one arm leaning against the mobile command unit, ready with his phone and script.

Huston called Taylor's phone, but she ignored it. *Not now, boss.*

"Can I get a SITREP?" Taylor said into her mic.

The spotter, up with the snipers, had been silent until now, but his mic flared to life, relaying movement in the house.

"Got an adult male, pacing. Living room. Kitchen. By the

stairs. Back to the living room. Thank God these curtains are sheer. I have a decent view."

"Do you have eyes on the girl?" she said into her mic.

"Nothing yet. Looks like he's alone."

Someone from the SWAT team who she didn't recognize unrolled a set of blueprints and slapped them on a hastily-erected card table, knocking a half-consumed cup of coffee to the pavement. Everyone dodged the splash, murmuring and glaring.

"Sorry," he said, his voice deep and low. "The house has a basement. It's possible the victim's down there. So be careful with the flashbangs if you start tossing them in. The place catches fire, she could be stuck underground, unable to get out."

Taylor's armor itched. She scratched the tender base of her throat and pulled the shield back into place.

"Okay. Lincoln and I will approach, and I'm going to do the knock. Y'all be ready, stay back so that they don't see you. But be close enough to come in right behind me if he overreacts."

The spotter said, "If we're doing this, we gotta move. Neighbors up your way are stepping out of their houses, we're drawing attention."

"We're going now. Linc? On me."

She wasn't wearing her uniform, had donned jeans and a turtleneck over her body armor instead. She knew there was a chance she was going to get reamed by Huston, but she did have her badge strapped to her belt. Lincoln was similarly set up, and with a nod of readiness, the two of them walked down the block to the address.

"Anything?" Taylor said, hoping against hope the spotter could see something, anything, that could tell her what she was walking into.

"Pacing's done, TV just went on. Looks like he's settling in to watch something now. He's seated on the couch, approximately two meters west of the front door entryway."

"None of the women are in there?"

"Don't think so. No movement or lights anywhere else on the premises."

Don't know so either, she thought. Shit. This felt sketchy.

They reached the concrete steps up from the sidewalk. The house was well kept, with a small garden in the side yard, the perfect place for flowers and veggies to soak up the southern sun. The garden was fallow now, ready for the colder weather to set in.

"Okay. Here we go."

She unsnapped her holster and let her fingers touch her Glock, then drift to her Taser. She had a small knot in her stomach, wariness, and something else. This felt wrong all of a sudden, but it was too late to pull back.

With a glance at Lincoln, she used her left hand to knock on the door, sharply, three times.

The spotter's voice in her ear said, "Movement, he's moving, he's coming to the door."

She stepped back to give herself some leverage if she needed to make a quick entry through the door. It opened, and the man she recognized from the photo as Theodore Burnkin looked at her quizzically, then in total alarm.

"Oh God," he moaned. "No. Please, no. Tell me she's okay. Tell me she's not hurt."

"Mr. Burnkin, I'm Captain Jackson. No one's hurt. We just have some questions."

"Oh, God. Thank God." He shut his eyes briefly, and she blew out the breath she'd been holding, starting to relax, just as Burnkin bolted. He slammed the door behind him, catching her knuckles, and she ripped her weapon from its holster and kicked open the door with a curse, bursting into the house after him, screaming, "Bring SWAT, bring SWAT." Lincoln took off to the left to circle around. Burnkin's feet pounded down the hall-way, and she was right behind him, three steps away, two... Her instincts told her to fire, to stop him, but she resisted. She wasn't going to shoot unless she had absolutely no choice. And she wasn't going to shoot him in the damn back, either.

Burnkin disappeared through a door, thudding down the basement steps, and she halted before tearing down after him, her back against the doorjamb. Lincoln pulled up opposite her, his Glock out. She could hear the rumblings of the SWAT team as they made entry, knew it was only a matter of moments before Burnkin did whatever he was planning and this would be over.

She held up her fingers to Lincoln in a silent *three, two, one*, then they dove into the stairwell.

THIRTY-SIX

CHAOS.

Darkness.

Screams.

The hot fire of a bullet, whizzing past her ear, then a barrage from behind her.

She hit the deck, and rolled up against something hard, boxes or a small table. SWAT was in now, the basement overrun with burly men and women, taking up too much of the small space. Lincoln was shouting; Taylor's ears were ringing from the close-quarter shooting. She couldn't hear, couldn't see.

Silence.

Just for a moment, just a heartbeat, but in the tiny pause, her senses righted themselves.

Theodore Burnkin was five feet from her position, on his side, mouth wide in a scream, stretching his arm toward a shiny object that her primeval brain registered as an explosive device.

She knew she screamed the word *bomb* aloud because there was another barrage of gunfire, and Burnkin went flat and still on the ground just as Lincoln yanked her backward by the collar and pushed her up the stairs in front of him, and then they were out of the basement, out of the house, into the street. SWAT poured out of the door behind them like drunken ants, and seconds later, a soft *whump* resonated, almost gentle, before it roared to life. The sound was followed by the percussion, then the whole house went up in a ball of fire that tossed everyone in the vicinity to the ground.

An hour later, the fire had been put out, and chilly water gushed through the street. Neighbors for two blocks around had been evacuated until the area could be cleared. The media, with their long-range cameras, were peering into the scene from any angle they could get. A chopper flew in tight circles overhead, broadcasting live.

Taylor did her best to avert her eyes from the curious gazes of everyone around. She still couldn't hear properly. She sat on the tailgate of an EMT's truck, a chemical ice pack pressed to her wrist. She was sore and bruised all over, her lip was split, and her chin sported butterfly stitches from where she'd hit the ground when the bomb went off. Her clothes were smoky and torn in a few spots.

But she was alive. Lincoln was alive. The entire SWAT team was alive.

Theodore Burnkin, though, was dead.

And if Carson Conway was in that basement, she was dead now, too.

She heard Huston coming before she saw her, which was saying something, considering the damage to her ears. She struggled to her feet, tossed the ice pack behind her.

"You!"

"Commander Huston. My—"

"Shut up. Right now." Taylor didn't think she'd ever seen Huston so pissed off. She looked like a tiny deranged bumblebee. "I want you in my office in twenty minutes." She stormed off toward the media scrum.

Uh-oh. This was not going to be good.

Taylor slid off the tailgate and followed gingerly. Huston had taken up a spot near Dan Franklin, and Taylor realized they were about to give a statement. She should be there. She caused this, this was her case, her mess. But Huston stared back at her, eyes shooting daggers. She pointed over Taylor's shoulder, jabbing her finger, mouth set in a grim line, and it was very clear that her presence was not being requested.

Taylor forced herself not to limp toward Lincoln, who was chatting with the spotter and one of the snipers, standing wary with baseball caps backward. They'd tucked away their long-range rifles—the public tended to get upset when they saw such sophisticated weaponry.

"Hey," she said. "You okay?"

"Better than you," Lincoln said, reaching for her wrist, which he touched gently. It was visibly bruising. "This hurt?"

"All of me hurts."

"I didn't mean to push you down."

"Linc. Trust me. You don't owe me any apologies. I owe you one. We should have—"

"Don't start that. We did this fine, turns out the guy was a squirrel after all."

"Yeah," the sniper said—his greens had the name "Marshal" on the pocket. "Righteous moves, all the way around. We'll back you up, don't worry. God knows what the dude was planning. We probably just saved a whole lotta folks."

"When will the scene be cool enough to get inside and see if she's in there?"

He shrugged. "Dunno. Twenty-four hours, at least. I thought I saw another person in the east corner, but things were chaotic. Hoping I'm wrong."

Taylor spied the media moving back to their vans and cars. The presser was over.

"I gotta run," she told Lincoln. "Command performance with Huston."

"I'll come."

"No. You stay here. Someone needs to keep this scene under control. She's just going to ream me out. She's seriously ticked off."

"Check in with me later, then. I want to talk with Simeon, see if he's found anything else on the phones. He's smart. I wish I could use him more, but don't worry, I won't let him get his feet wet. Maybe just a toe or two."

"Good. We're in enough trouble as it is. And Linc? Thanks. You saved my life. I won't forget it."

He hugged her gently in response. "Can't do this without you," he murmured. "Don't let her get too feisty with you."

"You know I won't." She tried to smile but it made her lip hurt to stretch, so she settled for patting him on the shoulder with her good hand and strode off.

Taylor's truck was two blocks over. She dug her keys out of her pocket, rather amazed that they were still there, and drove back toward headquarters. She stopped at Walgreens, grabbed a chemical ice pack, a bottle of Advil, and a stretchy Ace bandage, which she wound around her wrist. At least they had Velcro now instead of those stupid metal clips, which made it much easier to finish off. She was thankful it was her left hand she'd hurt. She must have fallen back on it, but the whole thing was a blur. She remembered the panic building in her chest as Burnkin went for the explosives, and then they were outside, she was on her face in the street, and the house was going up in a plume of smoke and ash.

She shook it off, literally, flipping her hair off her neck, bits of glass and wood hitting the ground. She was a mess.

When Taylor walked into her office, Delila gasped and jumped to her feet.

"Oh my goodness, Captain. Are you okay?"

She waved her good hand. "I'm fine. We're all fine. Just a little sore. Huston back yet?"

Delila's face fell. "Five minutes ago. She said to tell you to get in there the second I saw you."

"Off I go, then."

Huston was standing at the window, looking west to downtown and the darkening sky.

Taylor knocked on the jamb. "Commander?"

"Come in and shut the door," Huston said without turning around.

Taylor didn't bother sitting.

Huston opened with a killer. "I've half a mind to take your badge and gun."

"Ma'am—"

She whirled around and attacked, a small tiger in her fury. Taylor had never seen this side of her boss. It was unnerving.

"Shut up. You're listening, not talking. You went off-book. You endangered the people of this city, your team, SWAT. There are steps we follow. There are actions we take. You inform the proper chain of command. Do you have any idea how bad this looks? What were you thinking?"

Taylor didn't speak, only hiked a brow, and she could have sworn flames rose in Huston's eyes.

"You may answer, smartass."

"I was thinking I might have a chance to find Carson Conway. There was no way of knowing Theodore Burnkin had a basement full of explosives. The girl's phone pinged and we went for it. We were trying to save her life."

"You didn't follow protocol—"

And that was it. The simmering volcano inside Taylor lit.

"Fuck protocol. A girl's life was in danger. I did exactly the right thing, going in after her."

"You didn't know she was there at all. You had no confirmation. And you nearly got yourself and nine others killed, not to mention the suspect. And Carson Conway's probably dead as well.

"I know that. I'm beating myself up enough. I don't need your guilt trip, too."

That took some of the fight out of Huston. "Taylor. Listen to me. The FBI has had Burnkin under observation for weeks. They knew he was buying up explosives. They have a whole team on him. If you'd taken five minutes to explore things, you would have known that. Instead, you strolled right up to his house, panicked the man, and he blew himself up. And probably Carson Conway, too."

Shit.

"Listen, if the FBI is operating in my city, they need to fill me in. If they were watching him so closely, they should have known if he took Carson or not. And they should have flagged his file. We looked closely, and there was nothing to indicate—"

Huston ignored the latter comment. "Your city. *Your* city? Like the whole town revolves around you, and what you need? You have to play the game, Taylor. You need to start acting like a captain, not some rogue beat cop."

"I am not after your job, Joan."

Huston stopped dead, then leaned forward, hands on her hips. "Excuse me?"

"You heard me. Things have been weird with us ever since I took the captain position. Which you foisted upon me, if you recall. I was perfectly content running the Murder Squad. I don't want this." She waved a hand around the well-decorated office. "This isn't my end game. I am not your enemy. I am not trying to push you out so I can have control. I am better suited to the street, and we both know it."

Huston's voice was steady, but there was an underlying surprise that Taylor had never heard before. "You might not know this, Taylor, but I did you a favor letting you come back, bringing you into the leadership. You lost your nerve after the shooting, after the death of the Pretender. He got the best of you —of us all—but *you* especially. I wanted to make sure you still had a home on the force, so I gave you one."

"I did not lose my nerve. I got shot in the head, for Christ's sake."

"You don't get it, do you? That man was working with us for months, on the inside. The city leaders wanted your head on a pike. I did you a favor. I went to bat for you. And you aren't cut out for the street anymore. Today's debacle proved that in spades."

"That's completely unfair. I was following a lead and it went south. It happens."

"Not if you follow protocol. You are a danger to yourself and others, Taylor Jackson."

"I—"

"And you're off this case."

"Commander. Joan. You can't—"

Huston slammed her palm on her desk. "I can, and I am. I will not have this agency run amok under my watch. Things are tenuous enough as it is, we don't need the bad press this is inevitably going to bring. Not to mention another young girl is most likely dead, and a slew of bodies have been found. I am putting together a team who is capable of doing things the proper way. They will take over, and they will liaise with the task force in place, and with Carson Conway's family. Take a few days, Taylor. Think about what you *really* want."

"I *want* to solve this case. I want to find out why Carson Conway was stalked and kidnapped. I want to find out why Georgia Wray was killed. We are so close. Don't do this, Joan."

The setting sun gave one last spike of gold in the sky over

her boss's shoulder, blinding her for a moment, as if it was saying farewell.

"And *I* want you to disappear from my sight before I say something I'll regret. You are dismissed, Captain Jackson."

Taylor moved before she thought. Her badge was in her hand. Then her gun. She dropped out the magazine, which fell on the floor, pulled back the slide, ejecting the bullet that lived there, always ready and eager to take a life, and dumped both badge and gun on Huston's desk, slamming them down with an almighty clatter.

"You don't get to dismiss me, Joan. I quit."

THIRTY-SEVEN

NEW HAVEN

AVERY CONWAY'S new phone rang at 5:17 pm that Wednesday, and she knew, without answering, that the news was bad. That terrible sixth sense of motherhood, a curse as much as a blessing, that tied you to your child whether they were young or grown.

She was in the kitchen, staring at the pantry, hungry but not, trying to decide what she could throw together that would sustain her for another day. Food tasted like cardboard; it mattered not what she ate, nor how well seasoned—it was empty.

The phone was on the counter. It was in a midnight-blue case, the latest Apple model, nearly too big for her slender hands, definitely too big for her small jeans pocket. Somehow Santiago had programmed the whole thing, so when the ringer chirped crickets at her, she had the image of Carson conjured in moments.

She didn't want to answer it.

Alan was babysitting her at the moment and entered the

kitchen silently. He looked at her, then at the phone. "Want me to—"

"Yes," she said quickly.

He snatched it up. "Dr. Conway's phone. Yes. Yes, she's here. I'll put it on speaker."

A crackle and hiss, then a woman's voice. "Dr. Conway, this is Commander Joan Huston, Metro Nashville. We have some news. Your daughter's phone was tracked to a house in North Nashville."

"Did you find her?" Avery cried, grabbing the phone from the counter. "Can I talk to her?"

"Ma'am, there was an incident at the house. We're investigating, but it's going to be several hours before we will know anything. We tracked the phone to the home, and when the investigators attempted to speak with the resident, things went a bit sideways, and there was an explosion. The suspect is dead. We weren't able to ascertain if he was holding Carson at the residence or not. Once it cools down, the scene will be more closely examined, and we'll know if anyone else was in the home. I'm sorry I don't have more, or better news, at this time."

It was cruel, really. To know Carson might be dead—again—and at the same time, she might not. But the last nightmarish call had given her a stoicism she didn't know she had in reserve.

"Who was he?" she managed.

"His name was Theodore Burnkin. We're trying to establish a connection to Carson right now. This is a multifaceted case, and we're doing everything we can. I will be in touch as soon as we've cleared the scene and are able to determine if Burnkin was the only one in the house."

"Where is Captain Jackson? Why isn't she calling me? She and I have unfinished business."

A lengthy, charged pause. "Captain Jackson has another case to manage. We have a task force in place, which is being led by Lieutenant Lincoln Ross, who has been working closely with Captain Jackson. We're going to find out what's happened, Dr. Conway. I will be in touch the moment I hear something."

She rang off, and Avery stood gaping at the phone.

Alan was typing furiously on his, then raised the phone to his ear. "You heard all of that? Burnkin, Theodore. Yes. Yes. Get back to me."

Avery whirled on him. "Is he one of yours?"

"I've never heard the name before. We're checking now." His face softened. "Just because her phone was there, that doesn't mean she was. Don't lose hope." His phone rang and he put it to his ear, listened, then hung up.

"There is no connection that we can see. Burnkin is on the Feds' radar for possible terror ties, but he's not someone we have been tracking. They're saying a second body was suspected to be on site, but that can't be confirmed."

"So there's a chance this was just a fluke?"

"Phones can be manipulated. Someone could have dropped it outside that house. Sold it. Stole it. Faked the signal. So yes. There is a chance Carson is still alive."

Avery's legs buckled, and she sat hard on the stool at the marble counter.

"I don't know how much more of this I can handle."

"It won't be long now. Angelie has gone off-grid, which means she's hunting. She'll find Game, and this will all be over. I promise."

"I want to talk to Jackson. It sounds like she was shunted off Carson's case for some reason."

Alan nodded. "It does. But there are always two sides to the story. Hang in, okay? We should know more soon." He excused himself, leaving her alone in the kitchen.

She ran a hand over the marble. She'd never felt this much pain, not even when the New Haven police came to her door with the news about Richard's accident. *His murder,* her mind helpfully corrected. Having Santiago and Alan hovering over her while all of the chess pieces moved on a board she couldn't see... She was in over her head, but it didn't stop her from wanting to get back on a plane to Nashville and find out exactly what was happening from the captain herself. She hated the woman, was furious with her for how she was handling the case, and yet, her doctor's senses were on fire. There was something else going on.

She dialed the number from memory, steeled herself when a woman's husky voice answered.

"Captain Jackson? It's Avery Conway. I've heard about the explosion, and that you've been reassigned."

A pause. "Doctor. I thought you might be in touch. I'm sorry. I don't know what else to say."

"Was Carson in the house?"

"I honestly don't know. The situation is fluid."

"And you're no longer working my daughter's case?"

"No, ma'am. I'm not. I shouldn't be talking to you at all. But I think you're owed the truth. I don't know what you were told, but we tracked Carson's phone to that house. I was trying to save her life. I don't know more than that yet. I'm sorry," she said again, and Avery knew she meant it.

"What am I supposed to do now? Wait? Again?"

"Unfortunately, yes. The best people are on this. I trained them all myself. They'll figure it out."

"If she was your daughter, would that answer satisfy you?"

The smoky ghost of a laugh. "Of course not. I'd be furious like you are, and rightly so. But it's all I can give you, Dr. Conway. I promise, should things change, I'll be in touch. But I'm not giving up. I might be off the case, but I'm not giving up."

The urgency in the captain's voice sparked a nerve inside Avery. "Don't. I want my daughter back." Glancing over her shoulder, knowing she was alone, she whispered, "Look at Joseph Game," then hung up, setting the phone on the counter. It was foolish, they were clearly listening to her phone, but damn it, she wasn't content to sit back and wait anymore. As furious as she was, she trusted the captain—a total stranger—more than the men she'd been friends with for years.

She heard the babble of angry voices from the hall, and smiled to herself, even as Alan came into the room like an angry bull facing a matador and snatched the phone from the marble counter as if he could undo the call.

"That was stupid and reckless. The captain is a loose cannon. She tries to go up against Game herself, Carson will die, and the captain will, too. You may have just condemned them both. Do you have any idea what you've done?"

"Yes," Avery said simply. "I do."

THIRTY-EIGHT

NASHVILLE

TAYLOR COULDN'T SLEEP.

This in and of itself was nothing new. A lifelong insomniac, she'd tried every trick—melatonin, CBD, prescription drugs, alcohol—and finally agreed with Mother Nature that she would forever be a four-hour-a-night kind of girl and stopped trying. Besides, she often solved cases in the wee hours of the morning. She'd take the dark smudges under her eyes if it meant getting justice for the people of her city any day.

Tonight, though, her sleeplessness was well earned. Her wrist hurt. Her lip throbbed. Her chin itched. She kept replaying the fight with Huston over and over, a loop of righteous indignation. In the replays, she said all sorts of things to her boss, from reassuring platitudes to an all-encompassing "fuck you and the horse you rose in on."

Which, in a way, she had said. All of that. And more.

She replayed the moment over and over. The finality of it still shocked her. Before she could take it back, she'd stormed out of Huston's office, gathered up her things from her office, driven home, ignored all texts and calls, and seethed.

Huston had been incredibly unfair. And Taylor had overreacted. Possibly. Probably. Definitely. Not at all.

There was never going to be the right time to quit, but she hadn't wanted to burn down the house when she did.

She'd call her union rep tomorrow and deal with the fallout, but for tonight, she'd decided to smolder in her righteous indignation.

Taylor had at the very least wanted to touch base with Carson's mother, feeling a sense of responsibility, but knew better. Not only could it make the department liable, but it could also open Taylor up to a civil lawsuit. She trusted someone on Huston's new team would do that, was pleased that it was Huston herself.

So she was surprised when Avery Conway had called her instead, though she felt like a heel telling the woman she had nothing for her. Then Conway had whispered something about a game and hung up. Taylor had no idea what that meant, and she was too tuned up not to agree. This *was* a game to some, and that pissed her off.

Baldwin had left several messages and texts, having seen the news about an explosion, and when she finally connected with him on a video chat, he was about to teach the evening session and couldn't talk for long. If he felt dismayed at her decision, he was smart enough to keep that to himself. When she finished the recitation, including the explosive end to an already explosive day, he didn't hesitate to reassure her.

"You're okay, and that's all that matters. You can talk to Huston tomorrow, once you both cool off. She'll ask you to come back. You watch."

"Doesn't matter if she gets on her knees. I'm not going back."

Baldwin's brows furrowed, but that was the extent of the

reaction.

"I'm serious. This wasn't a fit of pique. You know I've been unhappy for a while."

"I do. And I support you making a change." Taylor appreciated the vote of confidence and told him so. He was quiet.

"But?" she asked.

"But." He laughed gently. "It's me being overprotective, but I'm worried about you going to work for Macallan."

"Why haven't you mentioned that before?"

He glanced at his watch. "We need to have a nice long chat about this, but unfortunately, I have to go. Just promise me you won't make any sudden moves before I get home, okay?"

"Any more sudden moves, you mean?" She twisted the simple diamond band around her finger, feeling closer to him as she did.

He laughed again. "You do keep things exciting, my dear. I'll call you later. Love you."

"You too." Then she called Sam, who whooped and hollered and cheered so loudly Thor woke up and started barking madly in the background. They had a good old-fashioned bitchfest about everything, and she hung up grinning.

Talking to them both made her feel better enough to have some dinner, though she pushed away her plate of spaghetti halfway through. Huston was right, she had screwed up royally. Though damn the FBI for not letting her know about their operation. And damn Huston, too.

She cleaned up the kitchen, showered, took a Unisom, and climbed into bed. She managed almost three hours before her eyes flew open, and she spent another hour restlessly staring at the ceiling, replaying the day, saying small prayers for Carson Conway and Georgia Wray.

Her beloved pool table had been a bitter casualty of the move—their building had a games room she could access any time, so she and Baldwin decided it was easier to leave it behind for the folks who bought their house. The billiards room here, with its dark oak paneling and bookshelves with green- and brown-spined leather books, was very British and very enjoyable, but taking the elevator down just wasn't the same. In the wee hours of the night, instead of playing, she'd developed the habit of pacing the condo. It had a similar soporific effect on her brain, an almost trance-like detachment that allowed other thoughts to rise and fall naturally instead of being forced into being. Like a novelist who gets a great idea in the shower, the mindless activity rewired the avenues of her brain. Movement meditation, Sam called it, and Taylor thought her best friend wasn't entirely wrong. Lord knows Taylor couldn't stay still long enough to reap the benefits of an actual seated meditation —she'd tried, it was *not* for her—but the walking meditation worked wonders.

She climbed from the cloud of a bed Baldwin had bought and started into the living room. She smelled something subtle, the gentle notes of hyacinth and rose. She stopped, senses suddenly on high alert. The scent was familiar in the abstract way of olfactory memories—she recognized it but didn't know why.

She eased back into the bedroom and lifted her backup weapon from its spot in her night table drawer as quietly as she could, chastising herself as she did it—*you've become too paranoid*—but felt better with the weight of the small Glock in her palm. She hugged the walls as she moved toward the living room again. In the reflected lights from the building next door, which beamed blue and red slats in her shadows, she saw a bouquet of flowers lying on the living room's glass coffee table.

Her first thought was *Baldwin* and a brief moment of joy sparked within her. Just as quickly, she thought *Maryland,* and her gun was up, pointed at what now looked like a female shadow on the couch.

"Hello, Captain."

THIRTY-NINE

HEART THUNDERING, Taylor tamped down the adrenaline rush, fighting the urge to simply squeeze the trigger. There was a glint of metal, and she realized she was looking at the wrong end of a pistol. *Shit*, she thought, finger tightening just as Baldwin's face flashed in her mind, and she was comforted that the last thing she'd ever see was an image of him, the one thing in her life that truly mattered, had a heartbeat to think *Oh, Baldwin, I'm so sorry* when Angelie Delacroix stood, gun in hand but now at her side, and said, "Please don't shoot me. I am here with a business proposition."

There was a beat. A pause. A moment.

A million responses flowed through Taylor's synapses at the same time, mainly the fact that she was already pressing the trigger and needed to stop, but was this a trick, some sort of weird assassination, and if so, why hadn't Delacroix just shot her the first time she started into the room, and what the hell was up with the flowers? Realized just as quickly it was an advance warning system so that Taylor could be armed before she faced her assassin, because Angelie Delacroix somehow knew—understood on a basic level—that if Taylor had come across a woman with a gun sitting in her living room unarmed she would have felt like a failure, and though it could have been Delacroix's way of laughing a bit, it was also a way to let Taylor save face. Taylor didn't know if that was better than being killed outright, or if it was just one of those stupid things that her brain latched onto in the moment, the beat, the pause, before she released the pressure on the trigger. She didn't lower the gun, but she relaxed her stance and slid her finger out of the guard.

When faced with a terrifying situation, a normal person panics, and often freezes. When a professional who's been trained over a lifetime to be able to laser focus in a life-or-death situation is faced with the same, it would be a lie to say there isn't fear. Of course there is. But the amygdala of a modern, trained combatant is more in tune with its ancestral brain chemistry. If a caveman hesitated, he or she would be eaten by the saber-toothed tiger that caught them unawares. They lived in a state of constant readiness. Always ready, always alert, always on—that was how Taylor had lived for almost her entire adult life, and she knew the woman across from her had as well. There was fear, yes. But there was also a burning curiosity about why she was still breathing when an assassin of Angelie Delacroix's caliber had drawn down on her at close range.

"What in the hell are you doing in my house?"

Angelie Delacroix smiled, white teeth feral in the darkness. "Thank you for not asking how I got in. That would be an insult to us both. These systems are so easy to overcome if you know how to manipulate them. I'm putting away my weapon. Would you mind doing the same?"

The voice was cultured, with a French accent and a baffling hint of humor in its tone.

"So I can trip over a wire and be blown to pieces instead? Sure."

"I assure you, Captain Jackson, if my interest was seeing you dead, you'd be in heaven already."

The bitch of it? The woman was right. Taylor had been lulled into complaisance by the elaborate mechanics of their new security system. She should be dead, she knew it, so what did she have to lose at this point?

"Why now?" she asked.

"We'll get there," Delacroix replied, drawing her legs underneath her like a cat settling in for a nap. "Sit." Another pause. "Please."

Taylor sat, the Glock loose in her hand. But still there. Still there.

"I need to tell you a story," Delacroix said. "Would you like a glass of wine?"

Flowers. And yes, a bottle of white wine.

"Are you trying to seduce me?"

Angelie Delacroix's laugh was surprisingly joyful for a woman of death. "In a way, yes, I suppose I am." Her face shifted in the gloom, and her voice was now a bit husky. "Would you like to be seduced? You are a beautiful woman. I could make you feel things your FBI agent never imagined."

"Thanks, no. Get to it, will you? I have other things to contemplate tonight."

"Ah, yes. Sweet Carson. Another beautiful girl missing from your jurisdiction. One might think terrible people target your city simply to involve you in their worlds."

Taylor was intrigued enough to ignore the slight. "You're here about Carson? Do you know where she is?"

"As I said, I'm here to tell you a story." Delacroix reached out and Taylor tensed for a moment then realized she was just going for the glass on the table. She took a deep sip of the wine and set the glass back with a tiny clink. God, she'd been in the house long enough to help herself to the wineglasses, too. Silent as a cat. A lucid thought. *Thank God Baldwin isn't here.* While

Angelie Delacroix might be extending grace to Taylor, she doubted that would go for Baldwin. His teaching gig had saved him, of this she was sure.

"I'm trusting you with my life," Delacroix said suddenly. "Thierry says I can, and while Thierry and I have a long history, some of it very grim, as you know firsthand, I do respect him. And he respects you. So for now, I must, too."

"I'm honored."

"Sarcasm doesn't become you, Captain."

"Quit calling me that and I'll stop being sarcastic."

"A bargain." She took another drink, deeper this time. Taylor sensed the woman was gearing up and was reluctant to share what she was about to.

"A story," Delacroix said again, softly this time, and started to talk.

FORTY

SOME FAR-FLUNG LOCALE

THERE WERE FIVE OF THEM. Angelie, Santiago, Richard, Alan, and Joseph Game. She was used to working with the men, and rarely had issues in the field, though Game would be just as willing to bed her as he was to work by her side. She didn't like him, never trusted him fully, but told herself it was just his demeanor, just the way his shoulders were set, as her mother used to say when she took a dislike to a man. *"The set of his shoulders tells you everything, Angelie. Whether he is kind, or brutal. Pay attention to how he holds himself when he is relaxed, and you will always know what sort of man you are dealing with."*

How she remembered this sage advice, given when she was possibly five years old after a man had leeringly accosted them in a shop in Varennes, and her mother had shooed him off with a few sharp words that made his leer turn ugly, was beyond her. She'd given up trying to remember her parents. The only images that came when she thought of them purposely were filled with blood and bone and shattered glass. Deep, corrosive fear. The sharp ping of bullets hammering into the side of their car. Her father, telling her to live.

Angelie did not dwell upon them, instead welcomed the strange unbidden memories that came with a sight, or a sound, or a smell.

The first time she'd met Joseph Game, her mind had taken her to the leering man in the store in Varennes and her mother stepping between Angelie and the brute with a snapping "asshole" in colloquial French and the man's angry face. She looked at Game's shoulders, how he was rounded a bit, hunched forward toward her, and identified him as a predator. So long as he wasn't hunting her, she was fine with him on the team, especially since after one small hint that he wouldn't mind a taste of her, she'd dealt with it so firmly and devastatingly fast he never glanced at her sideways again.

But a man like that always holds a grudge.

At first, it was little things. Retrieval times miscalculated. Backup weapons missing. Egress vehicles on the wrong street. Sloppy work, work she complained about to the rest of the crew over beers after jobs were complete, who agreed. Later, when it was clear he'd stopped worrying about retribution for pissing her off, it got more specific. A cut strap on a parachute that she only caught at the last moment. A backpack full of empty magazines when she was alone in the forest with no backup.

But when he leaked her real name to a client, that was the last straw. She had to eliminate the client, then had it out with Game in an abandoned warehouse in Kuala Lumpur, which left them both bruised and bloody. He'd managed to slither away, and when she staggered out, barely alive, she went to Thierry and insisted the man be terminated.

Thierry cut Game from Macallan but didn't put out any paper on him. He was allowed to live. It infuriated Angelie, who felt he was a danger to all of them. But she was overruled.

Regardless, Game did not take the news well. He made many threats, oblique and concrete, and then he disappeared.

It was always a bit disconcerting to have a highly trained assassin fall off the radar. Not that they were looking over their shoulders, but still. One likes to know where one's enemies are.

The crew heard rumors, now and again. He'd joined up with a group of Colombian drug lords, was murdering his way across their borders. He was working with the Russians on destabilizing the US government before the 2016 election. He was in Hong Kong, fomenting dissent and organizing protests. He'd died in Haiti after the assassination of the president in 2021, which was proved false when he was caught on film at the airport in Kabul at the Abbey Gate, shoulders deep in the evacuating masses, the same day thirteen US soldiers were killed.

And they all knew he'd been in New Haven. Richard's death was just the beginning of Game's retribution. He was being patient, and he was going to be thorough.

Taking Carson Conway guaranteed Santiago and Alan would get involved. And Santiago's first call had been to Angelie.

Two birds. One stone.

NASHVILLE

Angelie finished her story and waited expectantly for Jackson's reaction.

Finally, Jackson shook her head. "I don't know what this has to do with me."

Angelie tamped down the rising frustration. "Avery Conway decided to read you in when she gave you the name Joseph Game. I need to know what actions you've taken to discover his whereabouts."

A moment of confusion flew across the captain's pretty face before recognition set in. Angelie didn't know what that meant, and it made her uncomfortable.

"I require this information. Game is dangerous. Retrieving Carson unharmed is my only goal here. You will help me."

Jackson's poker face was back in place. "You just told me you can access anything. Why don't you just pay someone off and break into our databases?" She stood and flipped the wall switch, bathing them in light. Angelie flinched but did not move. The avenging angel was back, eyes narrowed, hands on her hips.

"I don't appreciate you breaking into my house. I'm sorry you have an issue with this former teammate, and I'm sorry you lost your friend. But I can't help you. We have nothing. We have no idea where she is, and I've never heard of Joseph Game."

"Ah, but that is not entirely true. I heard Avery tell you to look into him."

"She whispered something about a game. That's all I heard. I didn't realize she was giving me a name to investigate."

"Game killed the singer and her boyfriend. Surely you've put that together."

Jackson still had the Glock in her hand. Angelie tracked its progress. "Why do you think so?" Jackson asked.

"He died of a suicide, correct? It is one of the easiest ways to murder, and a favorite of Game's."

Angelie watched Jackson's forefinger tap against the gun. "What do Carson Conway and Georgia Wray have in common?"

"Coincidence."

"I don't believe in coincidence."

"And yet, it happens. Daily."

Jackson shook her head. "Nope. Not good enough for me. I'm happy to put your man's name into our database—"

"He is a ghost. He will not be in your database."

They stared at one another for a moment until Angelie was

certain she could read the Valkyrie's mind. "You were looking for me, were you not? I was nowhere to be found. I am very good at my job, Captain Jackson. As is Game. We would never be so sloppy."

Jackson gave her a little smile.

"No? I wouldn't be so sure. You left quite the mess back in Maryland. Even the best can't help it when their sweat lands on their lover in the act of congress."

"C'est impossible."

"*Non impossible*, at all." Jackson's French pronunciation was surprisingly good. "I have your DNA. And I bet, as careful as you've been over the years, you've left a trace here and there. I put it in the system, who knows what might pop." She put the gun into the waistband of her yoga pants, sat down, and crossed those impossibly long legs. "No one is a ghost. What's the real connection between the girls? Tell me that, and I'll know you're serious."

Angelie was struggling for self-control. Was Jackson bluffing? Did she truly have a usable DNA sample? Chances were it wouldn't matter; even if something showed up, Thierry could make it go away. But the trouble that would cause—she might lose the château, and that was anonymity she was not willing to lose.

"I don't know that there is any connection," Angelie answered, honestly. "I genuinely believe it was bad timing for them. If you dig deep, you'll see Carson was being tracked. It's a favorite ploy of his. He likes to play with his prey. He followed her, probably for weeks, intending to take her, and when he found the perfect spot, was surprised by the singer and her boyfriend. He had to eliminate the threat."

She watched Jackson think this through and pressed her advantage, leaning forward, dropping all pretense.

"I am not playing around here, Taylor. The daughter of a man I knew, a man I greatly respected, maybe even loved, is missing, through no fault of her own. I may not be an honorable woman in your eyes, but friendships are rare and treasured. Game killed my friend, and he's going to kill the girl because he knows it will draw me out. He's playing his end game, and I can't let the child be hurt. She's innocent, and I want to save her. That is all. I need your help. You know the world here. You have information. You are my shortcut. Time is running out for her, I can feel it. Game is a sadist. God knows what he's done to her already."

She got to her feet. Jackson tensed, but Angelie held up her hands.

"Men like this make our lives hell. We are grown women. We can handle a man like Game on our own. Carson is a child. She will be scarred for life because of this, but perhaps we can mitigate the depth of her horrors. But only if we move quickly, together, to find her. You are a very good investigator. I would appreciate your help. And Thierry wants us to work together. He feels we need a fresh start if we are both to work for him. Believe me, I will go it alone if I must. I'd rather have your help."

Jackson was playing with the tips of her ponytail. A nervous twitch, a tell? Angelie didn't know, but she thought she had her on the hook. Finally, Jackson said, "You're supposedly retired."

"Not supposedly. This isn't a job. It's a personal mission."

"Then I'm sure you already know Carson's phone pinged at a house today. A house that blew up. We don't know if Carson was inside or not."

"She wasn't."

"How can you be sure?"

"It is not his style. That was a diversion, at best. The man in the house was being investigated."

"I wasn't aware of that until after the fact. How were you?"

Angelie smiled. "If I knew it, so did Game. What better way to get you off his back than send you into a lion's den, the home of an unstable man who is planning an attack on the city? Allow you to be a casualty of your own desire to do good. From what I can see, he nearly succeeded."

Jackson touched her split lip self-consciously. "Then where has Game taken Carson?"

"That is what we must find out. I believe she is no longer in the United States. I have managed to get Game's most recent telephone number, and am tracking it, but because of a...situation I was involved in, Game now knows I am in the US and hunting him. He will divest himself of all the items we can use to track him. But. There is a man I know who will have information. He has worked Game's jobs in the past, handling money and papers. We must go to him, together, and he will tell us what he knows."

"Call this person. Call him right now."

"There is no phone in the world that he would answer. Believe me. He only works face to face."

"But you know where he is?"

"Yes."

"Then tell me. Quit playing games."

"It has to be my way, Taylor. My rules. This is my world you will be entering. I know the players. I know the landscape. You will have to trust me. This is what I do, and you need to learn how to maneuver safely in this space, for both our sakes. Thierry wants that. I... Well, I am interested to see how you operate. You add an air of...legitimacy to my project."

Jackson yanked her hair out of its ponytail, wound it around her fist, and pulled the elastic over the ends, capturing the mass in a thick bun. A sign of frustration; Angelie recognized it from their last meeting. There was a bandage around her wrist. She had been hurt in the explosion. She must be both furious and terrified.

"How in the world can I trust you, Miss Delacroix?" the Valkyrie asked.

"Thierry trusts me. That should tell you all you need to know."

"I saw you stick a knife into Thierry Florian, remember? You're just as likely to kill me as help me."

Angelie took a deep breath in through her nose. Her patience was fraying. "If you help me, I will give you information. No strings, as you say."

Jackson recrossed her legs. "About what? What could you possibly have that a cop from Nashville needs?"

It was Angelie's turn to smile. "Help me, and I will tell you where John Baldwin's son is."

FORTY-ONE

TAYLOR FELT FAINT. She tried not to show her shock, but knew it was for naught; at the offer, the assassin had leaned back, finally relaxed, like a cat contemplating settling in for a nap. Taylor's thoughts raced.

Baldwin's son. He will die of joy if we find him.

His son with that horrible woman.

What would happen if we found the child?

Would he come home to live with us? Can I be a mother to Charlotte's son?

She couldn't imagine that Baldwin would walk away from his son if he was found. Which meant she wouldn't have a choice.

Hell. She'd cross that bridge when she got to it.

She palmed the Glock in a heartbeat, so quick the assassin tensed. "What do you know about Baldwin's son? Tell me right now, or I will shoot you dead, I swear it."

"No, you won't. We are all aware of John Baldwin's illegitimate child with the profiler who worked for him. Charlotte Douglas was *trés fou*, insane in the head, as you well know. We are all well rid of her. But the child...*oui*, I know where he is. I am willing to trade that information for your help. But I will not give it until Carson is recovered."

"I can't guarantee the girl is still alive."

"I know you can't, nor would I make that a part of the bargain. But she is. I know it. This situation is meant to draw me to this moment. Game is a terrorist, but he's not stupid. He took Carson from Vanderbilt so I would come here, murder you, and get myself tangled into his web. I am not as reckless nor hot-headed as he believes me to be. I have no desire to kill you. Not anymore."

Taylor ignored that little aside. "Baldwin's. Son. Now."

"You will help me?"

"If you tell me, and I can verify you're telling me the truth? Yes. I will."

Delacroix let out a breath, and Taylor realized she was still in control of this situation. The assassin did need her help. Which made Game an even more frightening proposition.

"The boy is in London at the moment. He is safe. He has a loving mother who is a doctor. She's with Médecins Sans Frontières. He travels with her and has known no other world since he was born. She's had him the whole time. She has raised him, and he is well."

"Who is she?"

"Her name is Tamsin. Now, that is all you get until we find Carson."

"I have to tell Baldwin. Please."

The assassin shook her head. "No, no, you don't. Besides, I know he is not reachable. The boat he is on does not have personal cellular access outside of the port, and he will not be in port for three more days. Three days, that is all I ask. If we have not retrieved Carson by then, I will give you the rest, and you can tell him everything."

Taylor was disconcerted yet again by how much Angelie Delacroix knew about her. But not everything. She didn't know

Baldwin was back in port and very reachable. At least Taylor had that little bit of backup. She wondered for a moment if Angelie was behind Charlaine getting sick and Baldwin being assigned to the conference too but decided she didn't want to know.

"I can't hold this from him. It's a betrayal."

"Like he did not betray you by not telling you the truth when he learned of the boy's existence?"

"Stop," Taylor said. "Stop peering into my life. I don't know why I'm even in this room with you. You're an assassin. You are the kind of person I hunt. The kind I put behind bars. You are not allowed into my world."

"Ah, and yet, here we are. I am in your living room, drinking your wine, from your glasses, talking to you about your most intimate situations—the son of your lover—and doing a business deal with you. Perhaps we are not so different, you and I. You could be considered an assassin as well, could you not?"

"I could not. People don't pay me to kill."

"Then why are you joining Macallan?" Angelie leaned forward, spitting out the words. "You are no better than me. You and I are the same. You are cloaked in righteousness, but in your heart, your soul, you are a killer, just like me. You take life when you need to, just like me. That is why you are struggling now. That is why you want to leave your precious job and throw in with us. Because you are tainted. I, too, am tainted. This world, it breaks us in too many ways, and we are bound by our consciences to do what is right, even if it is wrong in the eyes of some."

"I am not any of those things."

Delacroix tipped her head and gave Taylor that infuriatingly knowing smile. "You are all of those things, and more. This is why we will work well together. We will hunt the bastard who hurt my friend's child, and then I will give you the location of John Baldwin's son. Will you agree to help me?"

Taylor forced herself to breathe. Absolution. Angelie Delacroix—murderer, assassin, terrorist—was offering her absolution. God damn her eyes, she was going to take it. *For Baldwin,* she whispered to her soul. *For the boy. For Sam, and the twins. For them all.*

"All right. I'm in."

With a small exhalation, Angelie relaxed. "*Merci,* Taylor Jackson."

"Don't thank me yet. What's the plan? How are we going to track Game?"

"Through the money. He sent a ransom demand to Avery. We're going to give him the money and take him when he comes to retrieve it. Simple."

"Simple. Right. He's not going to be expecting that at *all.*"

Angelie's eyes narrowed. "I have a few things I'll need to set up. Be ready by noon tomorrow. Pack for three days. Leave your firearms. We will have all we need upon our arrival. I have taken the liberty of having papers made for you. You may need them."

She handed Taylor an envelope. Taylor peered inside, saw a passport, driver's license, a tidy stack of euros contained by a rubber band, and a burner phone. "Presumptuous."

"Prepared."

"Where are we going?"

"France. Paris, to be exact."

"Paris. And what am I supposed to tell my boss? I'm in the middle of two cases, a murder and a kidnapping."

"Get sick."

Taylor laughed briefly. Another test failed. There *were* limitations to Angelie Delacroix's information—she didn't know about Baldwin returning to port, and she didn't know Taylor had quit the force. "You don't know me very well. I rarely get sick, and I work when I do."

"Not in this environment you don't. Here." She handed over a triple-wrapped plastic bag. "It is a positive COVID test. Tell them you woke feeling ill and tested yourself out of precaution. They'll have no choice."

"Keep that. I can't lie like that, it's too easily verifiable. I'll think of something more plausible."

"Fine. Do as you like. But make sure you will not be bothered. Leave your phone, too."

"No. I will not waltz off with you without a phone or weapon."

"You have the burner. I have no idea if your phone is compromised. The number has been spoofed to yours. No one will know the difference but me."

"I am not—"

"This is not a negotiation. You agreed to the deal. You will do it my way."

Taylor realized there was a stiletto touching her ribs and stopped breathing. She hadn't even seen Angelie move, and here she was, pressed up against her, Taylor's life in her hands. Again.

"Do you understand? Quit wasting my time. I will not harm you. I am a woman of my word. But you cannot defy me at every step. We don't have time to waste. No phone, no guns. Noon. There will be a car waiting for you on the corner of Fourth and Broadway."

The pressure left her ribs. Taylor watched carefully, saw the stiletto go back up Delacroix's sleeve.

"Neat trick."

Delacroix ignored the glib comment. "Tomorrow," she said, and left.

This is crazy this is crazy this is crazy.

She now understood Avery Conway's whispered warning. It wasn't that they were playing a game. It was about Joseph

Game. And with a ransom demand, Avery Conway was aware of what was happening with her daughter. It explained so much about her odd actions—the trip to DC, the strange phone call, the lack of parental panic that Taylor was used to seeing. Avery knew a stranger hadn't taken her daughter, Taylor would bet her life on it. She was terrified, though, waiting for something to happen. With the other teammates hovering over her, that's why she hadn't been able to tell Taylor straight up about Game.

Damn these people.

Taylor stalked around the condo, running the past hour through her mind. It was fragmented, pulling apart. What had she just agreed to?

Finding Baldwin's son. That's what. Finding Carson. That's what.

Redemption, in all its many forms.

Angelie Delacroix was right. Taylor was planning to chuck it all and join Macallan. She'd agreed to work with Thierry already. This was her test drive. And it wasn't like she could do anything here, watching from the sidelines.

But she also wasn't stupid. Haring off with an assassin without telling anyone what she was doing, regardless of the warning she'd received, without proper weaponry or a phone, was downright idiocy.

The first thing she did was make duplicate copies of the identification she'd been given. She also wrote up everything Angelie had told her, turning off her WiFi before quickly typing it all up on her laptop. She wrote Baldwin an extensive letter, explaining her rationale both with Macallan and agreeing to work with Angelie to find Carson—stopping just short of telling him the whole truth about his son. That was something she had to do in person. But if something happened to her... In a separate file, she documented the conversation about the boy, citing the doctor, Tamsin, in London, who worked for Doctors Without Borders and had supposedly taken him in. It was only right that Baldwin have some way to get the information if she couldn't be the one to relay it directly.

She didn't mention Angelie had managed to get into a secure building and past their layers of security without blinking an eye. That trick, she wanted to dive into with the assassin herself. Though she was pissed off about it, she wanted to see exactly how Angelie had managed to circumvent their precautions.

She filled envelopes with the papers, the identifications, the letters, and sealed them. She placed the letters about the child in her "SHTF" file in the gun safe—Shit Hits The Fan was their morbid reference to the personal files that would be opened in case something terrible ever happened to one of them. It contained wills, letters, bank account information, passwords and PINs, and now, a hint to help Baldwin find his son. The other letter she left under his pillow.

She downed a granola bar and a Diet Coke—gingerly, her lip was even more swollen than it had been, though thankfully her wrist wasn't hurting as much. Packed three days' worth of T-shirts and underwear, a spare pair of jeans, and a sweater, grabbed her black leather jacket, and shoved her feet into her favorite battered Lamas. Now that she'd made the decision, she moved with purpose, even alacrity. She was taking a chance, yes, but it was a calculated risk.

Justify it to yourself, why don't you.

She sent Baldwin a text, telling him how much she loved him, that she might be hard to reach for a couple of days. Put an "MC" after, with a winking smiley face, knowing he'd get what she was trying to say.

It was well past dawn now, and she shut everything down, grabbed her bag, and took the elevator to the street.

She had a stop to make before she met Angelie's car.

FORTY-TWO

TAYLOR FELT like she owed it to her team to explain in person what was happening since she was pretty sure the rumor mill had spun off into the stratosphere.

She texted Lincoln, who grabbed Marcus and Renn and met her at Pinewood Social. They got a booth in the back, ordered breakfast, and sat back, waiting. They watched her, confused, upset. These men had been her life for so long that she didn't know how she was going to leave them. Doubt spilled through her, but she just as quickly pushed it away.

She took a fortifying sip of tea and dove in. "I'm sure you've heard already, but I've resigned. I owe you an explanation."

"You don't have to explain anything, Taylor," Lincoln said, reaching a big hand over to cover hers. "Yesterday was my fault. I've already told Huston that forcing you to turn in your badge and gun was a mistake, and—"

"Linc, hon, that's not what happened. This was all me. And it's not about what went down yesterday. That was simply the breaking point. I've been planning to resign for a while. I don't like being in the brass, and I really don't like taking orders from Huston. She's changed, and we will never see eye to eye. I have another opportunity, but I haven't accepted their offer just yet." At this, she met eyes with Marcus. "The moment I do, you'll be the first to know." He nodded and looked at his lap, a small smile starting on his lips. She wasn't forsaking him, and that made him happy.

"You'll still be here in town, won't you?" Renn asked. "We might have someone who'll want to see you."

"Of course, I will. You can take me out of Metro, but you can't take me out of Nashville." She laughed, surprised at how true this felt. She'd never thought about it before, but it was right. "This is my home, and it always will be. I might be traveling a bit more, but this is my base, no matter what."

"Good. We're going to miss you."

Lincoln shook his head. "First Sam, now you. I wish things could have stayed the same, but I suppose that's impossible." His phone lit up with a text, and Taylor saw the image of Flynn on the phone's screen. She gestured toward it. "No, Linc. Nothing stays the same."

He smiled softly, and she marveled again at how having a child in his life had gentled him.

"That might be true, but we all adore you, and if you stop coming around for BBQs we'll hunt you down and drag you back to the house. You hear?"

"I hear."

"Good. You want an update on the nest case?"

She grabbed a piece of toast and nodded. "Hell, yeah. I admit, this wasn't exactly the right time to bail, especially when we've got a possible serial. I'm sorry to leave y'all in a lurch."

Marcus chimed in. "It's all good, Taylor. We get it. So we have IDs on the women in the grave. All four are documented missing person cases. Renn has been reaching out to the families."

"Hated like hell to do it," Renn said, breaking a piece of bacon into crumbles. "You know how much I dislike doing notifications, but this, this is different. They've all been so grateful to have an answer at last."

"That happens on long-term cases like this," Taylor said. "Families hold out a tiny bit of hope but know in their hearts when someone is gone. You get to give them actual peace of mind. It's sad, but it's a relief for them, too."

"Yeah. That's what I sensed. So the oldest case is from ten years ago, the victim's name is Bailey Staubach. I spoke to her mother, down in Mississippi. Apparently, Bailey came to Nashville after a huge fight with her family. She thought she could make it big in the country music scene."

Taylor set down her toast. "Go on."

"That's as far as I've gotten on her. But the most recent, the girl we pulled from the top? Similar story. Name's Krista Bush. She's from Arkansas, stopped calling home six months ago. Last they heard she had recorded a demo and was making the rounds on Music Row. Family's broken, she doesn't come from much, but they insisted she had a voice like an angel."

"You have my attention," Taylor said.

"Marcella Nieves, third down in the grave. Originally from Puerto Rico, came to Miami with her family in the early 2000s. She sang in clubs all over the South, got into drugs, and the habit ate her up. Went into rehab, got clean, and struck out for Nashville. Got a band together, played around the smaller venues and honky-tonks. When she went missing, the family pushed, hard, for our help. There's a decent case file with a lot of legwork, but nothing ever came of it.

"Finally, the second one we pulled out."

Taylor had chills racing up and down her arms. "Let me guess. Another singer?"

Renn tapped his nose. "Close. Backup. Sessions only. She was a guitarist by trade. Name is Cindy Hynds. She has a few credits on some albums, was working steadily before she disappeared. So yes. They were all in the industry."

"Damn," Taylor breathed. "There's no way Justin Osborne was responsible for their deaths, is there?"

"We might could make a case for his involvement with Krista Bush. The other three? He would have been very young. I think we're looking at someone older. Someone who came across all five of them. I think Georgia was the fifth victim of a serial killer who has been preying on Music Row for a decade. Justin was in the wrong place at the wrong time. He followed Georgia up that mountain, and argued with her, but he didn't kill her. Someone else was there, someone who wanted Georgia dead."

"So how does Justin get GSR on his hands?"

"The suicide was staged. You've always thought that. The notebook paper, the angle of the gunshot, the idea that he'd kill Georgia then go home and kill himself...your gut was right on. I think he ran. And the killer realized he'd been seen and had to get rid of him. The argument the Vandy girls heard? Was probably between Georgia and the killer."

"It was personal," Taylor said. "Whoever killed her knew her. This wasn't a stranger."

These revelations blew Angelie Delacroix's theory out of the water. Joseph Game wasn't responsible for Georgia and Justin's deaths. It also felt so much more logical to Taylor. Carson stumbling onto the crime was a horrible coincidence. Nothing more.

A lucky one, too. If she hadn't, they might never have found Georgia's body, not to mention the rest of the women. Taylor kept that to herself but shared O'Roarke's find at Osborne's house. She called him while they all sat there.

"Taylor, I heard—"

"I know. It's true. But let's circle back to that. Were you able to track down the audio from that smart speaker?"

O'Roarke was clearly excited, his voice boomed through the line.

"I sure was. Waiting on one more warrant to come through,

but I hit pay dirt. The company has gotten more cooperative when a serious crime is involved, and they honored the warrant quickly, though they only gave us a small window of time. You gotta hear this. Can you come by the task force offices? Is that allowed?"

"No. But I'll get somewhere private. I've got some folks with me, they'll want to hear, too. Call you back in twenty."

They paid the check and jogged to Taylor's 4-Runner, piling in. It was like old times, a car full of cops about to catch a big break on a case. For a moment, she second-guessed herself—*you can't leave them, you know your soul is here*—but within five minutes they were in the elevator to her condo, and then inside the space. She tried not to look at the flowers on the coffee table. Why she hadn't thrown them out, she didn't know.

She called O'Roarke back, put him on the speaker. "OK. We're ready. Go for it."

"I can send you the whole thing, but I've got it cued up to the relevant moment." There was background static, but the clarity was good enough to hear a conversation between two men. One sounded cruel, the other was sobbing.

Voice 1: "You're an idiot. You always have been."

Voice 2: "Why did you do that? Why? You didn't need to kill her."

Voice 1: "I most certainly did. You should have stayed away. This is all your fault."

The report of the gunshot was loud enough that Taylor jumped.

Voice 1: "Good damn riddance."

And the recording stopped.

When her heart slowed a fraction, she said, "Play it again."

O'Roarke did, without saying a word. She could hear the scuffle now, moments before the shot.

"Again. Please."

When it clicked off the third time, he said, "You were right. Jason Osborne didn't kill himself. He was murdered."

"It certainly sounds that way," she agreed.

"There's more. Remember you were pissed that the dumpster was moved? I was able to track down the company, and they gave my forensics team access to the dump site. Lucky for us, the dumpster was still there, intact, waiting to be sent to the landfill. They only go once a week and take all their construction dumpsters at the same time. Guess what we got?"

"Tell me."

"A pillow. Remember that piece of fabric from the autopsy report? It was duck cotton, and the ME thought it was from the shirt Osborne was wearing? It's also a match to this torn-up pillow."

"Huh. So you think the killer tried to muffle the shot through the pillow? You'd think we'd have a lot more debris on the body than a tiny piece of fabric."

"I know, I've never seen something like this that was so clean. There were cotton fibers recovered from the body, but again, they were attributed to his clothing and Georgia's. The pillow is that heavy canvas cotton, fake-down polyester interior, and the bullet went right through. It's as clean as a flesh wound, seared it, there's a burn mark where it melted the interior. He must have had it pretty close to the weapon. What was the estimate on the shot?"

"Thirty-four inches, to be exact."

"Well, our killer moved fast, to be able to hold Justin down and shoot him. They were arguing, clearly. I don't know how he did it, but at least we know Osborne wasn't alone when the gun went off."

"So who was that with him?" She looked around the room. "The voice sounds familiar, doesn't it? Play it again, O'Roarke. Please," she added. They were doing her a favor now, she needed to remember her place.

O'Roarke complied.

And it was Marcus who said the magic words. "That sounds to me like Travis Bloom."

They all spoke at once.

Lincoln: "The head of Georgia's record label? I will be damned."

O'Roarke: "Her parents said they were having problems."

Renn: "Gosh, you think he's responsible for all of these murders?"

Marcus: "We have to keep this quiet. He has means. A plane at his disposal. We spook him before we get evidence, we'll lose him."

Taylor: "The guitarist in the band warned me about him."

The conversation jumped around, and Taylor watched them play it out, pride and sorrow mingling. She'd never do this with them again, at least not in this way. Theories flew fast and furious, but it was O'Roarke who clinched it. "I just pulled a VICAP report. Plugged in the parameters—fifteen-year window, women in their early twenties with connections to music. You aren't going to believe this. Guess where there's another cluster of missing persons? Five, to be exact, over the same time frame."

"Los Angeles?" Taylor suggested.

"Give that lady a prize."

Marcus had his notebook out. "Travis Bloom has a house in Santa Monica, and the label's headquarters are on Sunset Boulevard. You think he's been killing in both places—California and Tennessee?"

"I think we may have just broken this case wide open."

Taylor was in the middle of giving the whole team high fives when Baldwin walked in the door. She intercepted him with a hug, to the wolf whistles of her former team.

He kissed her soundly, then arched a brow. "What am I missing?"

They filled him in, and he agreed, it sounded like they had a pattern. "Get yourselves some DNA from the bodies and the suspect and it's a done deal."

After a few more minutes of chatter and coordination, hugs were given all around, and the guys happily trooped from the condo, off to their respective jobs and leads to follow. When the door closed behind Lincoln, and they were alone, Taylor glanced at her watch, swallowed back the emotions, and told Baldwin what she was about to do. Most of it. She tried not to see the abject horror on his face.

"Absolutely not. You can't go off with her. She's an assassin, Taylor. Unpredictable at best, dangerous as hell. No. You can't."

"I can. And I am. Trust me. I know who she is, and what she's capable of. But she is not going to hurt me. We have a deal."

"You can't make a deal with the devil, Taylor. He always has an ulterior motive."

He ran his hands vigorously through his hair, a gesture that caused something inside her stomach to pull.

"This devil is a she. And I think I understand her."

He looked utterly miserable. She wrapped her arms around his waist. She was tall, but he was taller, and she looked up at him, trying to make sure he understood. "I need you to trust me."

"I do, Taylor. But—"

"Seriously." She pulled back, focused on his sea-green eyes, trying like hell to see past the pain and confusion. "I'm doing this for a very good reason. I need to find Carson Conway. She is a tool in a bigger struggle, and that pisses me off. But it's more. Angelie...well, she claims she needs my help, which I hardly believe is true. But if I'm going to work for Macallan, this is a chance for me to see how things are done. Saving Carson is my goal here, but I can answer some lingering questions for myself, too."

"There's more you aren't telling me."

She hated when he did that. Like he could see right through her, into the core where she kept things hidden. She supposed that's what loving someone was about, letting them past the shell and into your heart, and she loved Baldwin very, very much. It still unnerved her when he peered inside.

"Please don't ask. I need to do this. You'll understand why when I find Carson."

He kissed her lightly, not commenting on her bruises, the split lip, just brushed his lips against hers once, twice, and stepped out of the embrace, crossing his arms on his broad chest. "I trust you implicitly, Taylor. Just promise me you'll be careful. It would kill me if something happened to you."

FORTY-THREE

IT ABOUT KILLED Taylor to leave Baldwin, but she had made this decision, and she was going through with this plan. As promised, the car was at the corner at noon on the dot, and a pristine white Gulfstream V with a long black stripe was waiting at John C. Tune Airport. Taylor mounted the steps, expecting Angelie to be inside, but found the plane empty except for the pilots. One man and one woman, both wearing uniforms.

"Captain Jackson, I presume. You all set?" the woman asked, her voice redolent of the Deep South. "We're all gassed up and ready to rock."

Taylor handed over her bag. "Just Taylor. Am I flying alone?"

"That's what the manifest says. Deadheading a single."

"All right. Where, exactly, are we headed?"

"Connecticut. Be there in an hour. Have a seat, buckle up. Drinks are in the fridge toward the back, so's the head."

The female pilot smiled and took her place on the left side of the cockpit.

Taylor grabbed a Diet Coke and a bag of almonds. The seats were warm and the leather luxurious, and she happily settled in. The flight was short, but after her snack, she managed to doze, her long legs thrown onto the seat opposite hers.

They landed gently in New Haven, taxied for a few minutes, then stopped. The male pilot opened the door, and Taylor stood up.

"Stretch your legs if you want, but don't go far. We're off again as soon as we're gassed up."

Taylor was surprised by that. She stuck her head out into the crisp northern air only to see Angelie striding toward the plane, followed by Santiago Diaz-Rooney. Neither carried a bag. The assassin waved her back inside, ran up the steps, and spoke French to the female pilot—*"Allons-y."* The pilot nodded and took her seat, the engines revving.

Diaz-Rooney entered, sized up Taylor—looking up, as many did; she was six feet tall in stocking feet, and the Lamas gave her two more inches. "Diaz, if you don't remember," he said, sticking out a hand.

"Jackson," she replied, taking it briefly. "I do. Might have filled me in a little when we last met, though."

His eyes were colder than she recalled. "Don't criticize. You just got read in."

"Now, now, Santi. Play nice," Angelie crooned, taking the seat opposite Taylor. Both Taylor and Santiago rolled their eyes. Santiago retrieved a bottle of water and took the bench couch.

The pilot came over the intercom. "We expect to be on the ground in Paris just after 2400 hours local. Smooth flight."

The plane began to move, and things inside were quiet. Having flown commercial to Europe on several occasions, Taylor was pleased to hear the time of the trip was cut almost in half by the big Gulfstream's capacity. She snuggled into the seat and watched Angelie pretend to sleep.

Not so quick, lady.

"So, Paris?" Taylor hinted.

Nothing.

"Paris is lovely this time of year, I hear."

Again, nothing.

"Any particular *place* in Paris? It's a rather large city."

"The Seventh," Angelie said, without opening her eyes.

"Any particular part of the Seventh?"

"A building."

"Come on, Angelie. You have to brief me on what you're planning. If we're going to work together, you should know I do like to think through what I'm doing before I just ride off into battle."

After a beat, Angelie's eyes opened. She glanced at Santiago, who nodded.

"She has the right to know."

"You have gotten soft, Santi," the assassin said, then looked at Taylor directly.

"D'accord," Angelie said. "Fine. We are going to pay a visit to a man in the Seventh arrondissement who has worked with Game very recently. He is going to give us access to Game's bank account. Santi and his people will do a forensic accounting, which will give us the locations he's most recently visited and any holdings he has where he might be hiding Carson. While that happens, you and I will talk with the man directly. He is known as La Boulanger."

"The Baker? Let me guess—because he cooks the books?"

The assassin's eyes narrowed. "I did not know you spoke French, Taylor."

"I don't. Not really. I had an *au pair* from Avignon when I was ten. I barely remember a thing."

Angelie continued studying her, but Santiago laughed. "Better watch what you say, Ange. You never know who's listening."

The assassin ignored him, instead eyed Taylor speculatively. "It must have been lovely, growing up with your family."

"Did you hear me say *au pair*? I was raised by a series of young women. Strangers. My parents had better things to do."

"But your parents were in proximity to you? You lived with them, had meals, yes?"

"I might have shared their house, but if you know anything about me, you must know that my family and I don't get along."

"Yes, I do know. Still. You had the option." She looked out the window, and said gruffly, "Get some sleep. We will be there in four hours."

"Not until you run me through the actual 'plan.'" Taylor made little quotes with her fingers, feeling both reckless and exhilarated. She was poking the bear, she knew this, but damn if she was going to let the assassin play games with her. Diaz was clearly enjoying this byplay, but Angelie sighed in annoyance before sitting up and cracking open a bottle of water.

"As a member of Macallan, it is expected that you will have accounts that are both untraceable, and accessible at all times, from anywhere you might be. This allows you to move freely throughout the world. With a call to La Boulanger, a wire transfer happens, and your money is available, anywhere, anytime. He is discreet and subservient, and we have enough information about him to keep him in line should Interpol or another agency ever come calling. They never have, and part of that is his natural discretion. The other, of course, is Thierry's influence. Many of us use La Boulanger for this purpose. Game most certainly does, this I have confirmed."

"Okay. And?"

"We will go in and set up your accounts. It is something that must be done in person, with a reference. He would never take a new client otherwise. You will pose as my assistant. We cannot bring weapons, we will never get past the guards and the electronics. The house is camera-heavy, too, so you're going to want to be aware of your posture and the angle of your chin. We're not trying to hide you, but you don't need to be staring at the cameras, either. Once we're in, you'll distract him while I get what we need."

"Distract him, how?"

"With your arm around his throat, preferably." That feral grin flashed, the one Taylor was starting to recognize as the wolf inside Angelie. At Taylor's narrowed eyes, she waved her hand dismissively. "He will give us what we want. When we have access to Game's accounts, we can ascertain who's been paying him, and where he's been. All of his life will be revealed. Once we know that, we will be one step closer to finding where he's stashed Carson. Kidnapping and hiding people, it takes money, and resources. It will all be in his banking records."

"How do you know, though? And as a part of your former team, wouldn't he expect you to come looking for the money trail, and change bankers?"

Angelie smiled sweetly. "Game overestimates his cleverness. And he may expect this of me, but he would never, ever, expect it from you, which is why we need you to go in."

"But you'll be with me."

"Not through the front door. I will come in later."

"A man like La Boulanger, who does banking off-book...I assume he's been threatened before."

"We will not threaten. We will explain, and we will offer a deal. Once we know what Game has been up to, we will be in the power position. That's what Santi will be doing while we go on whatever errand La Boulanger asks of us. You've heard the term *quid pro quo*? The little shit will give us what we want, but only if we give him something in return."

"I'm curious, how would the money give you these details? You said everything was done with anonymous wire transfers?"

"They are. But Game is an idiot. He likes Bitcoin, and with that, every transaction is traceable, given the appropriate knowledge and leverage. With the source of the transaction identified, we'll be able to find where he had the money wired."

"But if Game kidnapped Carson to draw you out, what does tracing the money have to do with it? You don't think he was paid to kidnap her, do you? That would mean someone else was involved."

"*Non.* I believe he is acting alone. But I do think that he's spent a great deal of money slipping her away. Money is always the best place to start when you're searching for someone."

Taylor shook her head. "It's too simple. Hack his accounts, and find where he's been sending and receiving his cash? If he's remotely good at what he does—which I assume because he was once your teammate, he is—that feels sloppy. Also, if he's made a ransom demand, and you're planning to give him the money...that also doesn't fly for me. Now, if you're planning to rob the man of his assets to get his attention, that would make more sense. You can trade his money for the girl, even-steven. Then you can hunt him down, and Carson won't get hurt."

The assassin gave her a completely new and appraising look.

"If this was a normal situation, we might do just that. I'm not saying we won't skim a bit, just to make things easier for our own movements. But if we steal too much, he'll just kill the girl and then come after us. Our primary goal is to get Carson back unharmed. He knows this. He won't hesitate to ruin things for us."

"What will he trade her for, though? Money? A physical showdown with you? I don't get what he has to lose by just killing Carson and walking away."

"Other than his life? He kills her, he's a dead man walking, and he knows it. No, he wants to punish us, to belittle us, embarrass us. This is a pride issue."

Taylor cracked open her own water. "But is it? Really? You're coming for him regardless. He has to know that. In my experience, when a killer wants to play, he plays. Kidnapping Carson pissed you off enough to come out of retirement to go after him

—that's playing. But why the subterfuge? Game doesn't feel like the kind of show-off killer I'm used to, the kind who think they're smarter than us, need to show us how smart they are, and genuinely believe they will get away with it. Game can't possibly think that by drawing you out, he can win against you head-to-head."

Angelie bowed her head. "Thank you for the compliment."

"I don't know that it was one. But the point stands. What does he think he's going to get out of a direct confrontation with you? If he was looking for a showdown, why didn't he just kill Carson straight up and let you come after him? He's after something else, isn't he? Something you have or can get for him. What is it?"

Santiago and Angelie traded a glance.

"That, my dear captain, is what we need to figure out."

PART THREE

"It is very beautiful in Paris and
very lonely at Christmas time."

—Ernest Hemingway, "Christmas at the Roof of the World"

FORTY-FOUR

SATURDAY: FAUBOURG SAINT GERMAIN, PARIS

AT THE CORNER of Rue de Grenelle and Rue de Bellechasse stood a building that fairly screamed Paris. A Haussman edifice—elegant masonry, tall wooden doors, wrought-iron balconies—it was a quintessential Parisian residence, a dream for any Francophile. What lurked inside was something altogether different.

Their car was waved through the courtyard entrance of the building down the street that was attached to the one on the corner. La Boulanger owned the whole block. Taylor thought it would have been a lot more fitting if the bottom floors of the corner building housed an actual patisserie, like the one across the street, but when she said this to the assassin, Angelie didn't crack a smile. The sky was gunmetal gray, and Taylor shivered inside her jacket.

"Are you prepared?" Angelie asked.

"Yes. Are you?"

Angelie just jerked her head.

Taylor climbed from the back of the vehicle, only slightly

disconcerted when it slid away; her bag was inside, with her passport—her real passport—and back through the gates into the city. It was quiet in here. A few tables and chairs, some desiccated greenery spilling from urns—someone hadn't attended the garden. An early and unexpected snow had begun to fall, whispering from the sky to gather in her hair and on her shoulders, and Taylor was happy she'd grabbed the sweater from her bag before she got into the car. She shrugged into it. As romantic as Paris could be, adding in a deep chill wasn't as special.

She adjusted the bag on her shoulder. The drive into the city from the airport had included two stops, both buildings that Angelie disappeared into and returned carrying a plain black duffel bag. These bags, Taylor soon learned, contained money, papers, and weapons. Lots and lots of weapons. She had a flashback to one of her favorite movies, *The Matrix*, when Neo and Trinity go through the metal detectors to rescue Morpheus, and their bags are opened, showing a variety of weapons filling them to the brim. If they needed to go up against an army, Angelie had them covered. It made Taylor wonder just what, exactly, to expect from the next few days.

Taylor was not given a weapon, which made her uneasy, but she understood. She would be checked, both by a metal detector built into the jamb of the front door to the building and after she entered the third-floor offices. It was this secondary chokepoint where the security system would be disabled to allow her entry, and when that happened, Angelie would slip inside from the building next door. She couldn't chance being seen on the cameras.

Taylor had her short script memorized, and a piece of paper in an envelope with a numbered account for the transaction. All of this was just for show, though. Her main role, insofar as she could understand it, was to act as a decoy simply by walking into the offices of La Boulanger.

She squared her shoulders and stepped to the entry, where two men in suits stood. Her practiced eye picked out the telltale bulges that indicated shoulder holsters. Apparently, everyone but her would have a gun today.

Get it over with, Taylor. Remember why you're here.

"Bonjour," she said prettily to the guards at the door. *"Je suis attendu."* I am expected.

The guard on the right gestured, and she lifted up her arms and turned in a circle. He grunted acquiescence and jerked his head toward the stairs. She walked up and through, not pausing, directly across the ancient marble floors to the impressive staircase. She wound her way up two floors and was met with the unsmiling visages of two more guards.

Only four? Surely there's more.

There were, of course there were. Angelie had described in great detail the setup inside the building. The rest of the boogeymen were concealed behind the doors, ready to spring out like characters of a terrible horror film. No, on its front, this was meant to look like a regular home and personal office. One that belonged to a respectable Parisian, not one that belonged to a terrorist moneyman.

She grinned like a tourist and gestured to the intricate moldings. *"Très jolie."*

Nothing. It was like speaking to a couple of sphinxes. Fine. Stick with the script.

"Je suis attendu."

Their hands were businesslike, professional, and a bit too thorough. She suffered them. She had nothing to hide. They knew this already because she'd made it past the highly sensitive magnetometer downstairs, but they were paid well not to take chances.

"Satisfait?" she asked. Satisfied?

"Oui," the guard on her right answered, and she watched carefully as he spoke into his wrist. A loud clunk, like the

sound of a bank vault opening, and the doors before her split apart.

She hoped like hell Angelie was paying attention.

Inside the sanctum was another set of doors, these leading to a regular office, though this was windowless. No way for a sniper to take a shot. The room was expansive, paneled, and split into two areas: a large desk with two chairs facing it on the west side of the room; a large leather couch with two wing chairs squatting in front of a gas fireplace on the east side. The fire was lit, making the room cloyingly warm. The man she was meeting was at the desk. He barely looked up when she entered. He certainly seemed comfortable with strangers.

She waited for a moment, then cleared her throat. The man still ignored her.

Where the hell was Angelie?

A shout. Ah.

The commotion was quick. Taylor heard a suppressed pistol bark once, twice, then the doors swung open again and Angelie strolled through.

"Bonjour, Frederick."

The man behind the desk merely waved a hand, still intent on his ledger. Taylor was mildly impressed. He couldn't not know what was happening, not after the gunshots, yet he was playing it calm and collected.

Finally, he capped his fountain pen and deigned to look up. His face was bored, but Taylor sensed a flicker of fear in his reptilian eyes.

"Comme c'est incroyablement impoli de tirer sur mes gardes. Savez-vous combien il est difficile de trouver une bonne aide de nos jours?"

Angelie twirled the gun in a circle. "I had to get your attention somehow."

"Oh, we're speaking in English. Fine. What is the meaning of this intrusion? You could have called. There was no reason to eliminate my guards. I happen to like them. Do you know how hard it is to get good help these days?"

"Frederick. I don't care. I need information, quickly."

The man's gaze slid to Taylor. "Who is your friend?"

"Natalie Johnson. She is my new assistant. She needs access to an account."

"Ah. Well. If only my assistants were such beauties." He followed with a flowery speech in French. Taylor caught the words *lovely*, *heavenly*, and what she thought was a very deviant sexual position, and tensed. So the great La Boulanger was a bit of a pervert.

She must have guessed right, because Angelie was across the room with the barrel of her pistol again the Baker's temple a moment later. "No, she does not have enough French to understand your disgusting suggestions. No more games. I need the accounts of one of your clients. And you're going to give them to me—all of them—right now, or I will splash your brain across this expensive desk and leave you here to rot."

"I give you a client's information, and they will come visiting to do the same as you threaten. *Non*. I will not."

Angelie knifed him in the thigh, and the man howled. Leaving the knife deep in his flesh, she pulled a baggie from her pocket and dangled it in front of his face. There was a syringe, a spoon, and a lighter inside, plus a prescription bottle.

Great. The Baker was a pervert and an addict. "Remind me never to keep funds here," Taylor said, trying to keep calm and not leap to the man's defense. Damn it, why did Angelie have to get physical?

Another test.

"Quiet," Angelie shot back, turning to the wounded banker. "The files for the man you know as Gareth Maughan. Now, Frederick. You give them to me and you'll get your treat. And I won't cut your throat."

Gareth Maughan? Taylor knew that name. That was the

angel investor who'd offered so much money for Simeon Chase's app. Some of the pieces of the past few days started to fall together. Taylor began to speak, but Angelie gave her a nasty look.

"Now, Frederick. The files."

The little man was muttering curses and sweating hard, blood dripping down his chair leg, but started typing. "He thought you might come calling. Why don't you just transfer the money he wants? It's nothing."

"Shut up and give me the transactions. If I needed to steal something I wouldn't have bothered to come here."

Finally, the man handed her a thumb drive. He pulled a handkerchief from his pocket, yanked free the knife with a hiss, and pressed the cloth to his thigh. "Be gone, *salope*, and never return. You will be killed on sight."

"*Merci beaucoup*, Frederick."

Angelie shot him in the left eye. Taylor started at the small report. The suppressed Walther cracked like a whip.

La Boulanger fell to his desk, and Angelie immediately began to move, graceful as a dancer, gathering up files and notepads.

"What. The. Hell?" Taylor snapped the words, trying, and failing, to keep her temper in check. "Was that necessary?"

"Check his hand."

Taylor looked and sure enough, he had a small silver pistol in his left palm. It must have been taped under the desk. *Stupid, girl. You have to pay better attention.*

"Oh."

"Yes, *oh*. I had no choice, he was about to shoot you. Now hurry. We need to download everything we can before the rest of the guards wake up, so Santi can tear his files apart. Frederick never has meetings that last more than ten minutes. We're already seven in."

Taylor, still furious, handed over the bag, and Angelie dug

the small thumb drive out of the zipper where it had been loosely sewn. She plugged it into the laptop, deftly reaching around the dead man, and clicked a few buttons. "The data is transferring. Get ready. We may need to be creative leaving."

"Maybe if you hadn't shot the man... For God's sake. You've taken out five people since we got to Paris. You lied to me. This is not what we discussed. This is not how I work."

Angelie didn't bother looking at Taylor. " Would you rather be dead right now?" When Taylor didn't answer, Angelie continued. "When it's your job, you do things your way. He would have called Game the second we left if I'd left him alive. It was safer this way. And if you'd actually understood what he wanted you to do to him? You'd have shot him yourself. *Bien. C'est finis.* Done." Angelie tossed Taylor the gun, dug another out of the holster under her arm. "You go first. I'm right behind you."

Taylor slid to the doors, looked out. Nothing. This was too easy. She knew things were about to go to hell. Her heart pumped once, hard, and she fought back the ill-timed adrenaline rush and made for the stairs. She was three-quarters of the way down when she smelled smoke. She turned back in horror to see Angelie flying toward her. "Go. Go!"

The car wasn't in the courtyard. Taylor realized she was counting silently in time with her running steps. Five. Six. Seven. They were on the street now, the guns away, and Angelie practically scurried into an alleyway on their right. Ten. Eleven. Twelve.

There was a large stone wall in front of them. "Keep going," Angelie hissed, turning again, this time to the right. Left. Right again. Left.

Angelie stopped hurrying, pulled a baseball cap from her back pocket. She pulled her hair through, slung her bag across her body, and immediately looked so American Taylor almost laughed. Angelie murmured, "Into the Rodin. Now."

She had a set of passes—Taylor recognized them as the multiday museum passes that allowed tourists to jump lines and enter the sites unmolested. A minute later they'd passed through the house proper and into the elegant green gardens of the Musée Rodin.

Sirens began to wail, but Angelie simply darted toward the first epic bronze sculpture and posed. "Get in here, girl, take a selfie with me," she called in a credible but cringeworthy southern accent.

Taylor walked over to her and fake smiled for Angelie's bent arm. "No one our age talks like that. Can we just..."

But Angelie was off. The gardens were quiet, and nearly deserted. It was too cold for most sane people to enjoy an afternoon outdoors. Fake selfie by fake selfie, they made it to the far wall. Angelie dropped the stupid grin. Taylor was momentarily taken aback by the fact that she missed it. Angelie was charming when she smiled. Her normal expression was so serious as to be dour.

"Over the wall," Angelie said.

There was a wrought-iron bench under the willow tree. Taylor dragged it to the wall, climbed over the white stucco, and carefully dropped to the sidewalk on the other side. Angelie was with her seconds later, and the car slid to the curb. They were inside and off before anyone noticed them.

FORTY-FIVE

IN THE CAR, Angelie called Santiago on the encrypted phone. “Are you prepared? Good. We have everything we need. We will be there shortly.” She tucked the phone away and crossed her legs casually, as if this was simply another day, another Parisian afternoon with snow falling from the sky like petals in the wind. Her nonchalance was alarming. The silence was too much for Taylor to hold back any longer.

“Why the hell did that just happen?” She was steaming mad, but Angelie didn’t seem to care. She answered casually, calmly, dispassionately.

“I did what I had to. And we got what we needed.”

“Bullshit. You’d planned to take him out all along.”

Angelie cocked her head to the side like a spaniel hearing a strange noise. She was not accustomed to having her orders, nor her barbaric methods, questioned.

“And if I told you I was going to eliminate him, you would have reacted poorly. As is evidenced by the tension you’re feeling right now. Take a breath before you have a stroke.”

“This isn’t funny.”

"I wasn't making a joke. Your face is red, and you've nearly pulled your hair off your head. Settle down."

Taylor bit back a retort and untangled her fist from her ponytail. She hated it when people pointed out her hair tic. It was an unconscious thing, and people who cared about her didn't mention it. Angelie's observation of it felt like a loaded gun to her head. This whole thing was going sideways, fast.

Angelie caught Taylor's gritted teeth and with half a smile, chose the moment to continue her elucidation. "Sometimes, Taylor, when you are in the field, you will have to act in ways you don't expect. You're wrong. I wasn't planning to kill him when we went in. He was about to shoot you."

"Oh, don't you pretend for a moment you did that for me. You took out the guards—"

"Also unplanned. When someone tries to shoot me, I shoot back and ask why later. If I hadn't, you'd be leaking all over La Boulanger's floor. Not only would that be a shame and a waste of a good resource, Thierry wouldn't take kindly to me losing you on your first mission."

That obsequious tone... "Oh, so you killed them to save *me*? This is not going to work. I will find Carson myself. Drop me at the corner."

"No."

The driver, in response to Angelie's curt answer, had the audacity to speed up.

"I'm serious, I will not—"

"Quit complaining and look at this."

She tossed a file in Taylor's lap. Taylor, too, was unaccustomed to having her authority undermined, and debated for half a moment about pressing the button to slide down the window and toss the file onto the street. She only stopped herself when she recalled the multitude of bodies they'd left behind. Too many lives had already been lost for this information.

Instead, she did as Angelie asked, took a deep, admonishing breath through her nose, and opened the file.

Joseph Game, aka Gareth Maughan, had a lot of money in La Boulanger's bank.

At first glance it totaled somewhere in the $150 million range. Investments, assets, the supposed stake in Bitcoin, plus good old-fashioned liquid money in a variety of currencies, mostly dollars.

"That's a lot of cash."

"We are paid well for our work."

"Disgusting," Taylor muttered.

"You really don't get it, do you? You, who only kills in the name of the law. You're no better than some Wild West sheriff who decides who lives or dies based on who the villain robbed. My work is more...elegant."

"That's utter bullshit. And I'm tired of arguing with you," Taylor said. "Let's just do this job, get Carson, and get her home, agreed? Preferably without murdering anyone else."

"I can't promise that," Angelie said, eyes darkening.

They drove for an hour before stopping. The snow grew worse the farther south they went. Taylor watched the signs as they drove, though she knew exactly nothing about the French countryside. They hit the village of Chevreuse, and a few minutes later, the car slowed, then turned into a rambling lane that led to a large, charming buttercup-yellow two-story farmhouse with gabled windows along the expanse of the mansard roof. The snow had gathered prettily over the gravel courtyard, and Taylor was annoyed all over again. After the events of the day, staying in a lovely house in the French countryside felt obscene to her.

Angelie trudged out, along with the driver, who had yet to

introduce himself. He opened the trunk and took the bags while Angelie stalked directly inside. Taylor followed, trying like hell not to appreciate the very old and exquisite door she entered through.

It was as lovely inside as the exterior foretold. Santiago was set up in the kitchen, a laptop and stack of papers in front of him, feet bare on the warm terra-cotta tiles. A fire roared, making the room cozy, and dinner was waiting for them in the oven, some sort of chicken and vegetables with plenty of onions and garlic, from the smell of it.

Taylor went to the kitchen window and glanced out at the dusky sky. She could see the place had a pool, gardens, and extensive grounds. It was off the beaten path, a good safe house. She shook her head. It was like overnight, she'd been transported into a spy novel.

But this situation was of her own making. So she needed to suck it up and do the job, regardless of the company she was keeping.

Baldwin's face floated into her mind, only slightly mocking. *Told you you'd hate it.*

Hush, she told him back. *I'm doing this for you.*

Suddenly the charming hostess, Angelie stopped and gestured toward the stairs. "Your room is upstairs on the right, Taylor. Your bag is already there. Would you like to freshen up, or are you ready to eat?"

Taylor glanced at the stairs. "I'll be back in five minutes."

She needed the alone time. If only to rationalize with herself for the hundredth time. Every step up the thick oak treads was a new recrimination, answered with a justification.

You're doing this for Baldwin.

You're doing this for his son.

You're doing this for yourself.

You're bored.

You're not as outraged as you seem.

You don't care that she killed those men.

You are lost.

The room was perfect, of course, with timbered beams and whitewashed walls, a double bed piled high with downy pillows and crisp linens. She hopped in the shower, rinsed off the acrid scent of anger, and dressed quickly. Damn if she wasn't hungry, and the food, whatever it was, smelled incredible.

Yep, put away your conscience, girl. Apparently, you can't afford to have one anymore.

She'd always been so sure of what was black and what was white. What was evil, and what wasn't. Now she was cavorting in the shadows, dallying in the gray space, and it was damn uncomfortable.

When she entered the kitchen, Angelie and Santiago merely pointed at a chair. The driver, who was also some sort of servant, brought plates to the table, along with a couple of crusty baguettes that were clearly homemade. *Santiago owns a bakery, that's right.* Well, she wouldn't die for lack of carbs, at least. She took a seat at the table, trying to keep her mouth from watering.

"Coq au vin?" Taylor asked, spying the telltale pearl onions and the roasted chicken in sauce. It smelled ridiculously good, all wine and thyme and onions.

"Santiago has been cooking all afternoon," Angelie said with a smirk.

"Shut up. It's my love language." Santiago passed Taylor the butter, a crock of fresh yellow goodness, and they dug in.

FORTY-SIX

WHEN THEY WERE CREAKING FULL, Jackson finished off her wine and sat back, hands folded on her stomach.

"So."

Angelie imitated her posture. It wasn't that she wanted to needle the detective, but Jackson was just so ripe for the picking. "So?"

"What's next?"

Angelie waved a hand at Santiago. "We stay up all night crashing through the records until something jumps out at us. Legwork. Similar to what you do with your team, I suspect."

"What can I do to help?"

A decent meal seemed to have tamed the beast. Jackson could be a righteous bitch, but Angelie suspected that deep down, she was more interested in getting the answer to Carson's disappearance, regardless of the cost.

"Sleep. We will handle this part."

"No way. If I'm in, I'm in. Give me a stack and let me help."

"Suit yourself," Angelie said. "This might be your last

chance to rest, though. I doubt Game is far away. We find him, we're rolling immediately."

"Without a plan?"

"We'll plan on the way."

Jackson shrugged. "I'm fine. Just...give me something to do. I can't just sit here."

Santiago peeled off a fist-sized stack of papers. "I'm cross-referencing transactions with phone records. So far, I know he's in Europe and has been for nearly a week. He's supposedly been all over, Denmark, Amsterdam, Edinburgh. He's masking his transactions so we'll chase our tails trying to track his movements. He's simply using IPs and false flags to lure us into following him all over the place while trying to stay off Interpol's radar. But we've been trained in the same tactics. We aren't stupid. We are not cats chasing a piece of string. One of the locations will be legitimate. We just need to find the right spot. We find Game, we find Carson. He will have her stashed close by."

"Why not try to negotiate?"

"Because that's what he thinks we'll do. We have to surprise him by knocking on his door before he expects us. So we're laying in our own false flags. Making it look like we're following his trail of bread crumbs, so he doesn't realize where, exactly, we are. While we do that, you can cross-reference the transactional data."

Jackson accepted a highlighter, looked at it with a spark of amusement.

"All this technology, and this asshole will be thwarted by a generic study tool." She toyed with the plunger for a minute, popping the fluorescent tip in and out of the pen. "Game's been playing a long con. He took the time to get to know Carson, to find the right way into her world. He hacked her phone, but not before doing research on the developer of an app that Carson ended up using. As Gareth Maughan, he offered the developer a ton of investor money to gain access to his code, citing due diligence, and hacked in from there. He took over the app, and the app downloaded bad software onto everyone's phones who were a part of the community. Then he waltzed right through the open door and started following Carson's every movement. He timed her kidnapping with the delivery of the notes to Avery Conway, plus used Carson's phone to send a text to confirm he had her. Those aren't the actions of a hothead. That is calculated long-term planning."

"Your point?"

"The Game you describe is a tool. A blunt tool, at that. These plans have an elegance to them. They took time, energy, patience. More than just money, obviously."

Angelie said nothing. Jackson raised an excellent point, one she'd only partially considered.

"Are you saying you think someone is helping him?"

Jackson nodded. "I assume you have more enemies than friends."

That made Angelie bark out a laugh. "You could say that. There are any number of people all over the world who would love to see me dead."

"Then you should consider the bigger picture. Perhaps this isn't just about Carson, and drawing you out. Perhaps this is about eliminating you, period."

"It is possible. Though I see no reason to go to such lengths to kill me."

"If you've retired, you've turned down a number of jobs, I assume. Maybe this was a sure thing. Maybe someone wants retribution for a wrong you've caused them, and Game is simply a means to an end."

Angelie watched the blond head bend over the papers and sighed inwardly. The constant barrage of Jackson's principles and scruples and insights was getting to her. Especially because they were logical and sound.

Few rational people decide to take lives for the fun. Some are monsters. Some do it for money. Some do it for revenge. But the rational people, people like Angelie? She was not a monster and fell squarely into both remaining categories. She'd had her vengeance on all who'd wronged her, though. That was how she met Jackson in the first place. She'd been poised for revenge and instead learned the truth about her childhood and her parents' demise. She'd taken care of business, and she'd genuinely thought this was behind her.

Yet here she was, seated across from the very sort of person she steered away from at all costs, after a surprisingly companionable meal and a bottle of wine, working together to solve a problem.

She should kill Jackson immediately and walk away forever.

She knew she wouldn't, and that made her all the angrier.

Angelie was getting soft. She was no longer the striking cobra, but a tool for Thierry and his Macallan cronies. She wanted this partnership less than Jackson did, she suspected.

Santiago stepped into the living room to make a call, leaving the two women alone at the table.

A few moments later, Jackson looked up. "Why are you staring at me?" she asked warily. "I can't work under your basilisk glare."

Angelie laughed. "Thinking. We are an unlikely pair."

"You said it." But there was no heat in the recrimination.

"I only want to recover the girl. Then you and I will go our separate ways. I will honor our time working together by not cutting your throat in your sleep and adding another scar to your collection. I hope you will offer me the same promise."

Jackson set down the papers and highlighter and regarded Angelie thoughtfully. A hand went to the thin white line on her neck, then to the puckered flesh on her temple. Angelie knew both scars were souvenirs of attacks by killers Jackson was tracking. She'd put her life on the line more than once in her quest for justice. Angelie could respect that.

Jackson's mismatched gray eyes were even more dissimilar in the shadows of the kitchen. An unusual woman. Beautiful, but not in a conventional way. Angelie was neither plain nor stunning, just a woman who could disappear in a crowd. Jackson would never have that advantage. It would make her work with Macallan difficult.

"I quit my job," Taylor said finally.

Angelie tried not to show her surprise. "Why?"

"I'd already planned to retire. Thierry's been after me for a while, and the gig seems interesting enough. I like the idea of being proactive, investigating people who come across the radar, stopping their crimes before they happen. But things have been...off, for a while now. I never expected to live in the same world as the kind of evil I've come across in the past few years. People have lost themselves. It's not only the world, which is its own problem. It's smaller. More personal, more devious. Did you know that in Nashville, some of the bartenders help roofie women? If you slide a hundred dollars to the right person, they will hand over a drink that knocks out a woman for the night. And we're meant to look the other way. We can't police anymore. We can't stop the evil. It's terrifying to me to see the breadth and depth of the depravity. It has multiplied, morphed, become something so tangible I can't hope to contain it. Nor am I allowed to, in many cases."

"I will come back to Nashville and murder them all."

Jackson's lips quirked. "Don't you think I'm tempted? Don't you think that infuriates me to the point of no return?"

"It doesn't, not if you don't act on those emotions."

"I don't have that luxury. I simply have to lead by example and try to make people follow. Try to make them choose to do the right thing instead of the wrong one."

"How could you ever control another human's decisions?"

"Good question. Deterrence used to work, at least a bit. I could sit down with a troubled kid and put the fear of God into him. Now? I try that? I'll get sued and lose my job. I can't stand by and watch it happen, either." She shrugged. "I had to get out. It's no longer a space I can function in."

"And Macallan is?"

"I don't know. I certainly can't do what you do and live with myself."

"You could learn. Trust me."

"No." The emphatic tone was tempered by a quick smile. "It's not who I am. I suspect there is a strength to you that I am missing. You were born in blood. Thierry told me how your parents died. I'm sorry."

Angelie didn't respond, and Jackson went on. "I was simply trained to react to the atrocities I saw. No, I couldn't take a life for money. In defense, yes. I have. Lord knows I probably will again. But I could never hunt someone down and eliminate them."

"Why are you telling me this?" Angelie asked. She was intrigued, to say the least, but sensed Jackson was leading her somewhere.

"Because I don't like who I am with you around. The wolves inside me turn dark. So yes, Angelie. I will honor our agreement. I will not slit *your* throat in your sleep. But when we're done here, when Game is dead and gone and Carson back home with her mom, I don't want to see you again. Deal?"

Angelie nodded, surprised by how sharply the big woman's words sliced.

"Do not worry, Taylor. People like me don't have many friends."

"Good."

They worked in silence then, the only sounds the crackling fire and the whisper of paper.

Near dawn, Jackson handed over a piece of paper, scribbled with arrows and lines of yellow. "I found him. Just outside of Geneva, in a town called Prévessin-Moëns. It's about twenty minutes west of the city. He's rented a house."

"He rents a lot of houses."

"This one has a name."

Angelie felt that tiny tick of adrenaline that said something was about to happen, something she wasn't going to like. "What's it called?"

"Les Chambres des Anges. The Angel's Rooms."

FORTY-SEVEN

MONDAY: GENEVA, SWITZERLAND

THEY WERE wheels up at noon and driving into the Geneva suburbs an hour after that. Santiago and Angelie had an arsenal waiting when they landed, a black Land Rover packed to the brim with weapons and materiel they'd need to assault the house.

Geneva was experiencing a clear, cool day, the sky an unearthly blue, the air as crisp and clean as the snow that was surely on its way soon. They crossed through the city proper silently, Taylor watching the Jet d'Eau reliably spewing water into the sky and the tour boats swinging ever closer, just enough so the delighted tourists could feel that chilling spray but not get soaked.

She was starting to have serious doubts about the situation she'd found herself in. She'd been trying not to think about Nashville, about what it felt like to lay down her badge and gun on Huston's desk. The moment of freedom, of vindication, was quickly turning into a gnawing question: *Did I do the right thing?* While Angelie's long history inspired some confidence, Taylor was not at all thrilled to be riding into battle with the assassins. It went against everything she'd always thought she believed in.

At the same time, a girl's life was at stake. And she would do anything she had to in order to make sure Carson Conway got home safely. Not to mention the opportunity to reunite Baldwin with his son.

So did that make her different from Angelie and her ilk? Or the same?

The thrum of energy in the car was almost too much. Both Santiago and Angelie had done little but grunt orders at her since she'd found the house, and their intensity along with Taylor's wandering thoughts was becoming oppressive.

"This is a little overkill, don't you think?" Taylor asked. Her legs were bent nearly to her chin to fit in between the cases of guns.

Angelie stayed staring straight ahead, as she had since they'd discovered Game's possible location, teeth clenched and hands on her knees. "This is a trap, you do understand this? He is thumbing his nose at us, wants us to come in quietly, to try and sneak Carson away. We will not. We will drop a bomb on this house and drag his sorry ass kicking and screaming on fire into the dirt of the road."

"Temper," Taylor said. Angelie shot a nasty glance over her shoulder. She looked like she might just scream again. "I agree it's a trap," Taylor continued, trying for a reasonable tone. "Why else would he rent a house with your name in it? But maybe we don't have to blow up the whole block to get in. Maybe we could be a little more stealthy."

Angelie fully turned in her seat and looked at Taylor scrunched in the back seat. "It is a suburban neighborhood, Taylor. Of course I'm not being literal." Disdain dripped from every word.

Santiago huffed out a laugh. "She's blowing off steam so

there's no adrenaline left to get in the way. You should try it. Scream."

Taylor rolled her eyes. "I don't need to scream. I am just fine."

"You should. You'd probably feel better. I could bounce a quarter off you, you're wound so tight."

"You're welcome to keep your observations to yourself. I feel fine," Taylor said, surprised to realize she meant it. She'd talked to Baldwin briefly before the plane left France, and as always, hearing his voice had settled her nerves and recommitted her mentally to this job. *Remember that, girl. It's just a job. You can figure out the rest later.* "I find preparation to be the most soothing part of an op. So why don't we cover what happens when we get to the house."

"We'll park in the lot of the grocery down the street. Santiago and I will take our weapons and hike in. You will then proceed to the end of the street to wait for our egress." Angelie's dismissive tone grated on Taylor's nerves.

"If it's a trap, doesn't walking in the front seem...foolhardy?"

"We're going to go in through the neighbor's home. It is less than fifteen meters from the target. They share a pool, a sidewalk, and a drive. They also share a basement door, which is where we'll come in. The owner of both homes is the same, he rents the house next door to travelers visiting Geneva. Game has taken the south-facing home. We go in through the basement, find Carson, dispatch Game, if he's there, and leave."

"Too easy," Taylor said, feeling a spike of annoyance. "They'll have the door between the two houses reinforced. He'll expect you to come in that way."

Angelie snorted. "Then, by all means, Taylor, you plan our ingress."

"The roof." Taylor shoved her phone toward the front seat, where a satellite image showed remarkable detail of the property and surrounding neighborhood. "See the solar panels?

There's a widow's walk behind them, so there must be an access there, on the western edge, next to the third array. The view must be lovely from that angle."

"Too exposed, and there's no guarantee we can even get it open," Angelie said dismissively, but Santiago laughed.

"Go down the chimney like Santa fucking Claus, why don't we? It's not a bad idea."

"Thank you for the vote of confidence," Taylor said dryly. "There will be stairs down, either into the top floor or the attic. You can access the roof from the house down the street. There's a tree with plenty of branches. We don't even need to be on the road the house is on. He won't see you coming from above."

Angelie flicked through the shots, magnifying the screen, making it smaller, turning it this way and that. "This one?" she said finally, pointing to the house Taylor was suggesting they start from.

"Yes. This is a working neighborhood, according to the brief. Many are with The Hague and use these homes for vacation rental properties when they're not in town. If we want to try now, with luck most of the people will still be at work. But not for long. We should wait until dark."

"Hmm." Angelie twisted the phone around a few more times, then handed it back. "Okay. We'll try it your way. We stage and wait. There's no sense trying to do this in the daylight." She looked Taylor over critically. "You're too big of a target."

Everything went fine until Santiago stepped wrong off the last tree branch and slid right off the roof.

Taylor watched him land hard through the night vision scope they'd left her, a blurred shape in the darkness, and was out of the vehicle and hoofing it down the hill before he managed to get to his feet. When he did, he grimaced and stood with his left foot up like a flamingo.

"Is it broken?" she asked quietly, slinging his arm around her shoulder.

"Fuck if I know. Damn it."

She stood quietly for a moment, taking the smaller man's weight easily. "Doesn't seem like we've disturbed anyone. No lights, no movement when you fell. They mustn't be home. Let's see that ankle."

She put a pen-sized flashlight into her mouth and took a look, pulling down his sock to a hissing noise through his teeth that told her if it wasn't broken, it was at least very badly sprained. The ankle was swelling before her eyes, bruising beginning along the shin and heel.

"This is going to need attention."

"Forget about me. Get on that roof, girl. She needs your help."

"You can't walk, you idiot. Let me at least get you back to the truck."

"I'll make it. But I can't climb that damn tree again. Go. Seriously, I'll get to the vehicle and we'll swap roles. I'll be ready for you when you bring out Carson. It's my left, thank God, I can still drive. Just be careful by the gutter. There's a soft spot, I stepped right in it and it twisted my damn leg. I was off the roof before I could blink."

"I know, I watched."

He handed over his machine pistol and ammunition pouch. She hesitated only a moment before nodding, slinging the weapon around her shoulders so it lay crosswise over her chest, checking the clip, then jogging to the tree.

She hadn't climbed a tree since she was a girl. Doing it armed was certainly a new challenge. She managed, grateful for the natural toeholds and her regular workouts. Angelie had shimmied up the tree like a leopard. Taylor was decidedly more of a ground cat.

Careful not to make the same mistake as Santiago, she moved onto the steeper roofline and stepped carefully. Angelie was at the widow's walk already, and Taylor could see her posture change when she, not Santiago, scrambled into view. Her head was shaking immediately.

"What the hell?" she whispered when Taylor got to her.

"Santiago fell. His ankle is trashed. You've got me instead. Let's go."

Operational Angelie was laser focused. She didn't hesitate again, eased open the door. Sure enough, the stairs were there, just as Taylor had suggested.

They went quietly, one step at a time. The treads didn't creak; these houses were relatively new and hadn't settled yet. It was dark, but Taylor had the penlight and she shone it down by her leg, careful never to let it go horizontally. It took seven steps to hit the door. Unsurprisingly, it was locked.

Angelie gestured and they went back up the stairs to the roof, stretching out against the shingles so they weren't easily seen from the ground.

"What do you propose?" Taylor asked, but Angelie was already digging in her bag. She pulled out a small leather bundle.

Lock picks.

"I propose the old-fashioned way," she said, grinning like a pirate, and shimmied back down the stairs.

FORTY-EIGHT

ANGELIE MOVED QUICKLY, her motions born of years of practice. Insert, insert, twist. They were through the door a heartbeat later, weapons at the ready. She would have much preferred Santiago on her six, but the big woman could hold her own. She hoped. She also hoped Jackson didn't get a wild hair and shoot her in the back of the head.

They crept through the hall into the laundry room, eyes adjusting to the gloom. The house felt empty. Neglected. They cleared room after room on the bottom floor, finally traversing the stairs and entering a spacious tiled living room. Angelie looked for traps, but there was nothing.

It was Jackson who said, in a strangled voice, "I don't think they're here. But he left you a message."

Angelie shone her light onto the table. A delicate fingertip, wrapped in what looked like a lock of thick blond hair, sitting atop a three-by-five card.

"Le salaud," Angelie cursed. "He is hurting her to hurt me."

"There's a note."

"Finally. What does the bastard want?"

Taylor was already wearing nitrile gloves; she swung the

weapon across her back before handling the note and the girl's finger.

"All it says is *the storm on the sea*. Below it, *trade*. What does that mean?"

Angelie started to laugh. "It's a painting. Rembrandt. *The Storm on the Sea of Galilee*. It was stolen in 1990 from the Gardner Museum in Boston, along with several others. He's always had a thing for it."

"And you know where this stolen painting is?"

Jackson sounded downright prim, which made Angelie laugh again. It felt good. She was relaxing too much, though. She couldn't afford to drop her guard; that's how people got killed on assignment.

"I do, actually."

"Did you steal it yourself?"

"But of course not. I am not a thief. We happened across it on a job once, though. It's impossible. He's out of his mind."

"Where is it?"

"That depends on where the current owner is. It moves."

They're protecting it?"

"Not exactly. It is on a plane. The owner of this plane is a very rich man, who loves to play with fire. A Saudi sheik. It is not as if we will be able to bargain with him. To get the painting, we will have to steal it."

"Steal a painting from a plane. That doesn't sound too difficult."

"We can only hope that is true. We must hurry. I don't want to linger here."

The egress was easier knowing no one was there to stop them. They found Santiago in the truck, sweating bullets, his ankle three times normal size. "I'm off the mission," he said, and Angelie couldn't help but agree. He was going to need medical attention, quickly.

"Alan can be here—"

"*Non*. That is not necessary. We know what we need to do. He's hurt Carson, but she is still alive."

"You hope," Jackson said.

"I hope. He wants that damn Rembrandt. He'll trade it for the girl."

She gave him the note, and Santiago eyed her dubiously. "How do you propose to make this happen?"

"We find Ahmad Abdullah. His plane will be close by. Where might he be?"

Santiago scratched his chin. His normally olive skin was pale; he was clearly in pain. "Well, we're getting to the end of the continental polo season. Maybe we get lucky and he's in England. I'll get Alan on it."

"You need this ankle worked on, my friend. We'll need to leave you with James."

"James? Who's James?" Jackson asked.

"A doctor. He'll meet us at the safe house in Chevreuse, and we will plan the op. When we find Ahmad's plane, we will go there immediately. We will take the painting, and we will get Carson back. By this time tomorrow, this will all be wrapped."

"You sound awfully sure."

Angelie smiled and put the truck in gear. "Trust me."

Two hours later, they were back in France. The doctor met them at the house, and assured them Santi's ankle was not broken, only a very bad high ankle sprain. He casted him and gave him painkillers, which Santiago manfully declined. Angelie shoved two in his mouth anyway, and he was sound asleep upstairs with his foot resting on a pillow. Jackson had been quiet all the way back, and once they'd arrived, had excused herself to take a shower. Once the doctor was paid and sent on his way, Angelie was left alone downstairs, searching for a madman.

Sheik Ahmad bin Abdullah was a handsome rake who brokered in stolen treasures, flying them around the world, slipping through customs like water through a sieve. He had money to burn, zero conscience, and a smile that could make angels weep. Damn if Angelie didn't like the man. But she was wary of him, too. Ahmad would not take this slight lightly. Even if they were only borrowing the painting for a short time, he would come after her, and see her dead.

The best choice was to make sure he didn't know the painting had been stolen in the first place. Especially not by Angelie.

It would be a neat trick to steal the painting, trade it for Carson, murder Joseph Game, and return the painting—without Ahmad realizing it was gone. Not impossible, but close to it.

But Angelie always did like a challenge.

She plotted long into the night. Alan was in regular touch, searching for Ahmad and his flying grift. Around midnight, Jackson wandered into the kitchen. She poured herself a glass of wine, glanced at Angelie's empty glass, brought the bottle over, and splashed some red into the crystal. Then she joined Angelie at the table.

"So?" she asked. "Where are we going?"

"London. Looks like he's in a slot at Northolt for the week. Only presents a slight challenge, as it's the RAF base. Crawling with security. Which is why he likes it. Plus, you know that sort of man. He gets a level of excitement from thumbing his nose at authority. The government is protecting him while he's stealing from them, and they don't have any idea, that sort of thing."

"How can he stay off their radar if he's so notorious?"

"He's only notorious in certain circles. The public persona is one of great respect and admiration. Above reproach."

"So what's the plan?"

"We get into the private jet area, to his slot, and we take his plane."

Angelie had to admit, it was almost worth dropping that bomb to see the shock on Jackson's face. If she weren't already lost in thought on how, exactly, they were going to pull this off, she might have even laughed.

"That's impossible. You want to steal a G-Five—"

"Not a Gulfstream. A 747-800. Fully customized. Bought from the factory and retrofitted to his specifics. It's a flying palace. There's an *Atlantic* piece on the renovation, very detailed, very specific. It gives me the new layout. Incredibly stupid of him to allow, because now he's operationally insecure."

The incredulity written on Jackson's face was priceless. "Angelie. I'm not the kind of woman who would second-guess you in your chosen field. But that's simply not going to happen. We can't steal a 747."

Angelie began to laugh. "Oh, if you could see your face. Of course we aren't going to steal the plane. We're simply going to take the painting. Then we will fly to the location Game gives us, exchange Carson for the painting, and we will disappear. Forever, probably. I can't imagine Ahmad taking kindly to losing his prized possession. If he finds out who was behind it, we'll both lose our heads."

"Ha ha. Great. Lovely. How are we going to take the painting?" Jackson shook her head. "I can't believe I'm even having this conversation."

"The painting is built into the plane. Behind bulletproof glass. It's wired and alarmed. For most people, they would not bother. It is too much trouble to steal."

"Then Game is just trying to get us killed. He must expect us to remove the painting from the plane, right?"

"Perhaps. Perhaps he believes the challenge is one we cannot accomplish and is laughing at us for even considering it.

It is difficult, yes, but not impossible. We have a high-end tactical micro explosive that can sever the wired connection. It's very small. If placed properly, it will release the locks. Then we'll be able to cut the glass with a laser. There will be a pressure-sensor alarm inside, but with luck, I can circumvent that, as well. We remove the painting, make our way back to our plane, and fly out, with none the wiser. Easy."

Jackson cocked a perfect eyebrow. "Easy. Bulletproof glass–cutting lasers and tactical micro explosives. What is this, a James Bond movie?"

"You lack imagination. The writers of those movies get their ideas from *my* operations."

That got her. Jackson actually laughed. Angelie continued. "But I don't care about these inconsequential details. That vile man killed my friend. He kidnapped a dead man's daughter—an innocent—and cut off part of Carson's finger to taunt me further. I am no longer willing to play this game of his. We are wheels up in three hours. I suggest you get some rest. I need you sharp."

Jackson looked like she wanted to ask more, but Angelie needed to focus. She didn't need the constant mosquito patter of the oh-so-ethical cop right now. She watched the big woman finish off her wine—deliberately sipping until the glass was empty—pour a fresh glass, then march up the stairs, annoyance bleeding off her.

Jackson was going to have to unlearn quite a lot if she wanted to succeed in this world. Was the woman an intuitive investigator? Yes, absolutely. But the constant second-guessing, trying to find a path that wasn't illegal, that didn't contravene her morality...Angelie would go mad, faced with much more of that. She couldn't imagine Thierry would put up with it, either.

At the thought of Thierry, Angelie tensed. What was he up to? Why was he trying to bring this woman into the fold? It made no sense, not really.

Stop fretting, she told herself. *There is more than enough worry to go around.*

She turned back to her computer, and the plan ahead.

Get through this. Kill Game. Save Carson. These are the only things that matter. Then you can go home, and start over.

FORTY-NINE

TAYLOR TOOK HER WINE UPSTAIRS, shut her door, and dialed Baldwin. She needed a distraction. Angelie's plan was audacious, crazy, and loaded with treachery. There was no way it was going to succeed. Who steals a stolen painting from a 747, for heaven's sake? Especially off a Royal Air Force base? Clearly, the assassin had lost her mind.

"Everything okay?" he asked without preamble.

"Not even close. How are you?"

His voice warmed. "Missing you, as always. When will you be home?" There was a slight challenge in his tone, which she ignored.

"I'm not sure. We haven't accomplished our goal. Soon, though. Moving on...have you spoken to the boys?" Baldwin paused as if he wanted to argue, and she said softly, "Tell me. I need the distraction."

"Marcus shot me the series of murders to profile, 'just for fun,' as he says. I've leafed through them. In my professional opinion, you certainly have a serial killer in this man. The MOs are similar, the victimologies are similar. All the women had ties to the music industry, all went missing over the past decade. So far, there's no physical evidence that ties him to any of the women, nor have they found anything digital, though it's early days there. He's incredibly organized, but he has patterns —the gravesite at Radnor is clearly a touchstone for him, and I bet there's a nest of some sort in the LA area, as well. He's been at this a while, which means he's good at compartmentalizing —he's the head of a major music label, with a lot of eyes on him. Which also means he's the kind of man who panics when he's found out. The question is whether these are premeditated murders or simply transactional, whether he stalks and kidnaps, or kills impulsively. Georgia Wray's murder didn't seem well planned—or it was and the boyfriend just got the better of him and was eliminated later. These might not have a sexual component, but they are all about power. You'll get him from that angle, I think. My advice to Marcus was to rattle his cage, watch him, and see what he does. Chances are he'll give us what we need to charge him. Right now, though, it's all circumstantial."

"Even with the voice recording from Justin Osborne's? You don't think we can't do voice recognition and match it to him?"

"You can, but you know that's not enough. That audio could be spun as Justin shot himself just as easily."

"Damn. I was hoping you'd see it differently. All right. I'll give Marcus a call, and—"

"Taylor. This isn't your responsibility. This case isn't yours. You don't work with Marcus anymore. You quit. Remember?"

She took a deep breath. Of course she remembered. That didn't mean she didn't care, that she didn't want to see justice done. It was bad enough to lose Georgia and Justin, but that there was more, a murderer hiding behind the veneer of a successful businessman with the means to travel the world and kill indiscriminately? It pissed her off.

That little voice inside her: *No different than Game, Taylor. No different...*

"I've hardly forgotten. I just...maybe I should have waited until we had this case wrapped, you know? I feel responsible."

"They are more than capable of handling this without you, my dear."

"Ouch."

"Taylor, you trained them all. They're going to take every single step you'd take yourself." He was silent for a moment. "This is bigger than that, isn't it? You're rethinking the decision to leave Metro?"

"No." She answered so quickly she surprised herself. "No, I'm not. I just want to see this case to its conclusion. Both of them. Carson is starting to lose body parts. We need to make our move, right away, or we're going to lose her. And I can't lose her, Baldwin. I can't."

"Do I want to know how you're going to find her?"

"No. God, no. You want to stay as far away from me—from this—as you possibly can."

"Are you breaking the law?"

"With that woman at the helm? Regularly."

He huffed out a laugh. "Maybe we should wait to discuss the details until you get home."

"That would be wise." She played with the end of her ponytail, wrapping it around her finger. That just made her think of Carson, and the pain she must be in, the coil of blond hair around the delicate fingertip, and she loosened her grip.

"You can come home now, babe." Baldwin's voice was soft, and she yearned to be next to him, to have his strength holding her up. "You don't have to do this. You don't have to be responsible for them all."

If he only knew...

"I do, though. I'll be home soon. This is almost over. We

aren't playing around anymore. So don't worry. I've got it all under control."

"That's what has me worried," he said. "Just...don't compromise yourself too much, Taylor. You lose your moral compass, and you'll have nothing left."

"I hear you. And I love you. I'll call you when it's done."

She hung up before he could say anything more and dialed Marcus. He answered on the first ring.

"I was hoping you'd get in touch. Everything okay?"

"Okay enough. I hear you're getting a profile that matches your gut instincts. Where do we stand on Bloom? Where do *you* stand, I mean? Baldwin already told me his conclusions."

"Man, this is going to take some getting used to."

"Tell me about it."

"We're going to do what Baldwin suggested. Spook him and watch him run. We have cops in LA on alert, and we have eyes on him here, too. He's scheduled to come back to Nashville tonight and be back in LA by the weekend. Sometime in the next few days, we need to hang this on him. Lincoln has a line into his computer and phone. O'Roarke is working on the voice recognition, though without video or other evidence, it's going to be a difficult path to have it hold up in court. We're trying to get paper to go into his house here, but it's taking forever. The audio isn't going to be enough, we need more."

"Agreed. I'd reach out to both Georgia's bandmates and her parents, let them know there's a development. See if they have anything else to add to this. What did her phone give us—you?"

"All the texts between her and her folks. There's nothing illegal on there. Just complaints—he's controlling me, made me break up with Justin, need to get out of the contract. Nothing that implicates Bloom in the murders."

"There has to be something else, Marcus. Something we're missing."

"Agreed. We're working on it, Taylor. The second I get the

paper, and we're up on his phones, his houses, everything, we'll nail him. Everything good with you?"

"Good enough. I'm going dark, though, so I wanted to check in before I did. And no, you don't want to know. Well, maybe you do, but it will be a story for our grandkids one day, okay?"

"Just let me know if there's anything you need. Seriously. I don't care if Huston fires me. If you get into trouble, shout and I will drop everything. We all feel that way, you know."

"I do. You're a good guy, you know that? Hang in there. Talk soon."

She hung up and stared at the phone for a few moments, then went to the window. The grounds were charming, and she wasn't tired. She decided to take a walk, burn off some steam.

Angelie Delacroix did not *need* Taylor for this job. Yes, she had come in handy when Santiago hurt his ankle, but they had plenty of people on their team who could have slotted in for backup. She was starting to wonder if maybe Thierry wanted Taylor compromised in some way. Hunting down a killer was well within her purview. Stealing things, murdering people who got in her way—that was not.

But if she wasn't an official law enforcement agent...she no longer had that cover.

Hunting a killer wearing a uniform was no different than hunting without one. Game was no different from Bloom. From the Pretender, from the Snow White killer. Those who would see them punished were different, but the basic premise? Rid the world of those who do harm to innocents: that had been her mantra for as long as she could remember.

She lapped the garden twice. Thinking. Thinking.

Admittedly, she was getting tired of having this argument with herself. She was as willing as anyone to bend the rules if it meant getting the job done. She'd done so more times than she could count. Was the resistance she was feeling simply a function of taking orders from someone she didn't respect? Or something more?

That wasn't the right word, either. She did respect Angelie, albeit grudgingly. She was a devoted friend, and one hell of an operator. She was quick on her feet, and if Taylor was being honest with herself, certain of her path. Angelie wasn't making laps around a fragrant garden, wrestling with her conscience. She was making plans to remove her enemies from the world. Which meant she was ten times more effective at her job than Taylor. Besides, who was she to judge Angelie Delacroix?

Ah, but you're judge, jury, and executioner, Taylor. That's your job. It's always been your job.

Then why in the world was she going along with this?

Oh, that one was easy. To save the innocent. That was always the reason. It mattered not whether she could sleep at night so long as innocents didn't have to suffer.

The gardens were quiet, perfumed with the last of the season's roses and a smattering of bougainvillea fighting for purchase before the chill stole the blooms for good. Well-established swatches of night-blooming jasmine, too—whoever built this garden was a romantic. The gravel crunched under her boots, and as she paced in the moonlight, she felt a peace steal over her. These past couple of years had been hard. She'd nearly died at the hands of a serial killer, then at the hands of a terrifying madwoman who almost managed to drive her insane. She'd been forced to question everything she believed after that. She'd lost people she loved. These things change a person. You begin questioning the ways of the universe. How could she not wonder if her path was supposed to be altered?

It was. She knew that. And it was time to stop fighting herself, her conscience. She would always do the right thing in the end. There was no reason to worry anymore.

Taylor made one last turn and started toward the house,

just in time to see Angelie tearing out the door, calling her name.

"Jackson? We need to go, now. Now!"

Taylor jogged the rest of the way to the house.

"What's the matter?"

"Game. The *salaud* is changing the rules. Avery is missing. Alan feels certain Game has taken her. He is no longer willing to wait for us to meet his demands."

They were in the house now, where the gear was already stacked by the door. Santiago was downstairs, pale but upright, his foot on the chair next to him, typing on the laptop and talking to Alan on a sat phone.

"Jackson is here. Tell her what you just told me."

Alan's voice was strained; though she'd never spoken to him, she could hear the stress in his tone. "You know she's been upset about how we've handled everything. Said she was going crazy locked in the house. I agreed that she could go for a run, and she was out the door before I could stop her. That was three hours ago. I got worried after hour one and took a lap, found her phone by the bushes at the end of the street. I pulled the cameras from the intersection. A black SUV stopped and snatched her. I couldn't get the plates, they were covered."

"Damn it. That means Game is in the States, while we're chasing him here in Europe," Taylor said.

"You're assuming he's working alone," Santiago said.

"A dangerous assumption," Angelie said quietly.

"So what do you want to do?" Alan asked.

"We get to the plane and get that damn painting. Santi and Alan will keep tracking Avery, see if she shows up anywhere. The pilots are gassed up and waiting for us. Stay in touch, Alan."

The call ended, and without hesitating, Taylor shouldered three bags of gear and started for the door.

"What, you aren't going to argue with me?" Angelie called after her.

She looked back over her shoulder. "Nope. Your show. I'm along for the ride to help however I can." She clattered into the gravel drive and dumped the bags in the back of the waiting SUV. "Tell me what you want me to do, and I'll do it."

Angelie joined her at the tailgate, tossing in two more bags. She watched her briefly, then laughed lightly. "Uh-oh. I think I might miss the old Jackson."

FIFTY

AVERY CONWAY CAME to with a blinding headache. Darkness surrounded her. She took a moment to figure out why—was she masked? Blind? Or was it simply an absence of light so complete it was like being inside a coffin?

Don't think that. That was one of her worst nightmares, being buried alive. Her heart rate ticked up. Why had she gone there? She knew better than to give her fears free rein.

It was coming back to her now, in bits and pieces—jogging, being struck from behind, the sharp pinch of a hypodermic needle in the crook of her elbow.

Oh, my darling Carson.

Is this what her daughter had experienced as well?

She started to move, to struggle, and realized she was tied to a chair. She tried to shout—she was gagged. Impotent. Helpless. At the mercy of whoever had taken her—and she knew exactly who. That bastard Joseph Game had stolen her daughter and now had Avery, as well.

Why?

What was he trying to accomplish? What value did the two women have?

Anger filled her. In the years since Richard had died, she'd asked "why" a thousand times. Why her? Why him? Why was their family marked for tragedy? A ridiculous accident; a life snuffed out in a heartbeat. You never stop to think it might be the last time you have a chance to say something nice. *I love you. Drive safe. Have a good day.* She'd spent years bullying herself for not saying the right things the morning he left.

Now, all her anger was *at* him. *What have you done to us? What have you done to your daughter? This is your fault. You have killed us all.*

She heard a hinge creak and felt a draft. A door had been opened. She smelled yeast.

Yeast? The bakery? There was a proofing room in the basement, was she being held there? In her husband's old business?

Alan. Oh my God, what have they done to Alan? She couldn't lose any more people she loved. She just couldn't.

She screamed behind the gag, but all that came out was a whimper. She heard something drag across the room, like the leg of a chair, scraping the cement with a screech. She could feel someone coming closer. Someone—or something—was down here with her, and she was deathly afraid.

Before she lost her head completely, she breathed in deeply through her nose. Her adrenaline was on overdrive, swamping her body with panic. She needed to keep her wits about her. She wasn't going to go down without a fight. She owed that to Carson, at the very least. She knew in her heart her daughter was fighting. She would, too.

A sharp pain ripped across the top of her wrist, and she smelled her own blood. She began to struggle, screaming again behind the gag, her voice only making little "ugh ugh ugh" grunts.

"Scream again, and I will cut off your hand."

That voice. So familiar. Amused. Yet so harsh, so cruel.

The voice of a friend. The voice of a trusted companion.

"Do you agree, Avery? I'll take off the gag if you promise to behave."

She nodded, and the gag came loose.

"Alan? What are you doing? Get me out of here."

"Soon enough," he said, and the horror of his nonchalance gripped her spine.

"I don't understand, Alan. What is happening?"

Three things, at once. A shout. A gunshot. And a sudden fight, one of such intensity she shut her eyes against the disequilibrium of movement. When she opened them, she saw two shadows, fists flying, moving so quickly it was like she was watching a movie, a staged sequence, a choreographed scene. Only one of the men was better than the other, that was readily apparent. The weaker one went down, and a sickening crack echoed through the room. She knew a neck had been broken.

Whose?

A light swung into her eyes and she was blinded, her senses on overload. She screamed, and a soft voice shushed her.

"Are you okay? My God, Avery. Tell me you're okay."

She was imagining things. It couldn't be. It *couldn't* be. She was dreaming. Of course, she was dreaming. This was a nightmare. She was going to wake in her bed, feeling foolish for the spark of hope and joy that filled her at this very moment. Hope and joy and fury.

He was dead, had been for years.

A bottle of cool water was pressed to her lips.

Her vision cleared, and a face shone in the gloom, the light from below his chin like a campfire ghoul telling a creepy story. The face of a stranger. The face of a lover. The face of her very dead husband.

Not so dead, after all. Richard stood before her, a little thinner, a little older.

And very much alive.

The water must have been drugged because she was floating, drifting, and as she slid into darkness, all she could think was *You bastard. I am going to kill you for this.*

And then, as she disappeared: *Richard. Oh, my darling Richard.*

FIFTY-ONE

TUESDAY: LONDON, ENGLAND

THE PLAN WAS SIMPLE, as far as plans went. Even Taylor had to admit it had a certain kind of elegance. But elegance and reality were two different things.

Fly their jet into Northolt—it was a more and more popular business aircraft destination as well as the RAF base, so a Gulfstream wouldn't stand out at all. This shift in Northolt's policies worked in their favor across the board—Macallan had enough clout to have multiple airports to which their aircraft was welcomed. No, the landing wasn't the issue. The issue was getting into Ahmad's plane. It was under guard, in a hangar, being serviced, while Ahmad played in the end-of-season polo matches. They had to get past the guards, into the hangar, and steal the damn painting, then get back to their jet and fly the hell out.

Taylor had bit back a thousand reasons why this was a *very* bad idea and was only slightly reassured when Santiago called to let them know he'd pulled the plane's maintenance records and they were getting really damn lucky because the service was finished and a flight plan had been registered for the following day. Ahmad was moving on to Brazil, and they were catching him just in time. Getting in and out of Brazil unnoticed would have presented more problems. Not insurmountable, but a much more difficult operation. So the plan was solidified—while Angelie and Taylor made their way to the 747, Santiago would lay in their cover should they be stopped: they were there to repossess the 747 for the bank.

Apparently, this was a relatively common occurrence. When Taylor questioned this, out of genuine curiosity, Angelie explained.

"We often pose as plane repo men. Jet repossession is a huge business. You'd be amazed at how many people can't afford their jets. It's a lucrative industry, and all the private airports are aware that it happens. We come in under the auspices of taking the plane back for the bank. It gets us into the airports, and on the ground, in many areas we would otherwise have trouble getting into. Some of the more private airports are rarely surprised when a group of us fly in and steal whatever is sitting there, looking out of place. Gets us into trouble sometimes, too, when the owners are expecting the real repo men to come and they fight back, but it's a solid tool."

"That's clever," Taylor said, and Angelie laughed.

"Only when it works. Which is half the time."

"And the other half?"

Angelie jacked the slide on her pistol and didn't say a word.

"Great. What else do I need to know for this?"

"Just follow my lead, and have my back if things go south. Santiago would normally be my partner on a job like this. We've worked together for so long we don't even need to talk."

"I have that relationship with my men as well. They anticipate my every move."

Angelie nodded. "You must promise me that if I give you an order, you will obey it, no questions asked. I like you, Taylor. I think we could work well together, given the proper circumstances. But there might be shooting, and there might be death. I need to know you aren't going to be second-guessing my every move."

The pilot, whom Angelie had introduced only as Jean-Paul, came over the speaker, interrupting them. "We'll be on the ground in ten," he said.

"Roger that," Angelie replied. She turned back to Taylor. "So?"

"It's your show, and I'll do what's needed. Okay?"

"D'accord. Merci," she added, and Taylor smiled. My God, she was practically taming the damn shrew.

As warned, they touched down ten minutes later. The plane taxied to its assigned slot, and Taylor and Angelie stepped out onto the tarmac into the cool London air. A mist hung in the sky, not a falling rain, but Taylor instantly had droplets of water on her leather jacket. They weren't drawing any attention at the moment, so she shouldered her backpack, which was full of specialized equipment in various foam-lined boxes, and followed Angelie. She could see streams of people in knots moving from the many planes on the tarmac toward the jet center, where their private cars would be waiting. They joined that flow for a hundred feet, then Angelie gently nudged Taylor's shoulder and stepped aside. Taylor followed.

They started west. The hangar that housed Ahmad's plane was approximately five hundred meters down the tarmac. Angelie hurried, and Taylor tried to ignore the eyes she knew must be on them. This was much more open than she'd expected. Two women hiking down the tarmac? Hardly inconspicuous.

Angelie ducked off the main channel and they were between the buildings now, with much more cover. Taylor felt better. So far, no one had given them a second look. She knew there was security, but also knew Santiago had that covered. He and Alan were doing all they could to keep Taylor and Angelie safe. She had to trust them.

Though her watch said the sun was setting, the light was gray and milky. A very British day for a heist.

They were one hangar from their target when Taylor spotted the guards. She grabbed Angelie's arm.

"Hold up. They look like they're on alert."

"Of course they are. Don't worry. We're going in the side, here."

She hauled open the door—Taylor couldn't believe how lucky they were to have found it unlocked—and they entered the darkness, pausing a moment to let their eyes adjust.

Lights played on the plane itself and shone in the hangar's second-floor office, where gentle music played. But on this side of the huge building, it was gloom. They froze and listened, and the footsteps of a guard rang clear. He was pacing approximately twenty feet from their position. Why guard the door when you could be inside out of the rain, and closer to the light?

Taylor whispered, "We can go around. I looked at the blueprints. There's another entrance by the western gate."

She wasn't quiet enough. The guard snapped his head to their position and took a step toward them. *Shit.*

"Non."

Angelie moved like a cobra. She was on him in a heartbeat, before he had a chance to raise the alarm. The suppressor on her pistol coughed. The guard fell to his knees, then crumpled to the ground. The shot had taken him in the throat, right above his body armor. He twitched several times as his brain got the message that his body was dying, and his gaze went deep into a darkening sky no one could see but him. Blood began to pool under his shoulders, and Angelie gestured to his now dead form.

"We need to move him."

"Damn it, there was no need to kill him. You could have

disabled him, and we could have gone to the other entrance. My God, Angelie. I thought we'd agreed you wouldn't hurt anyone who wasn't trying to hurt us first."

Angelie sighed.

"I agreed not to hurt *you*. You must understand, Taylor. We are on a schedule. We do not have time to seek ingress elsewhere. And if you keep wasting my time, I might renege on our deal, simply shoot you, and leave you in the gutter. Take his arm."

Taylor took his arm.

They dragged the man to the side and moved deeper into the hangar. The plane was a hundred feet ahead. They were in luck; the door to the plane was open, the movable staircase already nestled up against the opening. The trick was going to be getting up the stairs unnoticed—they were on the office side of the hangar. And a man was wandering nearby, whether a guard or a maintenance worker, she had no idea. But he turned, and she saw the bulge of the weapon under his arm. Damn. Another guard.

"Well?" Taylor whispered, once the guard was well out of earshot. "What would Santiago do in this situation?"

"Kill the guard before he realizes his partner is down."

"Any other options?"

Angelie looked at her watch. "We have a five-minute window before we need to be inside that plane. We will wait here."

"Thank you," Taylor said softly.

To which Angelie snorted, "Let's hope he decides to take a bathroom break." Her voice was low, barely discernible over the music coming from the hangar's office in the back. "I've been thinking about your reluctance to do what is needed without thinking about the consequences. I believe I can explain in a way you might understand. You see, I'm what your literature professors call a Byronic hero. I do things someone else might consider an illegal action—"

"Yes, murder for hire might fall into that category. As well as murdering innocent people indiscriminately."

Angelie ignored the interruption. "—but have a higher purpose, and benefit the masses. An immoral action for a moral reason. This is what makes the job interesting, and gives my position gravitas. It is why we are paid so well, because we do things most people cannot. I am helping rid the world of the vermin who breed in the darkness. Now you..."

The guard started to move their way again, and Angelie tensed. Just as quickly, he turned and made his way to the office. They both relaxed. Now was their chance.

They ran on quiet feet, Taylor up the stairs with Angelie covering her, then Angelie.

No shouts. No bullets. They'd made it.

The plane's capacious interior was dim; the lights from the hangar illuminated the interior through the windows.

Angelie was already moving, pulling tools from her bag. She had gotten downright chatty at this point, something Taylor recognized from their operation in Geneva. She talked when she got nervous. *Nervous* wasn't the right word, of course, Angelie Delacroix was not nervous. Excited, maybe. Channeling the lightning passing through her synapses as she weighed every possible permutation. When she was alone, it must be a party in her brain. She moved through the plane's luxurious living room past the stairs that led to the second deck, gear in hand, mouth going a thousand miles a minute like they were chatting over coffee.

"As I was saying, you are just a plain old-fashioned hero. You are boring. Predictable. And your predictability will get you killed. Your enemies know how you will react in any given situation. You will always hesitate. You will consider the consequences before you act. You will only do what you believe is right, what is just. Those traits may seem noble to you, but to someone like me, someone who understands the need to act—"

"Without conscience, without honor, without any semblance of decency?"

"You are quite judgmental, do you know this? Also what makes heroes boring. As I was saying, I understand the need to act and can do so without peppering my soul with a million questions as to the legality and/or the morality of the given situation. It is why I am still alive."

"So now you're giving me morality lessons?"

"I am simply making an observation."

A noise sounded behind them, and Taylor turned just in time to see a guard sticking his head inside the plane's door with a look of utter incredulity on his face.

"Watch it," Taylor said, and Angelie shot him from fifty feet, dropping him where he stood. They ran back to the door. Taylor stepped over the body of the guard, careful not to get blood on her shoes, and looked out to see if anyone else was coming. Nothing. The hangar was silent again.

"Pick up his arms, *s'il vous plait. Merci.*"

They dragged him inside the plane and set him gently against the first leather sofa.

Damn it.

Angelie blew out a breath, put her hands on her hips, and assayed the scene, toeing the guard's shirt with her boot. "This man, for instance. I didn't want to kill him. He was in our way and a danger to our mission. Eliminating him was logical."

"And what about his family? His wife? His kids? He was just doing his job, and you ended his life because he was in your way."

"I've told you before, that sort of thinking will drive you mad," Angelie said softly. "The painting will be in the bedroom. It's in the nose, under the cockpit. Follow me."

They started toward the bedroom again, but there was a

noise behind them. Taylor swung around, her own weapon at the ready this time. It was one of their pilots from the Gulfstream. Angelie rushed past her and seized his arm.

"What are you doing here? We—"

"We have a problem. They know we're here."

Angelie huffed a deep and angry breath through her nose. "*Merde*!"

Taylor knew this was not good. It was one thing for the hangar guards to go on alert. But the pilot was supposed to be with their jet. That was their way out. Without him, without the plane...

Angelie had her comms up to Santiago. Taylor was wearing an earwig too, but it was around her neck. She plugged the plastic into her ear to hear Santiago's voice running, smoothly excited but totally professional, no different from the comms of any op she'd ever been on with her own team when something went awry.

"—breaking into the Northolt air traffic control now and altering the flight plan, getting you clearance for takeoff. I will make it apparent the bank is taking the plane and they won't stop you. That was the original cover, you're just going to have to make it happen. We'll forfeit the Gulfstream for now, we can circle back for it."

Angelie was a blur of motion.

"You, Jackson. Push off the stairs and shut the door. Do you know how to secure a plane's doors?" When she shook her head, Angelie snapped her fingers at the pilot. "Help her. I'll get the engines going. We must leave now. Santiago has everything ready. The hangar doors are open, we will not be stopped."

"Go? In this?"

Angelie tossed her a pirate grin. "It is a plane, Taylor. It will fly."

"We're stealing the sheik's 747? Is that wise?"

"You promised no questions."

Fuck.

The set of boarding stairs they used was against the plane's fuselage. Taylor pushed it away hard, grateful it was on wheels, then slammed the door into place. The pilot reached for the lever and locked it. Well, that was easy enough.

Taylor watched out the porthole window—somehow, no one had caught wind of their actions outside of the two hangar guards. Would that stand as they moved the big plane onto the tarmac and took off? *This is utterly insane.* Her adrenaline was pumping, and she barely noticed the pilot had left her, running up the stairs to join Angelie in the cockpit. Taylor was torn—go for the painting? Or head up and see what other nonsense Angelie was going to get them into?

The latter won. She had no idea how to use the micro explosives properly anyway.

Taylor climbed the stairs as the engines roared to life. She made her way forward in time to hear the pilot call, "We're ready."

Angelie appeared by her side. "Come," she said to Taylor, pulling her by the bicep into the cockpit. Angelie took the copilot's seat and gestured for Taylor to take the jump seat behind her, buckling herself in.

Taylor didn't want to think about the lack of preparation—she knew pilots always checked out their planes from top to bottom before they took off—just hoped like hell they were going to get lucky. The plane had been getting standard maintenance, which was allegedly finished, but still. If she died in a plane crash stealing a 747, she thought Baldwin might just march into the afterlife and kill her himself.

The pilot and Angelie spoke in a shorthand Taylor didn't understand but sounded official. The engines rumbled excitedly as the pilot got the plane moving. How they'd gotten lucky enough that the hangar doors were open, she didn't know.

The plane went right onto the tarmac like a dog off its leash, heading for freedom. They taxied to the queue of planes waiting to take off, Angelie cursing under her breath or calling on the gods for help, Taylor didn't know which.

She picked up a pair of headphones, set one speaker to her free ear. Now Santiago was speaking on one headset, the air traffic controllers on another. The plane taxied, moving down the row. Three to go. Two to go. One. And then it was their turn.

"Prepare for takeoff," the pilot said, lining up the plane, and gunned it.

Taylor had always loved flying , and especially the moment when the engines revved into a higher gear and the plane starts to leap forward. It normally gave her a sense of hope and excitement. Now, she found herself chanting little prayers in time with the deep *thwapping* of the great tires on the tarmac. Forty seconds. That's all it would take for them to get in the air.

She counted down backward in her head. When she got to one, the plane soared into the sky.

They'd made it. My God, they'd done it.

She was still grinning when the gunshots rang out.

FIFTY-TWO

IT WAS BEDLAM IMMEDIATELY. The plane still rocketed toward the sky, but the pilot was now slumped forward, blood spraying from a neck wound on the windscreen in front of him. Angelie was fighting with the controls, screaming at Taylor to "find him, find him!" as the plane dipped right, then left.

Taylor flung off her harness and palmed the borrowed Glock 40 that she'd stuck into the holster in the back of her jeans. Angelie had plenty of guns, but this was the one Taylor knew best. She dove through the now open cockpit door into the body of the plane, yanking the reinforced steel closed behind her.

The pilot hadn't bothered turning on the plane's interior lights—one less thing to draw attention—so it took her a second to get rid of the imprint of the runway lights burning in her vision. She wasn't exactly excited about shooting at random into the darkness, either—she didn't think planes took well to bullets.

Her thoughts were answered by a roar, extremely loud in the close air, that gave a supersonic whistle by her ear and slammed into the cockpit door. Thank God she'd thought to pull it closed or that bullet would have gone right out the front window. Or into the back of Angelie's head. She heard a clatter of feet, then silence.

Unlike the commercial jets she was used to, with rows of seats and compartments, this plane was broken into living areas, and she could see the width of it now that her eyes were adjusting. This upper deck was more of the same from downstairs—casual living that ended in a staircase. Chances were whoever was shooting at them had fled back to the main level of the plane. The private area, Angelie had said. That's where they'd been heading before all hell broke loose. The lower deck housed the bedrooms, a private living room, a conference room...and the painting they were trying to steal.

This is crazy, she said to herself as she made her way carefully down the stairs, weapon up and at the ready. *Crazy, crazy, crazy.* Each step gave her a moment to assess what was happening.

Someone had shot their pilot as they were taking off.

Whoever that was must have a death wish, because if Angelie hadn't jumped on the controls, they would all be very, very dead now.

Does Angelie know how to fly a damn airplane? That brought her up short for a moment. It would seem so; the plane was still climbing, the angle of ascent steep enough that Taylor was bracing her arm against the railing as she went down the stairs.

Focus. Find the shooter.

She slowed as she drew closer to the bottom. The shooter had the advantage, that was clear. All she could do was lay down fire to clear her path or explode into the space and hope like hell she didn't get popped before she could locate and neutralize the threat.

The second option seemed like the best one. She controlled her breathing, which might be for naught; surely he could hear her coming, then gave herself a *go, go, go* countdown and launched herself into the space.

It was dark, thank goodness. And she didn't get shot. She rolled to her feet and duckwalked slowly forward, toward the nose of the plane, to what Angelie had said was the bedroom. A step forward. Another. She heard something move and two decades of instinct had her dropping to her stomach just as a barrage of bullets pummeled the couch where she'd been standing.

Damn it. Heart racing, she crawled forward using her elbows and boots to balance. Another shot, right above her head. She didn't have a choice now. She rolled to her right into the clear space and got off three shots just as the door in front of her closed.

Okay, okay. You've got this. Now he's the one who's trapped.

She inched ahead, moving as soundlessly as she could. She reached the door. She could see the puckered spots where the bullets had hit—the door was lined with steel or Kevlar, something. She supposed a sheik couldn't take any chances.

She put her hand on the latch, praying it was unlocked, counted off again, and flung it open.

Darkness.

She took a step into the room, then a second. Strained to hear anything. Sense anything.

It was still. Too still.

As her eyes adjusted to the darkness, a frisson of energy spiked down her spine.

There.

The fist came out of the darkness and Taylor ducked just in time. It hit her shoulder instead of her jaw, and she spun around, slapping at the wall for a switch. She could smell him now, acrid and angry, but he'd retreated into the gloom. She could just make out a second, smaller room off the first as the door slammed. She lunged for the door, twisting the handle before he could get it locked, using her weight and momentum to smash it open.

She tumbled through, rolling to her knees. A bullet whistled past and she hit the deck, marshaling her breath. If she'd been standing she'd be dead. But the shot gave away his position. She could see something—someone—tucked into the corner.

A shadow, which became a man.

A man who was holding a gun to the head of another, smaller shadow.

A man who snarled, "Send that French bitch down here, or the girl dies."

Taylor didn't think. She didn't stop to wonder if she was making the right decision. She didn't harangue herself, or debate with her conscience. She didn't stop to ask if it was right, or wrong.

Taylor Jackson pulled the trigger. Once, twice, thrice.

The man-sized shadow collapsed to the ground with a *thump*.

There was a startled cry from the girl, who scrambled away from her captor.

"Get the lights," Taylor said, and when she heard the click of the switch, shut her eyes for a moment against the sudden glare. When she opened them, a mellow lamplight filled the space— a bedroom, she realized—and soft sobs filled her ears. The girl was dirty, her shirt bloody, her eyes luminous and terrified.

"Carson? Are you Carson Conway?"

"Yes."

"Are you hurt?"

"No." A deep, soul-cleansing sigh. "No, I'm not. Not really."

"Good. Go upstairs, right now," and the girl disappeared without a word.

Taylor approached the target. The man wasn't dead yet. She'd shot him as she'd been trained, heart and head. But it seemed he was wearing body armor, expecting her to come in guns blazing, and had turned, or ducked, when she moved. The headshot had caught him in the neck, below the ear. He was bleeding heavily, she must have nicked the artery, but he was still alive and conscious.

She inched forward carefully, ready for him to spring to his feet and attack her. He didn't. She kicked away his weapon, eyes locked on his, anticipating his next move. His arms were splayed out to his sides unnaturally, and she realized the bullet must have either hit his spinal cord or flown close enough that the swelling was paralyzing him.

She took her first full breath in minutes and gestured with the gun.

"You're Joseph Game, aren't you?"

"Fuck you." Blood started frothing on his lips as he spoke.

"No, thank you. You're an idiot—why would you shoot the pilot?"

"Was trying to...hit the bitch. Plane...jerked. She should... be dead."

"Looks like you're the one who's going to die today. That's a nasty wound."

"You kill Angelie... instead. I'll pay."

It all came into focus.

"So this was just a setup all along? You lured Angelie here to steal the painting, but you were just planning to murder her?"

His lips moved in what might, in other circumstances, pass for a smile. His teeth were rimed in red.

Taylor went down in a crouch. "Well, you blew it, buddy. Looks like you're in a bind. Bleeding out, paralyzed? Can you move? Anything but your mouth, that is?"

She lifted his arm and it flopped to the floor. She'd definitely clipped his spinal cord.

"She will...hurt you."

"Doubt it."

"When you...are no longer...of...use. Discard...you. Kill..." He shut his eyes. He was going gray, the blood oozing now instead of pumping. He was not going to survive without immediate medical intervention, this she knew. She could help him along and save them all a lot of trouble. But that was Angelie's style. Taylor was still Taylor. If there was a chance for him to live, to see justice, she was willing to risk it.

She fished her handcuffs out of her back pocket, slapped one around Game's limp wrist, and almost carefully, rolled him and cuffed the other. At least on his stomach he wouldn't drown in his own blood before Angelie could talk to him. And he wasn't going anywhere under his own steam.

"I'll be back."

Up the winding staircase, carefully, in case there was something else waiting to jump out at her. The lights were on now. She didn't see the girl, kept her weapon up and steady, just in case. At the cockpit door, she banged her fist three times, hard.

"It's Jackson. Game is neutralized. Let me in."

The latch released. Angelie was sitting at the copilot controls, more relaxed but wary enough. They were above the clouds, the sky a deep purple, spreading out like a blanket of night ahead of them.

"Tell me."

"First, can you fly this thing?"

"Obviously," Angelie drawled, gesturing to the controls.

"Okay. Game had Carson downstairs, she's somewhere on the plane. I need to go find her. I shot him, he's down, but he's not dead. Paralyzed, I think. Do you want to talk to him?"

To say the look Angelie gave Taylor was one of surprise was a misnomer. Shock, actually, quickly covered by her usual sneer, but shock, nonetheless.

"He claims he was shooting at you, not the pilot. Accident."

Angelie glanced at the dead man next to her. "Can you move Jean-Paul? I...liked him."

"Of course."

Taylor unlatched the harness, got the man under the arms, and pulled him from his seat. He was heavy in death, and it took all her leverage to get him out of the seat and into the main cabin. She laid him on the floor by the sofa.

"You want a shot at Game?"

"Of course I do."

"Then put this thing on autopilot and go get him."

The stillness from the assassin was remarkable. Like a wolf in the forest, setting its feet to leap at the throat of the elk five feet away. But the moment passed. Angelie shook herself slightly.

"There's no time. We need to start the landing sequence.

"Then I'm going to find Carson, make sure she's okay," Taylor said, turning from the cockpit.

"I'm here," a voice said from her left, startling her. "Is that man...dead?"

Taylor followed the girl's eyes. She'd lain Jean-Paul on the floor just outside the cockpit, and his head was lolling to the side in a very unpleasant angle.

"Yes, unfortunately."

"I can't stay here."

The girl was turning green, and Taylor felt bad for her. "Go sit in the cockpit, on the seat behind the woman flying."

"Who are you?"

"Oh, sorry. Taylor Jackson. Nashville...formerly captain of the Metro Nashville Police. That woman is my partner. She'll tell you who she is if she wants, but don't ask, okay? She's not as nice as me."

"Maybe I'll just stay here with you, then," Carson said lightly. "How long have I been gone?"

"A little more than a week. Your mom is going to be mad with joy that you're okay."

The smile was tired but genuine. "You met my mom?"

"Of course. She came to Nashville immediately when you went missing. Want to tell me how Game took you? And where he's been keeping you?"

Carson gestured to the plane's spacious interior. "I've been here for a while, I think. He locked me in a closet. Of course, the closet on this thing is bigger than my dorm room. He's been drugging me, too. I've been sleeping a lot. I think...there was a Jeep. Following me. I was scared, I ran. Then I woke up here. That's all I remember." She touched her head. "Ouch."

"Let me see."

The girl was dutiful, she came to Taylor's side and bent her head, parting her dirty hair. There was a small cut, healing.

"Your hand?"

The girl's face was pale. She held up her bandaged finger. "I woke up like this. I... I haven't looked. It doesn't hurt too badly now."

"And he didn't..."

She shook her head. "No. He wasn't interested in me like that."

"Thank God for small mercies."

"Yes," Carson said, voice soft. "Can we call my mom?"

"Yes, but let me talk to our pilot first. I bet there's food and drink in one of the cabinets around here. Why don't you find us a Coke?"

She watched Carson walk off toward the cabinets and went back into the cockpit.

"She's okay. Full of questions. Wants to call her mom. Where are we headed?"

"Back to France. Santiago got us clearance to land at Le Bourget. We'll be on the ground in ten and the driver will meet us. We will go to the safe house to plan our next move."

"What do you want me to do with Game?" Taylor asked quietly.

"Will he live?"

"Not for long. Not without help."

"Guard him. I will deal with him once we're safely landed."

Taylor nodded and started away. She hesitated a moment, then put her hand on Angelie's shoulder.

"I know," said the assassin.

FIFTY-THREE

AVERY WOKE TO SUNLIGHT. She was in a soft bed, with a pillow under her head and cool sheets pulled up to her shoulders

A dream. What a dream. At once glorious and frustrating. What she wouldn't do to have it be real. She stretched, lingering in the happiness of seeing his face again. It had been a long time since she dreamed of Richard.

"You're awake."

Startled, she jumped to a seated position, pulling the covers with her.

Her husband sat on the edge of the bed, staring at her in bemusement.

God, he's real. This is real. She was face to face with the man she loved, a man who'd died, and her brain was simply not working. Not comprehending. How could this be?

"Richard?"

"Hi, Avery."

She didn't know whether to laugh or cry. She knew she couldn't touch him or she'd disintegrate.

"You have questions. And I have answers. But first, I have something for you."

The door opened, and Carson practically flew into the room and launched herself onto her mother's bed, wrapping her neck in a hug. "Mom!"

"Carson? Oh, my God, Carson!"

There were tears then, joy and pain mingling, Carson crying too, and Richard watching them patiently. Finally, Carson moved to the side, holding her mother's hand.

"Dad's alive."

"I see that. Richard? I—"

He pulled a chair to her bedside. She could tell he wanted to touch her, and with a deep breath, she moved her free hand to the edge of the bed. With a smile, he took it, tears in his eyes.

"You're real."

"I am."

"But you died."

"I had to."

"You faked your own death?"

He nodded. "I had no choice. Joseph Game was going to kill you. He threatened you, and he threatened Carson and the boys. I didn't know how else to keep you safe. If I was out of the picture, then he had no reason to come after you. Santiago and I found a way to make it work. We staged the scene, doctored the autopsy, all of it. And it did work, for a long time. You have no idea how much I've missed you. How much it killed me to be away from you. But I had to keep you safe."

"Then why did he take Carson?"

Richard's eyes grew flinty, becoming those of a stranger. Or perhaps that was the real man, and the warm and sunny person was the fake, the one she thought she knew. He was forever going to be a stranger to her, she knew that. They would never be the same people that they were before.

"Someone talked."

"Who? Someone who knew you weren't really dead? Where have you been all this time? How could you have left us all alone like this?" Her heart was hammering and her voice was rising.

"It was Alan, Mom. He betrayed us."

"What?" Avery realized she had shrieked the word. *You're losing control. Calm down.*

Richard continued the story. "Santiago discovered a series of messages between Game and Alan. Alan figured it out somehow. They plotted to take Carson to draw me out. Alan is dead, by the way. I had to eliminate him when he took you. He put you in the basement of the bakery, and God knows what the plan was at that point. I had no choice."

That neck snapping. She'd hear it in her bones forever. "Oh my God. This isn't real."

"It is real. Mom. We were both kidnapped, and we're both safe. We're in France, and Dad's going to take us to a secure place he knows. We are all going to start over. As a family. Rory and Jules, too, if they want. They work with Dad."

At the look Avery knew ran across her face, Richard put up a hand.

"They don't work with me, but for the same organization. And they didn't know either, hon. I swear it. I sacrificed myself so Game would leave all of you alone. When he discovered my trail, he went to Alan first, knowing that he would be the weakest link. I don't know what leverage he had over him, what he said, or how he compromised him. Santiago might find traces one day if he looks deeply enough. But Alan helped Game stage Carson's kidnapping."

"The note. A note came to the house. We never could figure out how the kidnapper could be in Nashville and in New Haven at the same time. It was Alan, all along. Jesus."

She dropped their hands. "Now what? I'm supposed to just

forgive and forget? Do you have any idea what we've been through?"

The sadness on his face told her yes, he did. "I wish there was another way. But for now...we disappear. We go so far away we never have to look over our shoulders again."

"I need to get up."

Richard hesitated only a moment before standing and allowing her to move her legs. "The bathroom's over there," he said.

He still knew her. Knew she didn't like to show strong emotion in front of him, and especially in front of Carson. He slung an arm around Carson's shoulder, and the two of them watched Avery move to the bathroom and slowly, quietly shut the door.

Too much. This was too much.

In another life, she would admire the charming blue and yellow tile that lined the floor and walls and know she was in a foreign country by the placement of the bidet, but at the moment, she registered nothing. She started the shower and stared at herself in the mirror.

All that matters is they are alive.

Nothing else.

They are both alive.

She opened the door to the bedroom, just to check.

Carson was perched on the edge of the bed, chattering at her father, who was watching her with tenderness and amusement. Their grins were heart-stoppingly similar, and she was almost afraid to smile back for fear that they would both disappear.

They were real. Safe. Hers.

She and Richard would have long conversations about all of this, soon. But for the moment, she recognized one thing. Her prayers had come true.

She rushed across the room and threw her arms around them both, laughing, grateful, overwhelmed.

"I love you," she said. "I'm still furious with you, and I'll probably never forgive you, but I love you."

"I love you, too," Richard replied, and kissed her.

FIFTY-FOUR

THEY FLEW the 747 back to Northolt as conquering heroes. Thierry had made a few calls, massaged the narrative in their favor, and it all went away.

The story had to be amended here and there, of course. The official record was they'd been lured to Ahmad's plane, kidnapped along with Carson, fought for control over Game and his crew, then safely landed and reported immediately what had happened. The sheik, being a man who preferred to take care of business privately, was so grateful for their safety—and that of his plane and his priceless stolen painting—that he was happy to overlook the damage from the shootouts. And overlook the theft of his flying palace. And happy to deal with the body of the dead man in his bedroom. He had never liked Joseph Game, he told them over an exquisite bottle of champagne. The man had crazy eyes. And he'd been wanting to change that rug anyway.

Taylor actually liked the sheik—he was handsome, sporty, full of tallish tales, and whether he believed their cooked-up story or not, remarkably gallant about the whole thing. This was certainly a world she was going to have to get used to, should she agree to work with Macallan ever again. She was still having doubts.

She didn't have Game's death on her conscience, though. Angelie had taken care of that. When they landed, while Taylor ushered Carson from the plane and into Santiago's waiting arms, Angelie had gone into the sheik's bedroom and emerged fifteen minutes later, a look of horror on her face. She'd gone straight to Santiago, pulled him to a quiet corner, and shared some news that made the man pale. They left him there, standing over his crutches, and Taylor could have sworn he was crying.

Taylor would find out the whole story later, that his husband had been in on the kidnapping, that Richard Conway was miraculously alive, that he was on his way to the safe house with his rescued wife, waiting for their rescued daughter.

But for now, Taylor's part of the deal was done, and Angelie was getting her back to Nashville forthwith. The Gulfstream had been rescued from its temporary slot, new pilots assigned, and would be leaving as soon as they finished their "drinkies" with the sheik. His word, not hers.

Taylor was feeling pleasantly mellow when at last the bottles were empty. She had to admit, the people who ran in these circles did have excellent taste in wine. She accepted the sheik's hand and promised to be in touch if she ever needed anything, then followed Angelie from the plush living room down the stairs to the hangar floor, trying and failing to ignore the ghosts of the men they'd killed during the operation.

On the Gulfstream, Angelie gestured for Taylor to take a seat. She went to the back of the plane and returned with a file folder.

"Payment," she said, smiling as she handed it over.

Taylor flipped it open and saw the heartbreakingly adorable face of her fiancé's son. There was no question whose child it was, he was a carbon copy of Baldwin, only with his mother's red hair. Something inside her cracked, and she closed the folder and set it gently on the seat next to her.

"All the information is there. Thank you, Taylor Jackson. I fear things would have gone very badly if you hadn't been a part of this operation. You will make an excellent operative for the Macallan Group."

"I don't know about that."

Angelie crossed her arms. Taylor knew her well enough now to know she was impatient to be gone. But there was something Angelie needed to know.

"Are we secure?"

Angelie raised a brow. "No one is listening."

"Thierry was in touch with me earlier. He asked me to do something. Something I don't particularly want to do. He asked me to eliminate you. That you were a liability Macallan could no longer afford. That you were too sloppy on this operation, that too many things went wrong. You were out of the game too long, he said."

There was a weapon in the Gulfstream's seat. A Glock 40. It had been left for her when she'd received her assignment. She lifted it from its hiding place, letting it rest in her palm.

A slow smile spread across Angelie's face. "He does not understand you at all, does he?"

Taylor smiled in return. "No. He doesn't. I think he was expecting me to jump at the chance."

"Did you tell him yes, or no?"

There was a bit of tension in the assassin's shoulder now. Taylor took a deep breath, watching her. She popped out the magazine, pulled the slide, caught the bullet that was ejected.

Laid them on the seat.

"There was a time, Angelie Delacroix, that all I wanted was to see you dead. Not anymore."

"And there was a time I wanted to see you dead, Taylor Jackson. Not anymore."

"So what do we do now?"

Angelie sat down. "Well, that depends on you. Are you going to join Macallan? Has Thierry earned your loyalty?"

Taylor laughed. "No. He has not. I don't trust that man as far as I can throw him." She settled for a moment, crossing her legs as she got more comfortable in the seat. "This isn't my world, Angelie. Yes, I can operate in it—I can operate in any scenario. I've trained for it my whole adult life. But I am my best self in Nashville. Fighting for the people of the city. I don't think I can take on the world. Certainly not without you by my side."

"We made a good team, did we not?"

"Shockingly, yes. But I don't want to operate in that space. I like rules. I like being boring, and predictable." She put a hand on the file folder. "I think we're going to have quite a lot to deal with for the time being."

Angelie nodded. "You will. And you will do the right thing. I have no doubt."

"I don't know if there's a right or wrong when it comes to Baldwin's child, but I'm willing to try. So what will you do about Thierry?"

"What should I do?" Angelie asked, and Taylor sensed genuine curiosity in her tone.

"My honest opinion? He is a threat, and you should eliminate him."

"Goodness, Taylor. How cutthroat of you. But I'm so glad you said that. You're not wrong." Angelie was practically purring.

"Well, I'm not exactly proud of it. But he can't be trusted. I've never had a good feeling about him. And if he wants me to kill you, and I do, then when is it my turn? When I balk at his orders, when I chafe at the bit, he'll come for me."

"He won't."

"How can you be sure?"

"Because I knew what he was going to ask of you."

"How?"

The look on Angelie's face told her all she needed to know.

"Yes. Your instincts are right. Eventually, he would need to silence you. He did the same to me when I joined. My predecessor was in the way and was my first assignment. But you have nothing to fear. I've taken care of this situation. Thierry is dead. And the Macallan Group is dead with him. And I am officially a ghost."

Angelie stood, and gave Taylor a little salute. *"Bonne chance, mon amie."*

"What if I need to reach you?"

Angelie walked out of the plane, laughing in delight. "You won't."

Jesus.

The woman was ruthless.

And damn if Taylor didn't like her for it.

The pilot approached her seat. "Are you ready, ma'am?"

Taylor looked at the file folder again, playing with the edge. "Another ten minutes, if you don't mind."

"Certainly."

She flipped open the file and looked at the address. Tamsin lived in central London. Taylor could be there in less than an hour. She could see Mason for herself. She could wrestle her emotions and decide, once and for all, if she could handle this.

But that wouldn't be fair. Mason was not her blood. This was not her decision to make.

She closed the file and called, "I'm ready."

The pilot responded by asking her to buckle up, which she did. As the plane shot into the sky, she called Baldwin.

"My God, I've been worried sick. Are you okay?" he asked.

"I'm fine. I'm heading home, actually. We did it. She's safe."

He blew out a huge breath. "Thank God. Will you tell me—"

"Not a good idea, especially on a mobile. Even if this network is secure. Maybe on a beach somewhere."

"I like the sound of that. What did you have in mind?"

"An island. Where no one can bother us. No one but Sam and Xander, I mean."

The silence was deafening. "Taylor," he said, voice breaking. "Are you saying what I think you're saying?"

She spun her engagement ring around her finger. "Yes, I am."

"When?"

"Now. As soon as possible. Book the flights, and I'll call my maid of honor."

"What about Macallan? Your new job?"

"Oh, that's not happening. In the end, I came to my senses. I have another idea."

"Metro?"

"Nope. I'm done with that."

"FBI?"

"Definitely not." She laughed.

"Then what?"

"I'll tell you when I see you. Which should be in about five hours. I love you, Baldwin. Let's go get married."

"It would be my honor," he said, voice deep and rumbling, that tone that made her body tense in delicious anticipation. "I love you, Taylor. I'll see you soon."

She thumbed the Off button, then dialed a number she'd never dialed before. A woman answered, voice clipped and assured.

"Sky? This is Taylor Jackson."

"Well hey, Taylor. What can I do for you?"

"You mentioned a job when we spoke last. I thought we could talk."

Twenty minutes later, with meetings planned with Sky and her aunt Joy upon returning from her honeymoon, Taylor hung up and held the phone lightly, amazed at the peace stealing through her. She hadn't lied when she told Angelie she wasn't suited for her line of work. What she was good at, damn good, was investigating crimes. If she couldn't do it for the police anymore, and wouldn't do it for the spy world, it was time to do it for herself.

Her phone chirped with a text, and she looked down to see Marcus's name on the screen.

I know you're out of touch, but if you get near a TV? We got him.

There was a television embedded in the wall across the fuselage, and she turned it on. It was set to a twenty-four-hour cable news network, and the screen had a breaking-news alert Chyron spinning.

Music Man Serial Killer Apprehended

She turned up the volume, smiling.

EPILOGUE

THE GRAVES of the men who've wronged her are hidden deep in the forest, where they will never be found.

She walks there sometimes, just to reassure herself. Walks over their bones, each step a reminder of how they'd nearly bested her.

The château is finished now, the renovations years in the making helped along by a massive influx of cash. It's easier to restore a château when you aren't piecemealing it back together but instead can afford to have every decent craftsman in the area throw their backs into it.

She doesn't know if she will be able to live here, so near the ghosts of her family. She has decided that she no longer wants to be sad. She wants to find a way to live a life. To move into the world without looking over her shoulder. No one knows where she is, but people talk. The rich-widow cover will only work for so long before someone from her old world gets suspicious.

If they're looking for her.

The few remaining, the ones she trusts, swear no one is. That she's in the clear.

But they, too, are in hiding. They, too, look over their shoulders.

This world, this château, these grounds, this restoration drawing to its conclusion, this is the life she's chosen, though she never expected to live to see it to fruition.

But she has eliminated all of her enemies. And now, as she walks over their bones, she wondered if maybe, there is a chance for her, after all.

She owes her life to a woman half a world away. An enemy who became, in many ways, a friend.

The sun moves lower in the pink sky, and the fields of lavender beyond the edge of the forest wave it goodbye.

"C'est impossible."

The assassin straightens her shoulders with a sigh and leaves the forest of the dead.

She cannot afford friends.

AUTHOR'S NOTE

As I was finishing the editorial on this novel, Nashville suffered a terrible tragedy. The shooting at The Covenant School has rocked us all.

I am honored to write novels that deep dive into the lives of the fictional heroes of Metro Nashville. And I am so grateful that our real men and women on the force personify the very best traits of my fictional characters. They do not hesitate. They run toward the bullets, not away. They are remarkable, well-trained, and heroes in every sense of the word. But you don't need to take my word for it. The whole world saw the bodycam videos of the shooter being neutralized by the outstanding heroes of the Metro Nashville Police Department.

I offer my deep and humble thanks to Officer Rex Englebert, Detective Michael Collazo, and Sergeant Jeff Mathes, who did it by the book, along with the rest of the responding officers. You are why I write these books.

And in memoriam, may those that we lost be forever remembered:

Evelyn Dieckhaus (9); Hallie Scruggs (9); William Kinney (9); Katherine Koonce (60); Mike Hill (61); Cynthia Peak, (61).

Rest in peace, and know your deaths were not in vain. Real change is coming.

ACKNOWLEDGMENTS

Saying "thank you" never seems quite adequate when it comes to creating a novel, especially one that was so many years in the making. But allow me to try:

Laura Blake Peterson, an astounding agent, friend, cheerleader, and all-around amazing woman, for standing by me as I struggled through this one.

Metro Nashville Patrol Officer Aldridge for indulging my curiosity on a Saturday night in Lower Broad.

Donna Christie, who allowed me to turn her into a forensic anthropologist K9 cadaver dog handler extraordinaire.

Jayne Ann Krentz, brilliant writer and friend, who helped me figure out how to make the bakery work, and helping me send Avery to Nashville.

Barbara Peters, owner of the Poisoned Pen bookstore, who never ceases to amaze and gives the best advice, and the rest of the indie booksellers who champion my work!

Laura Benedict, forever sounding board, for never once saying don't do it.

Ariel Lawhon, for helping me recognize when it's wrong and when it's process. And oodles of Wordles!

Patti Callahan Henry, for the shop talk, the encouragement, and the never-ending inspiration.

And the rest of The Porch: Paige Crutcher, Helen Ellis, Anne Bogel, Lisa Patton, MaryBeth Whalen, for the zooms, the emails, the support, the pens, the true-crime documentary recommendations, and the love. And the tulips!

My betas: Anna Benjamin, Sherrie Saint, Joan Huston, all of whom gave me such brilliant advice.

Kim Killion, who created the most amazing art yet, and Phyllis De Blanche, for the excellent editorial (and cat photos).

Mom, this one is for you! And Daddy–you are magnificent. How lucky am I to have parents who encourage my creative life? Jay and Jeff, you are the best brothers a girl could ever hope for. Jimmy and Jo–thank you for all the support and love. You're wonderful in-laws and much adored.

Jameson and Jordan, the thriller kittens, need their own line item thank you for bringing joy into our lives every day. It's hard to believe they are as old as the gap between this Taylor book and the last.

Finally, my darling Randy. As I have realized, one can't be thanked enough. But I will do it, yet again, because without you, Taylor would never have come into being, and I would not be the woman I am today. Thank you for being my fate.

Everybody lies. Even those you think you know best of all...

ABOUT J.T. ELLISON

photo credit: KidTee Hello Photography

J.T. Ellison is the *New York Times* and *USA Today* bestselling author of more than 25 novels and the EMMY® award-winning co-host of the literary TV show A WORD ON WORDS. She also writes urban fantasy under the pen name Joss Walker. With millions of books in print, her work has won critical acclaim, prestigious awards, been optioned for television, and has been published in 28 countries.

J.T. lives in Nashville with her husband and twin kittens, where she is hard at work on her next novel.

Join J.T.'s Monthly newsletter
jtellison.com/subscribe

facebook.com/jtellison14
twitter.com/thrillerchick
instagram.com/thrillerchick

ABOUT TWO TALES PRESS

Two Tales Press is an independent publishing house featuring crime fiction, suspense, and fantasy novels, novellas, and anthologies written and edited by New York Times bestselling author J.T. Ellison, including the award-winning Jayne Thorne, CIA Librarian fantasy series under J.T.'s pen name, Joss Walker.

To view all of our titles, please visit
www.twotalespress.com

CPSIA information can be obtained
at www.ICGtesting.com
Printed in the USA
BVHW041611050523
663676BV00003B/13